THE
BLACK
CROWN

ALSO BY H. M. REINHARD

The Black Hand

THE BLACK CROWN

H. M. REINHARD

THISTLE QUEEN

PRESS

Cover Art by Nevena Jevtić

Editor: Charlie Knight, cknightwrites.carrd.co

Thistlequeen Press

ISBN 979-8-9894291-3-4 (paperback)
ISBN 979-8-9894291-5-8 (hardcover)
ISBN 979-8-9894291-4-1 (ebook)

*For a younger Hannah, more at home in fantasy than reality.
Now they can all see your dragons, too.*

N
W
E
S
CORAVEN
NERO
SOL
SIEREN
ISLANDS
OF SAMA
FYALL
MOUNTAINS
ROHLEACH
TAMHAIN
SGUDAL
DESERT
RAMAL
PYESAK
ZARAK
MERGUR
VINGARD
EWITHWARK
ELDUR
HYTHE
RÖKKUR

PRONOUNCIATION GUIDE

Arix Sable: Air-ix Say-bull
Michael Woodhale: Michael Wood-hail
Revena Kali: Re-ven-nuh Call-ee
Celeste Ayala: Sell-est Uh-yall-a
Orion Karcharias: Uh-rye-un Car-care-ee-us
Lakai: Luh-kai
Lord Bardon: Lord Bar-done
Gaelan Ulfur: Gay-lun Ool-fur
Endar Em Abbas: En-dar Em A-bahs
Nesrin Yara: Nes-rhin Yar-ruh
Esme Halotus: Ez-may Ha-lotus
Ro Laris: Roe Lair-us
Semmer Kloevendirr: Sem-mehr Klo-ven-deer
Doral Kel: Doe-ral Kell
Lydia Skonos: Lydia Sko-no-s
Delphine Vod: Del-feen Vawd
Maer Dáinn: Mare Day-n

THE REALMS & WARDENS
Rökkur: Ro-koor
Nero: Nee-ro
Sieren: See-er-en
Sol: Soul
Warden Uellen Vod: Warden Oo-ellen V-awd
Tamhain: Ta-wen
Rohleach: Ro-lakh
Warden Aliska Sviengard: Warden A-lis-ka Svee-en-guard

Zarak: Za-rock
Pjesak: P-yes-ock
Ramal: Ra-mall
Warden Los Ke: Warden Loss Keh
Eldur: El-doo-r
Vingard: Vin-guard
Ewithwark: Eh-with-wark
Hythe: Hai-th (rhymes with tithe)
Warden Reuben Corrigan: Warden Roo-ben Kor-i-gahn
Mergur: Mehr-goo-r
Fyall Mountains: Fyell-uh Mountains

THE GODS
Kaoss: Kay-aws
Aion: Eye-on
Arduinna: Are-doo-ee-na
Vulcan: Vuhl-khun
Zephyrus: Zuf-eye-ruhs
Nereus: Neh-rus

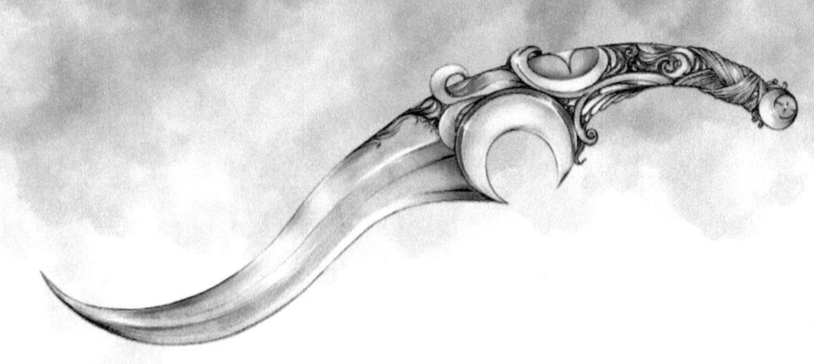

PROLOGUE

My lungs are on fire.

Everything in me is screaming, tearing, biting, clawing violent-ly to get away. To scramble, without thought or awareness, as far as I can get from the fire in my mouth, my nose, my blood.

I've felt pain before. Pain so deep and aching that my whole body throbbed. Pain that made me cry out, that made me pass out. But this pain is different.

The room I'm in is large, dark though lit with flickering can-dles, and filled with people I know. They watch me and I wait for them to rush forward, to help me, but they do not see the pain that circles my head like a crown, the goosebumps that race across my skin. The taste of death sits on my tongue, eating its way down my throat like acid. There is a hollow darkness swallowing me whole, and I can do nothing to react, nothing to stop it. I cannot even move.

The crowd below the steps doesn't see. They do not know.

I'm only vaguely aware of the hand that takes the now empty chalice from my frozen fingers, leading me away from the cheer-ing and the garbled voice of someone speaking. My face set in total indifference, as though I'm not being burned alive from the inside out. A hand on my back as I'm escorted away from the eyes of the court, away from the eyes of the new king. Orion.

I'm trapped within my own body, screaming myself raw and hoarse. I want to black out. I want to escape this torment and let sleep overtake me. But my body won't let my mind shut off, and no matter how hard I fight inside, my body is behaving as though nothing is wrong.

I am burning.

Stairs now. Walking up them, my arms slack at my sides. I vaguely realize there are three men walking with me. One walks ahead, opening doors and ushering us through with a backward glance. The crystal blue of his eyes are crinkled at the corners with worry. The other two walk on either side of me, hand under my arms and at my back, walking me forward. I can't turn my head to see who they are.

My body is slowly starting to catch up, as if it's only now re-alizing that my mind is in torment. That *I* am in torment, trapped deep under the curve of my ribs in agony. My hands shake first, then my chest and shoulders. My knees begin to buckle. I'm stag-gering down the hall, my body beginning to convulse with spastic waves ripping me apart. Before I crumple, there are arms lifting me, and I'm being held like a babe to someone's chest. My head lols and I see now it's Abbas who carries me, dark skin and long locs and taller than a mountain. Out of the corner of my eye I get a glance at the third man. It is Ulfur, hand gripped tightly on his weapon.

Then my eyes roll back, and I'm staring into myself. A tearing sound rings in my ears, but I know it's not coming from anywhere but inside me. My very muscles are ripping themselves to shreds. My veins are snapping, curling up under my skin, my bones splintering and healing and splintering again and again. Each old fracture sticks to my insides, causing minuscule tears more painful than any cut of a sword, more painful than if each organ were being peeled back layer by layer. Wave after wave of pain hits me, and each one ricochets through me with the same intensity as the one before it.

Goddess. Kaoss. Please.

Help me.

Then there is a final pop, and all is silent. I think for a moment that this quiet is an easement to the pain. In the next instant, I know I am wrong.

The silence is worse.

I have been locked into a box of my own body, dark and silent, even though my lungs are tired from screaming, my throat hoarse. Inside my mind, I tear at this cage, this darkness, all while feeling my limbs hang limp in Abbas' arms. I flail, scratching at my own skin, slivers of flesh wedging themselves under the curves of my fingernails. I tear at my hair, ripping out chunks that come attached to bits of my scalp, runny red with blood. The blood is mixed with sweat as it dribbles down my neck and spine.

When Tanis had poisoned me with Witch's Envy, it burned deep, dragging me kicking and screaming into terrifying dreams and wishes of death. If only I could sleep now.

I'm drowning in anguish, drowning in my own pain, suffocating in darkness. I have torn myself to shreds in an attempt to end it all, and yet outwardly, I am as still as stone.

Neither sleep nor death will claim me.

The deep dark has no end.

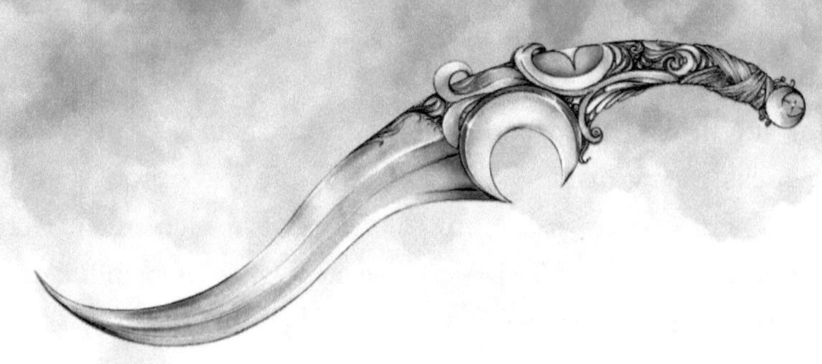

ONE

The world was being born. From inky black nothing, the world grew, slowly shaping into form and detail. It happened so slowly that for a long while, she thought she was imagining it, her mind finally having given up on trying to save itself, and simply creating a new paradise. A world inside her mind free of splintering pain and cavernous, echoing silence.

She sighed. At last.

At first, the colors of the world were dull, gray things that barely stood out from one another, the lines between them blurring the spaces where one thing ended and another began. But then there was light. Bright and orange against the gray, making the world a smoky haze of color bleeding in on itself. Green trees, blue sky, and red, so bloody that she did not want to see it.

The woman lowered her gaze from the color to stare down at the hands that rested in her lap. But they were not her hands. These hands were pale and clean, the nails manicured, fingers interlaced on a lilac-colored bed of the embroidered fabric of a dress. *Her* hands were covered in blood and flesh, worn down 'til bone poked through flesh from trying to claw away from the darkness.

These were not her hands.

Slowly, she raised her eyes again, shifting her gaze to the left. Beneath the dress was the wood of a bench, and beyond that, a cluster of emerald leaves and a crisp red rose.

A song broke through the silent world. High above her, hidden in a trellis, a bird was singing. Brown feathers intermingled with blue stood out against the foliage. Then there was another, a different song in a different tree. And something cool caressed her cheek.

With a start, she realized it was a breeze.

It was jarring to have lived in silence for so long, to not even hear the sound of her own breathing, and now be surrounded by small individual echoes of a world she had almost forgotten. How long had she been gone? Decades? Millennia?

It was a garden she sat in. Around her, red blossoms peeked from the bushes, their petals crisply flayed to show their bloody centers. Beyond the hedges, the fountain spewed water, its lilting notes as startling as shattering glass.

"Lady Arix?"

That had been her name once. Long ago in a life that felt lost to her. So long she could hardly remember.

A face came into view, caramel brown hair swept neatly, a simple brown dress and crisp white apron hanging from her frame. She was young, but her hands were rough, and she wore lines around her hazel eyes that should have belonged to a woman much older.

"Lady Arix, can you hear me?"

Arix blinked against the sound. The girl was familiar. Perhaps a dream from back before the darkness swept her up.

There was squeezing pressure that forced her to look down. The girl was holding her hand, kneeling in front of her on the white stones of the path, her face expectant.

"It's me, Wren. Nod or blink twice if you can hear me."

Blinking. Moving. All things she had not done for years. Arix forced her eyelids down, squeezing them over her sockets, then opened them abruptly. When her eyes closed there was too much darkness. Too much of a reminder. She blinked again, but faster this time. The darkness was barely noticeable when she did it quickly.

A great sigh of relief came from the girl, and she promptly stood, water sliding down her cheeks. "Thank the Goddess."

The girl squeezed again, and Arix relished the feeling of someone else's skin on hers. Then the girl was calling, and Arix's ears splintered at the sound. She clapped her hands over them and ducked her head, eyes wide and staring at the ground. She felt the vibrations through the wood of the bench as more feet approached. Then someone was kneeling, pulling her chin up.

Arix's insides flooded with sunlight. But she did not know why. It was yet another face she couldn't quite place.

This time, it was a man looking at her, a crinkle between his brows as he examined her. Slowly, he took hold of her hands, lowering them to her lap where he grasped them tightly within his own.

"Arduinna."

This was also her name, she knew. Though it felt different. Her heart felt lighter at its sound.

The man's black hair was swept back from his face to show the hard lines of his jaw, the steel blue of his eyes. She must have known him in her life before the darkness, but she couldn't quite remember.

"Has she spoken yet?" The man asked the girl who called herself Wren, though his gaze never strayed, his eyes piercing her own.

"No, Your Majesty. I asked her to blink or nod if she could hear me and she did so. She was looking around at the flowers."

"Arduinna? Can you hear me? Can you speak?" He asked, his brows still furrowed.

That, Arix knew, she could not do. She had forgotten how.

Some kind of sign must have shown on her face, for he righted himself slowly, bringing her with him until they both stood together on the white stone path.

"I will escort Lady Arix back to her rooms. Send for Lakai." They began walking, and as an afterthought, the man said quietly, "And summon the council. Tell them the Black Hand is awake."

~

The walk through the building was strange. It was familiar, yet foreign enough to leave her guessing at the path they took. They passed a window and for a moment, Arix felt as though she should linger. Something important happened in this window seat. A flash of features skittered across her mind, and a vague recollection of a man smiling flit through her skull. Her insides clenched as she forced herself to remember. But every time she reached, the memories skittered away out of reach, leaving her empty. She knew she should remember. She knew it was important, but everything, even in the darkness of the stone hallways, was bright and vivid, causing a headache to form behind her eyes.

But then as quickly as it appeared, it was gone.

They entered a room overflowing with soft sunlight, the window open to let in the breeze that carried with it the heady rose scent of the garden. She was escorted to the window seat and slowly eased down into it. They were treating her like she were made of glass. As if any small, jarring motion would cause her to shatter. Maybe it was true. One wrong move, one wrong motion, would cause her to spiral back into the pit of darkness and shatter into a thousand pieces.

"Arix."

She looked up at the man who had spoken. He stared, searching for something in her eyes. She wanted to reach out, to touch his face, cupping his cheek in her palm. To somehow reassure him. Instead, her grip tightened and loosened in her lap.

"She hears you, Your Majesty. Speak to her."

The man sat in the chair opposite her, searching her eyes. Arix noted that he didn't bring the chair closer, keeping the space between them.

He cleared his throat. "Arix, do you remember what happened? Do you feel any different? Stronger?"

She wanted to answer him. She knew he wanted to hear her voice, but she had lost it years ago. She did not know what she sounded like anymore. Even if he begged, she wouldn't know where to go looking for it. And even if she found it, she didn't understand his questions. She didn't understand what he meant.

His face was hopeful, searching. Arix couldn't stand to look at it.

Instead she focused on the hands in her lap. The hands that were not her own.

"Please speak to me. I was so worried about you, I've been frantic." His voice was a little louder now. He sounded panicked, as if years of worry were leaching into him now and he felt them anew. "Give me anything, a sound, a grunt. Let me know you hear me. That you understand me."

He knelt on the floor, pulling her hands into his. But the motion was harsh, and a wave of fear raced through Arix's veins. She didn't know him. She didn't remember him. Even if she knew him once, she did not know him now.

His grip was tight, painful. He pulled her to him, off the chair and onto the floor. Her knees cracked against the stones, rattling her bones. A thundering rush of darkness yanked her back, and Arix snapped away from the man's grip, eyes wide and frightened.

"Enough!"

Arix's gaze flickered to someone new. An old man stood in the doorway, eyes pained. His long gray hair tangled with his beard, blue eyes crystal in the light from the window. She knew him. The darkness within her calmed. This one was different from the rest. Energy pulsed through him, dull, muddied purple, yet there nonetheless. She could see the lines that laced his arm, the soft glow of something familiar.

"Your Majesty, please," the old man continued, stepping further into the room. "Give her space. She has drunk from the chalice. There will be much she does not remember. She will need time and space to heal her mind and her body."

He stood painfully slow as his eyes blinked and his jaw tightened. "Of course. Lakai, I leave her in your hands."

Something told her she should feel something, an emotional pull at the strings of her heart at his expression, as he slowly moved to leave, the door clicking softly behind him. But there was just confusion. Confusion and emptiness.

The gray-haired man took a seat in the vacated chair by the fire, turning it to face her as he leaned forward. She was suddenly nervous, wringing her fingers in her lap, twisting and squeezing. His gaze traveled down to them, watching as her knuckles twisted back and forth.

"Good afternoon. My name is Lakai. You are probably feeling a lot of things right now. You might be confused or frustrated. That's alright. These feelings are normal."

They didn't feel normal. They felt foreign. Even the feel of her own hands was strange to her. It was all wrong. She was not herself. Did she even know who *herself* was?

"It's going to take a bit of time for things to start feeling comfortable or familiar. It's important to take things slowly. If it offers any hope to you, know that it all will come back." Lakai smiled, and something about the action made Arix's stomach tighten. It reminded her of something. Black curls dancing, an emerald green scarf. Fire and the taste of ash and bone. Arix shuddered.

"For today, I'd like to have you drink a bit of water. Do you think you can do that?"

She wasn't thirsty. But Arix nodded anyway, the motion jerky as her chin dipped.

"Good." He turned to the girl named Wren. "Please fetch us a pitcher and a cup. Wooden, please."

As the girl hurried from the room, a piece of Arix relaxed. The girl's nervous energy made her veins feel too tight in her arms, at the inside creases of her elbows. Strange, that she could feel—no, *hear*—the pulsing of her own blood. Arix glanced down, noticing for the first time how pale her skin was, how porcelain white it seemed. She reached, gently gliding the tips of her fingers along the thin gray line under her skin.

Minutes stretched by as the two waited silently for the water to come. Lakai watched her, and she watched herself. Listened to herself. Listened to the blood streaming through her. When Wren returned, Lakai filled a quarter of the cup and held it, outstretched, in the space between them.

Arix reached for it, but the cup slipped between her fingers. In endlessly slow motion, it teetered from her grasp and slammed into the floor, its contents splashing onto the toes of her shoes. As the water pooled and Wren moved to pick up the fallen cup, Arix simply stared.

"It's alright." Lakai smiled. Arix wasn't sure if he was reassuring her or the girl. "That's why I asked for a wooden cup. Your fingers still need to get used to themselves. Let's try again."

Once more he filled it a quarter with water and held it out to her. Instead of taking it, Arix only stared.

"You can do it, Arix. Take your time and move slowly."

After a moment, she moved again, this time taking care to place both hands around the cup, grasping it tightly before moving to take it from the man's hand. This time it did not fall. Raising the cup to her lips, she took a slow, deliberate sip, letting a few drops settle on her tongue.

It was not like she remembered. She remembered water to be tasteless. Refreshing on a hot day, but void of flavor and depth. Empty. This was different. It felt as though droplets of diamond sat on her tongue. Earthy and rich, tasting of crushed stones and minerals. How long had it been? How long since she had tasted?

The cup tipped of its own accord. The water splashed across her face and down her neck, pooling across the fabric of her chest, slipping between her breasts and down to her stomach.

Wren gasped, but Arix ignored her, lost in the ecstasy of the water. She had not felt something so precious in a long, long time. She stared down at herself, at the drops that remained on her skin, tiny crystalline beads that glimmered in the sunlight.

"Arix?"

She glanced up. Lakai was watching her with curious calm.

"How long have you been gone from us?"

Wren's voice was barely above a whisper as she began, "Sir, she—"

"Wren, please." Lakai cut her off, never taking his eyes from Arix's. "Let her speak."

Arix knew that she could not. How could she tell him of the years that had passed? The decades locked in darkness and pain so overwhelming it had brought no end of torment. That she had given up hope long ago of ever coming back. Of ever living again. Of tasting water and feeling the wind against her skin.

A sound escaped her. Crackled and raw and formless. It was not a word or speech, not a moan or whimper, but something else entirely. She had lost her voice so long ago, this strange sound was alien, yet ecstatic. She blinked in surprise.

"Arix, I'll ask again, and please take your time. Don't try and force yourself. How long have you been gone from us?"

Arix opened her mouth, pushing air between her teeth as the sound came forth again, formless. She moved her tongue, pushing it into her teeth as she tried again. This time it sounded like something. Her blood screamed, tearing through her veins as her heart picked up speed. She was speaking! *Almost.*

Once again, she tried moving her tongue around her mouth, tried to speak for the first time in forever.

"Long."

Out of the corner of her eye, she saw Wren place a hand over her heart.

"How long, Arix?" Lakai continued.

It was coming back to her, the patterns of her mouth, the shape of her lips, forming thought into speech. Frustratingly, disturbingly slow, she jostled out the word from her throat.

"Long...time."

She tried at a third word, but it got tangled in her throat, and her hands slammed against the window seat in frustration.

Lakai's hands went up to calm her. "It's alright, Arix. Slowly. Give yourself time to find the words. Don't rush it. You have time."

She took a deep breath, trying to quell the rising panic. "Years."

Wren's raspy voice filled the space again. "What?"

Lakai ignored the maid's outburst, motioning for Arix to continue.

"Seven. Teen."

No one moved as the complicated word made its way out.

"Seventeen?" Wren whispered.

"Wren, please." Lakai shushed.

"Days."

"Seventeen days?" Lakai repeated, piecing the words together.

"Six."

They waited expectantly.

"Months."

"Six months?" Wren's voice squeaked. Lakai didn't quiet her this time, his eyes still trained on Arix's mouth as she continued forming words.

"Thirty…" Arix screwed her eyes closed in concentration then forced them back open, trying again. "Thirty-one."

"Thirty-one? Thirty-one what?" Wren's eyes were as wide as dinner plates as she stared at her mistress, horror carved into her features.

Arix took a deep breath, her throat catching on the last word. She'd already spoken more than she thought she could. Desperately, she looked to Lakai, begging with her eyes for him to

understand her meaning. He leaned back slowly, looking as if years had been drained out of him as he stared at her.

"Seventeen days, six months, and thirty-one years. That's how long you've been gone."

Her brows pressed together as she gave him a small shake of her head. "Stopped. Counting."

Lakai only blinked, the understanding dawning. "It was longer than that? You stopped counting after thirty-one years?"

Arix slowly nodded.

"How is that possible?" Wren was blubbering now, her words mumbled, slipping through her slack lips. She spoke more to herself than to Lakai, her gaze at the floor as she went on. "How could she think she'd been gone for so long? It was only a week? What in the Goddess' name has happened to her? She—"

Her mumblings came to an abrupt halt as Lakai stood, filling the space between her and the now trembling Arix. His gaze tore into the maid, and she quieted, her mouth still gaping mid-sentence.

"Out. Now."

With one terrified look back at Arix, the maid turned and left the room, leaving Lakai and Arix alone.

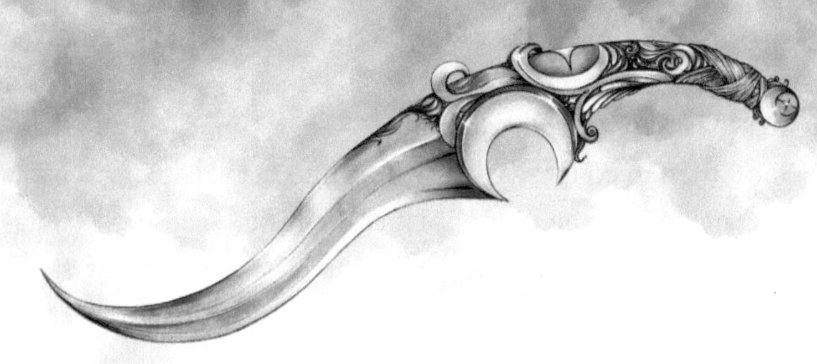

TWO

"More?" Arix held out the cup to Lakai, her hands gripped tightly so that it would not fall again.

Slowly, he filled it and settled back into the chair to let her drink.

Arix tipped the glass slowly, feeling the cool water slide down her throat. She felt it descend through her chest and hit her stomach, and she could almost hear the slosh as it settled there. She drank until the cup was empty, every last drop of sweetness smoothed across her lips.

"Would you like more? Perhaps some food?"

Arix held the cup out, which he filled, and she drained again.

And food? She was hungry, yes. But something else was wriggling like a worm in her mind.

"She…" The words stuck in her throat. "One week?"

Lakai settled the half empty pitcher on a small table and crossed his fingers in his lap. "Wren? Yes, she said one week. The passage of time you have experienced and the time we have experienced is different. How does that make you feel?"

Arix blinked. Time passing was something she knew. Something she had felt in her bones. For a long time it had been the only thing that had kept her alive and sane—*was she sane?*—in the darkness. She'd tried to count. Carving marks into her skin, chipping her bones, scratching on the insides of her eyelids to keep her best account of time slipping past her. Only when she'd run out of space had she stopped tallying the days.

But…

"What…happened?" The water had smoothed the ridges of her mouth, and words were making their way through her. Her mind was unclogging itself, untangling. She needed to know, to understand what had caused the darkness. What had put her there.

"Your outward body has been catatonic for about a week now. You haven't eaten or slept."

A week? It had only been a *week?* No. Her arm twitched at the thought.

"What do you remember?"

Flashes of seething pain, agonizing and torturous, ripping her body to shreds. Her fingernails flaking off as she clawed at the walls of her prison.

Arix flinched.

"Bad. Dark…ness. Pain."

Lakai winced. "Yes, I'm afraid that is how the transition starts. But I mean before the darkness, what do you remember?"

Trying to push through all those years of torment was like slogging through tar, and for a moment, Arix feared she'd get dragged back down into it again. Her breathing quickened, her heart racing in her chest.

An old man.

Why was she remembering an old man? She fought for the memory, desperately dragging it back into her consciousness.

"The king is dead."

"Yes, he is."

"I killed…him."

"Yes."

People…staring at her. They had stared, some with horror. And she had tasted…What had she tasted?

"I…" She tried to move past the visual of the memory, not just what her eyes had seen but the taste on her lips. "It tasted… like…death."

Tipping the chalice, the metal cold against her mouth, icy cold. The thick taste of death. It had been so sweet, like syrup. Black.

"I am the Black Hand." A strange sort of relief settled in her at the thought.

Lakai smiled. "You are."

But there was something—no, *someone*—missing.

"Where is Michael?"

She was looking past Lakai, past his chair and the pitcher on the table, at the room they now sat in. The bed and the stones of the floor, the furniture… All so familiar. She stood.

"Michael?"

Lakai was already moving to stop her, getting in her way as she pushed herself off the window seat and towards the door.

He had to be here. This was his room, wasn't it? She'd spent hours here, hadn't she?

Whole nights and early mornings spent sprawled across these floors, the chairs, the bed. Laughing and studying and throwing small acorns across the room with magickal force.

Curly black hair, soft brown eyes.

Ash and burnt hair.

Arix choked, throwing herself to the floor as she vomited the water back up. She was coughing, gagging on spew that was nothing but that clear crystalline water. But all she could taste was ash and bile.

Strong arms pulled her away from the puddle on the floor

'til her back rested against the side of the bed. She gasped for air and howled out a strangled cry, but she refused to shut her eyes. Refused to see the darkness.

Lakai let her weep. Let her feel these things she had forgotten, these friends she had let slip away amongst all the pain and all the torment. The darkness had been a prison. But was freedom from it any better if this was what she remembered?

Scenes filled her mind, of stone and straw, the creaking of a ship around them as Revena rubbed her back. The look on Michael's face as his eyes scrunched together, then hurled himself off the roof with them, feather-falling to the safety below.

And red.

Fire so red in filled her vision, and blood that pooled between her fingers.

They were gone to her. Burned away into nothing but the dry taste of ash on her tongue and the warm slick of blood between her fingers. How she had fought for them both. How she had cried for them both.

Gone to her now.

How could she have forgotten about Michael and Revena?

A blonde braid coming loose, pain in her shoulder, a glint of a silver dagger. Celeste? The tests seemed so long ago, but the pain was fresh all over again, cracking open her ribcage and gutting out her heart.

Then the tears were over. Dried up. Wren returned to clean up the mess, and Lakai moved them elsewhere, walking the hallways of the castle. A few of the windows were open, breezes filtering across the stones and over Arix's face as she walked. She did so slowly, arm wrapped around Lakai's as they moved. They walked for almost an hour in absolute silence, turned down staircases and looping back onto hallways that were becoming familiar again.

Again, she passed a window alcove, and this time, Arix remembered why it was so important. So many hours spent studying, or rather talking, with Michael and Revena. Whispering about their tutors and classes.

And then she was pulling away from Lakai, following her old route up to the roof. The sun was spilling across the trees now, shining across Michael's overgrown vegetable beds. She stepped up to the edge of the terrace, peering down the ground so far below.

Lakai's hand rested on her shoulder. "You can never forget them, Arix. All the magick you learned was learned with them, and as long as you have magick, you have them with you."

"I know."

"You're remembering it all."

Yes, she was. Every tiny detail was coming back. The good, and the bad.

"It will take time for all of it to come back. The lessons, the faces. But the words will be there for you, and so will the magick. Here. This might help with that."

He held out a small vial stoppered with a round cork. The contents were black, inky darkness. Arix took it from him, tracing the edge of the glass with the tip of her finger.

"It will help, I promise. It will help you remember."

She uncapped the bottle, and when she tipped it, the liquid that slid over her tongue was familiar. Like drinking sweet, honeyed death. Tangy and acidic, but in it was also clarity. With each drop, her mind cleared.

"This too. I've been keeping it safe until you awoke." He held out a clenched fist, and she cupped her hands beneath, the slide of cold metal cascading down into her palm.

"Hello, again."

The final piece of her that had been missing snapped into place, and all the gaps in her memories filled themselves back in. All the time she had spent in the darkness was still there, but her time before it was clear again. And wrapped up in all that clarity was relief. The sudden aching relief of knowing who she was, and feeling finally at home in her own skin.

"My necklace." Words were easy now, flowing out of her. "And Michael's ring? I want that back."

"I'm not sure if—"

"You will give it to me." Arix turned to Lakai. "It's mine."

They stared at each other for a moment, time seeming to stretch endlessly. Lakai nodded. "Of course."

"And my magick?"

She didn't need to ask. Not really. She could feel it, feel the power in her veins, thrumming as she settled the necklace around her neck and back into its place over her heart. Though it was day, though she'd been comatose for a week, lost in herself for even longer, she instinctively knew the moon's phase. She could feel the threads of elements woven into the plants on the roof, the breeze that tumbled through her hair. She could feel the fire in the sun, could almost *see* how it seeped into the ground, into her, warming her skin. All the little things that she'd known before, all the puzzle pieces, were so clear to her now. Impulses and instinct as easy as walking. As easy as flying.

She'd studied before. Studied to understand and see the threads that bound them, her to magick and magick to her. Now, she knew, without knowing, that she could snap her fingers and the cants she wanted would come to her.

"It is yours. Your core will help you access it as before. I would go slowly though, as you're still healing from the—"

Arix threw herself from the roof.

She heard Lakai's gasp of breath as she fell away from the castle, plummeting to the ground below, but her descent was already slowing as the magick flowed through her. It was as easy as breathing to cast the cant and float to the grass below. No feathers necessary. Not anymore. Now she could see the currents of air, bend them how she wanted. Magick was different. Almost easy now.

As her feet touched the ground, Arix let out a long, slow breath. She was tired. She was hungry.

In the darkness she had neither slept nor ate and it felt strange to think she could have both now. Already, the darkness seemed to be slipping away like a dream.

Lakai was waiting for her by the front entry of the castle when she approached the doors, and pushed her way past him.

"I guess you're feeling much better than you were an hour ago."

"I am." Arix fingered the stone inset in her necklace. "This helped."

"Good. I hoped it might speed up the process but wanted to give you a chance to try and get there on your own."

Arix glanced up at the new banner that waved from the grand staircase. It was a new stylized version of King Taurus' coat of arms, a five headed black dragon with sword clutched in one claw and a goblet in the other. The red, black, and silver colors of Taurus' emblem had been changed, a brilliant gold having replaced the former red background, any traces of silver gone altogether. "It seems there's a lot I still need to catch up on."

"Yes."

Arix glanced over in surprise at Lakai's tone. The old man's face was grim as he turned away from her.

"Yes, there is," he muttered as he walked away.

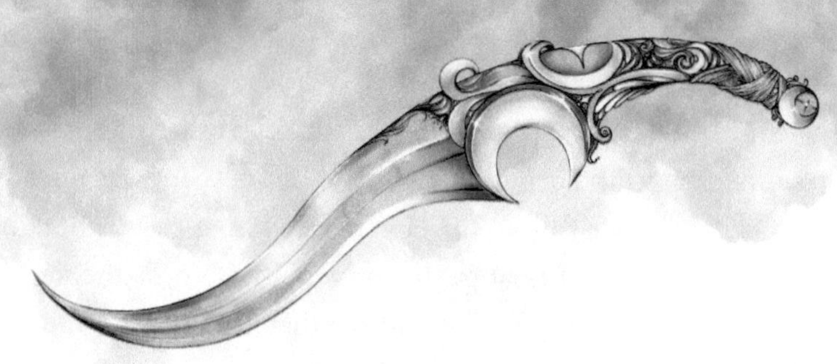

THREE

Her hair had turned white.

Arix ran her fingers along the snow white braid that circled her head, watching as the person in the mirror followed her movements. It was strange, seeing a reflection of yourself that was not your own. Her skin no longer held a light pink glow, but was closer to alabaster, and the veins at her wrists were no longer pale blue, but light gray.

She had stopped in the front hall, barely a few steps through the main door, and caught her reflection in the grand mirror that hung, floor to ceiling, between two ornate tapestries. Her eyes too had changed, the vibrant green muddled into a pale green that was closer to the color of dead grass.

"When did this happen?"

"It's been a transition since you drank from the chalice." Lakai watched her, his reflection from over her shoulder mirroring her own. "It's normal."

Arix let out a dry chuckle. "Normal?"

Their eyes met in the reflection, and she found a twinge of regret in his eyes.

"There will be more. More things to discover about your new

self. Things you do not yet know."

Finally drawing her gaze away from the mirror, Arix turned. "You thought I would have doubts if I knew the whole truth. Doubts about becoming the Black Hand."

Her tutor shifted slightly, doing his best to hide his discomfort. It was slight, but Arix noticed it anyway.

"Yes."

The more she stood in the hall, the more cold she became. She'd lived here, trained here, for over a year. She'd fought and won. She'd lost too much. And now, it seemed, she hadn't been told even half of what she'd hurled herself into.

She was the Black Hand. But what did that even mean?

"You said I had a lot to catch up on?"

Lakai turned without saying a word, and she followed him. The echoing of their shoes scuffing against the stone floor made Arix's shoulders tense, but she followed silently.

The familiar steps towards the throne room had Arix watching the more subtle changes in the interior of the castle. There were more guards posted, a couple at almost every major doorway, and as they stepped through into the grand room that held the dais at the far end, six more. Had it been only a week since she had stood there beside Orion in front of the whole court and drank from the chalice? Only a week since she had been proclaimed the Black Hand in front of them all?

"They all know now." Arix reached the dais, mounting the steps and leaving Lakai below her on the main floor. She turned slowly, standing beside the throne and placing her hand on its armrest.

There was a look of unease on his face, his forehead creasing and a tightness at the corners of his mouth that betrayed his annoyance. She was standing where she shouldn't. Making assumptions about what was allowed her.

But she knew where her place was. Arix raised her chin slightly, and the unease on his face only grew.

"Hmmm." The voice of the necklace in her mind was lazy and relaxed. *"What unsettles him, do you think? Your confidence, perhaps?"*

"They all know I am the Black Hand? Has there been an announcement?"

Lakai clasped his hands behind his back, still staring up at her. "There has been an announcement of the King Taurus's death, Osiris guide him. There is to be a coronation for King Orion, and there you will be announced as his Black Hand. Though, unofficially yes, they know who you are now."

"Good. As far as the people know, it's been a year of silence. They deserve to know that there is someone watching out for them now."

Lakai said nothing.

She took the steps back down from the dais slowly, purposefully, until she was back at the same level as her disgruntled tutor. The banners here had all been replaced as well, the new emblem of King Orion hanging heavy from the walls and pillars. None of the candles were lit, and the light from the windows caused long shadows to fall throughout the cavernous space. In a strange way, it felt abandoned.

No, not abandoned. Just empty. Waiting.

A tingle of anticipation traced up Arix's spine. Soon, the hall would be overflowing with light, and they all would know who she was. They would all know what she could do, and she and Orion would change Rökkur with it.

In the back of her mind, thoughts of Michael and Revena still hovered, but instead of the rush of pain, the rush of regret and anguish, it was replaced with a calm. They watched her, encouraged her, she knew. She would not be here without them. She would not easily forget their sacrifices.

"I'm famished. Can we continue this over food?" She offered Lakai a smile and put a hand on his arm. "I want to know what else I've missed."

Lakai offered her a smile in return, some of the unease melting into sympathy. "Of course. I've had the cook lay out some food for us."

It was a familiar stroll back towards the dining room, though the tables had been rearranged differently, and now a head table sat at the far end, facing the doorway. A large chair, clearly for the king, had been placed at the center, and to the right of it, a similarly ornate seat, only slightly smaller that held a place setting.

"Is that for me?" Arix made her way towards it, only offering the question out of respect for Lakai's previous disapproval in the throne room. She knew it was her seat. Where else would the right hand to the king sit?

"Yes, it's for you." Lakai moved to take the chair beside hers, settling into the food that was spread out for the two of them.

Arix took her time settling into the seat, fingers gliding across the ornate wood carving across the back panel and down the cushioned black velvet. The chair was heavy as she pulled it out for herself and took a seat. A small part of her wished there were others to see her. Revena and Michael, knowing they would be proud. And Celeste, knowing she'd be livid.

For the first few moments, they ate in silence, digging into the steaming venison and garlic-roasted potatoes. The smell of everything was stronger, more potent in her nostrils. She could single out the rosemary and sage in the potatoes. Cracked pepper and cherries in the sauce that the venison had been cooked in. The bread had bits of olives baked in, and as she chewed she could taste the differences between each bite.

So her taste and smell had improved. Her reflexes too, as she'd thrown herself from the roof, it had been almost too easy knowing exactly where she'd land. What else had changed?

"You mentioned a presentation?" Arix asked between mouthfulls.

"The coronation, yes. King Orion wanted to wait until you were awake before hosting it. The recovery time varies for each Black Hand but never lasts longer than a week or so. Now that you have, invitations will be sent out, and soon, everyone will be gathered in Mergur." Lakai took a deep sip of his wine. "There will be a tour after that, and you'll travel with the king to visit the four realms and the Warden's homes. An introduction of sorts. Think of it as your victory lap for becoming the Black Hand. Once that is over, the real work will begin."

"And in the meantime?" Arix asked around another mouthful of potatoes.

Lakai settled back in his chair, clearly finished eating, as Arix continued to pile her plate with more food. "I'd prefer you take things easy for the next couple of days, and soon we'll get you settled in. Your office is prepared, and you're encouraged to hire an assistant. They'll be at your disposal to help with your schedule once things calm down and offer their assistance as need be."

"What kind of schedule?"

"You'll meet with the king and council every two weeks to discuss policy and current issues, plan events and discuss issues within the realm. You'll have to meet more often on a one-on-one basis with the Wardens alone, and of course you'll also be present at any meeting made with the king. While your lessons with Desirae and myself are not required, please feel free to seek her or myself out to assist you in expanding your knowledge of magick and your new status as the Black Hand."

Arix nodded along while Lakai listed the various duties of her new role, shifting her attention slightly as a server cleared out the used plates and placed a brandied pear steamed pudding in front of her, drizzled and glistening in a caramel cream sauce.

"You'll have your own affairs to attend to, and you'll have quite a bit of control, so the Wardens want to be sure that you don't make a mess of things."

The pudding was decadent and Arix was halfway through another mouthful before she realized Lakai was waiting for a response.

"Of course." She gave him a sidelong glance. "They want to protect the power they hold. I might be a threat to that power."

"It's more complicated than that."

Arix snorted.

Lakai placed a hand on her arm, pulling her gaze away from her dessert and back to him. "You've proven yourself, Arix. Over and over again, you proved that you deserve the magick in your veins. You deserve this position. But managing your magick or defeating the Carn is a vast difference from the day-to-day running of a kingdom. Which you are now in the position to do. Lord Bardon will continue to run the more mundane aspects of the ruling crown, but you represent the magick that the crown wields. That means that all eyes are on you. You won't have any room for mistakes."

She met his gaze with a determined scowl. "I won't be bullied by them."

"You won't be, no. The king is on your side, and so are many in the court. But you do have enemies here, Arix, don't forget. They all wait to see what kind of Black Hand you will become. I'm sure many hope you will sit back as a glorified bodyguard to do as the king commands. You and I both know that you are capable of more than that. They will be waiting for a reason to usurp you, to prove you aren't capable of your position."

Anger coiled in Arix's insides as she let it simmer. And as the moments passed and the steam from her dessert wafted into nothing, so did her anger quell slightly. Lakai was right. This wouldn't be easy. And without Michael's cool head and Revena's determination, she'd need all the help she could get in her new role.

Lakai was a built-in ally, already in her corner, ready to teach her and fight with her to claim the power and respect she was owed. But not everyone would be that way.

"I'm sorry." Her food forgotten, she turned to him, grasping his arm tightly. "This day has had a lot of ups and downs. You're here to help and I've been treating you like…"

"Like I'm beneath you?" Lakai finished for her.

Arix swallowed. She expected some sort of shame to fill her, but it didn't. She knew who she was now, in a way that she never quite had before.

He let out a resolved sigh, leaning back in his chair. "Technically, I am, Arix. But don't let this newfound power get to your head. It'll be easy for it to overtake you, and cockiness will only lead to your downfall. I hope that you will consider me as someone you can trust. As one of the very few you can trust. Take a couple days to ground yourself before you start toppling the kingdom."

"I don't need a couple days."

"You do."

"I don't. I've been resting for over a week. I need to get into a routine. I need to feel comfortable, to get my bearings. And the faster I know my job, the better I'll feel."

Lakai stood up slowly, fingers tangled in his beard. "I suppose I could show you your office."

"That would be great." She offered him a grateful smile. "While we walk, maybe you can tell me what was in that chalice and why I spent so many years stuck in my own head."

"I am sorry for that." He offered her a sympathetic look, the lines around his eyes deepening. "From what I understand, it's the mind's way of succumbing to the effects of the Well Water. It changes you from the inside out, and the results can vary depending on the Incantor that drinks from it."

"Well Water? That was the same thing you just gave me, from the vial?" Arix thought back to the taste of the liquid on her tongue, the sweet, acidic taste as it slid down her throat. "What exactly is it?"

They had made their way up the spiral staircase and back down one of the west wing hallways towards the council's meeting room. Lakai waited until they were past another set of guards before he answered her, his voice hushed.

"It's a delicate subject, Arix. Very few—and I do mean *very very few*—know about what you drank from the chalice. The king knows, as do I, Lord Bardon, and I believe Warden Aliska has an inkling, but she's the only one of the Wardens who has even the faintest idea of what transpired that night. The secrets of the Black Hands and the Conclave have been kept secret for a very long time, and for good reason."

"What is the Conclave?"

"A very small and very secret collective that protects the secrets of the Black Hand. Even I don't know all of their truths. It is the kind of knowledge that disappears if not kept alive. The Conclave was designed to protect that knowledge, protect the secrets." Lakai glanced over at her, white eyebrows pushed together. "I know you feel like all of this was kept from you, but it wasn't without reason. Sometimes, the truth has to be learned slowly."

Arix nodded but said nothing, tongue tracing the lines of the roof of her mouth. The flavors of the food she had consumed still lingered, but beneath it, that sweet taste of the Well Water from Lakai's stoppered vial remained.

They stopped in front of a large wooden door, and Lakai smiled as he pulled it open for her. "Your office."

The space itself was less of a singular office, but two rooms that split off from a small centralized antechamber that contained a small seating area and a desk at its center. Arix stepped inside, almost tip-toeing across the lush whorls of the embroidered carpet.

"Your assistant's desk." Lakai motioned to the small desk in front of them. "And if you have meetings scheduled, your guests can wait here."

Behind the desk was a fireplace that was open through the back, and through it, Arix could tell it offered its blaze to two other rooms. To each side of the desk were doors, branching off in a Y-shape from the small antechamber.

"What's through those doors?"Arix asked, motioning to the right one.

Lakai smiled. "Go ahead and have a look. It's yours to do with as you see fit. There's a design implemented already from the previous occupants, but feel free to rearrange it as much as you need."

Arix carefully pushed the right door open to reveal a study very similar in design to Desirae's office. A desk sat beside a large cross-hatched window, a comfortable but ridiculously tall, cushioned chair behind it. Another table was stationed closer to the center of the room, with no chairs around it, cleared across the top for maps. A skinny bookshelf on the side of it held pigeonholed sections with curled parchment rolled and organized within. In the corner behind the door was the shared fireplace.

"And this is mine?" Arix walked to the window, peering out and down onto the grounds below. This was higher up than Desirae's office had been, facing a different direction, and you could see more of the wall and the city beyond it.

It occurred to Arix that she should have a higher office in one of the lofty towers since she wasn't just a competitor anymore. It still hadn't sunk in yet, her sudden vault in station. And yet here she was, nonetheless, looking down upon her new dominion. And it was hers now, in some strange way. Orion might be king, but she was his Black Hand. With that there was a semblance of ownership, of responsibility to the people in Rökkur. How many of the people in this castle, the very ones who had watched her drink from the chalice, knew what she had done? Knew that she was the one who had brought Taurus' final fate? And how many had known what Orion was planning long before she did?

"Did you know?" Arix turned to watch Lakai's expression remain still, wary. "Did you know that he was Taurus' son?"

"Yes. But my interaction with the knowledge was minimal, and I only knew the scope of things about halfway through the tests. I suppose his majesty had decided it was time I knew what was coming. To trust me enough to let me in on his plans."

Arix pulled the chair behind the desk out, sliding into the soft cushioned leather and splaying her fingers across the flat, cool wood of the desk. "When you caught me in that alley last summer, you didn't know what he was planning?"

Lakai shook his head. "No."

"And what do you think now? Now that all of this has unfolded the way it has? How do you feel knowing who your new king is?"

The silence between them yawned, stretching as the two incantors studied each other.

"Or are you not in a position to discuss the matter?"

The old incantor stepped forward and slowly took a seat across from her. "Arix, you make the mistaken assumption that you can speak freely. That you can speak your mind, even here, alone with me. In your private study, you feel the freedom to speak so openly against the king, and I would remind you of this: Just because you are the Black Hand does not mean you are safe."

She felt a shiver crawl up her spine.

"You will have to be careful. More careful than you were before. You will have to watch your words and your actions and be aware of the things people will say about you and to you. Be careful of your friends. Be careful of the people you place around yourself. You are the Black Hand, yes. But remember that there were many people you may have stepped on to gain your current position. Favorites of the court are dead because of you, because of the tests. Tempers will not easily be dissuaded or cooled. You will have to be extremely wise and exceedingly careful."

Arix let the grin spread across her face as she leaned forward towards him. "Indeed I will."

Her abrupt change in mood seemed to surprise Lakai, and when she stood, he quickly joined her.

"You're right." She said, moving back out into the antechamber. "It's been a long day, and I'm tired. Maybe it's time to rest a bit."

Lakai nodded, leading the way back through the familiar hallways. It was a new path that they traveled, toward one of the spiraling towers. Two guards nodded to them at the bottom of the stairwell and two more waited near the top of the stairs, nodding to Lakai as he pushed open the double cedar doors.

"New rooms." Lakai stepped aside, letting Arix step into the space and take in the beautiful rooms around her.

The apartments were spread out, all branching off of the main antechamber. They speared off to a bedroom, washroom, large and overflowing closet, and a small reading nook. The main room at the center of them all was large enough to hold a small dining set at one end and a large lounging area at the other. It was more than enough space for just one person, and Arix couldn't help but wonder if she would even need half of it.

"The guards, downstairs."

"They're for your protection of course. They do rotate shifts, but they'll always be there and at your disposal. I can assure you that they're of the highest caliber—"

"I want Ulfur and Abbas."

Lakai blinked. "Who?"

"The guards I had before. Ulfur and Abbas. I want them as my personal guards again."

Arix was sure that Lakai was getting a headache from the way the man's cheek twitched. "Of course, I understand your attachment to them, but since Orion has taken the throne, some changes have been made."

"Undo them."

"Arix, please be reasonable. These guards have been selected for a reason."

"Lakai, please." She matched his tone and noticed the twitch in his cheek only deepen. "You just reminded me to be careful. To choose my friends wisely. And I'll take your advice, of course, because it's good advice. And for that very reason, I want Ulfur and Abbas to be added to the lineup of rotating guards outside my rooms. Here, outside the door. And the others, I'll want to choose them myself, if you don't mind. I need to know who will be guarding me."

"Alright. I'll see what I can do."

His voice was clipped. He was angry with her.

"He doesn't like not getting his own way."

Arix's hand went involuntarily to the pendant around her neck, fingering the gem inlaid in the black metal casing. The voice was right. Lakai had expected her to lean on him, to have felt out of her depth and intimidated by the new world that was heaping onto her shoulders. He had expected her to be meek, grateful to be in this new role.

"I appreciate that." She offered him her best winning smile. "If you're free, I'd love to meet with you again tomorrow, and we can discuss more of my new duties as the Black Hand. As you said, I'll need all the help I can get."

Her words seemed to soften him a bit, though the twitch remained.

"Of course. I'll let you rest."

And with that he was gone.

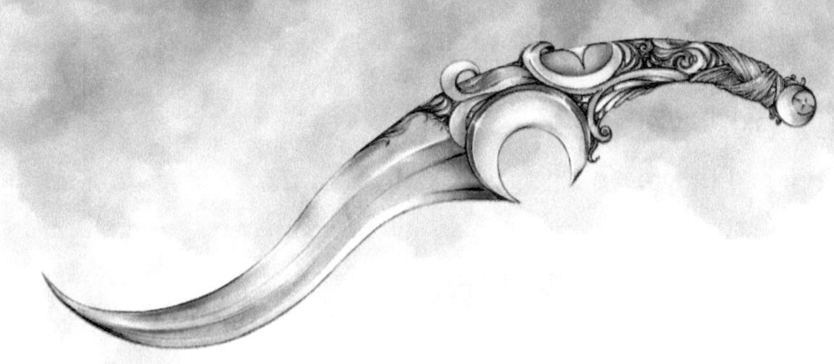

FOUR

It was only after she'd crept back down the stairs and stood on the main landing in the front hall that Arix realized she had no idea where Orion's room was. Her shoes were held in her hand to avoid making any noise as she passed the guards that had been posted along her tower. Not that she needed to tell them she was leaving her room; she didn't owe them an explanation as to where she was going. But there was an air of secrecy she wanted to keep. With an invisibility cant in place, they wouldn't be able to see her slip past them down the stairs.

As Lakai had said, this castle was always watching, always listening. And for what she wanted to do, she didn't want anyone's eyes on her.

There were always the old king's rooms she could check. Arix glanced back up the stairs, remembering the trek she had taken there the night she had become the Black Hand. Of course it would make sense for Orion to move into those rooms, they were the king's quarters, after all, but it felt wrong, and she was sure that no matter how Orion felt about his father, he wouldn't likely take up residence there so quickly.

That left only one other option.

She had only been there once before, in the week leading up to the final test with Celeste, but Arix still remembered the way, tiptoeing towards his door. The four guards standing at attention outside didn't notice her pass as she slipped through and came to stand barefoot on the rug inside the office doorway.

Orion was at his desk, a book in his left hand, his right loosely turning pages as he skimmed through the contents. He glanced up at her as she stepped further into the room, and their eyes met.

"You can see me?"

"I can."

A small smile curled at the corner of Arix's mouth. "You've had Lakai do a little cantwork in here, haven't you. Dampening any use of magick?"

He leaned back in his chair, watching her, his eyes warm. Crackles of heat radiated down Arix's spine at that look.

"It's smart. Something I was going to suggest, actually."

He slowly stood, coming around the side of the desk and reaching for her hand. She let him pull her into him, loved the feeling as he pulled her into a soft embrace.

"Goddess, how I've missed you."

His muscles were so taught beneath the fabric of his shirt, that Arix wondered if he wasn't holding himself back a little to keep from hurting her. Holding back to give her the space she needed, the time to heal. But Arix didn't want his light touches, treating her like an injured bird. She wanted to feel the weight of him wrapped around her, crushing their bodies together.

Before she could say a thing, he was already moving back, putting space between them, and instantly, she felt the loss of him.

"Are you well, Arix? Are you…" He trailed off at the look in her eyes. His eyebrows knit together, his jaw tightening. Like he knew the blaze burning inside her.

"I'm fine. Better than fine." Arix closed the space between them, hands resting on his chest as she pressed her body into his. "I'm on *fire*, Orion. There's all this fire in me, and the only thing I can think of to quench it is you."

His arms were around her in a second, pressing them together, his fingers tangling into the hair at the nape of her neck. Pulling her closer as their lips connected, soft and warm.

Catching his lip between her teeth, she bit lightly, tugging at the collar of his shirt with her hands.

Goddess, she wanted him so badly her ribs ached.

The fabric of her dress bunched in his grip as she pushed him back against the edge of the desk, and he dragged her up to straddle him. He let out a small groan as she pushed herself against him, feeling him beneath her. Dragging fingers through his long black hair, she pulled him closer, fisting his hair in her hands and guiding his head to move down to her neck. He kissed and nipped down her jaw to the soft spot on her collarbone, and Arix's head fell back at the rush of pleasure it elicited.

"Goddess, Arix, to touch you again…"

"I know, I know."

"It killed me to not have you."

His words were muffled against her skin, but his voice rumbled into her, leaving goosebumps across her chest.

"Have me now."

He pulled away to look at her, his blue eyes digging deep into her own. She could see that something warred in him, that he was fighting his urges, fighting what he wanted to do for the sake of some voice of judgment in him.

"Do you remember?" She traced her fingers along his jawline, across his lips, down his neck as she spoke. "Do you remember the day we came back from Sieren? After I'd fought the paramour, and you and I met in the chapel here in the castle?"

She watched his eyes darken as he stared at her, felt his breathing hitch as he recalled back to that day when he had stripped her bare and worshiped her with his mouth on the altar of Kaoss.

"Yes, I remember."

"Do you remember what you told me?"

He stayed silent, eyes trained on hers as she slid her fingers across his collarbone, sliding underneath the thin material of his shirt, tracing the hard lines of his skin.

"You told me that there would be time for us. That day had been about me and how you had wanted to show me how important I was. Now is that time, Orion. For us."

A feral grin spread across her face.

"You are the king. You can have whatever you want."

Everything in her sparked and shone at the look in his eyes. The look of hunger and want and desperation. She could tell how badly he wanted her, could *feel* how desperately he wanted her.

And then he pushed her away.

For a moment, she resisted, knowing she could convince him. But one look at his gaze and she knew that nothing would happen between them.

"Arix, you just came back to us. Lakai says you'll need a lot of rest, that you aren't yourself yet. That you still need time to come back to normal, to heal."

She could almost forgive him for the worry that streaked his brow. Almost.

"Can't we wait? Wait until you're feeling better?"

Her chest was tight. "I'm feeling fine."

Slowly, he pushed her back until they were no longer sprawled across the desk and standing back on their two feet. The concern that had only moments ago softened her heart had turned into determination on his brow.

"You think I'm being unfair." It wasn't a question.

Arix fought to keep the pout out of her tone. "Yes. I'm feeling fine, Orion. Really."

The embroidered thread on his jacket felt rough under her fingers; she traced the design of swirls and leaves, feeling every thread, every fiber, both the overall design as well as the individual threads that made up the whole. Her perspective was different, her senses acutely aware of the things around her. She *did* feel better, more herself now, but she also remembered the darkness so very clearly. She'd been alone for so long that all her senses had dulled; she'd been stripped of the world and forced into solitude. And there was no way in hell she was about to spend tonight alone.

"Fine."

She pulled from his grip and turned for the door. Maybe it was unfair, but she didn't care.

"Just know that I'm spending tonight in someone's bed, even if that person isn't you."

She heard his intake of breath, air sucking through his teeth. She felt the tension shift as he stepped forward and swung her back around to face him.

"You'd spend the night in some other man's bed because I won't fuck you?"

"Or woman."

His eyes narrowed slightly. "You're mine, Arix."

Heat rose up her spine, tingling across her scalp. "I don't remember agreeing to that."

Strong fingers ran up her arm until Orion had the back of her neck resting softly in his palm. He was watching her, blue-eyed gaze flicking back and forth as they traveled down along her jaw to rest on her lips.

And then he was hugging her. Pressing their bodies together as he nestled his face into the soft lines of her neck. His voice was muffled into her hair when he finally spoke.

"I have missed you, Arduinna. I have missed your smell and your taste, and it's taken more of me than you know to be away from you. To hold myself back from you."

"Then don't," Arix demanded, stroking her fingers up his back, feeling his hard muscles beneath his vest. His words were loving, sickeningly sweet. And maybe she would appreciate them later. But right now, there was a burning in her, hot and wild, and the sugared words he was speaking seemed to glide right past her.

"Orion."

His lips moved up to the soft curve of her ear, his breath light. "Yes?"

"I've been closed away from the world, locked away in a prison of my own mind for too long. Every moment you aren't buried inside me feels like a waste of time."

He leaned back, eyes darkening under the look she gave him.

"Do you promise to tell me if you want to stop?"

"I swear by the goddess and all her children."

His lips crashed to hers, and she groaned into him, the hand on the back of her neck crushing their mouths together. Orion was a man possessed, and Arix lived for it.

The stitching on his jacket itched beneath her fingers as she gripped his shoulder blades, hanging on for dear life as he nipped at her lips, moving down her jaw to bite her neck. It wasn't enough. None of it was enough.

"Harder."

Orion obeyed, digging his teeth into the soft flesh near her collarbone. The pain felt good, a reminder that she was alive. That she was here, no longer locked away in her own mind but real and flesh and bone, and in this moment, she was with Orion.

There were too many layers between them, too much clothing between their bare skin. She tore at the buttons on the front of his jacket, and at the same time, he mirrored her hands and went for the laces at the back of her dress.

The jacket was flung away the second his arms were free of the sleeves, and the light blue shirt underneath followed quickly. For all her rushing, for all her demands, Arix stopped for a moment, pulling herself back from him enough to admire his newly exposed chest. His muscles were defined, dark hair lightly leading her gaze down to the waistband of his pants.

A guttural exhale had Arix glancing back up to look him in the eye.

"I like it when you look at me like that." The look he gave her smoldered. "Like you could devour me."

"Maybe I will."

Their bodies came together again, and Arix moved directly to the lacing on the front of his pants. She wanted to see him, feel him, taste him.

Before she could finish undoing the laces, Orion spun them so that her thighs were against the desk, his hips grinding her against the hard edge. It hurt, but in the best way, her body heating up at the pressure, the control that he exhibited over her.

He must have noticed her wince because he pulled them away from the desk, moving Arix to an arm's length away. The heat was melting back into concern again, and it took everything in her not to groan in frustration.

She had to show him she wasn't fragile. She wouldn't break if he fucked her against a hard surface.

"Up to my room."

Arix blinked, the heat immediately spreading up her thighs.

"I want you spread out in my bed." His voice was deep, so heavy with desire. "A king's bed."

Before Arix could respond, Orion was already throwing the door open and pulling her with him down the hall. The guards stationed outside moved to follow him, but he waved them away, and with only the smallest hesitation, they stayed where they were.

The first hallway was fine.

The first staircase was harder.

By the second corridor, Arix felt like she was frothing at the mouth.

She dragged him into an alcove, pulling him against her as she pressed his back into the stone, hitching one leg up and around his waist.

Strong fingers dimpled the flesh of her thigh as he gripped her leg to hold it in place, his thumb tracing hard, rough circles on her inner thigh. It was so close, yet so impossibly out of reach. Arix squirmed against the touch, trying her hardest to encourage that thumb higher by just a few inches.

His breath was heavy in her ear as he ground his hips into her, all the while her mouth catching on the rough stubble of his beard along his jaw and down his neck. He'd left his shirt in his office, and her nails dug in slightly as she clutched his sides to pull him in closer.

He tasted so good; his smell of amber musk made her brain go fuzzy around the edges. Pieces of his hair had come loose from their clasp and fell across his face. She could feel how slick she was, how desperately her body wanted him inside of her.

Starting at his shoulder, she licked slowly up the side of his neck until she found his ear, sucking the lobe slightly into her mouth. Orion moaned, fingers digging into her sides as he held her closer.

"Goddess, that feels so good." Arix smiled against his ear.

That little pause was enough to get them moving again, and Arix once again found herself being pulled along towards the final staircase towards the king's tower. They made it past the guards at the bottom, winding up the stone staircase until they were out of sight.

They had hardly turned the corner at all before Orion pulled her towards him, pressing them down on the stairs until Arix was on her back, the cold, shallow stone cooling her through her clothes. He moved down her body, fingers skimming the skin of her calves, the dimple behind her knee, her thighs, as he pushed her skirt farther up and lowered himself down to taste her.

The first touch of his tongue was fire in her veins. Her hips rose of their own accord to meet his mouth, trying to grind up closer for more contact. But he was so slow, so deliberate, taking his time to stroke her open gently, teasing lightly. So light it made her want to scream.

There was no doubt that the soldiers below could hear them, her gasps and hiccuping breaths as Orion lapped his tongue against her. But there was only so hard Arix could bite her lips, teeth drawing blood as she fought not to let out a whimper. Her body felt like it was fighting her, trying to claw its way to a climax as she struggled to draw it out. She refused to let tonight be anything like last time, with Orion tasting her to climax while he remained fully clothed.

She wanted them both naked. And now.

"Orion." His name hissed through her lips, half demand, half plea.

She felt his warm breath press into her, his low, rumbling chuckle vibrating across her skin with enough power to make her back arch hard on the stairs. Goddess if she wasn't going to finish right here against the stone.

She panted her breaths as he lapped another lazy lick through her. "Orion, *please.*"

"Say it."

"I want you to fuck me." Her voice rose in volume, echoing down the stairs. The old Arix might have blushed at the thought of the guards below hearing her beg. But the new Arix wasn't afraid of saying exactly what she wanted from him.

"I will."

"Now."

The hair on the back of her neck prickled with goosebumps as he raked his fingernails down her legs to drag her closer to his mouth, holding her firmly as she writhed. He knew, damn him. He knew how close she was.

"I've missed the taste of you."

His words were so soft, she almost missed them. It was the quiet of them, the intimacy of those words, mumbled into her core, that pushed her over the edge into climax. He lapped, careful and consistent, as her back arched, and she rode his words into the abyss.

There was no muffling the moan that escaped her now, and it echoed around them, gliding like butter down the stairs to their audience below.

Arix found that it only filled her with more ecstasy, knowing they could hear her panting, her moaning. She was right where she wanted to be.

"Now," Orion said, finally shifting back to rest on his heels. "I'll fuck you."

The shivers rolled down Arix's spine again as he pulled her into his arms, her legs jelly beneath her, and took them the rest of the way up the stairs to his door at the top. Two more guards stood at the top of the stairs, ignoring them completely as Orion pushed past them into his room.

It was different than it had been when she'd been here last. None of the old furniture remained, all replaced with glossy new wood that shone in the candlelight. The huge window at the far side of the room seemed the only thing that held onto any of the memories she had of this place.

The old king was dead. Long live the new king.

Orion set her down carefully, turning her to better access the lacings at her back. He undid them so painstakingly slow that by the time he had finished, Arix was coming down from the high of her orgasm and already hungry for more.

He stripped her down, letting the dress pool at her feet, nothing but a thin chemise between them. He let her undo the laces on his pants, her grip settling around the waistband as she pushed them down to join her puddled dress on the floor. He was lean and hard, his skin soft as she ran her fingers gently down him, relishing his sharp intake of breath hissing through his teeth.

Goddess, she wanted to taste him.

But Orion's hands were moving to her now, hands bunched in the material of her shift, sliding it up and over her head.

He paused.

His fingers traced lighter than air down the delicate chain of her necklace, following the line of her collarbone to her sternum, resting between her breasts as he lightly moved the core aside.

"Is this…?"

Arix could hear the question in his voice and glanced down to where his fingers hovered a breath above her skin. Between the sloping curve of her breast was a spot.

Her own fingers trailed the darkened skin for a moment, star-ing as if, by some chance, she could explain away what she was seeing.

There, on the alabaster skin above her heart, was a black mark with branches of thin black veins stretching out in different directions. Arix blinked at the mark, tracing the lines with the tip of her finger.

"Does it hurt?" The worry was back in Orion's voice.

"No. I...I didn't even know it was here."

The mark had been hidden under her dress. Hidden behind the resting place of her pendant. She'd only woken up this morning—how could she have known it was there?

"Lakai mentioned..." Orion's voice died out as she glanced sharply up at him.

"What is this?"

He led her gently over to one of the candles near the window, pulling her further into the light. The lines were clearly black against her skin, like roots slowly growing from the center of her chest.

"A side effect from drinking out of the chalice. Lakai mentioned it vaguely, and I didn't press him for details. I figured we would wait until you woke up."

For the first time in the past hour, the voice of her pendant echoed in her mind. *"Another thing the old man kept from us."*

"What does it mean?"

Orion didn't have an answer for her. She asked again, this time channeling the question through her pendant, a shimmer of a cant locked behind the words.

As the magick fell into place, thoughts flit through her mind, tiny assurances, answers to a question that she wasn't even sure she knew how to ask. It felt jumbled. Like the voice could only help her so far to understand what the mark meant.

Notes of blood, images of the chalice, the Well Water that tasted like death. The magick, now amplified through her blood. And one word that overpowered all the rest.

Power.

"It's another change. To tell people who I am, that I'm the Black

Hand." She mumbled, fingers still sliding across the skin. The veins weren't raised, and if she'd had her eyes closed, she wouldn't have been able to tell the difference between her normal skin and the ebony lines.

Finally, she raised her gaze to meet Orion's. He was watching her, watching her piece together this new change to herself.

She pulled his fingers away, and he let the necklace fall back into place, resting over the new black lines.

"I'm different than how I used to be." It was a statement, but there was a question hidden behind it, asking him the thing she couldn't bring herself to say out loud.

Carefully, he cupped her face in his hands, drawing his fingers back until they were braced in her hair, angling her mouth to fit his perfectly.

"You are still Arix. You are my Black Hand." His lips grazed hers, nipping at her lip. "You are perfect just as you are."

Arix pressed into him, feeling his skin against hers for the first time. Slow at first, kissing gently and nibbling softly at her throat, and then his movements grew harder, the grip in her hair forcing her backward until the backs of her knees hit the bed, and she fell back into the pile of soft blankets and pillows. She liked him like this, rough and taking her how he wanted.

Arix gripped his shoulders, trying to drag him into her, to fill her up, but he moved her hands above her head and pinned them in place with one of his own. His other hand skimmed across her chest, thumb lightly circling around her nipple.

Goddess, every touch was electric. Raw.

She writhed beneath him, aching with want, demands turning into moans as she tried to angle her hips to force him into her.

His chuckle was dark and gravely as he leaned in to kiss her breast, tantalizing breaths moving across her skin. Biting lightly around her nipple, he sucked it into his mouth and slid into her in one driving thrust.

Her body clenched around him, fingers working into fists as he adjusted his grip on her wrists and plunged in a second time. His left hand moved from her breast to beneath the small of her back, raising her hips to drive in deeper, all the while sucking her nipple further into his mouth. He fucked her rhythmically, and each time he thrusted, it was purposeful, sliding into her again and again until she was practically crawling out of her skin with desire.

She dug her fingers into his back, pulling him up and forcing him onto his back beside her, and she shifted to straddle him. Her nerves were electric, and watching him touch her while she rode him pushed her closer and closer to another orgasm. Arix's body began to tighten around him, and she could tell by the look on his face that he knew it.

"Come for me, Arix. Come for your king."

Her climax hit her like lightning, traveling up her spine and curling her toes as he gripped her hips, thrusting into her when she could no longer hold herself up. Orion flipped them again to where she lay on her back, orgasm still rippling through her, legs locked around his waist as her back arched against the bed. He continued thrusting, pulling her past the place of pleasure into a mind-numbing ecstasy, and in moments he was growling out his own release, burying himself deep into her one final time.

Arix was only vaguely aware of the blankets that Orion draped over them, tucking her firmly against her chest. She should clean herself, fix her hair, say *something* to him. But all she felt was an overwhelming wave of contentment. Of realization that for the first time since she'd woken from the darkness, she felt *alive*.

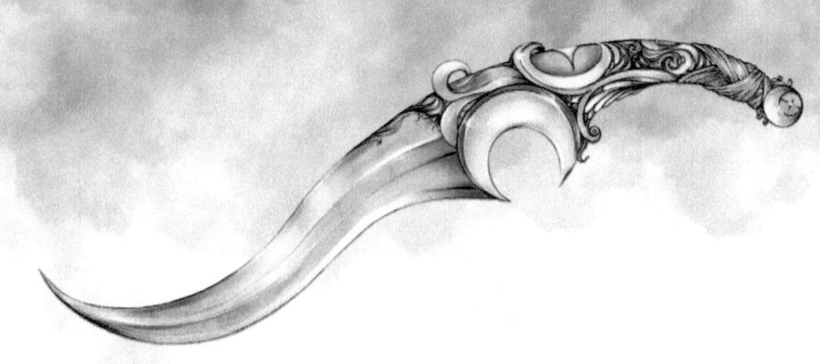

FIVE

Orion's strong arm draped slack across her hips; his deep breathing told Arix he was still fast asleep. She'd woken with the sun over an hour ago, watching carefully as the light in his room turned from inky black to that hazy lavender of early morning. Orion's windows faced east, giving her the perfect view as the sun stretched its rays over the distant horizon and reached out to hug the earth. The gray-purple light shifted in a blink to orange and gold; she could see the air in a way she never had before. It danced, the dust that floated in the air shimmering in the light of the new morning.

"You have awoken to a new world." The pendant at her throat whispered.

Arix fingered the metal of the necklace she wore, heavy on her skin. Indeed, she had. Whatever she had tasted from the chalice had awoken something in her. The air, the food—it all tasted different. Rich and earthy, she could smell and see things she had missed before. Even the light in the room had a richness of sunlight she hadn't seen before.

Beneath all things, there was a current.

She could see it now, in some places bold and deep, in others, light and airy as gossamer cobwebs. There was more to the world now, and she knew, as real as she was in this room, that the deepness she saw was traces of magick. It floated amongst the dust in the morning light and thrummed under the wings of the songbirds, pushing them in flight. Magick, however small or distant or faded, was woven into the tapestry of their world. Now that she could see it, it was impossible to imagine that the world could function at all without the trace elements of magick that flowed through it.

She, like so many others in Rökkur, had been under the impression that magick had died out, all traces wiped from the earth, the Goddess Kaoss taking back the gift she had given so long ago. Now that she could see it, *feel* it, pulsating around her, she knew they had been wrong. Magick was no more gone from this world than was breath or water or sky.

Carefully, she pulled away from Orion's grasp and walked to the window, swinging it gently open and letting the golden light of dawn seep across her naked skin. The air was crisp, with the chill of night ebbing away to the morning, and the smell of salt was light in the wind that swept across her skin. She could see the ocean, past the walls, and across the city below.

Stretching her fingers into the light, Arix extended her hand from the window, reaching towards the sun. Flexing and straining her hand, she watched how the sun glowed warm on her newly pale skin. Her freckles had faded down to where they were barely visible. She'd always loved her freckles, but now they were almost gone. Sadness rippled through through her as she trailed light fingers across where the marks had once been. The body she'd lived with for twenty-five years had practically disappeared. She almost didn't want to look down at the black lines over her heart. It wasn't a mar; she wasn't upset over the mark. It was like a new tattoo, symbolizing the change in herself. Except she hadn't ever asked for it. And she'd never been told it would appear.

She couldn't help but feel tricked a little at the yet *another* change she hadn't been warned about. What else was different about her that she had yet to discover?

The deep groan from under her ribs pulled Arix from her thoughts, and a quick calculation told her she hadn't eaten anything since that first meal when she'd woken up. Time for breakfast.

Arix pulled on her clothes and slipped out of Orion's room. The guards outside said nothing as she slipped between them and headed back to her own rooms in Castle Zma'ai. She was anxious to start her day, anxious to begin the new life she'd been gifted.

No, gifted wasn't the right word. She'd fought for this future, fought for the life that was now hers. She'd slit Celeste's throat for it and damned if she wouldn't make it her own.

There were things she needed to do, changes she needed to make. And first things first, she needed people around her she could trust.

After a quick word with Wren, a good scrub in her new bath-tub, and an absolute mountain of fresh fruit and scrambled eggs, Arix headed for the front gate. Every guard she passed watched her, their eyes following her across the gravel path as she entered the barracks and spoke with the guard commander.

He seemed startled to see her, glancing up from his desk and quickly rising, his chair scraping back from his desk. "The lady Black Hand, to what do I owe the pleasure?"

Arix smiled at the title, took his outstretched hand, and shook it. It seemed like a million years ago that she would have done anything in her power to stay as far from this man, or any king's guard, as possible. Now she was meeting with him, shaking hands with him. Much like yesterday, it felt right to hold a place of power like this. She was the Black Hand now, and she wasn't going to pretend that the thought didn't send a thrill down her spine.

"Thank you for your time, Commander Zaran. I'll be brief since I understand you're busy. I'd like to request that Ulfur and Abbas be added to my guard duty."

She didn't know their last names, she realized. Didn't know if Ulfur was a first or a last name.

The commander nodded curtly and gestured for Arix to take a seat, glancing at one of the soldiers who still stood in the doorway and giving him a nod. With a soft click, the door closed, leaving the two some privacy to talk.

"The Black Guard has been hand-selected by Master Lakai, and while Gaelan Ulfur and Endar Em Abbas are not on that list, I understand your desire to see them back at your side. I'll put in the paperwork right away and have them re-assigned." Commander Zaran took his seat again, straightening the papers on his desk and making note of something in one of the margins. His cool gaze found hers again over the top of the organized surface. "Will you be making any other changes to your guard?"

His tone was cool and purposeful, but Arix didn't get the sense that he was mocking her or looking down on her. This was a man who did his job well and efficiently.

"Possibly. We'll see how things go, and if I need any changes made, I'll be sure to speak with you about them."

Zaran nodded.

"I'd also like a list of the names of my…" Arix stumbled for a moment, trying to remember what he had called them. "My Black Guard. I want to know the men and women that will serve under me."

"Of course." He flipped through a ledger to his left and quickly copied down the list for her, blotting the ink till it no longer smudged. "Is there anything I can help you with?"

Arix stood, taking the offered list. "No, thank you, Commander Zaran. Can you have Ulfur and Abbas report to my office as soon as possible?"

Their arms clasped again over the desk as Zaran offered her a slight bow. "Of course, my lady Black Hand."

And with that, Arix moved out the door. She had eight other things to do today, and each was important.

~

"I need a *black* dress."

Wren pulled out another swath of light gray gossamer flounce, and Arix shook her head. "No, Wren. Not gray, not charcoal, not silver. Black."

Wren let out something between a sigh and a wail. "Lady Arix, there aren't any. It normally isn't fitting for ladies to wear black other than when they're in mourning."

"Except for me, I am the *Black* Hand, Wren. The Black Hand should own at least one article of clothing that's actually *black*." Arix collapsed back onto the bed, surrounded by bejeweled dresses with overly puffy skirts and ruffles that looked more like an oversized bow than an actual dress.

She filtered her fingers across the pile of fabrics around her. They were all beautiful, some more than others, but she'd hardly worn anything other than riding pants, simple skirts, and blouses for the past year. Other colors were perfectly fine—Arix was sure she'd wear the grey and the charcoal as easily, along with the blues and the purples—but she needed at least *something* black. She wanted to stand out now so that no one would mistake her for anything other than who she was. She wasn't about to let all of that bloodshed, the death of her best friends, to be for nothing. If she was going to do this, she was going to do this right.

If she was going to be the Black Hand, she was going to do more than play the part.

She would be the best gods damned Black Hand there had ever been.

"I can always send for the tailor. Have her draw up some new designs for you? Have something made in the style you want." Wren peered around the door to the closet, and the two women stared at each other for a moment, considering.

"I'm not even sure I know what I want. But I want clothes that will stand out. I want something different. Inspired by all four realms, unique but versatile."

"Who do we know whose clothing catches every eye that sees her?" the voice thrummed through her chest.

"Esme Halotus," Arix said, answering the unspoken voice in her mind.

"The high priestess?" Wren added two more dresses to the pile that surrounded Arix. "She certainly does have beautiful clothes."

Pushing aside the swathes of dresses and standing, Arix pointed at the small pile of dresses she had pulled to the side near the foot of the bed. "These we keep. I don't need eight million things in my closet, just a few good pieces I love. In the meantime, I'm going to have a little morning tea with the priestess."

Arix walked the familiar path towards the temple at the far corner of the castle, then veered towards the accompanying rooms that adjoined the main sanctuary. She hadn't been back to this part of the castle in almost three months, not since Orion had splayed her out and worshiped her on the altar of Kaoss. Heady incense filled the hallway as she stepped further towards the high priestess' rooms.

At the door, Arix paused. Was she supposed to announce herself? She rapped her knuckles gently on the door, pushing it open when a delicate "Enter" sounded from inside.

High Priestess Esme Halotus was reclined on a couch, a deck of cards spread out in front of her in delicate piles, some of the cards criss crossing over themselves. The priestess smiled without looking up from her cards.

"The Black Hand. What an honor. Please come in and have a seat. I'll only be a moment longer."

Arix joined the other woman on the low couch strewn with blue beaded pillows, crossing her legs underneath her as she watched in silence. Esme wore a creamy pale sheer dress with beautiful bell sleeves that ended in long cuffs at her wrist. Delicate lines of mother-of-pearl buttons held the cuffs closed. Embroidered into the fabric were bits of light peach shell that caught the light, making her look like a shimmering sandy shore.

Pulling another card, the priestess regarded it for a moment before placing it upside down in the center's empty space. Arix found herself transfixed by the woman's fingers. Long and delicate, tattooed bands across the tips, her nails, to Arix's surprise, filed to short points. Her hands traced the edges of the cards in front of her, making minor adjustments as she righted a card that was slightly askew.

Arix recognized a few of the cards, but she wasn't well-versed enough to understand their meaning. The silence between them spanned long, and with every passing second, Arix felt more out of place. She distracted herself by glancing around at the decorated room, the decor much inspired by Nero's colors and the beautiful mosaic tiles of colored glass in pale blues and greens.

Everything was swathed in fabric, too, sheer creams and seafoams hanging from around the windows and a sheer set of curtains separating this room from the one beyond. Arix could make out the bed, low to the ground and absolutely smothered in pillows. And twice the size of her own.

"I wonder what she gets up to in the candlelit hours of the evening," the voice noted curiously.

"Lady Black Hand."

Arix's gaze jolted back to the high priestess, who she found watching her with a small smile.

"Yes." Arix hurried to clear her throat, offering her own smile in return. "My apologies, I was admiring the room."

The other woman tilted her head, her chin dipping as her smile melted into one a bit more knowing. "It does cause that type of effect."

Arix glanced down at the cards between them. "What do the cards tell you?"

With one quick swipe, the cards were back together in a neatly stacked deck, and the priestess offered Arix a winning smile.

"Nothing to be worried about. Simply trying to listen to what the goddess is telling me."

She rose to a side table where she wrapped the cards in velvet and tucked them into a drawer. The way she performed the task was so graceful, lovingly even, the way she handled the deck, that Arix forgot for a moment why she had come. It seemed the priestess noticed the same thing, for she turned back towards the couch with that same knowing smile.

"What may I do for you, Arix?"

"I'm actually here for some advice, High Priestess."

"Esme, please." She came forward again, and instead of retaking her seat across from Arix, she slid in beside her, their knees grazing. "Now that we're on the council together, there's no need for such formalities."

Her throat had gone dry, Arix realized, all too aware of how close they were. This was the effect the high priestess had on everyone, the aura that surrounded her. The desire to reach out and trace the lines of Esme's neck split through her like lightning.

"Careful. She's cunning, remember?"

"I came because I need some advice on clothing." Arix was able to get out, pushing past the itch in her fingers. "The way you dress is so beautiful."

"But that isn't it, is it?" Esme challenged her, leaning back and resting her weight on her arm that crossed along the back of the couch. "It's more than just beautiful clothing."

Arix nodded, swallowing carefully.

"You want to be noticed."

"Yes."

Esme smiled. "I understand that need. We are women who hold great power. I use every asset at my disposal to remind people of that. You are a woman, but not only that, you are the Black Hand. You need to stand out. Our clothes do more than draw the eye; they remind people that we should not be so easily dismissed or under-estimated. That we know the power we hold, and we aren't afraid to wield it. By extension, the clothes we wear remind people what we're capable of."

Arix fought to let her jaw fall slack. She was good. Really good.

It would be wise not to underestimate this woman.

"I could easily go to the tailor or request new clothes, but I want to wear things that are unique. I want to wear pieces of art."

Esme stood, holding out a hand for Arix to take. She led her into the bedroom, pausing for a moment to ring a glass bell. Within a moment, a woman appeared in a simple blue wrap dress.

"Send for my tailor. He has work to do."

The girl scurried off as Esme pulled Arix the rest of the way into a side room that overflowed with dresses. They had all been organized in order of color, spanning from white at one end all the way to dark purple at the other. Three cloth figures stood in the corner modeling some of the dresses, their wooden arms outstretched in delicate angelic poses.

"Your hair is different now, which is good. The red was beautiful but tricky." Esme stepped towards the blue section and indicated for Arix to take a look. "Tell me what you like. What you don't like. It will help us find exactly what suits you best."

With the care she would have handled delicate ingredients in their glass vials, Arix filtered through a few of the dresses, careful not to snag any of the fabric or pull too hard on any of the skirts. When a teal and gold mesh dress caught her eye, she gently pulled it from the others.

"I love the gold here," Arix motioned to the mesh gold sleeves as delicate as silk that ended in a teal cuff. Gold lines criss crossed across the rigid corseted bodice, gold chain falling from the shoulders to meet the bodice between the wearer's breasts.

Esme pulled the dress from its place and held it out to Arix. "Try it on."

"Are you sure?"

"How will you know what you like until you try it on?"

For a split second, Arix thought she caught a look of challenge on the priestess's face. Daring her to dress herself in someone else's clothes. She was reminded of all the times she'd worn a disguise, a costume, in order to fit in and pretend to be someone she wasn't. This didn't quite feel the same.

"Can you help me out of this?" Arix turned her back to the other woman. She was perfectly capable of getting in and out of her own simple dress, but there was a strange kind of familiarity that surrounded Esme. A comfortability that lingered between them.

The tips of Esme's fingers grazed down her spine as she undid the laces, letting the dress slip from Arix's shoulders and pool to the floor. Arix slipped her chemise off, too, and it joined the dress.

"Careful now."

Arix turned around to face the high priestess, not moving to cover up her naked breasts, and took the gauzy gold and teal fabric from Esme. The priestess's smile had vanished, and there was absolutely no bashfulness in the gaze that roved down Arix's naked body. Her stare caught on the dark veins over her heart, spindly inky lines against pale skin.

Arix slipped into the new dress, realizing how high the thigh slit went up on her left leg, the fabric a combination of silk and mesh. The corseted bodice was sheer around her stomach and back, while the bust was more structured. This time, there was no way she would get into this dress without help. She turned again, silently offering her exposed back for Esme to lace her up.

She felt every twist and pull of the laces, wondering if the other woman was taking her time on purpose or trying to make Arix uncomfortable.

If the latter was her intention, she was failing. Arix's senses were heightened, and every touch of the other woman's tattooed fingers sent thrills through Arix's bloodstream, heating her insides with the tightening of each lace.

Esme's hands grasped her shoulders, turning her towards the full-length mirror beside the cloth figures, and Arix finally got a good look at herself.

She'd expected to feel beautiful, lithe, channeling cunning and whatever power the high priestess possessed when she walked in the room. On Arix, the colors clashed, washing her out, the beautiful effect lost against her newly pale skin and hair.

"You don't like it?" Esme sounded surprised.

In the reflection, they were the same height, Esme's dark skin in complete contrast with her own pale complection. The dark veins that branched from her heart were on full display with

the low cut of the bodice, but next to the teal and gold opulence of the dress, the duality of the two felt utterly disjointed.

Arix's fingers trailed along the gold chains that hung from the shoulders of the dress down to the bodice. "I like this. It looks like armor but without all the bulky weight. But these colors…"

The priestess stepped out from behind her, turning to stand beside the mirror so she could see Arix better.

"I think it might be the shade of blue." Esme mused.

"Maybe."

"It doesn't quite suit you." Esme leaned over to ruffle the skirt a bit, flouncing it out so that it lay out behind Arix in a wave.

The fabric was truly beautiful, and with the gold, they were a lovely combination. If Esme had been wearing the dress, she would have looked radiant. On Arix, it looked all wrong.

"Well…" Esme's fingers lingered a bit longer at the thigh slit of the dress. "Now we know what colors don't work for your complexion. And if you like the metal inlay, that's important to know."

Arix's attention had shifted. Instead of watching her own reflection in the mirror, now she just watched Esme. The fingers that had been trailing at her thigh moved up to the bodice, trailing the lines of boning and up to where the chains connected at the top. Arix sucked a breath in as Esme's fingers came in contact with the skin of her chest, where black veins bloomed across her heart.

"How does this feel?"

For a moment, Arix held her breath, forcing herself not to turn her gaze from the mirror. She couldn't tell if Esme was talking about her touch or the accent of the dress.

"The veins," the woman clarified.

In a whoosh, Arix let the breath slip between her teeth. "Oh. It doesn't hurt. I can't feel it at all, actually. New, since I've woken up."

"Do you want it covered? My tailor can design dresses that would cover it up if you'd prefer. But of course, that's completely up to you."

Before Arix could answer, a rustling sounded from the room behind them, and Esme moved away to usher the newcomers into the dressing room.

The man who entered was so spindly that Arix wondered if a light breeze wouldn't knock him right off his feet. His fingers were the longest she'd ever seen on a person, like the legs of a spider or the talons of an eagle. He looked exactly like she had expected him to, complete with tape measure draped around his neck and an embroidery hook holding his long salt and pepper hair away from his face. He took one look at Arix and scowled.

"Not your color. No, no, no. Take it off at once."

Arix faltered a bit. It was one thing to strip down here with Esme or with her own maid, but it was another thing to get naked for the tailor and his three young assistants.

With a quick roll of his eyes, the tailor turned on the spot, his back to her, and his three assistants stepped forward to help her out of the teal and gold dress and back into her chemise.

As she re-dressed, the tailor continued to talk. "Lylan Teal has too many yellow undertones and clashes terribly with your complexion. Something with a bluer undertone would suit you better but still wouldn't be right. And we'll have to stay away from anything too light, or you'll be washed out completely."

He turned again and tipped Arix's chin up to study the lines of her face. He peered into her eyes, then undid her hair to watch how it "caught the light," wanting to know what color the individual strands were in her hair. It all looked white to her, and the tailor refused to explain the difference between ivory and alabaster. Next were her measurements, which were marked down by an assistant, and then came the sketchbooks. The tailor had her flip through page after page of design, and Arix pointed out the details she liked and those she didn't. They discussed her black veins, the line between elegant and scandalous, and whether it was important that Arix need added adjustments for mobility.

It was exactly what she had hoped to achieve coming to Esme. The tailor asked her questions that she had never considered herself, and after an hour, the man departed, saying he needed to get back to his shop to finish sketching. He would send them to Arix's office for approval later that afternoon, and in two days, she would have her first dress.

During the endeavor, Esme stayed out of their way, hovering over the tailor's shoulder, making small comments and then retreating to the other room. The fact that she had given them space would have made another person feel comfortable, at ease. But it made Arix nervous.

In a small way, she was in Esme's debt for helping her with this. Offering up her own private tailor, without argument or pretense… It was a gift between two women who didn't really know each other.

And favor was still a favor, no matter how small.

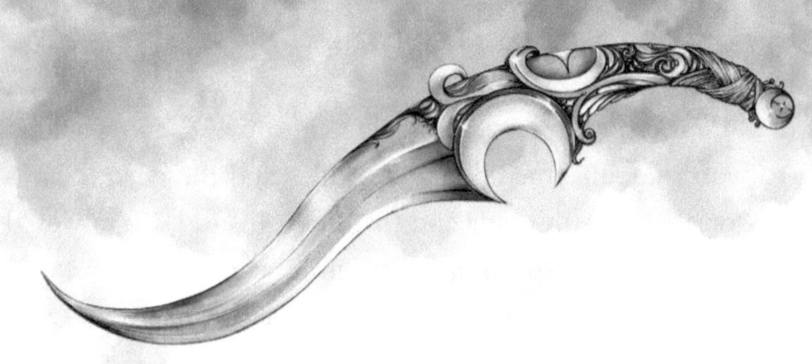

SIX

Lakai was talking, but Arix had tuned him out minutes ago.

She sat behind her new desk, fingers steepled across the mahogany surface as she watched the five figures that lounged in front of her. Lakai was still making their introductions, but Arix was only paying attention to their names. Their titles were useless—boring, nondescript court appointments that meant little to her other than that they had been raised in luxury and knew absolutely nothing about the world outside their castle keeps.

Before any of them had stepped foot into her office, Arix had cast a very low-level Cerebral Trap cant, allowing her to gain insight into the thoughts of those in the room. Lakai, not to her surprise, was already warded against that kind of cant, and Arix could read nothing from him. But that wasn't an issue; she wasn't worried about his motivations or internal thought process. It was the five new people in the room she wanted to know about.

To her far left was Colin, a ridiculously tall man with hair that was a tad too long past his ears. Either he was trying to grow it out or was in desperate need of a haircut. Arix assumed the latter. Lakai had introduced him as her Master of Word. The title made some sense;

he would be the one to help her acclimate to court. She wouldn't need to worry about remembering the titles and the correct honorifics associated with this lady and that duke. Instead, Colin would simply stand in her shadow to facilitate introductions.

The problem was that the man was an imbecile.

There was barely a thought between his ears as he stared blankly at Lakai. He was mentally reciting his new title, saying it in different ways, practicing his own introduction. Arix could hardly keep from rolling her eyes. How much help he might actually be would remain to be seen.

To the right of him was Lady Kel, to be her Mistress of Quill. A glorified secretary by the sound of it, which, again, might have been useful if the woman didn't look to be 102. Her beauty lingered even to old age, and the crystal green-blue of her eyes was almost disturbingly bright to look at. While Lakai droned, her mind was a blank slate. Not because she was warded, but because she had dozed off the moment she had nestled into one of Arix's tall-backed chairs, and Arix couldn't tell what the old lady was dreaming about.

Next was her Master of Coin, Harksten, who seemed the most competent thus far. He had been calculating numbers in his head since he walked through the door, and the best Arix could piece out, he was appraising the cost of the books on her shelf. Arix hadn't spent much time looking at them yet and, by the relative number in his head, she assumed that the books were nowhere near valuable.

The Cerebral Tap cant was a bit vague, giving Arix glimpses and themes of a person's mind rather than their exact thoughts. Incomplete images that helped her know a bit about the person's psyche but not necessarily a word-for-word exact accounting.

But Arix didn't need an exact accounting of the thoughts of the next in line to know that the woman despised her.

Anastiasa Asmund, her new Mistress of Maps, was an ambassador of foreign affairs. The woman was warded but not very well, and while her thoughts were much hazier than the others, her rage leeched off her in red waves.

Arix just grinned at her.

"And, of course, we have your Master of Woe, Tamsin Olsfair," Lakai continued, gesturing to the fifth person in the little lineup. "Tamsin's great grandfather was King Jaenil's original Master of Woe, though back then the title was a bit different..."

Arix regarded her Master of Woe, and he regarded her right back.

He was huge. Ridiculously huge, his forearms as big around as her thigh, and so tall, he seemed to loom even while seated. There was dirt under his fingernails, his clothing all ill-fitting in shades of browns and blacks. He looked like a brute.

His mind was anything but.

The thoughts Arix read from him were careful, calculated and pieced together quickly. Anyone who went up against him might easily miscalculate and assume that he favored brawn over brains. It was clear he was wasted as her Master of Woe. This man needed to be in a calculating strategic position. Not a dungeon master. He would be an excellent tool in her toolbelt.

"They'll be of service to you in your new role as Black Hand, of course," Lakai went on, completely unaware of the size up that had occurred in the last few minutes. "Consider them as the Fingers of the Black Hand. Whatever you need assistance with, they will be able to provide."

"Yes," Her Master of Word, Colin, cut in. "We are at your disposal, Lady Hand. Anything you need—"

"Lady Black Hand."

He looked startled, thrown off his train of thought. "I beg your pardon?"

Arix smiled at him across the desk, leaning on her elbows as she regarded him. "It's Lady *Black* Hand. Not just Lady Hand."

Already, she'd had to correct her Master of Word, and it had barely been five minutes. This would be a disaster.

"Ah, I…" Colin stuttered, blinking rapidly. Was the man about to cry? "My apologies, Lady Black Hand. I won't make that mistake again."

Lakai was staring daggers at Arix, but she purposefully refused to look at him. "Good."

She stood, and they all scrambled to stand along with her, Lady Kel jostling herself from her little cat nap.

"Well. I appreciate all of your help and your willingness to work with me. I do have another appointment in a few moments, and I wouldn't want to be rude." Arix pointedly stared at the door. Even with Lakai's wards in place, she could feel the frustration whistling off of him like an angry tea kettle. He could yell at her later.

The five filed out, Lakai the last to go, and it took everything in Arix's willpower to smile politely at them and wish them good day.

Four more people were already waiting in her foyer, and Arix's smile quickly turned from forced to genuine. Today would be chock full of introductions.

A stroke of genius had inspired her to ask Wren about some of the other maids who worked in Castle Zma'ai. She needed an actual secretary, but she didn't want anyone high-born. Wren had passed around the information to a few of the other girls, and four had requested to speak with Arix about the position.

She wanted someone who could write, read, and perform errands and small tasks for her. Someone who could keep her calendar, deliver notes and summons, and who knew Mergur well enough that Arix could send her into town without worry that the girl would be lost.

The interviews went even better than Arix had expected. All four girls could read and write, and all of them had grown up in the capital. Their mothers or aunts had gotten them jobs at Castle Zma'ai, and they seemed to know more about the inner workings of the court than those *five Fingers* who had been in her office a moment ago.

In the end, Arix hired all of them. One as her secretary, and the other three as informants. She made them sign contracts sealed in blood and magick, and each girl left with more than a little gold in her purse. Arix was nothing if not generous.

Nesrin was short, with straight black hair pinned away from her face. She was incredibly smart and very observant. She'd been working as a maid for one of the other competitors last year, one Arix had never bothered to learn much about, and had the great and powerful skill of remaining quiet and still and out of the way while keeping her ears wide open. The elite, as Arix already knew from her many years slipping her fingers into their pockets, regarded the staff as little more than tools. She was there to serve, nothing else. It never occurred to them that their servants might actually be listening to the secrets that they so quickly spilled behind closed doors.

Arix had known from the start that it would be next to impossible to sway a servant who was already loyal to their master, but someone like Nesrin was perfect. She held no allegiances other than to the castle and the king; she hadn't been serving any one lord or lady in particular, but she had worked in the castle for years.

The girl was unassuming, which was exactly what Arix wanted.

All that was left was for Nesrin to sign a contract.

There was magick in the paper, the pen, and Nesrin barely hesitated when Arix offered her the knife to open a vein and smear the blood onto the parchment at the bottom.

"I want to be clear," Arix continued before the girl could put down the final signature. "If you break this contract, if you break the words you've agreed to here, you'll be in terrible pain. You won't die…but you'll wish you were dead."

It would have been so ridiculously simple to make the pain of a broken contract death, but Arix wanted to be able to know when someone broke the contract. She wanted to be able to look Nesrin in the eye if the girl double-crossed her. Trust needed to be earned.

What Lakai had said was still ringing true in her ears, and even today, with the little bit of introductions that had been made, she was wary of all of them. She didn't know who her friends were anymore. She didn't know who she could trust.

Lakai? Most definitely.

"Orion?" The voice was so quiet she almost didn't hear it.

Now that was a question, wasn't it?

"I understand," Nesrin said quietly. Her gaze was calculated as she glanced over the contract one last time before she looked up at Arix. "I know what magick can do to a person."

There was so much weight behind the words, Arix was tempted to ask what the girl had seen, what she had experienced. But if this was going to be a relationship of trust, she would need to give the girl a bit of space. If Nesrin wanted to tell her, she would.

And if there ever came a time when she *needed* to know, she had ways to find out.

Nesrin signed her name with a flourish at the bottom of the page, the blood pooling against the curve of the letters.

"Let's get started."

They planned out Arix's week first—council meetings and individual meetings with each of the wardens. Then there were all the events she would need to be present at for the king's sake, any rendezvous with dignitaries or visiting lords. And then there was the ball.

Lakai had mentioned it during his introduction to her five Fingers, a way to introduce her to the court officially before the coronation. It was why finding the perfect dress had been so important and why it was more important than ever that Arix have people she could trust in her corner. Ulfur, Abbas, and Nesrin were only the first parts to that, the first pieces in making sure that the goals she had as the Black Hand were fulfilled.

There was much to be done, and Arix didn't intend to wait for someone to give her permission.

SEVEN

There were actual butterflies in Arix's stomach. She'd never felt this nervous before. Or at least, she hadn't felt this nervous in years. And it made her disgusted.

She was the Black Hand.

She had fought for this, fought for the chance to change things—to make Rökkur better in every way. It was going to take more than a single ball, of course, but this would be her official introduction as the Black Hand.

They'd kept her away from the court while she'd slept, but the gossip was rolling with tittering conjecture in her absence. She'd been locked in her darkness for two weeks. It was time for her to make her official appearance.

The dress that Esme's tailor had delivered this afternoon was transcendent. It surpassed Arix's expectations and more.

Arix ran her fingers down her body, the soft black velvet crushing beneath her fingers as she wove an enchantment through the design, pausing on each piece of embroidery as she whispered the words to herself. Stitched into the black velvet, hundreds of stars shone, now twinkling with the help of her magick. But as beautiful as the stars were, there was a hidden design, a hidden detail that drew the gaze down and held it.

All along the bottom hem of the dress and weaving upwards was embroidery in gold and silver thread of hundreds of eyes. Some wide and glaring, others half mast, practically closed. It was a subtle design, woven in among other motifs of shooting stars, but there they were nonetheless. And if you missed the design on the bottom of the dress, it was impossible to miss a single eye embroidered on the back of each hand as the sleeve came to a point by the base of her fingers.

The more you stared at the eyes, the more of them you saw. There were the obvious ones, yes, but hidden in the stars were others, small details hiding them amongst the starshine. And now she had incanted an illusion on the dress so that the eyes would *blink*.

It was macabre.

And Arix loved it.

It was the kind of dress that made you stare, and Arix wanted to be stared at tonight. She let Wren curl up the long white tendrils of her hair and pin them up to make it seem haphazard, ringlets falling in a cascade around her head. She looked like the fucking goddess.

When Arix finally stepped outside her door, she was met with a low whistle.

"Tha's our girl." Ulfur was grinning at her from the hallway, all dressed up in black armor. Abbas was right beside him, and even he couldn't hide the smile that spread across his face.

Arix dragged the two of them into a hug, albeit a little stiffly with all the extra layers the three of them wore. "It's good to be back."

"You are stunning." Abbas' deep voice sounded warmer than

it ever had, and Arix's heart swelled at the sound.

"Don't make me cry, you two." Arix carefully pressed her fingers around her eyes, doing her best not to smudge her carefully applied makeup. "We have a party to go to."

She led the way down the stone stairs where Nesrin was waiting. Her new secretary was dressed in a dark dress of her own, though far less fancy in design. Waiting near the end of the hall were her five Fingers, dressed in the colors of their realms. Tamsin Olsfair, her Master of Woe, was the only other person wearing black.

The entourage that followed her down the rest of the stairs felt strange.

Arix was late to the party, which was done on purpose so she could be introduced before Orion and be able to stay by his side for the duration of the night. Ulfur and Abbas and the rest of her Black Guard would stay at the entrances of the room, within easy distance should the need arise.

Orion was waiting for her at the door to the throne room, and when he saw her, his eyes went wide.

"You look absolutely amazing."

"So do you."

And he did. Orion was wearing the opposite of her. Gold and silver with black embroidered details into his long velvet coat. The sleeves widened and hung almost to the floor, black embroidered suns spearing up from the cuffs. She'd planned it, knowing what he'd be wearing, but hadn't realized they would look so startlingly perfect next to each other.

Like the sun and the moon, Vulcan and Nyx.

Her five Fingers settled in behind her as she took her place by the door, waiting for the announcement. Everything in her chest was quaking, quivering, and it took all her power to slow her breathing.

This was it. She was making her own history.

"Announcing the Lady Black Hand, Bellarix Sable!"

The doors opened, and Arix waited a second before stepping in, letting hundreds of eyes fall on her. With satisfaction, she watched their faces shift, some to unease and others to wonder at her dress, material shifting around her feet. She stalked forward, walking through the crowd that parted for her and closed the gap between her and the dais. It took practically no time at all, and yet, Arix felt like it was one of the longest walks of her life. She took her place beside the throne, all too aware that the unsettled feeling in her stomach had gotten worse. If she threw up in front of all these people, she would never forgive herself.

"Announcing his majesty, King Orion Karcharias."

They bowed for him, stooping at the waist or bending at the knee as he strode past them. But from where she stood, Arix could see that many of them still had their eyes on her rather than their new monarch.

The tightening grip on her stomach only grew.

It was thrilling, of course, but if she were honest with herself, Arix was terrified.

Only after Orion was seated on the throne did the tension die back a bit, and music began to play. Banquet tables had been set up along the sides of the room, overflowing with food, and guests began helping themselves as the center floor opened up for dancing.

"I'm about to do something you'll hate," Orion murmured out of the corner of his mouth.

Arix glanced over at him, but he was still staring out at the crowd. "What are you about to do?"

"I am going to ask one of the court ladies to dance with me." He stood, straightening his jacket before glancing at her. He had a small smile playing at the corner of his mouth. "Promise you won't flay me for it later."

Arix fought to hide a smile of her own as she turned back to face the crowd. "Do you really think I'm the jealous type?"

"Absolutely. But our roles are even more scrutinized now. No flaying allowed."

Something in his voice made Arix glance up at him again, and she found his gaze burning into her.

"These are the games we are destined to play, Arix."

Her gut clenched at that. "I know. We'll talk later."

As he strode down the steps of the dais and away from her, Arix wondered if she *was* jealous at the thought of him dancing the night away with all these preening court ladies.

The simple answer was no.

She wouldn't let something as trivial as Orion dancing with someone else bother her. He was the king. He had obligations to more than just her, but to the people here at court, dignitaries, the council—all full of people that he needed to woo and charm and dance with. She despised the kind of women who were so over-protective of their men that they needed to keep them at their side every moment of every day. Her lovers had always been free to do as they wished, and that practice wasn't something that Arix planned on changing. He was the king, after all. He could take as many or as few women or men dancing or to bed as he would like.

That was the simple answer.

But the more complicated answer? That was something she didn't like considering. Her whole chest felt like it was compressing as she watched him offer a hand to a woman in a lavender and gold sari and swing her into the next dance. To be jealous implied that what she felt for him was deeper than she anticipated, was deeper than she felt comfortable with. It was a thought she pushed from her mind.

A motion on the floor caught her attention, and Arix descended the steps of the dais to join Lakai as he waved her over. He stood with Lord Bardon and a few of the other councilors, who notably went quiet as Arix joined their ranks.

Stepping away from their circle, Lakai motioned to the rest of the room. "There's no need for you to stand up there all night, Arix. Enjoy yourself, eat, talk with your five Fingers. The cants are firmly in place, and there's nothing else to worry about. If the king needs you, he'll come find you."

It was clearly a dismissal as Lakai turned back to his group, their conversation starting right back up again.

Lakai had incorrectly assumed that her worry was about the cants they had placed on the throne room early that afternoon. They'd spent the better part of an hour warding the doors and windows, as well as the throne itself, from any magickal interference. Not that they had expected any, but Arix had insisted they do it anyway. She would prefer to have at least a little warning than none at all. The cants she had put in place would set off a signal if anyone tried to sneak in under nefarious circumstances and would keep certain areas, like the dais, free of magickal tampering by anyone other than herself.

The magick itself had been easy. Drinking the Well Water had opened something in her to see the ley lines of magick, the tracing criss cross web of the elements as they wove through the air. The incantations that formed the protections in the hall were as easy as tying two ends of a string together. Because now, Arix could actually see the strings.

The food at least looked enticing, and Arix hoped that maybe some of it might ease the death grip on her stomach.

Somewhere between Lakai and the food, Arix was joined by

three of her five Fingers. Lady Kel and Tamsin Olsfair were absent. No doubt the old bat had gone to bed early and her hulking Master of Woe was standing in a dark corner somewhere.

"Are you enjoying the party, Lady Black Hand?" Colin Calel asked, sweeping his arm and bowing slightly as Arix tried to step past him towards the food line. Her Master of Word put only the slightest emphasis on the word *Black*, as though to remind himself not to make the same mistake he had made in her office.

"I've been here barely a minute, Lord Calel. I'm sure I'll have something more interesting to say once I've had a chance to actually enjoy it."

"Ah yes, of course." Colin was quick to agree with her, offering the kind of saccharine smile that made her own teeth ache. "Allow me to make some introductions for you this evening, Lady Black Hand. Getting to know the right people in court could be a great asset to you."

"That would be most appreciated. Indeed, that is what you are here for, Lord Calel." Arix hardly paused a moment for him to re-spond and turned to her Mistress of Maps, Lady Anastasia Asmund. "Who is here tonight, Lady Asmund, that I should acquaint myself with?"

The woman clearly hadn't been prepared to be addressed, and her head snapped away from looking at something on the far side of the room to glance at Arix.

"Dignitaries are still arriving for the coronation, Lady Black Hand. It may be best to meet them all then. I wouldn't trouble your-self with any introductions this evening."

"But," Lord Calel, it would seem, had not enjoyed being side-lined and butted his way back into the conversation. "There are many that I should like to introduce to you. Right this way!"

He moved away, and after giving the food tables a longing glance,

Arix followed. There would be plenty of time to eat, and it would be important to make some introductions tonight.

Colin approached a small group of people who talked together casually, clearly in the middle of a story. Before Arix could stop him, he was butting into the conversation, interrupting one of the ladies and wedging his way into the circle.

"Pardon the interruption, of course, but might I make the formal introductions? The Black Hand to King Orion Karcharias. Might I present Sir and Lady Ciolot, Lord and Lady Brokersten, and Sir Go—" Colin stuttered a moment, and Arix flicked her gaze to him.

He was staring at the part of her sleeve that ended on the back of her hand, the large golden eye there in the middle of a slow blink.

Arix twisted her wrist, adjusting the sleeve, which brought her Master of Word back to the present, albeit with a bright red face.

"Ehem. Excuse me, and this is Sir Goreve."

There was a moment of awkward silence as they all bowed and curtsied. Arix inclined her head, wondering if she needed to bow at all. She did outrank them, technically. Lakai hadn't really mentioned how to perform correct introductions. She had hoped to rely on Colin for this kind of information, but so far, he'd proven himself an idiot.

Behind her, someone chuckled, and Arix's stomach grew even more uneasy.

"It's my pleasure to meet you all." She smiled, forcing her features to relax. Maybe if she could convince herself, she could convince them. "Are you all enjoying the evening?"

The woman to her left, Lady Brokersten, offered her a tight smile. "Why yes, yes, of course."

Another awkward pause.

As if the moment couldn't have gotten more strained, Colin started to laugh. Nervous, high-pitched, and incredibly irritating.

"Aha! Yes! It's truly a splendid occasion indeed! Sir Goreve, you are alone this evening? Where is your wife?"

If this was how her evening was going to progress, Arix wondered if maybe it would have been better if she'd stayed up on the dais all night.

The gentleman in question cleared his throat, glancing toward the others in their little circle as he shuffled awkwardly. "It's actually Sir *Tho*reve. My wife is preoccupied this evening and could not be in attendance."

Everything inside of Arix cringed.

Another chuckle caught her attention, and those in her group turned to look behind her.

"I hope I'm not intruding."

Arix turned to get a better view of the newcomer. A man a little older than her, he wore a bright indigo sheer blouse with a purple and gold vest and a black capelet draped across his shoulders. Gold necklaces hung in strands around his neck, and he wore a gold ring in his nose. His eyes were as brown as chocolate, and black curls hung around his face, falling past the gold hoops in his ears.

"I'd hoped to invite our Lady Black Hand to the floor. Lady Bellarix, would you do me the honor of accompanying me for a dance?"

Arix saw Colin Calel stiffen out of the corner of her eye. She smiled.

"I would be delighted."

He offered her his arm, leading her towards the dance floor as the music began to pick up again in a new song.

"If you don't mind me saying so," he said, fingers lightly holding hers as they began the dance. "Your Master of Word is an ass."

Arix fought the urge to snort.

"Is that so?" Arix matched his pace, swirling to the step of the song.

His expertly crafted black mustache twitched as he smirked. "Indeed."

"And you know this because…"

"Because any fool knows that *Lord* Calel,"—he mocked the word Lord as he said it—"is an idiot."

Arix fought a smile of her own. She was inclined to agree based on tonight's interactions so far. "And what would make you such an expert?"

The mystery man smiled, ruby lips smirking under his mustache. "I happen to know things that your Master of Word clearly does not. Mistaking a name is bad enough. It's another thing entirely to bring up the man's wife when it's a known secret that he keeps his wife at home and his mistress at court."

As they spun in another circle, the man's eyes purposefully shifted to look over Arix's left shoulder at a pretty woman in a magenta dress.

"Either your Master of Word intended to insult, or he is ignorant to what the majority of the court has known for years. Regardless, he is still an ass."

As the pair made their way around the circle, Arix watched her Master of Word as he continued talking with the little gathered circle. Those present were clearly uncomfortable.

"He was recommended to me," Arix noted, more to herself than to the stranger.

"Whoever recommended him clearly wants to see you fail."

That made Arix pause, eyes flicking across the room to glance at where Lakai stood. Had he chosen Lord Calel knowing it was a bad choice in the hopes that he would lead Arix astray? Or had he chosen Lord Calel to teach Arix to count on her own abilities rather than to trust the word of someone else?

"Lord Calel does seem to have ideas about who I should talk to and who I shouldn't," Arix said carefully, watching the stranger's face. "Who would you have me meet tonight if you were my Master of Word?"

He grinned. "I wouldn't have you meet anyone. You shouldn't have to introduce yourself to a single person; they should come to you. Let them seek out your favor, not the other way around."

Spinning her again, they wove between another couple, circling out and then back in again to join hands. The stranger cocked his head, glancing at the other partners that swirled around them.

"Anyone here worth their salt would know that to gain the king's ear, they will need to woo you first. And by flitting around the room from group to group, you put the power back into their hands." He leaned in, whispering across her cheek. "Don't give any of them even an inch of it."

She knew he was right. If Arix played into the game, introducing herself and making small talk, she would create a standard that told everyone in court that if they wanted the ear of the Black Hand, they need only sit back and wait for her to come crawling to them.

"I can see you agree with me."

Arix's gaze connected with his, sparking with mischief. "You talk of introductions or lack thereof, and you offer me advice so willingly. But I don't even know your name."

Her partner swept his arm and bowed as the music came to an end. "Ro Laris, my lady Black Hand."

She let him kiss her knuckles, his breath warm against her fingers. "Thank you for your advice. I look forward to our next conversation."

They parted, and when Lord Calel waved her over, Arix purposefully turned towards the food tables. The grating in her stomach hadn't ceased, and if she had to spend another second in her Master of Word's company, she might lash out irrationally.

Ro Laris had been right, of course, and Arix was annoyed that she hadn't thought of it herself. What kind of precedent would she be setting if her first night in court as the Black Hand was spent simpering and traipsing throughout the room having to introduce herself. They all knew who she was. If they wanted her to know who they were, they could come to her.

Suddenly, her dress felt too tight at the wrists, the fabric too close to her body. She was unnerved, and she didn't like the feeling one bit. Her entire life had been about control—controlling her circumstances, controlling people's perceptions of her. Carefully placed lies and well-guarded truths. And now, suddenly, she felt more on display than ever before.

She'd been able to hide behind a mask her whole life. And now, her whole self felt known, revealed to the entire court. There was no hiding behind her anonymity now.

They knew who she was. They could only guess what she was capable of or what kind of Black Hand she would turn out to be.

As Arix poured herself a drink, draining the contents to ease her stomach, she realized that even surrounded by people who looked up to her, maybe even feared her, she was well and truly alone.

Orion was here, sure, but he was doing what kings do. He was charming everyone in the court with his smiles and his confidence, and Arix was on the outskirts. It didn't bolster her with the confidence it used to, to be so removed from society and from the opinions of people. To view the world from above, with the clarity and perspective of distance.

Now, it made her feel empty.

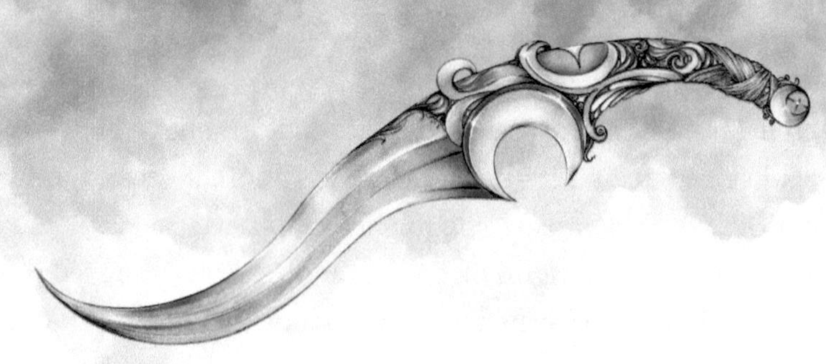

EIGHT

By the end of the night, Arix's insides were so tied up in knots that she went straight to bed after the party. There was a gnawing in her stomach that she might have assumed was hunger, but even the thought of food convinced her that if she tried to eat, it might come right back up again.

As she lay in the darkness, staring up at the ceiling of her new room, she tried her best to focus on anything else other than the disaster of an evening.

She'd done what Ro had suggested and returned to her spot beside the throne, waiting to see if anyone approached her. Now that she was trying to sleep, her mind was replaying every interaction, every met glance. Not a single person had come to speak with her, but was that any surprise? It would have been all but impossible for anyone to approach the dais without invitation, and she had remained safely out of all of their reach the entire evening. Her Fingers had hovered at the edge of the dais for most of the evening before they too scattered to dance or mingled with the rest of the court.

Arix could have easily stood closer to the floor or spoken to some of the council members, but she had chosen not to. At the time, she repeated Ro Laris' words in her head like a mantra, but in the end, maybe her fear had played a bigger role than she wanted to admit.

Like an unwanted horsefly that buzzed obnoxiously out of reach, a thought hovered at the edge of her mind, eating at her slowly until all confidence that she had had at the beginning of the evening had completely dissipated.

Revena would have been so much better at this. Even Michael, with the way he had been raised, would have been good at talking or dancing or *something*. He'd have danced with everyone, sampled the food, and known just what to say. Instead, she'd stood there like an oversized bulldog in a velvet dress, camped out beside the throne like the good scary guard dog that she was.

And…if Celeste had won?

There it was. The question that had nagged at her all night. If Celeste had won, she would have already known half of the court. She would have known the right thing to say, the right people to talk to, the right dances to twirl the night away. She'd been a favorite to win, Arix knew. How many of the people there tonight wished that Celeste was the one still here and Arix was the one rotting in the ground?

She groaned, fingers thumbing over the cold metal of her necklace in frustrated, anxious passes. The voice from her core had been uncharacteristically quiet all evening, and Arix wasn't sure if she liked the silence any better than she enjoyed the snarky commentary.

Goddess, she was too restless to sleep. She needed something to distract her if she was ever going to get a moment of peace from the anxiety that tumbled around under her ribs. Reliving the evening wasn't going to make it any better, and she needed something to do to distract herself before it kept her up all night long.

The stone floor was cold under her feet as she padded out of her bedroom and into her cavernous living apartments. Arix hadn't really had time to explore them or settle herself in since she'd come out of her eternity of sleep. She'd spent much more time in her office with Nesrin, going over plans and making lists. The past couple of nights had been spent in Orion's bed, but that wasn't a habit Arix wanted to start. She liked her space, her own bed, and however tiring her escapades with her new king might be, she much preferred to retreat back to her own apartments when they were finished.

With a flick of her fingers, three spheres of light appeared, hovering over Arix's shoulder and following her as she moved through her new rooms. For a while, she simply walked through the rooms, getting used to the feel of the space, fingers tracing along the lines of the furniture and the rich fabrics that made up the curtains. But after a while, Arix found that sleep still eluded her. With a sigh, she pulled on one of the long quilted robes from the closet and padded down the stairs to her office.

A fire crackled in the grate when she stepped into the small sitting area, the room draped in dark shadows and orange flickers. Nesrin sat behind her small desk, glancing up when Arix walked in. The girl immediately stood, her chair scraping back as she bowed slightly at Arix.

Arix waved at her to retake her seat and lounged out in one of the settees that had been placed against the wall, crossing her ankles on the low table in front of it.

"You're up late, Nesrin," Arix commented once she was settled. She noted that the girl only sat after she'd settled herself.

"Just wrapping up a few final details before we leave, Lady Black Hand."

"You can call me Arix when we're alone."

Nesrin offered a curt nod, shuffling the papers on her desk into two neat piles. "Can I provide any assistance, Arix?"

"No, I couldn't sleep. Figured I might come down and see if there was anything that needed doing. Seems I wasn't the only one who had the thought."

"Could I get you a cup of tea?"

Arix offered her assistant a small smile. "No, but thanks."

Nesrin went back to the papers on her desk, scribbling and taking notes, while Arix watched her, enjoying the quiet company. There were a few books in the office, maps and ledgers, but Arix didn't have any interest in looking at them, and after a while, the curiosity got the better of her. She raised her head to watch Nesrin work, then finally interrupted.

"What are you working on?"

"Correspondence. You've gotten a few letters just today; I'm answering the unimportant ones."

Arix raised an eyebrow at that. "What are the important ones?"

Without looking up, Nesrin motioned to a small stack at the corner of her desk. "These I was going to give you to look over. The rest are general letters of congratulation and introduction."

Striding over to the desk, Arix slumped into one of the chairs opposite Nesrin and picked up the stack.

"There's one from a Lord Vermoin, who asks if you might be interested in investing in his merchant shipping company. I thought you might want to look at it, though I don't think it's a good idea."

Arix picked through the letters until she found the one Nesrin was talking about, scanning through the letter. Seeing the signature made her grin.

"I know Lord Vermoin. Or at least, I met him once at a party." Arix mused. "Though, I don't think he knows that that was me."

"Shall I respond for you?"

"Burn it, for all I care," Arix answered, tossing the letter back onto the desk.

Nesrin didn't even blink; she took the letter, spun in her chair and tossed both the letter and envelope into the fire behind them.

Arix let out a low chuckle. "That solves that problem. Aren't you curious how I know him?"

A piece of dark hair fell across Nesrin's face, and she moved to tuck the stray strand behind her ear as she eyed Arix thoughtfully. "I don't want to pry into your personal affairs."

"My secrets are your secrets." Arix laughed, curling her feet up in the chair. "I once made an appearance at a party he was at and revealed some very damning secrets about him and his undertakings. There wasn't a riot, really, but things didn't go well for those at the party that night."

"Baron Edvard van Hourst's mid-summer soiree."

Arix blinked. "You know about that?"

Nesrin took her time finishing the line she was writing before she finally glanced up at Arix, a small smile playing at the corner of her mouth as she purposefully put her quill away.

"I've done a bit of reading on you."

Arix leaned forward expectantly.

"There isn't much record about your *exploits* before you came to Castle Zma'ai, but I've tried to piece together stories of a masked vigilante that matched your description. I suspected it might have been you at the Baron's party, but it wasn't confirmed."

"I should hope not!" Arix laughed, surprised at how much joy she felt that Nesrin had looked her up. "I was masked and had a daring getaway!"

Nesrin's eyes widened a bit at that, and she leaned forward to rest her elbows on the desk. "How did you get away? You were trapped on a balcony, and then you vanished."

"That I did," Arix offered with a twinkle in her eye. "That I did. Maybe I'll tell you one day. I have to keep at least some of my secrets."

"Fair enough."

"The rest of these letters," Arix said, tossing the pile back on the desk, "you can answer with a humble, 'no, thank you.' We're about to be out of the capital for months, and they can re-petition with their missives when we get back. I won't be making any alliances or rendezvous until then."

"There's one more thing," Nesrin offered. "I left it on your desk."

Arix perked up at that. "My desk?"

She pulled open the adjoining door that led to her private office and picked up the large box that rested on the polished wooden surface. Taking it back to her seat beside Nesrin's desk, she opened it carefully, running her fingers along the seams of the box and checking for any magick. There was none, but it didn't hurt to be too careful.

"I imagine this will be the first of many."

"Who is it from?"

Nesrin reached across the desk, swiping the small card attached to the wrapping. "The card says Bishop Elevin Forir."

Arix pulled the top off the box, pushing past the delicate tissue paper to the wispy fabric beneath. She had to set the box on the ground to pull the full dress out, an intricately embroidered gossamer cream and gold dress. Arix swung in a circle, the dress held up to her body as she preened. As the fabric caught the light of the fire, Arix smoothed a hand across the shifting colors, hints of lavender shimmering amongst the cream.

Nesrin came around the side of the desk and pulled a matching shawl from the wrappings. Gold tipped dragonfly wings in pastel rainbow hues wrapped across her shoulders to give the appearance she had wings.

"How do I look?"

"Beautiful. Especially with your hair down like that."

Arix beamed. "Now that my hair's white, I can wear whatever color I want. Red didn't go with anything."

"More will come."

"Dresses? Goddess, I hope so."

Nesrin smiled, leaning back in her chair. "Perhaps, though I meant gifts. From the council, from the lords and ladies… I'm sure there will be plenty to try and draw your favor."

"I'm sure there will be."

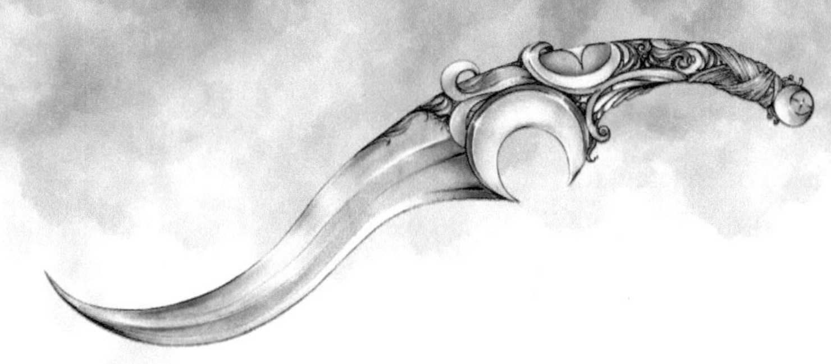

NINE

Mergur was lit up in gold.

Every street and every signpost was littered with streamers and flags of gold, fluttering in the perfect spring breeze. The sky was as crystal blue as the water in the harbor, the sun brilliant and bold. It was the kind of day that begged for brilliance, begged for glory and commotion and perfection.

It was the perfect day for a coronation.

After so much darkness and turmoil with a king who stayed locked away in his tower, it felt so fitting that the sun would shine so brilliantly today of all days. And when Orion was crowned, that golden band finally atop his brow, the whole court bowed before him, and Arix felt a lightness in her chest as she watched him.

So much pomp and ceremony, but so much wonder, too. Everyone had come to see this; every wide-reaching lord and lady had traveled to watch the crowning of the new king. He'd broken the tradition of wearing red on his coronation to wear gold instead, warm yellows traced through with glinting citrine thread. No one had fought him over it. None of the council members had warned him that it broke hundreds of years of tradition because they knew that this was a new dawn, a new era for Rökkur with a king that matched the dawn of the new future.

It was the day that Mergur and the people of Rökkur would begin calling Orion the Sun King.

Arix could not have been prouder. She rode behind him in the procession through the city, smile bright as she watched him wave to his people. They cheered and hollered, and somewhere down the main road through downtown, someone started up a song, and soon, the whole city was singing.

Someone threw a white rose, and Orion caught it and held it aloft. The crowd broke into cheers again as more roses came his way. These Arix did not allow to pass through the shielded barrier that she held around him, and the roses glided down in an arc on either side of him, paving the street in his wake with roses.

It was a beautiful sight.

The people loved him, and it was no surprise. There was nothing about his manner that said he was higher than them, more important than them, even though he was being paraded through the streets, wearing the crown. There had been very little Arix had had to do in preparation for this walk through the city. There was the shield, of course, which would be standard for any public appearance. With the security sweep she had done before the parade, and with the additional guards, there had been no planned attacks or resistance to the new king's coronation. There had only been a small group of malcontents upset at Orion taking the throne after his father had died, but none of them would be an issue during the procession.

It all had been surprisingly easy.

Osiris stomped, shifting slightly to the left as a stray rose almost caught him in the face, and Arix tightened her grip on the reins, running a soothing hand down his neck. She hadn't had much time to ride lately, and it felt good to be back in the saddle. Osiris had grown much too lazy now that their regular training had ceased.

"Starting tomorrow, you'll have to suck it up," Arix muttered to her horse with a smile. "We'll be traipsing all over the country, and you'll need to be on your best behavior."

The coronation tour would start in Nero, working its way up through the realm and into Tamhain, then back down again into Zarak and through to Eldur before returning to Castle Zma'ai in Mergur. The trip was supposed to be to visit the temples of the gods and goddesses, stopping in the capitals of each of the four realms to receive the four god-children's blessings, but the trip was also a political one. Their traveling party would be hosted in the Warden's homes, and the procession would allow the people to see Orion, to cheer and celebrate the new king.

Every stop that was planned along the way was calculated, a holy trip repurposed as bureaucratic.

Most of the court would be traveling with them, and with any luck, it would give Arix a chance to get more comfortable in her new role. A chance to host the king would mean a chance to have your pleas and requests met face-to-face, and every lord and lady within miles would be vying for a chance at the king's ear. An ear that Arix intended to guard exceptionally well.

As selfish a thought as it might be, she planned on vetting the requests that would be made, using her position as the king's Black Hand to push her own agenda. Isn't that why she had given in to the thought of being the Black Hand at all? To have a positive impact on the country, a positive impact on change.

It was time for those with the power to take the responsibility of implementing those changes. And she wasn't about to let the lords and ladies push for approvals of new lands and new titles when there were people starving in the city around them.

Orion would listen to her, and together they would make Rökkur the best it could be for the people in their realms, no matter what their station was.

And while they toured through the country, it would give Arix a chance to put another part of her plan into motion.

She would weed out the Carn once and for all.

~

It was strange being on a ship again. The last time she'd traveled this route, from Mergur to Sieren, she'd done it with Michael and Revena, and the journey had ended fighting the paramour. This time, the ship they traveled on was part of a fleet, and the cabin she stayed in was ridiculously spacious. Not that she spent much time in it anyway. Even though her cabin was huge, and Orion's even bigger, being below deck was suffocating. She couldn't seem to catch her breath no matter how hard she tried, and her stomach ached constantly.

It was all different this time, not the same seasickness she'd experienced on her first journey, hurling the contents of her stomach again and again over the side of the ship. This time, it was an ache that scratched at the inside of her ribs, curling a tight, cold fist around her heart.

She attempted to pass her days reading, but she barely made it past the first two pages of her book before she had to put it down and head back topside to steady herself.

At night, Arix found she couldn't sleep. Being wrapped in Orion's arms was too much, her throat closing up and forcing her up to the deck to pace under the starry sky. The weather had remained beautiful since the coronation, and crystal clear waters had met them thus far on the journey.

The wood was so cold under her fingernails. She gripped the railing as she leaned over the side of the ship, staring down at the waves that lapped beside them as they cut through the water.

She missed them.

It hit her so hard that Arix choked on the pain that bloomed in her throat. Goddess, she missed Michael and Revena so much. And now, going back to that place, Arix couldn't decide if she was ready to replace those horrible memories with new happy ones. Revena had struck the killing blow that day in the temple, and that night, all of Sieren had celebrated them as heroes.

Would any of them remember her? Last time, there had been over a dozen competitors, and now it was just her. Returning as the Black Hand to the Sun King.

Would she be able to do this without the guilt? The guilt of being the only surviving incantor? It felt like a betrayal, coming back to the sparkling sea city as a victor. But victory over what? Not the other competitors—no, it was too complicated to be that. It wasn't victory over the paramour; that was over and done with.

Victory of the new king?

She was proud of Orion, of course, but it wasn't a victory as much as it was the birth of something entirely new.

Arix's gaze followed the water until it met the horizon, black waves meeting black sky, and up to the stars above. She knew that this would be the hardest. Nero would be the hardest of all the realms simply because of the history this place held for her. Killing the paramour, Michael's assault, spending all night on the dock with him, and the long voyage home.

Had she ever opened up to Orion the way that she had to Michael that night?

The thought hit her, sobering the emotional wave that crested to slip out in a sob. She would never love Orion the way she had Michael. The two men were as different from each other as they could be, but still…

Arix cleared her throat, pushing down the ache that welled there.

She needed to sleep. She'd be useless if she was exhausted from the trip, and there was a lot she needed to be prepared for. Arix forced herself to go back down the creaky stairs, choosing her room instead of Orion's. As much as his presence should have been a comfort, in the bowels of the ship, it only felt constricting. If she wanted any sleep, she would need to sleep in a bunk of her own.

In the morning, they landed in Sieren's harbor, thousands crowded on the docks, ready to greet them. The procession was similar to the one they had had in Mergur, though this time, Arix's shield over Orion was stronger. She hadn't had the time that she'd had in Mergur, to check side roads and put preventative magick in place. Here, she would need to be on her toes.

While the excitement was much the same as it had been only a few days ago in the capital, Arix's inner emotions were vastly different. It was impossible to travel through the city and not see the temple that presided over them from the top of a hill overlooking the bay. Impossible not to feel it looming above her, staring down at her.

"It calls you back."

The stabbing in her stomach worsened. "I don't need you to remind me," Arix muttered.

The parade moved through the city, the beautiful tiled streets slanting a bit as they wove their way towards the Warden's house.

Movement to their right caught Arix's eye. Two men and a woman were moving through the crowd, hoods pulled up over their faces. They wove silently, pushing past onlookers towards the front where the crowd met the break in the path.

The woman glanced towards Arix and the two locked eyes.

Arix swore under her breath. The woman was already moving forward, grabbing her friends as they pushed faster through the crowd.

Urging Osiris forward, Arix rode past Orion, pushing her horse into the crowd after the trio.

The smiling and cheering crowd quickly turned to panicked screams as people rushed to get out of the giant horse's way. Arix kept her eyes on the three in hoods, but she was losing them as the crowd began to panic around her.

Gripping her reins in her left hand, Arix pushed out with her magick, locking in on the woman as the two men slipped out of her sight. The woman froze in her spot, the cant around her feet pushing through the seaglass tile to wrap tangled roots around her feet. Once she was caught, Arix shifted her focus back to the two men.

"Move aside!" The people in the crowd hurried to obey, but it was no use. She'd lost sight of them.

Arix hopped off her horse, shoving the reins at a bystander, and took off on foot. She'd need focus and her hands for the next cant. People cleared from her way as she ran, fingertips tangling together as she worked through the cant. A thin trail of gold appeared and she followed it as it twisted further away from the crowd.

As the throng thinned out, Arix pushed her legs to run faster. She chased the trail of gold down a side street and then up a long flight of stairs. She took the stairs two at a time, but already the gold line was fading.

Air wheezed through her teeth as she fought the splitting pain in her side. When was the last time she'd gone running?

The trail veered down an alley and across a small footbridge over one of the many canals that ran through the city. Streets were empty here, most of the city's populace back on the main road.

Arix slowed to a stop as the trail disappeared altogether.

"Fuck."

Her chest ached so badly that it took her a few moments to turn around and jog back towards the main street.

"They moved faster than your magick."

"Not possible." Arix wheezed in reply. "Can't outrun a Predator's Mark."

Arix blinked, forcing air into her lungs as she retraced her steps. As she turned the final corner, a crowd had gathered around the entangled woman, and a small force of her Black Guard kept them from getting too close. Ulfur was holding the reins to Osiris as she approached.

"The king?" She asked.

"Lakai stepped in, and they went straight for th' Warden's place."

"Good."

Arix moved forward to examine the woman, tearing the hood back from her face. Her lip was bloodied, and there was a new bruise starting to bloom at her temple. Around them, her Black Guard was holding back the crowd, angry eyes and clenched fists ready to strike again. Arix motioned for the guards to continue to hold the line, gaze twisting back to the woman. She glared at Arix through slitted eyes, mouth drawn into a taut line.

"I'm going to search you." Arix didn't bother to wait for an answer as she patted the woman down. Around her shoulder was a satchel, which Arix quickly removed and handed to Abbas. Other than that and the hood, the woman was dressed ordinarily, just another member of the crowd. No jewelry either, which Arix specifically looked for.

Just glancing, Arix knew the woman couldn't do magick. There was no fuzzy colored aura around her indicative of the kind an incantor would have. To double-check, Arix felt at the satchel on her side, pulling from it a piece of transparent glass. Holding it up to her eye, she surveyed the woman, confirming what she already knew. No magickal blood.

As the thorny branches receded, one of her guards clapped the woman's wrists in iron.

"Take her to a holding cell. I want to speak with her later."

Arix dissipated the thorny vines entirely and pulled herself back up into the saddle. Her breathing finally felt like it was returning to normal, and she needed to get to the Warden's house and make sure everything was well.

"Abbas, if you please." She held out her hand, and Abbas handed her the woman's satchel.

She flipped open the top of the bag and peered in. Vials and stoppered bottles were nestled along the inner lining of the bag, mutch like her own. Arix carefully pulled one of them out, examining the liquid. The viscous gray-green contents sludged against the glass. Arix placed it gently back in its place and swung the bag around her body. Without a second glance at the woman, she took off, hooves clopping on the road as she wove up towards Warden Uellen Vod's sprawling manor house. The crowd hadn't dissipated, and the traffic had started to pool into the road, making her journey slower than she would have liked.

As the house loomed up, a pang hit Arix in the chest. She remembered so clearly the panic she'd experienced the last time she had been here. When she had thought that Michael had ended his life. They had still lost a life that day, but it hadn't been Michael's. That panic still welled in her, but the fear was like remembering an old wound.

Orion and Lakai and a large portion of their traveling party were gathered in the inner courtyard, talking and bustling as groups were escorted off to their rooms.

The courtyard hushed around her as she neared the king.

She offered a nod to Lakai as she approached the group. "One caught, the other two got away."

"Would you care to tell us what exactly happened?"

Arix peered at Lakai, annoyed at his demanding tone. "Three people, looking like they were about to make an attack on the king. I caught one in a Tangle trap and chased down the others."

"Ran off, you mean."

The hair on the back of Arix's neck prickled, all too aware that their conversation was not a private one and too many people stood around them, listening in. She caught a glimpse of Ro Laris in the crowd, intently watching her interaction with Lakai.

"I did not run off."

Lakai scoffed, and it felt like a slap to the face. "You did. You have a Black Guard, do you not? You have men and women who are at your command, and it is your *duty*, first and foremost, to protect the king. What would have happened if I were not here? Hmm? You would have scampered off like an untrained dog and left our king alone."

Arix's cheeks burned, and it took all her willpower not to look to Orion for defense.

"I had eyes on them." Her reply was hushed, trying to keep the volume of their conversation between the three of them. "It would have taken too long to summon someone else and explain the situation. I acted, and now one of them is in custody."

"And the other two you have lost."

Wrenching the bag off her shoulder, Arix held the strap out to him, her grip tight. She replied through clenched teeth. "Have a look at this before you bite my head off."

Lakai took the bag and pulled out one of the vials. His eyes widened.

"Was she an incantor?"

"No. I checked."

"The other two?"

Arix shook her head. "They didn't have an aura."

Her teacher quickly returned the vial to the bag, hugging it towards his body protectively. "We can take a closer look at these later. It does not change the fact that you left the king *alone* and—"

Anger seethed down Arix's spine. "Enough, old man."

She didn't try to keep her voice down this time. If Lakai wanted a fight, then she would give him one. The courtyard went silent as her tone took on a clip.

"I did my duty today. I protected the king. This bag," Arix flicked the strap that hung out of Lakai's arms to punctuate the word, "contains bottled cants. Cants that can be used without the need for a present incantor. I don't know how, I've never seen this kind of magick before, but I can feel the power coming off them."

Her gaze connected with Orion, hoping that he would see what she meant without having to spell it all out.

"They were with the Carn." His voice was quiet.

"Yes."

That sobered them up, the courtyard absolutely silent as those around them heard the word.

"You did well, Arix." Orion offered her a small smile, clasping a hand on her shoulder. "Very well."

He turned, servants bustling behind him to escort him away to his quarters. Slowly the commotion around them surged again, and court ladies and lords began talking, ushering themselves this way and that as they dispersed.

Slowly, she tilted her chin to look at Lakai, her gaze hard and cold.

"You will never," Arix said, her voice low. "Talk to me in that manner again."

She took a step forward, gripping the canvas of the bag tightly until Lakai relinquished it.

"I am the Black Hand. I am not a child to be reprimanded."

Without waiting for a response, she snatched the bag out of his arms and walked away.

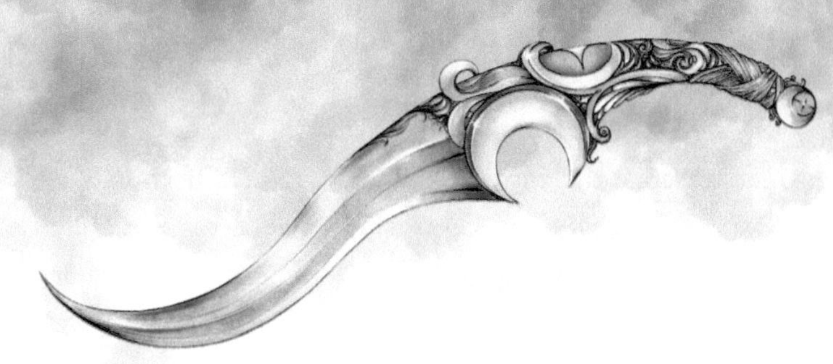

TEN

After everyone else had gone to bed, Arix stalked the outer edge of the Warden's home, following the outer wall and testing for traps or weak spots. She'd done this kind of reconnaissance before, hiding under the cover of darkness and feeling her fingers into cracks in stone walls, searching for the easiest places to gain entry or make a quick escape. Only a year and a half ago, she'd have been outside the wall, not inside it. She'd have been scouting her offensive. Now she checked for those same weaknesses in the estate's perimeter on the defensive.

The inner corridor was next, meticulously tracing the doors and the archways as she walked. To anyone watching, it might have seemed that she was just taking a leisurely stroll through the house and grounds.

It gave Arix a better sense of the layout of the house, and it helped in knowing exactly who was staying in which rooms. A large portion of the court was traveling with them on Orion's tour through the realms, and most of this trip would include elaborate dinner parties and lots of dancing.

"And intrigue, of course. So much can happen when a party travels so inti-

mately for so long."

A smile teased at the corner of Arix's mouth. "Of course."

Finally satisfied with the cants she'd placed on the hallways and the doors, Arix slipped into Orion's room, carefully sealing the magick closed behind her. Orion was at a desk in the corner, and he glanced up with a soft smile as she entered.

"Come to bed me after your little victory?"

The peace that Arix had felt while she'd done her rounds for the last hour turned slightly sour, and her smile faltered.

"You think my rescuing you is a little victory? I would have considered it a rather big one."

Orion laughed, standing from his chair and wrapping his arms around her. He tipped her chin up so that her lips met his own. "I have been saved by you, my Black Hand. I am in your debt."

Arix pulled out of the embrace and slumped down on the chest that sat at the foot of his bed. "Don't patronize me."

"I'm not! Arix, I'm sorry, I really am grateful for today." He knelt in front of her, slowly undoing the laces on her boots as his hands skimmed up under her skirts. His voice took on a rougher, deeper tone as the laces fell away, and he pulled one boot off and then the other. "And as any grateful king might be, I will repay my debts."

Hot kisses nipped up the inside of her calf and up her thigh as Arix leaned back against the bed. She wouldn't protest if he planned on showing his gratitude with his kisses.

Her breath hitched as Orion nestled between her thighs, teasing and tasting her, her legs cocked over each of his shoulders.

Annoyance melted away as warm electric zings of pleasure shot down her spine, curling her toes. Orion's dark hair grasped tightly in her fist, and she pulled him closer. His low growl vibrated against her skin, and a shiver ran down her spine.

"What would I do without you?" Orion's deep voice thrummed

through her, and she squirmed against the sensation. Tension was coiling in her, swelling with every passing second, taking her closer and closer to release.

"You'd be dead." Arix let the answer slip from her mouth without meaning to, just as she crested into ecstasy, back arching off the bed. She clung to Orion, holding him in place as she rode out the spasms that slowly reduced her to a shivering mess. She hardly felt Orion kiss his way down her thigh, rearranging her clothing and laying down beside her, pulling her into himself as he wrapped her in an embrace.

"Those people today," His voice was soft in her hair as he spoke, "Do you really think they meant to kill me?"

Arix fought the drowsiness that was beginning to catch up with her, turning in Orion's arms so she could face him. "Yes. The vials in that satchel are like contained cants. Made by an incantor and bottled with preservatives so that others can use them. I don't know how they work, if their potency lasts, or if they need to stay close to their maker to work."

"You think it was Maeve, the incantor with the Carn." It wasn't a question.

"Probably."

They lay in silence for a bit, Arix's breathing evening out until sleep began to overtake her. She almost missed Orion's quiet voice before she drifted off.

"Cowards."

~

Arix was up before Orion. She crept out of his room, heading for her own to bathe and dress. She was almost done changing when the knock came at the door. Nesrin opened it a fraction, her tone hushed. Wren was finishing fastening the back clasp of her dress when her secretary came back around the corner, mouth set in a grim line.

"What is it?"

"The woman is dead." Nesrin clutched at the ledger she held in her hands, her calendar of notes, and other papers she'd been collecting for their journey. "They found her this morning, her throat slashed. Unclear if she did it to herself or if it was someone else."

Anger crawled up Arix's spine, surging through her like white hot fire. She pulled away from Wren, stalking to the window to look out. Her rooms were situated over the innermost garden courtyard, giving her the perfect view of the splashing fountain below.

"Who was on guard?"

"The Warden's men."

"Ulfur and Abbas?"

"They're waiting for you outside." Nesrin moved instinctively out of the way as Arix stalked past her towards the door, picking up the bag of cant bottles on the way.

Ulfur and Abbas were waiting in the hallway, faces stony. Abbas remained composed, but Arix could practically see the smoke coming out of Ulfur's ears. They kept pace beside her, silent, down to the main floor and out of the Warden's house. The holding cells were near the wharf, and as they rode closer, Arix noticed the collection of the Warden's guards outside.

She barely offered them a glance, pushing past towards the cell the woman had been held in. Each cell was cut into the stone, a small window in the door offering the only light in the small space. The woman was laid out in the straw, arms still manacled to a ring in the wall. Her eyes were wide, staring up at the stone ceiling. A ragged deep cut marked the side of her neck, and the straw around her and her dress were stained dark, rusty-red with blood.

Her teeth ground, her jaw clicking against the force as Arix stared through the barred window down at the mess. She felt the movement beside her as a guard approached.

"Lady Black Hand, if you'll please—" "What the fuck happened here?"

The man flinched against her tone, shifting uncomfortably. "If we could talk in private—"

She cut him off again with a scoff. "No. We will not talk in private. We will talk here, in front of my men and in front of yours."

The look on her face was cold as she finally turned to face him. "Who was on duty?"

"I was, my lady Black Hand." He was the same height as her, but the way he stood, shrinking backwards, Arix towered over him.

"Did you fall asleep?"

"No, I—"

"Did you glance away for just a moment?"

The man stopped trying to answer, his swallow loud as the guards around him watched.

"Your belt surely better be heavier with all the gold you were paid in because if you were the one to slit her throat, I swear to the goddess…" Arix let the threat hang in the air.

Ulfur approached her shoulder, his presence offering support.

The guard in front of her shifted his gaze from her to the northerner at her side, and then back to her. "I can't explain it, I'm sorry. She was fine one moment and dead the next."

"Did she do it to herself?" Truth magick laced through the question.

"No."

"Truth." Her pendant whispered.

"And no one else was in the room?"

The man shook his head.

"Truth."

Arix let out a low breath, eyes glancing past him down the hall. There were other doors set into the wall, stretching down the long hallway. There was one way in and out, back the way she'd come, and no bars or windows to crawl through.

"I swear, my lady, I was standing right here, outside the door, to make sure no one came or went. I heard a sound like gurgling and turned to look through the door. She was already on the ground, bleeding out. She wasn't fighting, just laying there. She didn't have a weapon, and I searched her to see if she had an old nail or glass or something. I swear. I don't know what happened."

"Truth."

He looked so scared, so sincere, and all it did was fill Arix with frustration. If he looked guilty, or if he'd lied about leaving his post, it would have at least given her a starting point to work from. But an honest man who did his job well and still failed? That meant there was much more at work here.

"Get out."

The man glanced toward Ulfur and then back to her, hesitating.

"Everyone other than my Black Guard will leave right now. I won't ask again."

There was a scramble as the place began to clear, leaving just the three of them standing in front of the door. Ulfur held out a key, and Arix used it to unlock the heavy oak.

The tangy copper smell of blood hit her as she entered the small space. It didn't look like the woman had struggled, but by the jagged edge of the cuts, it had been sawed through with something dull rather than a swift cut with a blade. How the woman hadn't screamed out, Arix didn't know.

"There's more to this than meets the eye," Ulfur mumbled, still standing out in the hall, anger present in his quiet tone.

Arix nodded slowly, squatting down beside the woman's shoulder. "Someone didn't want her to talk. This," she pointed to the cut, "was rough. Hurried. Someone who was afraid and acting on their fear."

She had a suspicion that whoever had done the deed had used magick. The guard hadn't seen a thing, hadn't *heard* a thing, and yet here the woman was—dead. Arix sifted through the cants that immediately came to mind. She knew of one that could detect the presence of cants being used, but she couldn't think of any that traced the use of magick.

Bouncing her leg in frustration, Arix stood.

"The man spoke truth." Abbas was the one who spoke this time.

"Mmm."

"He will not be punished."

Arix turned, eyebrow quirked at her tallest companion. "Is that so?" There was opposition in the words, and Arix felt a flare of indignation that he would challenge her. Abbas didn't move to repeat himself, and he held Arix's gaze until she felt her frustration ebb away.

"No." Arix turned back to look down at the corpse with a sigh. "No, he will not be punished. I can't fault a man who told the truth and did his job. Magick did this, I'm almost positive. Someone could have snuck in, done the deed, and left."

"What about the woman?" Ulfur asked.

Arix rejoined the two men in the hall, staring down for a moment at the woman before turning back down the hallway to leave. "Let's wait for now. Don't do anything with her body just yet. There might be a way for me to confirm if it was magick at work here or not. I need to take the time to actually think about this, and I need to get back to the king right now. There's too much we don't know about what the Carn are doing."

Ulfur and Abbas stayed at her heels as she left the jail cells, stepping back outside. The sun was really and truly up now, and the sounds of the city awake for a new day echoed around them. Arix fixed the cinch on Osiris' saddle, fiddling with the reins as someone handed them to her.

"Keep this all quiet for now, within the Black Guard." Arix kept her voice low, making sure that only the two men stood beside her could hear. "If Lakai or anyone else comes asking, you direct them to me and me alone. Make sure the rest of our guard knows. We answer to the king first and foremost."

They nodded, and Arix swung herself into the saddle and headed back towards the Warden's house. All the way, she thought about the girl and the cell, trying to come up with a way to find out if magick had been involved in her death. The whole thing made her tired and frustrated. She still had a lot to learn when it came to coalescent magick, being able to mix and match cants and mold them into something new that met her needs. That had been Revena's specialty, and while she'd learned so much from her friend's journals after her death, there was still an element of natural ability, of talent, that Arix just didn't have.

It was a blow.

Knowing that once again, Revena would have been better at this job than she was. Lakai's words from yesterday echoed in her mind. She hated to admit it, but he'd been right. She shouldn't have run off the way she did. She should have thought smarter, used her magick. Her excuse to him had been true, yes, that there hadn't been enough time to warn her Black Guard, but she could have used her magick in other ways. A barrier, more tangled thorns, or anything that would have stopped them or obstructed their path. But instead, she'd run off.

How had Lakai put it? Like an untrained dog.

Arix huffed. Even if he had been right, he never should have called her out like that in front of the court, in front of the king. It very easily could have been a private conversation later when they examined the bottles. She reacted badly, too, Arix knew, and she regretted it now. But a wound for a wound. He'd embarrassed her, tried to put her in her place, and she'd done it right back to him.

If she let Lakai walk over her, especially in front of the council and the court, then everyone else would walk over her just as easily. She couldn't—no, *wouldn't*—allow that.

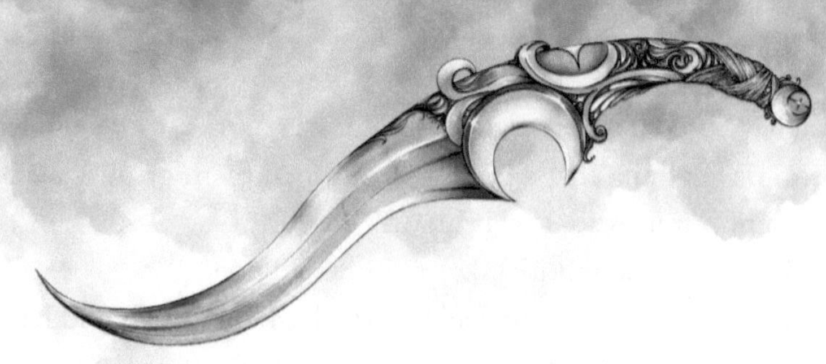

ELEVEN

Each step behind Orion was a labored one. Each step closer to the top, each step closer to death.

No, she had to remind herself. Not death, not anymore. Thanks to her and Revena and—

"Michael."

She couldn't think about Michael right now. Not as she was on the steps ascending towards the temple. Even as she wore his ring on her left hand, the green stone dark against the strange paleness of her fingers, she refused to think of the way things had been for him here. She would not muddy his memory like that. She would not disgrace his memory by thinking of him as a victim.

The last time she'd been here, she'd traveled up these steps with the other competitors as allies, their shortswords strapped to one hip and their cant ingredients strapped to the other. Everything about the temple was different this time. The smell of death and decay no longer lingered against the spotless white stone; the overflowing vases of flowers were gone. Too much sweetness, maybe, too much of a heady floral scent for a place that had seen so much death.

Instead of flowers this time, there was the soft smoke of incense, spicy and rich, that drifted down the steps of the temple like a shrouded mist. It mingled with the salty sea air, aloe, sweetgrass, and valerian. She would never have been able to dissect the scents like that before she was Black Hand.

Orion had come to be blessed by the goddess Nereus, the first of four blessings performed by a High Priestess in their god or goddess' temple. It was normal for a king to receive the blessings, but Orion had been adamant that each blessing be received in their proper temple. King Taurus had had the high priestesses come to him in the capital, but Orion said he wouldn't continue the ways of his father. The whole purpose was to show that he wasn't like the former king.

At the head of their group was High Priestess Esme Halotus. She carried in one hand an incense burner, swinging in step as she walked, her song carrying down the steps and echoing across the marble. Below them, thousands gathered to watch the ascent, waiting patiently until the ritual was done, and then they would cheer as King Orion emerged, newly blessed by one of the goddesses.

Arix's insides churned as they stepped into the cool marble interior of the temple. She'd scarfed down some breakfast when she'd gotten back from the wharf, but it felt like her stomach was still clawing at the insides of her ribs. It was taking more effort than she expected to control her breathing, and with every step further into the temple, her lungs constricted until she thought they might snap. By the time they had moved to stand by the final door into the inner room, Arix was nearly gagging on her own breath.

It was only after the double doors were pushed wide that Arix was finally able to strangle air back into her lungs. She'd expected to see the bodies tangled in on one another, husks drained dry of their life force, and the paramour herself draped in the bodies of the temple's servants as she languished on the stone altar at the center of the room.

Orgies were normal in the temples, she knew, but it seemed that today, with the blessing of a King, would not be a day for one.

"Small mercies."

Instead of the normal servants of the temple, the room was empty of people; the couches and pillows that had littered the area before were cleared away, leaving only the smooth, clean white marble beneath their feet. Everything about this place was different than how she remembered it. It seemed that perhaps she was not the only one who hated the thought of being in the temple as it had been before.

Arix didn't want to think of how long it had taken them to clean the sacred space. To remove the bodies, replace the scent of death with salt and sea air that twisted up behind them from the steps and flowed between the pillars and into the inner sanctum of the temple. How many days or weeks had it taken for the temple to be seen as a place of worship again rather than a place of death and horror. How many had died, in the end? How many still woke up screaming in the middle of the night after what had happened to them?

A hard and pressing ache crushed the back of Arix's throat, and she fought back the stinging in her eyes.

"King Orion Karcharias, step forward to receive the blessings of the Goddess of Water." Esme's voice echoed against the stone pillars, bouncing off the stone around them. Her voice had taken on a deep timbre, and Arix shivered as it enveloped her.

Orion stepped forward, dropping to his knees before the altar that Esme stood beside. Arix forced her gaze on her king rather than on the slab of stone beyond.

"Depths call to depths, ancient and old. It is water that binds the world, water that connects us. It is water that leads all men from birth, and it is water that keeps men alive." Esme recited the prayer, and Arix couldn't help but feel the push and pull of the words, like the tides that drew close to the shore and dragged bits of sand back out to sea with it.

"Great Goddess Nereus, lonely daughter of Kaoss, last of her siblings, patient goddess of the sea; we beseech you to ebb and flow the tide of your blessing over the reign of our king. Pour your wisdom atop his crown. Let your purpose spring forth in his heart, allowing his feet to wade through rivers of patience and perspective that he may lead us all towards the truth of the goddess."

Esme lifted a chalice of water above her head, her eyes trained at a point above them all as if she could see through the roof and up towards the goddess above, waiting for some unseen signal. The moment stretched in silence, and Arix fought the urge to look around them at the others in the room.

Something in the air shifted.

Pinpricks of cold traveled down Arix's spine, and she choked on the air lodged in her throat, the sound matching the gasps of the others around her as they felt the same presence. Esme smiled, the joy so obvious across her face that Arix could not look away. The high priestess slowly tipped the chalice, and water poured over Orion, pouring across his bent brow, tumbling through his hair and across his shoulders.

The water kept coming long after the chalice should have been drained, an endless wellspring that continued to tip from the lip of the metal cup. Orion angled his chin up, and Arix caught sight of his expression, raptured awe as his mouth opened to drink the water. It poured over him mercilessly, and after a moment Arix wondered if he wasn't drowning under the deluge.

Nereus was here—Arix was sure of it. The goddess was in

this place as if her very essence was being poured over the king, enveloping him. The stream slowly lessened until the last drop had been poured out of the chalice, the puddle around Orion spread out and still at last.

The king stood, bowing to the high priestess before turning to smile at the council of men and women around him, his clothes and his skin as dry as when he had entered. The blessing was complete.

Arix watched his eyes, so crystalline blue, more vibrant now, shifting colors slightly in the light. There was joy there, in his expression, and perhaps relief? Had he been worried that the goddess would not bestow her blessing on him for what he'd done to his father?

She hadn't thought it was even an issue, that the gods and goddesses might deny their blessings to the new king. Regardless, it was done, and Orion had a new kind of glow about him, a new kind of aura. Even without her magick glass, Arix could tell.

And then his face shifted.

His eyebrows knit together, and he stared at her in confusion. Arix glanced towards Esme, but the high priestess was staring at her as well, eyes wide and mouth slightly parted.

Motion caught at the corner of Arix's eye, and she glanced downwards just in time to see water pooling at her feet. She couldn't feel the wetness, but she felt its cool temperature as the water slowly began to rise up her legs. It was the feeling of slowly dipping your toes into a pool but without any of the actual effects. Her clothing remained dry, even as she watched the water travel and dance up her arms and across her chest. When it reached her chin, Arix tipped it upwards, as if to pull her mouth further from the water, but it followed her up, streaming into her mouth and nose as it rose across her vision toward the crown of her head.

It was like drowning without drowning. She didn't need the air; she didn't need to fill her lungs with anything other than the wellspring that filled her up. Immediately, the grating in her stomach ceased, and Arix was filled with such an overwhelming sense of contentment and totality that she breathed a deep sigh of relief.

She felt so full. Full of crystal clear abundance and the most staggering sense of peace. She never felt so connected in all her life. Connected to the water and to the others in this room, she could feel the thrum of the water in their bodies, could feel the thrum of the waves on the beaches outside. And above her, she could sense the moisture that gathered in the clouds high above Sieren.

It was the water that connected them all, and for this one moment, she was connected directly to it all. To the goddess.

And as quickly as it came, it was gone. The water splashed down around her, settling back into a puddle at her feet.

Pulled back into the present moment, Arix glanced up at Orion. He had a look in his eyes that she couldn't quite place, his eyebrows knit together and mouth slightly parted. Anger? No.

Hurt. He was hurt.

"It seems," High Priestess Esme Halotus's voice echoed around them, slicing through the silence, "that the goddess has blessed more than one today."

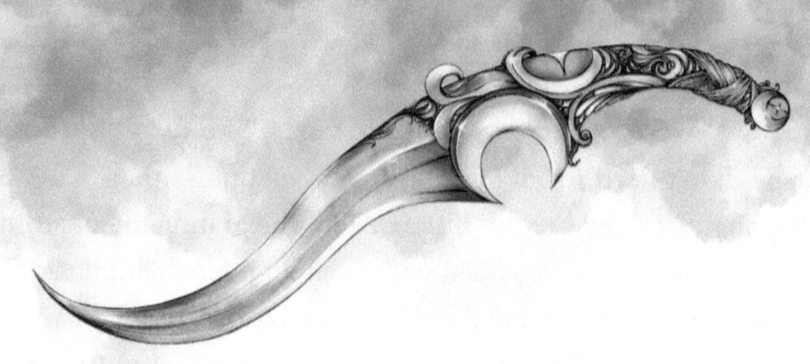

TWELVE

They emerged from the temple when the blessing was over, and just like she'd expected, Orion raised an arm to the crowd and they erupted into cheers. Yet while the excitement from below was electric, Arix felt the shifting gaze of the council and the lords and ladies that had traveled with them to witness Nereus' blessing upon their new king. They watched her in dipped chins and turned heads, but no one said a word. They would all pretend that nothing had happened here. They would pretend that a once-in-a-lifetime event had not just occurred.

The cooling calm that had pooled in her only minutes ago was vanishing quickly, replaced with a yawning, cavernous anxiety.

Arix did her best to keep her steps even, her pace calm as she descended only a few steps behind Orion. Below, the streets were lined for another parade, another spectacle to watch the king return to Warden Uellen Vod's home. There would be another party tonight, a ball to celebrate the blessing. Arix dreaded it.

There were no attempts made on the king's life this time as their horses clopped across the cobblestones. It was hard to focus on the crowd when it took more work to keep herself from hurling her breakfast across the stones. Arix kept her gaze trained on the faces, faces that smiled and shouted. Mouths that sang songs and hands that threw flowers. All of it, a distraction to keep her from letting her mind wander. To roam towards meaning.

Kings were blessed, their reign exalted. A blessing from the gods and goddesses was a blessing of long life, of victories in battle, of prosperity for all of Rökkur. But what did it mean when a Black Hand was blessed?

Arix wanted to ask Lakai, to gain his insight into what the miracle meant. But he hadn't so much as looked her way once all morning. High Priestess Esme, on the other hand, had not stopped staring at her.

It made Arix uneasy.

When they arrived back at the house, Arix held back, fiddling with her horse until the others had streamed into the house. She didn't want to talk to Orion or Lakai, couldn't meet Esme's piercing gaze, and didn't want to try to fight for answers that she just didn't have.

"It's never happened before."

Arix flinched at the High Priestess' voice. After a moment, she glanced back to look at the other woman. "What did it mean?"

For a moment, Esme was silent, the white gossamer fabric of her veil shifting slightly in the wind. "I do not know."

Arix let out a slow breath, waiting.

"It is a good thing. Nereus has blessed you. Don't look so terrified."

"Blessed me with what?" Arix finally stopped fiddling and handed Osiris' reins to a stableboy. She fell into step beside Esme as the two entered the courtyard.

Esme's voice dropped as they stepped further into the estate. "That, I don't know. But I will ask her to reveal her truth to me and let you know what I learn."

Without thinking, Arix scoffed. "Sure. Maybe ask her where the Carn are hiding while you're at it. Or if she'd sprout the flowers early."

"Just because you do not hear from the goddess does not mean she does not speak."

"Right," Arix muttered, but Esme was already gliding away, swathes of fabric billowing behind her as she disappeared from sight.

Fuck.

She didn't want to anger Esme. She didn't have many on her side, and Esme was one of the few on the council she actually liked. Within the span of twenty-four hours, she'd pissed off Lakai and Esme, and by the look Orion had given her at the temple, he was likely upset with her too. Not that she knew the reason why. So far, this trip was not turning out the way she had hoped.

~

The courtyard had been wreathed in candle-light, swathes of small white budded flowers and gray-green vines of dried sea lace draped between the pillars. Arix had opted for a dress that was closer to Esme's style this evening, dark blue layers of sheer fabric that clasped on her shoulder and fell around her shoulder like a cape. She entered just behind Orion, like usual, though he had yet to speak a word to her since this morning. Even in the quiet of the hallway, waiting to be announced, he wouldn't look at her.

He wore loose, billowing teal pants and a gold shirt with matching billowing sleeves. High collar and a matching vest, he looked so good dressed in traditional Neroian clothing. It was easy to forget that he had been born here. He just seemed to fit so well in the capital, it was strange to think he might prefer the customs of Nero best of all.

"Orion." Arix placed a hand on his arm, all too aware of how he stiffened against the touch. "I don't know what happened today. You have to know that I didn't choose for that to happen. I didn't ask for that—"

But he didn't have the chance to respond. The doors opened, and Arix steeled her face into perfect tranquility as she stepped into the decorated courtyard and hovered at Orion's shoulder, nodding and quietly conversing when spoken to. Once the dancing started, she stepped back toward a pillar and simply watched.

"I hope you're not bored?" The rich voice sounded from her left shoulder, and Arix glanced over to see Ro Laris.

"I'm doing my job."

"And a Black Hand can't have a bit of fun at a party?" Ro sipped his wine, then offered her the glass encased in gold.

For a moment, Arix only eyed the goblet, weighing whether or not she trusted Ro. Then she snatched up the cup and downed the contents, handing the empty glass back to him.

He chuckled, taking it. With a wave, he soon had two more glasses and handed her one. This one, she only sipped.

It was a honeyed fig wine, and her first glass hit her empty stomach like an anvil.

"I hear you've been blessed by our goddess of water."

The knot in Arix's stomach only clenched harder. "I'm sure everyone knows about it now."

"Of course."

"I didn't ask for a blessing."

"I know." Ro's response was soft. "Esme's been in the library all day."

Arix's gaze flicked across the room to rest on the high priestess. She was dancing now, smiling and laughing as Warden Uellen Vod stepped forward, their palms meeting between them. Even in a simple dance like this, the sensuality that Esme moved with was obvious. Arix fought against the pang of envy.

"Why? What did she find?"

"Why should I tell you?"

Arix glanced at him, the bits of gold threaded through his red jacket catching against the light. "You shouldn't."

Their gazes held for a moment before Ro smiled. "I know. Maybe that's the fun of things, deciding what pieces of information I want to give away for free and what pieces I want to charge for."

"Bold to assume that the information you hold is so valuable."

Ro Laris laughed, deep and musical. "Ah, but since I'm the one who holds it, it is I who decides if it's important enough to share with a Black Hand blessed by the goddess."

Arix held his gaze, refusing to look away. "What is your price, Ro Laris? What do you want in exchange to tell me what the High Priestess was looking up in the library all day."

Ro's eyes sparkled in the light of the candles that surrounded them. "Make me one of your five Fingers."

Arix blinked, caught off guard. "You…want to be one of my Fingers?"

It sounded strange to say those words, as if she was asking him to join hands with her, but regardless of how strange the phrase sounded, they both knew what it meant. The implications of what he was asking.

Ro's stance was casual, leaning against the pillar and as he sipped his wine, motioning with his cup toward the far side of the room where her Master of Word, Colin Calel, was currently coughing violently and beating at his chest. After a moment, he was able to cough up whatever he was choking on before turning an embarrassing shade of red and excusing himself from the party.

"Your Master of Word is an idiot. He doesn't know anything worth a damn, and he's already tried leading you astray." He turned back to Arix, a serious look taking over his features. "Fire him. Pick me instead. I swear to do a much better job at keeping you informed."

Arix considered him. "You realize that you'd be sworn to me. You couldn't lie or keep secrets from me. You'd be one of my elites and, by proxy, incredibly close to the king."

"Sounds like bushels of fun."

Arix twisted her cup between her fingers, watching the crowd twirl past. It was an interesting thought. Having him take Calel's place would be an easy switch, and she had no doubt that Ro knew more than Calel could even dream of. It would be a boon to have him on her side. She hadn't known him long, but the thought of him helping her, whispering in her ear of whatever the council and the court may be keeping from her, made her feel less uneasy.

"To be my Master of Word… This is what you want as payment? It seems I'm getting the far better deal. I'd gain from knowing what Esme was up to today as well as gaining your loyalty and your whispered secrets. What do you gain? Speak the truth."

Her fingers twisted around the bottom of her glass, forming the sigil that would force him to tell the truth. But he didn't fight the cant, and Arix realized he planned on being honest with her regardless of whether he'd been forced into it or not.

"After what happened today, I want better access to you. To your magick. I can feel a shift—the whole country can. It has always been my practice to keep my ear trained as tightly to the ground as I can let it. I hear the whispers, and I don't have to pay for information like other spymasters. I don't have to use magick to get people to tell me the truth; they just choose to tell me. And the truths I hear are this…"

Ro stepped closer, the fig and honey wine on his breath sweet on Arix's cheek. "The world is changing; something is different. Whether it is the king or the Carn or *you*, all that we know is about to shift. I simply want to be close enough to see the blocks begin to fall before the whole thing topples into the sea."

There was something about his words that filled her with a sense of dread. It reminded her too much of what Orion had said the night she'd become the Black Hand. The reminder that she was part of a new era, a new change.

"How is it that you always seem to know things before they happen?" Arix asked the question casually, doing her best to steer the conversation further from the apprehension that roiled under her ribs.

"It is my job to know."

Arix considered this.

There was no real need to test him. With the contract he would have to sign, he would be forced, at the risk of his life, to tell her the truth, to keep nothing from her. But a test would do more than prove his usefulness. It would prove fealty and prepare a foundation of trust. If she was to have Ro Laris as an ally—a contracted ally, even—she didn't want to simply use him. His request had triggered an idea in her head, one she'd already been thinking about. She wanted to build a group of five Fingers that she could trust. She wanted friends again.

Michael and Revena and Arix had been inseparable. They'd shared ideas and magick, and they'd been better incantors because of it. Even after both were dead, Arix had learned more from them as teachers, their deaths the inspiration to push herself forward and to fight for them. To prove their deaths did not mean nothing.

In part, her Black Guard was already being shaped by this

notion, by putting Ulfur and Abbas at the head of it. Building an elite team of people who would rally behind her gave her a sense of power and belonging, and she wasn't afraid to admit that she missed it. Belonging somewhere.

Arix's gaze shifted as she watched Orion move through the crowd, smiling and talking. After what had happened today, Orion's response to the blessing at the temple, it had only solidified one thing. She and the king shared a bond, yes, they had to. But there was also a deep chasm between them. A chasm Arix could not step across.

"Prove it," Arix said, taking a sip of her wine. "Tell me something I don't know. Something I should have been told, a secret, and prove to me that I need you."

She turned back to Ro, eyes boring into him. She was angry, she realized. Just a bit angry and quite a bit of something else. Something she wasn't quite sure about.

"Liar."

"I could tell you what the high priestess was up to today," Ro offered casually, not meeting her gaze. Instead, his eyes slid across the crowd and came to rest at a fixed point across the room. "Or I could tell you something far more important. Far more immediate."

Arix followed the look, peering through the crowd to see the far point he was looking at. Dancers swirled at the center of the courtyard, blocking her line of sight.

"Something that even the king has not decided yet. But he will."

The urge to arch up on her tiptoes to see who he was looking at itched at Arix's spine, but she held her ground, waiting for the dancers to move out of the way.

"Do with the information what you will, but know this…" Ro

leaned in, his voice quiet as Arix kept her eyes glued to the spot across the courtyard. "You can't let them know you know.

My spies are carefully crafted for a reason. Letting on that you knew would only jeopardize the network I've carefully put into place. A network that could serve us well if you would let me."

The music was slowing, the song coming to an end, and the dancers made their final rotations. Soon, the dance floor would clear, and she would be able to see. The dancers bowed, stepping across the tile, and finally parted, letting Arix see what Ro Laris was looking at. Who he was looking at.

"King Orion has a firm hold of the crown. A firm grasp of the kingdom. But all kings, no matter how strong they are, must bind the assurance of their reign. The king will need…"

Everything in Arix's stomach dropped as she stared across the courtyard. Orion had stopped winding through the crowd, stopping flitting between the members of the court, and had stopped to stand with Warden Uellen Vod.

He was smiling, tipping his head down to kiss the delicate fingers of the Warden's daughter. The girl beamed up at him.

"An heir."

And Arix felt her blood turn to ice.

"When?" Her voice sounded hollow against the backdrop of music.

"Before we leave Sieren. He'll take her with him. This will no longer be coronation tour; it'll be—"

"A wedding tour." Arix finished for him.

The dancers had taken the floor again, and her view of Orion was obscured. She slipped backward, stepping into the darkness behind the pillar, Ro Laris placing a hand on her elbow to steady her. She shook him off.

"Orion has chosen his queen," her pendant whispered.

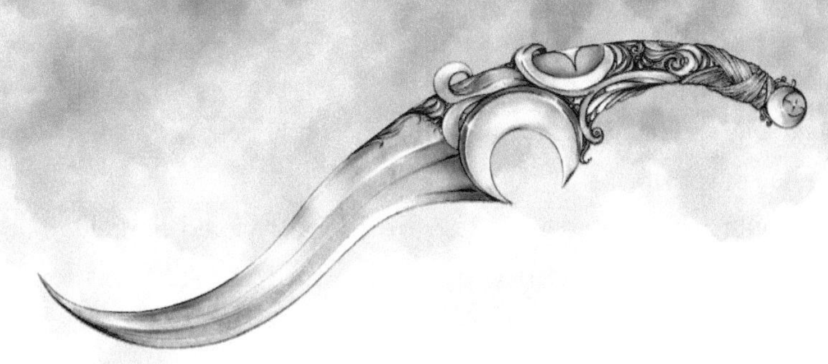

THIRTEEN

Arix wanted to leave the party early. She wanted to slip away down to the bay and sit on the docks and wait for whatever swell of emotion that was surging through her to come crashing out. She wanted to demand how Ro knew. Demand how he knew before she did. She wanted to pull Orion away, to demand that he tell her the truth. How long had this been in motion? How long had these plans been in place? To marry? To sire children?

But Arix did none of those things. Instead, she excused herself from Ro Laris' company and went to get another drink. And when her glass was empty, she walked the perimeter of the courtyard, double checking her protection cants. She ate, she talked, she danced. She kept her eye trained to the king, kept her eyes open, and watched.

She did what she'd done only a few months ago when Revena had died and what she'd done even harder when Michael slipped away in her arms.

She built a wall around her heart, around her emotions. She sealed them away, forcing herself to focus on her purpose, her job. She was the Black Hand. She'd fought to be here, fought for this place at Orion's side, as his incantor. She would not make another mistake like she had before. She would not let her emotions drive her from her purpose.

Stupidly, she should have known that this would happen. The king needed heirs. He needed alliances to further solidify his reign. And she hadn't even considered it.

Goddess, she was stupid.

When the night came to a close, Arix checked the incantations again, walking the perimeter of the estate, checking every wall, every doorway. She took the time to let her emotions envelop her, to sweep across her scalp and down her spine and think. To feel.

She didn't want to be a mother. That was something she'd always known. Even if Orion had asked her to be his queen, which she knew he wouldn't have, she would have said no. A queen and a Black Hand? It wasn't something she would have ever wanted.

Ro had said that even the king had not made the final decision yet.

This was the one thing she held on to. That if Orion had not made his decision yet, that was why he hadn't told her. Surely, he'd been about to tell her. To warn her of what was coming. But after everything at the temple, how could he? Maybe he was questioning his choice?

The rabbit trail of thoughts speared out in too many directions, and slowly, Arix stopped them all, forcing her mind back to the task at hand.

There was one simple answer. She had to talk to Orion. She had to find out what he was thinking and give him the chance to tell her his plans.

She trusted him. And if she trusted him, she had to give him the benefit of the doubt. Let him tell her in his own way, in his own time. And meanwhile, she needed to pretend she didn't know.

When her walk around the perimeter was done, she headed down the familiar hallway and approached Orion's door. She knocked gently and waited. When no answer came, she turned the knob to enter.

It was locked.

Orion knew she could unlock the door with a cant. That no regularly locked door could keep her out. But it was the knowledge that he had locked it at all that pushed her away, back down the hall and towards the courtyard. If he did not want her in his bed, she would respect that.

But it still hurt.

It was a strange space to be in. She and Orion were lovers, but was that all? He had told her he loved her the night she'd killed King Taurus. But he hadn't proclaimed the same sentiments since, and Arix had been grateful. Did his loving her make all this easier or harder? Or had he only said it in that moment, a quiet lie to force her hand in that final moment in the tower.

"And what of you?"

The voice was annoyed, persistent, as Arix stepped into the courtyard, the decorations still hanging between the columns. The sliver of moon was hidden behind the clouds, but Arix stared up at it all the same, wishing that a little of its light would sift through the coverage and burn crescent shapes into her eyes.

"You cannot escape the question. I am in you. I am you. Do you love him?"

Did she? If she compared her feelings to the ones she'd had for Michael. For her father so long ago. For the men and women she'd been with, thinking back to the relationships and the people who had wandered through her short life, she had to wonder if she was even capable of love.

She had loved Michael and Revena. That was certain. And when they had been taken from her, the hole in her chest had yawned so violently, she had done everything in her power to fill it back up again.

The pieces of her broken heart were still patched, and she missed them every day. But the love she'd had for them had been different. Michael had been engraved on her very soul. And losing him had been to lose part of herself.

But Orion?

His breath on her skin slid shivers down her spine; his nearness and his strength always gave her pause. The desire to be near him, to win his favor, to prove herself to him was so strong, but was it enough to warrant the word love?

No.

"Liar."

"I'm not lying," Arix muttered aloud, but even as she said them, the words felt hollow. "I just… I don't know."

"The truth."

A frustrated sigh escaped her lips as she tore her gaze from the clouded night sky and headed for the door.

"Who is the bastard king to you?"

"Don't call him that."

"What else is he, if not a bastard king? His mother was a hidden affair, a secret buried in Nero while Taurus reigned in Mergur. And who was she? This faceless mother, lover, and shame? Orion is the bastard son of a king who pretended to forget what he'd done. It is the truth of him, and the truth of you is this: You do not know whom you serve."

Arix ground her teeth as she pushed through the outer door of the walled estate, nodding to the guards who stood watch. She wandered down the street, heading nowhere in particular. The mosaic roads were quiet around her, the night too late for the people of Sieren to still be awake and too early for the fishermen and market makers to be rising for the new day. It was eerie, the dark gray light shrouding the buildings that lined the road in lines of charcoal. The blue and green tiles were muddied in the dark, and the ocean colors of Sieren were lost in the inky black of night.

There was no one to hear her talk. No one to listen as she whispered only half of a conversation with herself.

"I serve the king."

"Liar."

"Who else, if not Orion?" Arix's words were still hushed, muttered in anger under her breath as she walked. Pretending to believe her own words. "Lakai? I don't serve him."

The voice scoffed. *"The teacher is a fool. He doesn't know your power. He doesn't understand you anymore. No, not him."*

"The memory of Michael and Revena?"

"If you have to ask, then you already know it is not them."

"I'm not asking. I'm telling you. I serve their memory. I am the Black Hand because of them and their sacrifice. It was Revena's notes I learned from. It was Michael who died so I could face Celeste."

"He would have died anyway."

The words stung, cut deeper than Arix would have thought. Immediately, her throat constricted, forcing her to swallow down the ache.

"Shut up."

"He did not have what it took to be the Black Hand." The words were hard, but Arix could sense the voice softening a bit. *"He knew it. It's why he did what he did."* Tears sprang at the corner of her eyes, hot betrayal sliding down her cheek. She let the wet tracks lace down her face, sliding down her chin. Oh goddess, how she missed him.

"Then who?" The words came out defeated. Tired. Arix let out a shaking sigh. "If not for Michael and Revena or Orion, then who? What do I serve?"

An image flickered in her mind of the crowd that had gathered this morning at the base of the stairs at the temple of Nereus. Their roaring shouts as they cheered for their new king. Hadn't they been what she had fought for? When she'd slipped nimble fingers into great houses and heavy pockets and stolen back what was owed, she'd known who she was. A servant to the people of Rökkur, setting things right after so much wrong. She remembered the faces of the warden's family in Pyesak, terrified of what the Carn would do to them. She remembered the box engraved with the flowers Revena had taught her about, ready to detonate and bring the entire underground city to dust just to prove a point.

Anger, like hot billowing sand, stung at her insides.

"Do you truly serve them? The people? You did once, but now? I am not so sure."

Arix said nothing, not sure either. Her legs had finally stopped as she realized where she'd wandered to. The pale stone steps of the temple stretched up towards the reaching pillared entrance. Honeyed light spilled from the doorway, beckoning her upwards, promising comfort.

The voice of her pendant was quiet as she made her way upwards. As she neared the light spilling from the temple, the darkness behind her seemed to nip at her heels, making her wonder if this was all some terrible dream. If she might wake up at any moment and be back in the safety of her bed.

Arix shrugged off the feeling. She was the Black Hand. She had nothing to fear.

Candlelight spilled across the marble floor as she entered. An attendant in the antechamber nodded respectfully as she passed him. She'd never really spent much time in temples, and Arix wasn't even sure if she knew what to do.

The center of the temple was quiet. Cavernous. Expectantly waiting for her. So silent that Arix felt the need to shout, to cry out, to sing even, in order to break through that heavy silence.

Her feet had taken her here for answers. Taken her to the temple of the goddess to try and fill in the blanks in her mind, reveal some hidden piece of knowledge that might make her future fall into some semblance of sense.

"Lady Black Hand."

Arix turned abruptly, noting the shape moving out from behind a pillar. She was halfway through casting a shield cant before she realized who the voice belonged to and let her arms fall back uselessly to her side.

"Esme."

The high priestess joined her in the center of the room, and together, they stared at the altar, shadows cast across it flickering gently beneath the candlelight.

"You could not sleep."

"Neither could you, it seems." Arix shot back.

Esme smiled. "No, I have been seeking answers from my goddess."

Arix waited for her to continue. After a moment of silence, she offered a hesitant, "Well? Has she told you anything? Any hint as to what happened this morning?"

"An acolyte must be patient. It is not always in our power to understand the will of the gods."

It took everything in her not to huff in response, but Arix held it in. "Sure."

"What…" Esme's voice was soft. "…did it feel like?"

She turned toward Arix, a crack in her normally confident cadence. Arix found it hard to look at her, still not knowing herself what she'd felt, not knowing how to put it into words.

"It felt like drowning alive. Like my lungs were filled to bursting, but I could still breathe. Like being dragged away by a current without knowing where it will take you. Fear for a moment, and then…" Arix paused, frustrated that her words weren't portraying the feeling well. "And then the fear was gone, and instead, I just felt…"

"Peace?" Esme finished for her.

Arix only managed a nod in response.

Esme hugged herself tightly, her long fingers playing with the edge of the veil she wore. She took hesitant steps forward until she stood directly in front of the altar, staring down at the stone.

All the life Arix had felt that morning had been replaced by the cold indifference of the marble. It made her wonder if maybe she'd made it all up in her mind. If none of it had happened at all.

"You were blessed." Esme turned back to face her, her voice having regained its confident timbre. "I don't know why she chose to bless you both, but she did. The gods and goddesses speak in actions we do not understand. Sometimes, it is not until later that their purpose is made clear. But I do know this…"

Goddess, please don't say it. Arix took a step backward, heading for the door but knowing she would hear Esme's words anyway.

"You were chosen."

Arix's jaw clenched as she took another step back.

"I wasn't chosen," she spat out, anger and despair coiling in her stomach and tightening her insides into knots. "I was just the only one that was left."

And then she ran.

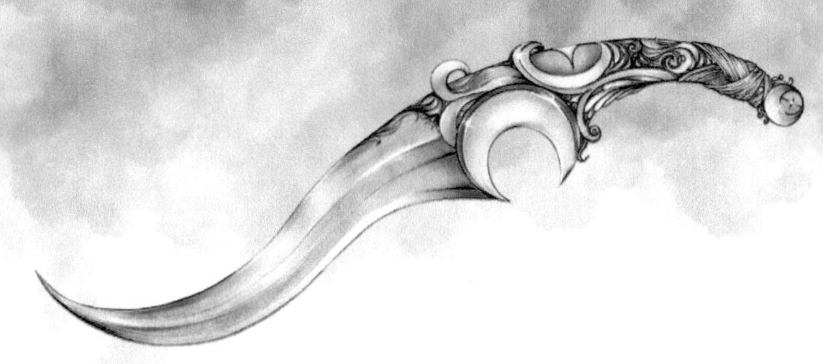

FOURTEEN

Orion was asleep when Arix slipped into his room. Fuck the locks, fuck whatever Orion was doing to put a barrier between them. She needed to know, needed him to tell her what he was going to do.

Stripping from her clothing, she climbed in beside him, curling her body to his. Whether in sleep or consciously, Orion wrapped an arm around her midsection, pulling her to him until their bodies were flush. But as much as she had hoped that being with him like this would calm her nerves or fill a hole in her heart, instead she was left with an acrid taste of bitterness.

Arix slept only a little, waking long before he did. But she stayed silent and still, waiting for his breathing to change as night slowly shifted to dawn and golden light filled the room. It wasn't long before Orion woke, placing a gentle kiss on her shoulder, his breath warm and reassuring.

"Good morning," he mumbled into her hair, the strangeness of yesterday seeming so far away now that she was wrapped back in his arms.

"Morning."

She waited for him to say something, anything. But he only nestled his face further into her shoulder, delicately tracing the lines of her shoulder blade with his lips.

"You locked the door."

"And you unlocked it." The words were mumbled into her skin. "I did."

Orion's fingers traced down her side until his palm was securely wrapped around her hip. He pulled her closer, pressing into her from behind. "Why?"

His tone was careful. Poised to be a question, but there was so much else behind the words. The instinctual reaction that rose up in her was to ask forgiveness, talk through what had happened at the temple yesterday morning, ask him about his choice in a queen.

Instead, she said, "I wanted to. To talk to you, and I didn't want to wait to have a strained conversation over breakfast with Warden Uellen Vod and the rest of the council."

He let out a frustrated sigh and bit down lightly on her shoulder. "Arduinna, don't be difficult."

Annoyance bloomed in her chest. "I'm not being difficult."

"Why are you like this? Always itching for a fight. I won't fight with you when you're convinced you're right."

Arix turned to lay facing him, pulling the softness of his lips away from her shoulder, and took his face in her hands. "I don't want to fight; I just want to talk with you. Don't lock me out."

His eyebrows shot up. "Am I not allowed privacy? I am the king, Arix. If I want to have my bed to myself, I'll have it." Sarcasm laced the question, and each word made Arix feel a mixture of annoyance at him and frustration at herself.

"Of course you are. And next time, if your door is locked, I won't bother you. But this once, I needed to say something to you."

He wasn't making this easy. She'd been thinking about it all night as the dusty dawn seeped in through the windows, and it had taken some self-reflection and self-analysis for her to come to her conclusion.

Orion let out a sigh but said nothing, waiting for her to go on.

"I think you should take a queen."

"What?"

Arix took a breath and repeated, "You should take a queen."

The look on Orion's face was unreadable. "Why are you saying this, Arix?"

"Because you are a coward."

"Because it's the right call. You'll need an heir, and you'll need alliances to solidify your claim to the throne." Arix spoke slowly, gaze trained on Orion's indiscernible expression. "And I won't be the one to give that to you. My job is to protect you, protect the kingdom. But I can't be your guard dog and your queen."

Something like relief flickered across his features, and he pulled Arix into him, her face fitting perfectly in the crook of his neck. He let out a long sigh, stroking his fingers through Arix's hair.

"Oh, Arix. I've been wanting to talk about this, but I wasn't sure how you'd take it." He pulled away, carefully stroking her cheek. "I didn't want to hurt you; I wasn't sure you would understand."

Strangely, that *did* hurt. He didn't trust her to understand the predicament they were in. Had he worried that he couldn't trust her not to turn into a jealous bitch about it?

"I do understand. I just want to make sure you and I are clear about where we stand. What it means for us moving forward. I'd serve you and your queen, give you space, step further into my role as Black Hand."

Orion's brow furrowed, his hand stilled on her cheek. "What are you saying, Arix?"

"I'm saying that I wouldn't get between you two—"

"No."

"Yes." Orion sat up, pulling Arix up and into his lap, wrapping her legs around his waist as he drew her closer. "I won't lose you to gain a queen, Arix. I won't. And if you plan on stepping gallantly away, think again."

Why did her chest ache? Why did his refusal cause even more of a yawning emptiness in her? He was telling her that he didn't want to lose her. Was that something his new queen would allow?

"And if your queen expects a committed king at her side? If she hates the idea of you bedding both of us?"

"I wouldn't choose anyone who wouldn't understand the situation, Arix. I won't disrespect you by hiding you away like some shameful secret and pretending I'm not in love with you all for the sake of a queen."

There it was again, him using the word *love* like it didn't make her whole insides shake. Like it didn't make her wonder if her feelings matched his.

"I'm sure, more than ever before, that you were meant to be with me, to help me rule. Yesterday in the temple was proof of that. The goddess blessed both of us—together. And together, we'll rule Rökkur."

Arix didn't know what to say. She'd wondered if he was angry at her, upset that somehow, she'd received a blessing along with him. Maybe it was better to say nothing. Already, this entire trip had taken a different turn than she'd expected.

"Do you know who you'd pick? For your queen?"

Orion thought for a moment, analyzing the look Arix gave him. His brow was creased again, and Arix knew he saw right through her redirection of topic.

"I've considered Warden Uellen Vod's daughter," Orion said slowly. "Delphine."

"Delphine Vod." The corner of her mouth quirked slightly into a half-smile. "Waters of the sea. The Neroians certainly do love their names."

"Indeed." Orion's tone did not match her mirth. "I've known her father a long time. I knew her growing up, and she would be less of a stranger than any of the other Warden's family."

Arix thought of the girl she'd seen at the party. Delphine had been dressed in swathes of rippling shimmery satin dyed in creams and pinks. The dress had made her look like one of the shells that lined the ocean floor, light peachy pink centers that shimmered in the sunlight. And she was beautiful, with strong shoulders like her father with the demure downcast eyes of the daughter of a powerful man.

"When will you announce it?"

"I don't know, Arix. I wanted to talk to you first."

"Liar."

Arix almost hushed her necklace out loud, forgetting for a moment that Orion could not hear the voice that rang in her mind.

"You should do it soon. Today. We'll be leaving Sieren soon, and she should come with us on the tour. Rökkur should have a chance to meet their new queen." Arix offered him a small smile, doing her best to cover up the turmoil that raged like knives of anxiety in her stomach.

She knew Orion was already planning this—or at least thinking about it—from what Ro had told her at the party last night. It felt like she was lying somehow, knowing what Orion was planning to do before he did it. But having the knowledge before it happened was a boon, wasn't it? It gave her time to come to terms with the decisions he made as king, and if she came across as the trusting Black Hand, didn't that help them both? In the end, wasn't it a good thing that she knew things before they happened?

"It's fast, Arix. Are you sure?" He took her hands in his, lips carefully brushing over the knuckles in a delicate kiss. "It would shift the focus of this trip, shift the focus towards me and Delphine. It would become—"

"A honeymoon?" Arix finished for him.

Orion nodded slowly.

"It's alright, Orion. Really."

And as she said it, she felt a strange truth to the words. She was fine. She still wasn't sure how she felt about Orion, about his regard for her or where they stood. She still wasn't sure if she loved him. It was the uncertainty of it all that made her chest ache, the thought that there was an imbalance between them.

"I'll settle everything today, then." Orion pulled her in, crushing her to his chest as he hugged her. This was where she was content. The tangible, the physical, of her relationship with Orion. Not the emotional turmoil of the last twenty-four hours.

His breath was even and sure against her hair, and Arix closed her eyes and reveled in the silence. Reveled in their skin pressed together. And selfishly, she was glad that, for now, she was the only one in his bed.

~

Uellen Vod agreed, of course. Could he even say no if he wanted to? But he didn't. His daughter would be married to the new king, securing Nero's alliance with the crown and making a statement to the rest of the realms. If there was any doubt in the question of the new king's plans, those doubts were put to rest. The new king would marry and sire an heir to secure his line.

If there was any objection to Delphine Vod, none voiced their disapproval to Arix. She wasn't surprised. There was a good chance everyone on the council already knew she'd spent time in Orion's bed.

But even if the council never voiced their concerns to her, she wanted to know their opinions all the same.

Ro Laris agreed to her terms, her contract of truth and loyalty, and signed in his blood, just as her secretary, Nesrin, had. She dismissed her Master of Word, Colin Calel, without a second thought.

"There's some discontentment, specifically from Aliska Sviengard," Ro offered, plucking a flower from one of the climbing vines that clutched the inner wall of the warden's home. He tucked it gently in his lapel before going on. "But that has more to do with the fact that she has her own daughter she would have put forward as a potential candidate. Usually, a king waits a bit before choosing a bride. I think Aliska expected to have more time to woo him over to her side."

Arix kept her gaze broad as she strolled beside him, watching to be sure none overheard their discussion. Together, they strode across one of the low footbridges that crossed a stream of water that ran through the grounds. She paused, noting a leaf tugged gently by the current, watching as it moved down, away, and out of sight.

"And the rest of them?"

"Watchful. Hesitant. No one wants to show outward disapproval of our majesty's choice. Lord Bardon seems to have been the one to suggest the match in the first place, so none on the council are arguing with him."

Arix dragged her gaze back to Ro and eyed him. "What are your thoughts?"

He smiled, the curve of his mustache twisting upward as he did so. "My thoughts are only of you, Lady Black Hand."

Arix didn't match his smirk. "Part of your contract with me is dependent upon you telling me the truth. Not what I want to hear, but your honest opinion. Don't try to mince words with me,

Ro Laris."

Ro's grin only deepened, and he bowed to her, his arm sweeping out at his sides. "Of course. You're absolutely right."

"And?"

"And I think our king is making a wise choice in a bride. Delphine is the oldest of eleven, and she comes from a good family. She'll provide the king with children, and her purpose will be fulfilled."

"But?" Arix needled, sensing he had more to say.

Ro turned, walking backwards as he faced her. "But she will be lonely. She may be content but not happy. Delphine is dutiful. She'll do what her father has asked of her, but she doesn't seem the type to enjoy the weight of a crown."

They had circled the garden once already, and at the hallway back to her rooms, Arix stopped, stepping further away from the sunny courtyard.

"You seem to care a lot about her welfare."

Ro's eyebrows quirked at that, rising slightly. "And you do not?"

"Not really."

"Why?" Ro reached a lazy hand to stroke the edge of one of the decorative colored tiles that covered the wall. "I thought your goal was to protect people. To care for them when others did not. Why is Delphine different?"

Arix felt the bite of the words, the smarting accusation beneath the question, and her defenses instantly rose. Before she could respond, Ro Laris continued.

"Don't misunderstand me, Arix. I ask because even after knowing you a short time, your ambitions seem clear to me. You are content to protect, to serve. But I do not think you will always be content to stay that way. One day, there will come a time of action. And I'm curious what that action will end up being. Who it will impact and affect. What do you truly care about?"

Arix faltered for a moment, not really knowing how to answer him. Strangely, it aligned with the questions that had reeled through her own mind the past couple of days. She was questioning quite a lot lately, and her purpose was a big part of it.

Her goal had been to help the people of Rökkur, but in a strange way, it had shifted. She hadn't really sat down to think about what she wanted, what she saw for her future. What did it mean to be the Black Hand?

She didn't have any frame of reference, no guide to help her find her path. If she'd been at home in Castle Zma'ai, she might have tried to find history books or past records or something that might offer her insight into her new role. By learning from the past, she could avoid pitfalls in the new role that was her future. Maybe the library would be able to help her find the answers she sought. Lakai certainly wasn't offering any sort of help.

Her mind drifted to the dead woman in the cells. The bag she had carried had been full of canted potions imbued with magick to somehow allow the user the use of cants without the necessity for any training or magickal capability. If the Carn had that kind of magick, then it was no wonder they were so hard to catch.

That thought pulled a tight grip around her heart, her jaw tightening at the anger that pulled in her.

Arix turned, stepping in close to Ro, her voice gruff and low. "I care about King Orion and the safety of the people in this country. I care about rooting out the Carn and crushing them." Slowly, she smiled. "The truth is this: I am still learning my purpose. But when I think about the good I might do, of the change I might make, I see the rebels wiped from our realms and their incantor dead at my hand."

She'd hoped to surprise Ro with that last bit about the Carn's incantor, but he only nodded slowly.

"I'd heard about her, but I wasn't sure how much was truth and how much was fiction."

"She's real. And she's using methods I'm not familiar with. I have to learn as much as I can about her, about myself, to end her."

"I'll do my best to collect what I can."

Arix felt herself softening slightly. Ro had heard her out and didn't judge her for the hatred she harbored towards the Carn. He didn't even blink when she told him she would crush the rebels and kill their teenaged leader. And instead of offering her flowery words or reminders for diplomacy, he'd simply understood and offered help.

"Thank you, Ro. I mean it. I've been…"

She didn't want to say lonely, exactly, but Arix desperately missed the companionship that she'd had with Michael and Revena. They'd helped each other, held each other accountable, and encouraged each other. She missed that.

He smiled, knowing. "I understand."

And then he stepped away and disappeared down the corridor.

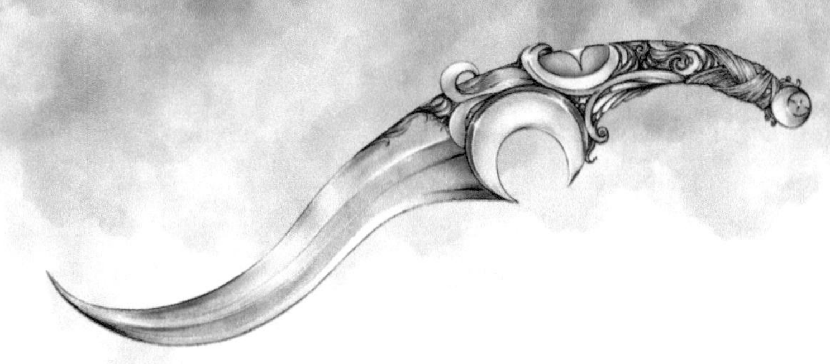

FIFTEEN

Delphine was dressed in coral pink today, her dress pretty but modest in cut and style. The perfect thing to wear on a date with the king.

The vice that squeezed Arix's insides tightened.

She stayed ten paces behind them as Orion and Delphine strolled the pier, smiling and chatting as they weaved their way between the stalls. Two of the Black Guard walked ahead of them, clearing a path, and Arix walked behind them, flanked by Ulfur and Abbas. It was all a show, playing up the story to Sieren that the king was courting Delphine. Their engagement still hadn't been publicly announced, and Warden Uellen Vod had suggested they take a walk, make an appearance to elicit some talk amongst the commoners.

All tactics and ploys just to get the people excited.

Arix had been the one to suggest her Black Guard as chaperones. She was sure the Carn had people in Sieren, and she wasn't about to let Orion out of her sight.

They suited each other, Arix realized. Orion wore more gold today, leaning towards a orange tone, and it complemented the peachy coral of Delphine's dress. She was wearing her hair simply, her locs carefully wreathed around her head and bound with a band of small shells. Delphine looked every part the Warden of Nero's daughter, listening intently to the king she walked beside, her laughs dainty and reserved.

Arix could not read the girl at all.

She couldn't tell if Delphine was dreading every step or if she was secretly enjoying their little display on the docks. Since her conversation with Ro, she'd had her eye on the Warden's daughter, watching for a crack in the facade. Something that might give her a hint into the girl's inner thoughts. She tried a quick mind cant, *just a peek*, she thought, but quickly realized the girl was warded. Now *that* was a surprise.

Maybe it was all the better if the girl was content to provide Orion heirs. If she had ambition, a desire for control, then it was a problem that Arix would have to figure out how to deal with. If she was happy to be left to a simple life as the king's quiet wife, it would be easier on her.

"When has staying quiet ever been easy for you?"

Arix's eyes shifted to glance at the crowd around them. She didn't know if it was her lack of sleep or the anxiety that constantly rose in her, but her insides tangled in knots. She was hungry, but the thought of food made her sick. She was worried, but even a simple elixir of meadow-thistle and lavender hadn't eased her nerves in the slightest. Ever since they'd been to the temple, a headache had worsened in her skull, and the throbbing of it made her want to gouge out her own eyes.

She hadn't told Orion. He probably would have thought that it had to do with Delphine and wouldn't believe her if she told him the headaches and the aching insides had started long before any conversations about a new queen. She considered asking

Lakai, but the two hadn't spoken since he'd called her a pup and she'd put him in his place.

Orion and Delphine paused at a stall selling jewelry made of bits of shells and pretty crystals. Arix ground her teeth, trying not to let the frustration show on her face. The day was sunny with bright, puffy clouds and a clear blue sky. The light, in combination with the fishy smell of the docks, was making Arix feel worse. Why couldn't the Warden have suggested they stroll elsewhere?

"Arix?" Ulfur's voice was low. "You a'right?"

She gave him a brusque nod, and he stepped back into place. She didn't need him worrying about her either.

But the sun was so fucking bright, and she knew she was squinting against the glare.

The happy couple moved towards the edge of the docks, stepping down the wooden stairs to the beach. Arix suppressed a groan. The sunlight reflected off the waves, lines of silver and gold dancing on each crest, each brilliant reflection hell-bent on shining directly into her eyes and stabbing at the pain in her skull.

There were fewer people on the beach, thank the goddess, but more openly stared—not just at the king but at *her*. Arix ignored the stares as much as she could, but it was annoying. She wondered if she'd danced with any of them that night, the night they'd slain the paramour. She remembered dancing a little and then sitting on the docks with Michael all night.

Reflexively, she glanced up, eyes following the rocky beach line towards another set of docks ahead of them. Pressure and pain spiked, and Arix felt it lance down her spine. She was on her knees before she knew what was happening. There was a ringing in her ears, echoing distantly. The edges of her vision flickered dark, punctured only by the blinding light that seemed to reflect off every surface. It even made Ulfur and Abbas' armor seem silver rather than black.

There was an arm around her shoulder, a voice faintly calling, but she couldn't form the shape of it. And then Orion's face, forehead furrowed in concern as he cradled her in his arms.

It felt like someone was squeezing the life out of her lungs, sitting on her chest, pressing and pressing, her ribs curving inward and scraping at her.

Then the blackness crept in.

And the last thought she remembered was total and complete emptiness.

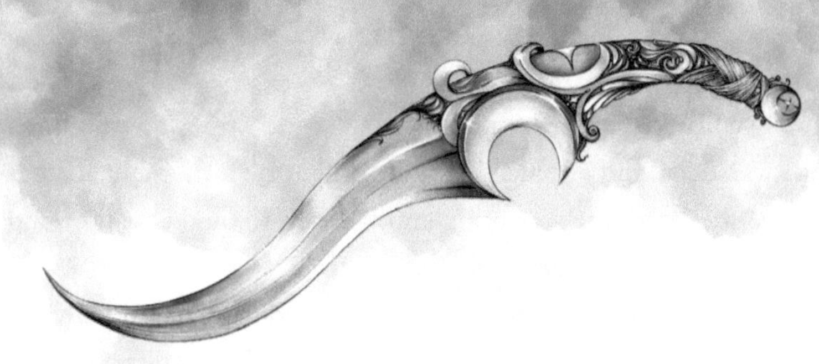

SIXTEEN

How many times was it now? That she'd woken up only half aware of her surroundings, half aware of the world around her and the people in it?

When Lakai had first captured her for the competition, turning her escape route against her, she awoke feeling like her skull had cracked open, vaguely aware she was in a wagon being taken to the castle. When Tanis had poisoned her with Witch's Envy during the tests. She'd woken in her bed, wishing she were dead. And then again, when she'd drunk from the chalice and become the Black Hand, she'd awoken, not even remembering who she was anymore. So much time had slipped between her fingers while she'd been trapped away in her own mind, the Well Water rewriting her very soul.

It seemed silly, the amount of times she'd been unconscious, waking slowly and groggily, needing someone to explain just what had happened to her.

This time, there was no ascent into consciousness. No slow, dawning realization and hushed voices. This was violent and immediate.

Arix launched herself from the bed before she even realized

she was standing, her back pressing against the opposite wall. Each breath was deep and agonizing, and it only took a moment for her to realize the headache was gone and her chest could expand again without feeling like her lungs clawed for air.

Lakai still hovered by the bedside, eyes wide at her sudden vault upwards. At the foot of the bed, Orion stood, shock still etched on his brow.

"Fuck."

Arix pressed her fingers into her eye sockets, massaging the space where her four-day headache had been nestled. Now, it was gone completely.

"Fuck," she repeated, forcing her eyes to blink rapidly as she stared at the two men. "What happened?"

Lakai was the first to speak. "You passed out on the beach. King Orion brought you back."

Arix was nodding. Unlike the previous three times, the details were perfectly crisp. "Yes, yes. I remember that. What I mean was, what the fuck happened to me?"

"You're still very new to the power in your blood, Arix." Lakai's voice was steady, patient. "Your body is still getting used to the new changes. How long have you felt ill?"

"Since before we left. I mean," Arix rushed to clarify, "since the coronation, that introduction ball before we left to come to Nero. It's been slow, but it didn't become noticeably worse until we got to Sieren."

For a moment, she thought she saw a shift in Lakai's expression, a line of worry crinkle on his brow. But just as quick as she saw it, it was gone.

"I've been telling you to take it easy." His reprimand was a gentle one. "I've given you more Well Water to help; you should be feeling better by now."

"No."

Lakai and Orion exchanged glances. "I can give you more if you—"

"What is in the Well Water?"

Lakai went still.

Arix took a step forward, closing the distance between herself and her old teacher. "What did you give me, Lakai? Nothing I've been taking has worked, and all of a sudden, I wake up feeling ten times better?"

She was in front of him now, the personal space between them shaved down to barely a breath. His eyes glinted ocean blue as he stared her down.

"Arix." Orion's voice was quiet, drawing her back to the present.

Arix blinked, realizing belatedly that her hand had moved to rest on her belt beside her sword. When had she done that?

Lakai's voice was soothing when he spoke, like he was speaking to a startled animal rather than to her. "You know what it is, Arix. The Well Water is what awakens your magick to turn you from simple incantor into the Black Hand. It's what helps your mind stay clear. Unfortunately, it is the consequence of the power you now wield. Without the Well Water to sustain you, your body will begin breaking down."

Carefully he reached toward the bedside table and picked up a glass vial. The liquid that swirled within was black as night. He held it out to her, and she took it.

"I've brought a supply with us for the journey, and you'll need to take more every time you begin to feel weak. I didn't realize you were suffering, or else I'd have given you a few vials much earlier."

"Sorry," Arix mumbled, fingertips rubbing over the glass. With a sigh, she dropped to the mattress, resting her head in her hands. "I'm sorry. I don't know why I reacted like that."

The tension in the room eased, Lakai moving to sit in a chair across from her.

"I think I'll leave you two to talk." Orion placed a hand on Arix's shoulder and gave a reassuring squeeze before he left, the door clicking in place behind him.

The silence between teacher and student stretched long, neither choosing to say the first word. Things had shifted so dramatically between them, Arix didn't really know where to start and where to end. How much of their relationship was ruined because he wanted her to be something she was not? How much had changed because she'd found that she no longer trusted him like she had before?

"Arix, I know you are settling into your role here," Lakai finally said, his voice tentative. He still spoke like he was worried she might jump up and head for the door at any moment. "You're making the role of Black Hand your own. You're straining against the guides and leashes that bind you in place, and I hope you know that it is not I that holds you back. I've been trying to shield you, I think. Shield you from moving too quickly, from being too hasty in your decisions."

Looking up, Arix saw his jaw set in worry, his gaze on the floor between them.

"If I've come across as suffocating, it's only because there is so much you still need to learn. Before, I thought I could teach it to you, but it seems you've learned much of it on your own." Lakai finally raised his chin to look at her, a small smile on his face. "Or maybe, you already knew it, deep down, from the beginning."

There it was again.

That implication that she was chosen to be Black Hand, a force of destiny and fate rather than pure luck. Irritation clawed at the back of her throat.

"I remember the first day I met you, in that little corner of Mergur. Do you remember?"

"How could I forget?"

"I'd tracked you for so long, flitting from city to city, following the trail of magick you gave off, so slight that I kept losing you. And then, out of nowhere, I found it. Right when I'd given up and come back to the capital… There you were."

Arix grinned. "You cracked my ribs that day."

"I did not."

"You did."

Lakai's blue eyes crinkled in amusement. "Maybe I did. Then, you stood in the great hall and laughed. I thought they might shoot you right then and there, you know."

She remembered. She'd laughed out of desperation and fear. The thought that she might be more, that she might be special… It had terrified her.

"I should have known that you were different."

Arix was already shaking her head.

"I should have known we would end up in this place, with you as the Black—"

"No. Lakai, stop." Arix leaned forward, weight pressing her elbows into the tops of her thighs. "You're acting like I'm special. Like it was destiny that I became the Black Hand. But that isn't it. It just isn't."

The look on Lakai's face told her that he didn't believe her, that he thought she was being modest.

"I didn't become the Black Hand because of destiny or fate. No powerful hand led me here; no goddess drew out my path before me. I am here now by sheer luck and will and the blood of my friends."

Arix held out her hands to him, palms facing up. The lines of her hands were calloused, the faint hint of black veins visible through the thin skin at her wrists. Emotion choked her as she looked at those hands. Hands that had been covered in her own sweat, in Revena's ashes, in Michael's blood. Dusted with chalk and oil and herbs, cut with knives and stained with ink.

Finally, she looked up and met his gaze.

"To say that it was destiny that I become the Black Hand belittles all the others who fought for this. It reduces their sacrifice to mere pawns in a larger game. And I can't believe that.

I can't. Because if I do…" Arix fought the tightening in her throat, fought the hazy blur around the edges of her vision. "If I believe that I was chosen for this, then I'll forget what I am. Who I am. Underneath all this power is just a girl trying to do the best she can one day at a time."

Lakai nodded slowly, taking her hands in his, his grasp warm and sure. "I know you see it that way, and I understand why."

She waited for him to go on, but whatever he had wanted to say died, and he just smiled instead.

"I'll let you rest a bit. If you're feeling at all ill again, drink the Well Water. I've left a few vials for you on your desk. Just a sip is all it should take. If you run out, ask me for more."

"But what is it? What exactly am I drinking?" Arix held up the vial, the light from the window splaying against the glass. Even in the warm, glowing sunlight, the liquid inside stayed dark as pitch.

"I don't know," Lakai answered softly. "But I can tell you this, Arix. No Black Hand can live without it. No Black hand ever has. The magick will eat you up inside if you don't."

"And the veins?"

He sighed. "The black veins will only grow. Even though you've woken up from your sleep, you are still changing. Your magick will grow, and the more it does, the further the veins will spread. Do not see it as an omen, Arix. It is simply a sign that you are different."

There was a mirror in the corner of the room, and Arix rose and approached it, peeling back the collar of her shirt and undoing some of the buttons until she could see the black veins that spiked across her skin. They were growing, inching their way across the porcelain of her chest.

"Do you hate them?" Lakai's voice was so quiet that Arix almost didn't hear him. Probably wouldn't have heard him if her senses hadn't improved since becoming the Black Hand.

"No." She traced her finger across the lines before buttoning her shirt back up. She turned back to him with a small smile. "No, I suppose not. But I wish you could tell me more."

He offered her a smile of his own in return. "I wish I knew more to tell. But eventually you'll uncover the information, and you'll understand the secrecy. After the tour, there will be answers waiting for you at home in Mergur."

Then Lakai rose, leaving the room with a quiet click of the door.

He had told her to rest, but she didn't feel tired. She felt awake, ready to do something. Sieren was boring her, already too stifling. There were bigger things at play that needed to be set in motion, questions that remained unanswered, and she didn't like the idea of languishing in Nero any longer than they needed to. There were still three more temples to visit, three more realms until they returned to the capital. Mergur was now more than just home in her mind, but it held the answers she still needed. Answers about the past Black Hands, the Conclave, the Carn, and about the Well Water. Answers that most likely waited for her in the library, shelf after shelf of tomes to provide the explanation she craved.

If she was being honest, Arix had half hoped another attack would be made against Orion today at the beach. Obviously, she didn't want to see him or Delphine hurt, but another attack from the Carn might give her something to work with, more information to add to what she knew.

And what did she know? Nothing.

Three members of the Carn had attacked on their first day in Nero, and she'd captured one. The others had somehow made an escape, regardless of the magick she'd cast to track them. And they'd disappeared into the city without a trace.

That irked her. The Carn had outsmarted her somehow. But then again, there were so many of them, and she was just one Black Hand. Powerful, yes, but still just one person against a whole hidden army of rebels with magick she didn't understand.

And the girl.

The girl had died from mysterious circumstances, and Arix still hadn't had a chance to look at the body and figure out if the wounds had been caused by a cant or not.

Arix poked her head into the adjoining bedroom and found Nesrin quietly reading a book.

"Nesrin? Where did you put the rebel's satchel?"

While the girl grabbed the bag, Arix laid out her own bottles and jars and pulled out the few notebooks she'd brought with her. One was the copied notes she'd taken from Revena's journal, and the others were notes she'd made of her own. Nesrin brought in the bag right as Arix sat down on the floor, the books to one side of her and bottles to the other.

"I'll take that." Arix settled the bag in front of her on the floor, vaguely motioning towards the desk. "Can you bring me that tray and bowl? Oh, and an eyedropper. Thanks."

Carefully, she removed each vial and set it on the floor in front of her, then grouped them by order of colored contents. There were eight bottles in total, each no taller than her index finger, and it seemed there were multiples of each liquid. Three of the sickly green, two red, two faint purpley gray-ish, and one a milky white. The glass was thin, and if thrown against a wall or a cobblestone street, would shatter easily, the contents splashing free of their confines.

Separating one of the green bottles from the rest, Arix set it in the center of the tray and cast her first incantation. It was a more complicated version of an identification cant, meant to root out the source of something, to surmise the sum of its parts. The cant would give her a glimpse into the danger of these vials, their possible threat, and maybe even the ingredients they were made with.

Instantly, foreign thoughts drifted across her mind's eye, images of clouds, of choking and boils lining the inside of someone's throat. Arix fought the urge to swallow at the thought. Next, she moved to the red bottle. Again, images and ideas drifted into her, this time of a spark igniting into a flame. Bales of hay combusting in a field. The gray-ish purple vials gave her visions of healing, small burns melting back into smooth, unflawed skin, and the white potion gave her a vision of speed, bodies moving at immense speeds and disappearing from sight.

"That was weird," Nesrin mumbled from her seat at the desk.

Arix glanced up to look at her, and the girl's eyes were round as she stared at the Black Hand on the floor.

"What was?"

"You. You went all glassy for a moment there. Like your eyes were unfocused. Was that magick?"

The corner of Arix's mouth twitched up into a smile. "Yes. Do I really do that?"

Nesrin nodded. "Like you slipped away for a moment. Your body obviously stayed right there on the floor, but your mind just kind of…" Her fingers wiggled as she moved her hand upwards away from her head.

"Weird." Arix realized that she'd never really paid attention to other people when they'd cast. She'd always practiced with Revena and Michael but never stared intently at them while they worked.

"I'll have to work on that."

"Why?"

"Because," Arix turned her gaze back to the bottles in front of her. "I don't want my facial expressions giving away that I'm incanting."

Very carefully, Arix unstopped one of the sickly green bottles, removing a few drops before closing the vial back up. The liquid was viscous, thick and goopy. Putrid, like rotten eggs and bad shellfish, filling the space around them.

"What's that one do?"

"Poison." Arix carefully placed a single drop of the green liquid into the center of the bowl Nesrin had given her. As soon as the goop hit the bowl, it evaporated, turning into a small cloud the size of Arix hand. "Shit. Nesrin, close your mouth and nose. Don't breathe in!"

The cloud wasn't big, but the thought of those boils growing on the insides of Nesrin's throat made her feel sick. The girl clapped her hands over her nose and mouth, eyes wide as she leaned back in the chair, further away from the bowl on the floor.

Arix held her breath, and her eyes watered slightly as she snatched up Revena's journal and flipped to a page she recalled near the back. Revena had made notes about coalescing a Resistance cant with Ascertention cant, allowing an incantor to identify and study something without being manipulated or affected by it. Revena had made a note in the margin that this type of magick could be used to study poisonous plants without any of the nasty side effects. It made sense that something like that could also be applied here.

With the toe of her boot holding the journal open to the right page, Arix repeated the words aloud, stumbling through the trickier bits. She cast it on herself and Nesrin, feeling instant relief as her vision cleared against the cloud.

She let out a slow breath and motioned for Nesrin to do the same. "You're safe. None of this will hurt us now."

Still, it took another few seconds before Nesrin lowered her hands from her face, sniffing carefully before wrinkling her nose. "It still smells bad."

"Sure, but it won't do the kind of damage it was meant to. And this is just one drop. Imagine what kind of harm this could have done if the whole bottle had broken."

"What about the others?"

Arix pointed to each glass vial as she named them. "Poison, fire, healing, and speed. I'm guessing the speed is how the other two got away so fast. That, or they might have had other bottled cants like these to help them."

"I've never heard of bottled magick before. Is that common for incantors?" Nesrin had joined her on the floor now, on her hands and knees staring intently at the white vial.

"Not that I'm aware of."

She knew the notebooks at her side were useless. She'd never run across this type of magick before, and she'd poured through Revena's notes enough times to know that if her friend did know about bottled magick, she hadn't written about it.

"Would High Priestess Halotus know?"

Arix slowly shook her head. "I don't think so. I could ask Lakai. I *should* ask Lakai."

"*No.*" The voice in her head was firm.

"Then why don't you?"

Arix glanced up and met Nesrin's gaze. For a moment, she faltered, unsure if she could trust this girl when, in the same moment, she was hesitant to trust her own teacher.

Arix avoided the question and tapped the side of the bowl where the green smoke cloud was just barely dissipating. "Luckily, we have these. We can study them, figure out how they were made, and replicate them for ourselves."

Before the cloud completely vanished, Arix cast another Ascertention cant, more images dropping into her mind, some familiar and some foreign, of the ingredients used to create the bottled poison cloud. She glanced up at Nesrin, a wide grin splitting her face.

"Grab some paper. Write down everything I tell you. We'll figure these out. Tonight."

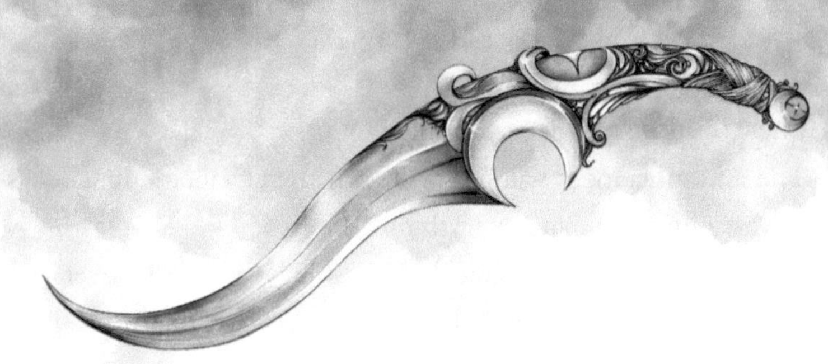

SEVENTEEN

The two stayed up all night, slowly dripping parts of the bottled cants into a bowl and studying the contents. By morning, Arix had a good sense for each of the bottles, instructions and ingredients carefully written out in Nesrin's neat and tidy handwriting. The only problem was…something seemed to be missing.

They'd tried multiple times to recreate any of the potions, mashing and mixing ingredients without any real result. Crushed herbs and ingredients still needed an incantor to cast them, and it was driving Arix mad that she couldn't figure out the last step.

She needed to imbue the potions with her magick, but she couldn't figure out how. She tried spit, blood, rubbing the ingredients between her palms, and she'd even tapped off a sliver of the gem from her core necklace for the task, but nothing worked. In the end, her versions were just muddled ingredients that lacked the spark.

While Nesrin tumbled off to bed, Arix washed her face and then headed back to the jail cells, finally ready to take a look at the dead girl's body. She'd spent all night staring at cantwork in jars and needed to look at something else. Something a bit more tangible.

Ro Laris caught her on her way out of the courtyard and followed her to the stables as she saddled up Osiris.

"The announcement will be today. For the engagement. There's going to be a luncheon and everything."

"That was fast." Arix chuckled, pushing the bridle over her horse's head and fixing the bit in his mouth. "You'd think they'd want to take things a bit slower."

"The incident on the beach might have hurried the plan a bit."

That stopped her. "Why?"

Ro just blinked.

"It wasn't that big of a deal." Arix couldn't keep the grumble from her voice. "I'm fine."

"You fainted."

Arix snorted. "I said, I'm fine."

Ro held the reins for her as she moved on to the saddle. "Around thirty people saw you collapse on the beach and, more importantly, saw the king rush to your side. Luckily, your guard stepped in, did some crowd control, and brought you back safe and sound. I've heard that our great king caught you before you ever hit the ground."

Arix finished off the last buckle before glancing towards her new Master of Word. "He did?"

"You don't remember?"

"I *fainted*," Arix said with a small smile. "Things went all blurry, and then I woke up in my room."

"Well, he did. And while normally I don't think it would have been a problem, there's been some…talk."

"What kind of talk?"

Ro waited until she'd pulled herself into the saddle before he spoke, leaning into Osiris' side. "Some think you're pregnant."

Arix stared down at him in horror.

"Look, everyone knows that you and the king are close. There's no doubt about that. And while no one much cares if he takes you to bed, they do care if the heir of our bright and shining new king is a bastard."

"I'm not pregnant."

"You did faint. The great and powerful Black Hand fainted on a beach, and her lover, the king, ran to her side to prevent her from being dashed to the rocks. You have to admit it looks bad."

"I'm not."

"Are you sure?"

Her eyes narrowed as she stared down at Ro, Osiris shifting beneath her and stomping a hoof. "It's none of your business."

Ro offered her a small, slow smile. "Ahh, but my Black Hand, it is my business."

"Then fix this."

His smile only deepened. "Of course. And how would you like me to *fix this*?"

Osiris threw his head, snorting, and Arix tightened the reins to steady him. "You're my Master of Word. You'll know better than me what kind of tales to weave. Just get the attention off of me. They should be focusing on Delphine's engagement to the king."

Ro stepped back, fist over his heart as he bent slightly in a bow. "As you wish."

"Ro Laris."

He straightened with another winning smile.

"I have bigger issues I need to worry about. I don't need people thinking that the king is marrying because he needs a legitimate heir. I mean…I'm not pregnant. I just…" For some reason, she was having a hard time getting the words out. It didn't matter what people thought of her. And yet…

He placed a soothing palm on Osiris' neck and stroked the mane a bit. "I know."

Arix could tell by the look in his eyes that he did. He knew what she was trying to say, knew what she meant. And more importantly, he knew the role that he needed to play to help her.

"Off you go. I'll take care of everything."

~

The body had already started to stink. The girl was laid out on a stone slab, the cool air of stone slowing her decomposition, but not enough to keep the body from showing its signs of death. Arix didn't need long anyway. She'd soon be back at the Warden's house and would maybe take a well-deserved nap.

Rosemary to cleanse, sage and cedarwood for clarity, benzoin rocks to channel the magick, and plenty of salt all laid along the edge of the stone slab. In her hands, Arix held one of her larger pieces of golden glass, holding it up to her eye and peering through at the body.

This cant, Arix knew, was complicated but not a powerful one. Yet, the magick was giving her immensely good readings. Whether that was because she was the Black Hand, or maybe she was just more sure of herself this morning, she didn't know. Now that she had all the pieces, they fell into place easily enough

"What do you see?" Abbas' deep voice echoed in the stone room.

Ulfur was with a few of her other Black Guard back up at the Warden's home, doing a walk-through of the grounds, but Abbas had been waiting for her at the dungeons, his quiet presence provoking a calming effect as she did her work.

Arix peered a bit closer to the girl's neck, getting a good look at the gash that had split her open.

"I need to see the cell again." She straightened, tucking a piece of her white hair behind her ear. "But I think I know what happened."

As they walked back to the girl's cell, they stayed quiet. Arix smiled to herself, glancing sideways at Abbas as they kept pace together. He knew she would explain her findings when she was ready. He was patient, she realized. So very, very patient.

The door of the cell had the same waviness to it that the cut on the girl's neck had, and that cinched the final puzzle piece into place.

"More magick." Arix finally offered. "Whoever killed her snuck in here using invisibility magick, then used a Whisp cant to step through the door."

"A locked door?"

"Watch." Arix performed the cant on herself, and her form turned wispy and translucent. Easily, she stepped through the locked door to the other side. Drawing one of her blades, she held it out so Abbas could see it through the small window in the door. Her blade, along with everything else she was wearing, was transparent as well. Slowly, Arix focused on the tip of the blade, and the translucence faded away, the tip becoming corporeal again. Stepping back through the door, Arix dropped the cant and returned her blade to her belt.

"Magick leaves a trace behind, and sometimes it's hard to see. But the door and the cut on the girl's neck both have leftover hints of this cant, so I'm positive that's what our killer used. There's only one problem with all this."

Abbas didn't ask, staying silent as Arix sagged against the wall and gave him a humorless smile. "It could have been anyone. As long as they had a bottled cant like the ones from the girl's satchel, anyone could have used this magick. Whisp is an easy-to-modify cant if you've been trained properly, and invisibility magick could be anything from a cant to a special cloak, a necklace, or anything that might carry the power. Items like that still exist, they just aren't very common."

"How do you know about these items?"

"I read a book about it from the king's library when I was doing research for my final test with Celeste." She reached up and touched the spot on her shirt where her necklace hung beneath, pressing against her skin. "I carry something similar."

Abbas' gaze flicked down the hallway where one of the Warden's men was standing guard at the far end. He lowered his voice. "You are saying that anyone with these items may be able to perform magick?"

She offered him a small nod. "I think so. It seems the Carn have found a way to bottle it up. Make it available for anyone to use, regardless if they have magick in them or not."

"This is not good."

"No, it isn't."

Sighing, Arix pushed herself away from the wall and headed for the door. She and Abbas rode in silence as they headed back to the Warden's house. It was cloudy today, dark skies threatening rain. Arix wished it would; she needed a break from all the blinding sun for a moment.

Without a second thought, she turned Osiris and headed across one of the canal bridges in a different direction. Abbas turned with her, his chestnut horse falling easily in step with hers as he followed her out of the city.

There was a place near here, a place she'd been to a long time ago, back when she was only a thief slipping through windows left open at night. It wasn't far outside of Sieren, just enough removed from the bustling streets and canals and far enough away from the docks that there were no ships blocking the view of the horizon. And there was a tree…

Arix smiled as they turned along a bend in the road, and she saw it. A beautiful hulking olive tree that leaned out over a small drop in the rocks straight down into the saltwater. She slipped from Osiris' back and took off running, unlatching her belt and kicking off her boots as she went.

She was suddenly overwhelmed with the sense of freedom as she ran, the smooth rocks biting into her feet as she neared the short cliff. And then she leapt.

She'd never learned to dive because the cliffs that had surrounded the beaches she'd been a child on were hundreds of feet high. But she'd seen other people do it with pointed toes and straight arms. The drop was only about ten feet or so from the top of the rocks to the deep salty water, but those ten feet felt like a million as she fell towards the sea.

It was cold. So very cold that it took every thought from her mind. The shock flowed through her whole body, pushing just one thought to her mind: breathe!

And so she did.

The saltwater flooded her mouth and filled through her lungs, and she coughed, the taste so foreign. She felt the water settle in her lungs for a moment before she blew it out, opening her eyes and glancing up toward the surface above her. Light danced on the crest of each ripple of the surface, and she felt the tide pull at her hair as it streamed out behind her, coming undone from the loose braid it had been in. Her limbs glided through the water, and each movement propelled her forward or backward.

When she breached the surface, she choked on the air, laughing at Abbas' face as he watched from the short cliff face above. She pointed to the skin along her cheek and held up a hand so he could see the webbing that had grown between her fingers. It didn't matter if she didn't know how to swim; she certainly couldn't drown with gills.

Arix let the current pull her back down beneath the water, noting that droplets of rain had started to fall, marring the surface with tiny ripples. The fish had run from her when she'd dived off the rocks, but now they were returning, coming to catch a glimpse of the new thing in their little corner of the sea.

Slowly she sank to the rocky floor, the slabs of stone smooth across her back as she stared upward. It was so similar to laying on the roof of Castle Zma'ai with Michael, both of them staring up at the stars and talking late into the night. That old ache was there in her chest, but this time, it wasn't quite as strong.

She pushed against that ache, feeling the edges of it line her heart, and wondered if she was forgetting him. Forgetting him so soon. How was that even possible? She could never forget him, surely. But maybe, with all she knew, all this magick to fill the spaces, the hurt lessened a little. Her new life filling in the cracks of her old one.

The girl that she had been so long ago was dead. Died the night she'd drank from the chalice, consuming the Well Water, and became the Black Hand. And the person she was now was so different, somehow both more and less alone than ever before. How much of the real Bellarix Sable was really left at the end of everything? She didn't know.

But she liked her new self. She liked the person she'd become. More detached from the world, yet somehow so much more connected to it. She felt the water slide through her gills and filter through her lungs and exit as bubbles, and in that act, simply of breathing the water in and out, she felt more connected to this world than she had in her twenty-five years of life.

And it was good.

Eventually, she pushed her feet underneath her and shot towards the surface, aiming closer to the edge of the rock. As her face broke through, she dissipated the cant, the gills and the webbing replaced with smooth skin and human lungs. She clung to the rock with all her might, laughing and calling for Abbas to haul her back up. The rain had made the rocks slick, but he held out his hand, and she crawled up the rock face, slipping and skinning her shin on the way back up. After he'd hauled her to safety, she lay on her back, staring at the sky as the rain hit her face. Just as she had been lying on the floor of the sea twenty feet below only moments ago.

"When was the last time you just sat out in the rain, Abbas?" she called to him.

Abbas was standing with the horses underneath the olive tree, mostly protecting him from the drizzle.

"I have never purposefully sat out in it."

"Now would be a great time to try!"

He hesitated for a moment, then, to Arix's utter surprise, he joined her, his back against the rock and his face upturned to the raining sky.

How many moments like this were there in the world? Where time seemed to stop and make space for a silent moment in the rain. Any second, reality would come crashing back, and they would have to return to the Warden's home. But now, for this heartbeat, time had waited for them. Waited for her.

As if Kaoss herself were allowing it to be so.

"And in the stillness, in chaos and in peace, She is there," Arix whispered to herself. The prayer was old, as common as any bedtime story or lullaby, but for some reason it sprang to her mind.

Arix smiled and gently placed her fist over her heart. A silent salute to the mother goddess in her heavens above.

And somewhere far away, the goddess Kaoss smiled back.

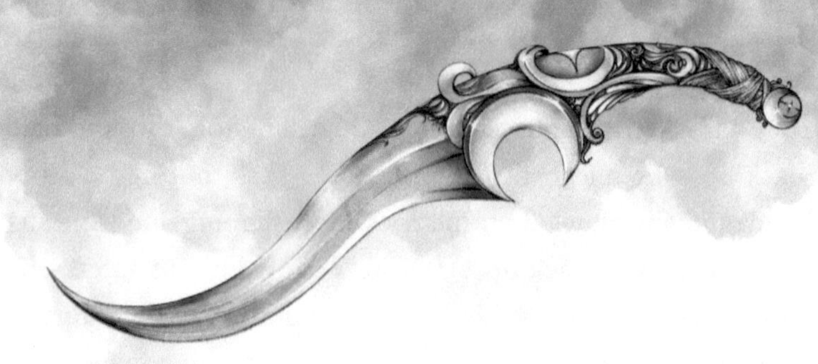

EIGHTEEN

They were finally leaving. The king, his Black Hand, the council, and all the court that had travelled with them were finally leaving Warden Uellen Vod's home in Sieren. Arix had hoped that they would be leaving Nero altogether, but they would be traveling to Coraven first, where the wedding of Delphine Vod and King Orion Karcharias would be held.

Only after the wedding would their merry band be heading northeast into Tamhain and towards the second temple in Rohleach to stay at Warden Aliska Sviengard's home at the base of the Fyall mountains.

Delphine's mother was planning the celebrations, and according to what Ro and Nesrin relayed to her, the woman was driving everyone mad with her details. The joining of Orion and Delphine would be on Beltane, the May Day celebration of fertility and love, performed at the temple where the River Helene split around the city. Messengers had been sent ahead of them to prepare, and everything would fall into place once the king and his soon-to-be bride arrived.

Arix did her best to stay out of the Warden's wife's way. The woman busied herself around the estate and then busied herself around Delphine as the party set off. Unfortunately, since it was Arix's duty to ride near Orion, it also meant she rode near Delphine and her mother and the plethora of ladies that accompanied her. As excitable as Delphine's mother appeared, Delphine herself remained as tranquil and demure as ever. Eyes downcast, a small smile on her lips when her mother berated her with wedding details. They rode in the carriage that Arix traveled beside, and there was no avoiding overhearing every single detail.

Only a few days into their travel, and that dreaded headache was back.

"If anything," Arix muttered to Nesrin, whom she had fallen back to ride beside, "Delphine is freeing herself from her mother. The capital is a long way from Sieren, and she'll finally be free of that horrible woman."

"I'd heard that Yvette Vod will be moving to the capital indefinitely to be close to her daughter," Nersin added cheerfully.

Arix could not suppress her groan of frustration. "You mean I'll be stuck with her?"

"Unfortunately, yes."

"No sympathy from you, huh?" Arix gave her secretary a sidelong glance. "You're supposed to be on my side."

"And here I was thinking you hired me to do my job, not to agree with everything you say."

"Rude."

"If you say so." Nesrin offered casually, but a small smile played at the corner of her mouth.

Most nights along their journey to Coraven, they stayed at estates that were more than happy to host the king and his new bride. Arix opted to stay outside, camping with the rest of her Black Guard and other members of the court who weren't important enough to merit their own rooms. Orion had refused at first, but she'd convinced him. He was on the way to his wedding, traveling with his new bride. If there was any time to put nasty rumors to rest, it was now.

She had expected to dislike this part of the trip, riding all day and sleeping on the ground all night, but after the stuffiness that had been building within her in Sieren, it was a nice change to spend more time outside than in the walls of a great estate. It reminded Arix of the old days when she'd spent her entire life on the road, traveling between towns, sleeping under trees and the vast open sky. And it gave her a chance to get to know her Guard better, the men and women she'd chosen to guard her and the king. Of course, they all knew Ulfur and Abbas quite well, but all this traveling gave her the chance to show herself as a leader to them. As someone who commanded soldiers. They listened to her, sure, but she wanted them to *trust* her.

As they sat around campfires at night, she stayed quiet and let the others tell tales of their adventures or how they had joined the service to the king. She had better stories than them, even though she was younger than most. But if anything, Arix knew that listening and laughing along would mean more than a hundred of her harrowing tales.

Besides, there was a strange sense that these days spent on the road with her Black Guard were going to be a balance. A balance between earning their trust and creating a persona of how she would be perceived. Arix was now more consciously aware of how she sat, how she smiled, how she laughed and talked and engaged with the men and women around her. Was she smiling too much? Looking too pleased at their stories? She didn't want to appear too eager. Ro Laris' words were still echoing in her ear from that very first ball.

Let them seek out your favor, not the other way around.

It was still good advice.

But if she was being honest with herself, Arix also wanted to create a persona for herself. She wanted people to look at her and see power. Not the kind of boisterous power that was flaunted by the lords and ladies that she used to steal from. But the kind of power that didn't need to be stated. The kind of power that made people stop and stare without having to utter a word. No grand proclamations or gestures, just quiet confidence that they were the most powerful person in the room.

And since Arix didn't have that kind of confidence, she faked it.

Her smiles were encouraging. Her laughs were reserved. It would have been easy to fall into a casual friendship with the rest of them, as she had with Ulfur and Abbas. But each time, she caught herself and reigned in the urge to meet their energy levels, to match their companionable revelry.

It wasn't until they had passed Sol that Ulfur finally spoke up. "They like ya."

Arix glanced over at her riding companion with a smile. "I like them."

He studied her for a moment before offering a contemplative, "You're diff'rent, ya know. Not like the lass who danced with me at tha' ball so long ago. Seems like ages now."

"Michael said the same thing near the end. He told me that I was harder. Angrier." She let out a long sigh. "He might have been right."

"I donna think you're angrier. Just more cautious, ma'be. Like you're holding back more o' yourself. Letting less o' the real you out."

Arix reached out of the saddle and leaned over to punch Ulfur in the shoulder with a grin. "I'm still me in here; I'm just more careful with who I let see it. There are more eyes on me now.

More people watching what I'm going to do and waiting for me to mess up."

Ulfur shoved her right back, and Arix almost lost her balance, scowling as Ulfur cackled. "And what'll they do, eh? What'll they do if ya do mess up? It's not like they can get rid of ya—you're the bloody Black Hand!"

It sounded like maybe Ulfur wanted to say something else, and Arix studied him, waiting.

"Yes?"

His brow furrowed as he watched the road stretch out ahead of them, the carriage wheels grinding softly in the dirt behind them.

"I's nothing."

"It's something. Out with it."

"You said it feels like they're waiting for you to make a mistake. But what could they do to ya, really? You're one o' the last incantors in the world. What do they do to people as powerful as you?"

Arix laughed lightly. "While I appreciate that, I'm not as powerful as you might think I am. I still have weaknesses. I still have to sleep and eat; my food could be poisoned. They could put my hands in iron mitts so I can't cast, put a bit in my mouth to keep from talking. I might have magick, but I'm not almighty. Since when did you become so pessimistic, anyway?"

"I'm not. I guess I'm just wonderin' if you're guarded enough." Ulfur looked around them at the open road that stretched in front of them, then turned in his saddle to look at the long train of carriages and wagons and riders that stretched out behind them. "You have us, yes, and I kno' you've got magick and the like guardin' tha king. But how much o' that magick are ya using to guard yourself?"

"Are you saying you won't protect me?" Arix needled him, grinning.

His gaze connected with hers, and she realized just how serious he was from that look. Her laugh faded.

"I'll protect you with my life, lass."

"It won't come to that."

"But if it did," Ulfur continued soberly, "Know that Abbas and I would rather die than let a single hair on your head be hurt."

He was so serious, the lines between his eyebrows furrowed in absolute assurance. Arix shivered, goosebumps rising across her arm, and the necklace burned warm against her sternum.

"Thank you, Ulfur. That means a lot."

"I donno 'bout the rest of the Black Guard, each one individually, but I know the others feel a lot the same."

The warmth in her chest grew, and for a moment, it was spliced with fear. It was a strange sense of responsibility to know that there were men and women who would die for her. She'd been thinking about power and perception since she'd become the Black Hand, all too aware of how she needed to look and act in front of other people. But this was something else. Was it blind faith, or did they see something in her that she didn't see herself?

Had she tricked them all into thinking she knew what she was doing? Or did they see beneath the facade and recognize the good she could do? Arix wasn't sure.

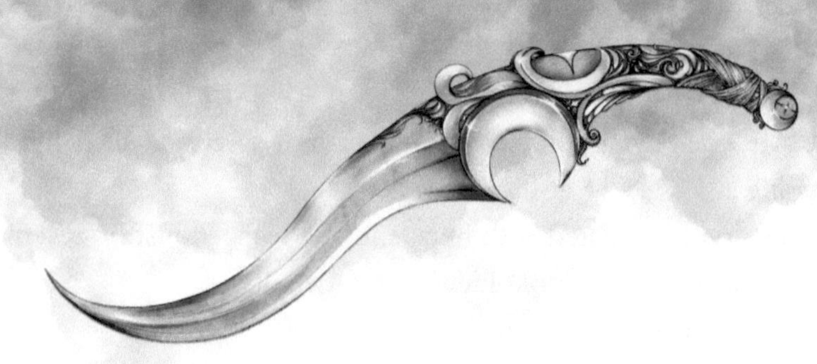

NINETEEN

Arix had to hand it to Delphine's mother. This wedding was beautiful. She traveled in the back of the boat, standing upright, her legs locked by a small binding cant to keep her from tipping over the side, as the family traveled towards the temple at the split of the River Helene. She'd offered the cant to the rest of the occupants, but Delphine, along with the Warden and his wife, had declined. Though the boat rocked slightly as it cut down the river, Delphine sat before her, shoulders pulled back and relaxed as they slid through the water. Ahead of them floated the boat carrying the Vod family, balanced as they stood at the center of the small craft.

All along the banks, people had gathered, throwing white and pink water lilies into the river, the petals floating with them towards the temple. Arix watched the banks, eyes flitting from person to person, looking for a sign of trouble. But all she saw were smiling faces, some cheering and shouting Delphine's name, others blowing kisses and singing blessings on the new couple. The bubbled dome of protection Arix had cast around the boat shimmered in the perfect morning sunlight as the sun eased her way over the horizon and basked the city in light.

Yet, among all the well-wishers and the many people with their eyes trained on the woman dressed in a long flowing veil, many eyes turned toward Arix next. They wanted to see the Black Hand who had been blessed by the Goddess Nereus, who had been blessed as equally as their new golden king.

Someone had leaked the information about her blessing. No matter how hard Lord Bardon had tried to keep it a secret, by the time they had arrived in Coraven, the streets had been teeming with the news. She suspected it to be Ro, but when she'd asked him, he'd merely taken a sip of his drink, eyes sparkling behind the rim of his glass.

When Arix had first realized that they were staring at her as much as they were staring at Orion's new bride, she'd expected to feel embarrassed or awkward at the attention. But no such feeling arose.

Instead, she beamed.

She had opted to wear her black armor. So very deep black that instead of glinting in the bright sun, it turned even darker. Arix had incanted it to pull light rather than reflect it, and the effect was off-putting enough that it made her look even more intense. Instead of braiding her hair or putting it up in an intricate twist away from her face, she'd instead left it down and straight, combed back away from her face without ornamentation. The effect made her look fierce, a silent protector, a dark shadow that guarded the warmth and joy of the day.

Focusing on the image she'd created for herself let her keep her concentration on the actual events of what was happening today. Kept her from thinking about the fact that Orion was about to get married. A new queen would stand by his side, and Arix would act as guardian over them both. She focused on the pride of that feeling, of being a protector, rather than the sinking in the pit of her stomach and the ache beneath her ribs.

She hadn't slept the night before. Her insides had started to ache again, and food was making her sick. Since she wasn't about to disturb the wedding by fainting on the temple steps, she'd asked Lakai for more Well Water. It worried her, her lack of knowledge of the thing she was drinking, but the ache that ran along her bones, the scratching and hollow scream of her insides, and the pressurized ache in her head all reminded her too much of the dark prison that she had passed so many years in. And it was better to drink more, even sips at a time, than to feel those aches again.

But even after she'd downed half the bottle, Arix hadn't been able to turn off her mind as it swirled with what this day would mean for her and Orion. They'd hardly gotten a chance to speak since the engagement had been announced, and she'd spent most of the travel to Coraven with her Black Guard. Orion had offered, again and again, for her to stay with him, sleep with him. But she'd refused.

Not only would people notice that the king had someone other than his betrothed in his bed on the nights leading up to his wedding, but Arix couldn't bring herself to accept him. It wasn't that sharing him was a problem. It was that this was so very public, this engagement to Delphine, this wedding, and the future of their marriage. And her life with Orion would always be hidden. Always be pushed into the dark. She was his Black Hand. His incantor and the protector of the realm. She was at his beck and call, his right-hand weapon to crush the crown's enemies. And her role as his lover wasn't a part of the public image she wanted to garner.

The rumors that flowed around her and Orion needed to stop. What better way to do that than to escort his new bride to the altar?

She glanced down just as Delphine twisted back to look at her.

"Lady Black Hand?" Delphine's voice was quiet, as meek as a mouse, the lilting notes of her voice sounding like silver.

"How may I serve you, Lady Vod?"

"I would ask a favor of you this day."

"Ask it."

"Say a prayer with me? Before we reach the steps?"

Ahead of them, the temple was approaching, steps coming up from the water as the river forked around the outside edges of the marble building.

Arix felt herself smile. "Of course."

"The days of blessing—do you know it?" Delphine had turned back around, facing forward, but her voice still carried soft within the bubbled dome of protection that Arix had cast over them.

Arix faltered slightly. "I'm not very religious, my lady. But I'll do my best."

Delphine whispered the prayer, and Arix did her best to speak the words she only half knew.

"May Nereus grant me the peace of still waters. May Arduinna make me as fruitful as the orchards. May Zephyrus give me the humility to serve. May Vulcan bestow strength upon a quivering heart."

At the end of the prayer, Delphine paused, and Arix stepped forward in the boat, finishing the final line.

"May Aion bless you with years. May Kaoss bless you with children. May Osiris turn his eye from you."

Delphine nodded before muttering a soft, "Thank you."

As the boat docked against the bank, the Warden and his wife stepped out first, holding a hand out to their eldest daughter as she approached. Delphine stepped gracefully onto the dock, the swathes of fabric from her dress and veil billowing lightly in the wind. Arix stepped out behind them, the guard dog to protect the new queen.

She almost smiled.

Orion was standing on the steps, dressed all in gold, his dark hair pulled back and a simple gold crown on his brow. He kept his gaze on Delphine, but as she finally took his arm, he glanced past her to Arix.

In his eyes was an apology; the slightest crease between his eyebrows, his smile faltering just a little as they locked their gaze on each other. Suddenly, the swell in her ribs expanded, and Arix felt the squeeze of her heart as Orion's look burned into her. She wanted to offer him a small smile, a sign that this was alright. That she understood the decision that was being made today. That she was better than simple jealousy, better than the basic instinct that raged in her screaming that he was hers.

Because he wasn't. And in that moment, a strange sort of calm enveloped her.

"She will never truly have him. Not the way that you do." The voice was so quiet, so filled with emotion, but Arix refused to listen. Refused to let that anger ruin things.

Today was a great day. It was a day where duty would be fulfilled. Delphine might be the one on his arm in front of the roaring crowds, but Arix held his heart. She knew it.

Did she love Orion?

Did it matter?

He loved her, and at the end of the day, it was she whom he would take into council rooms and onto the battlefield, and it was she whom he would confide in.

In a strange way, it gave her a sense of peace.

She had no quarrel with Delphine. They were both pieces on a chessboard of the new Rökkur that Orion was building. She wasn't so ignorant that she believed she was special. And lately, it felt like everyone was trying to tell her she was. But the sense of pride that guarding Delphine and Orion's backs gave her somehow felt equal to all the times she'd stepped in to right a wrong in her old days of thieving.

Her thoughts flickered to what Ro had asked, why she didn't seem to care about Delphine when she claimed to worry about the people. Delphine, regardless of her family, was something that she should protect.

Odd, how things changed. From stealing from the rich to protecting them.

Arix lightly shook the thought away and focused on the wedding. Orion didn't fall into that category of simply rich for riches' sake. He was the king. If he wasn't the way he was, if his plan was to sit back and extort the role he was in, Arix knew things would be different.

But *Orion* was different. It made him a good king. A king that Arix trusted.

The couple moved up the steps of the temple, and as Arix followed them into the cool marble interior, the din of the crowd outside settled and was replaced with the low harmonizing of the priestesses as they sang.

Billowing clouds of fabric hung between the pillars and the ceiling, draping the yawning space above them with gossamer clouds. When the song came to a close, Orion and Delphine knelt before the High Priestess, and she placed garlands on their heads and wrapped their hands together with cord.

As the prayers were said and repeated, and more songs were sung, Arix felt her mind drift. Instead of listening to the marriage ceremony, she watched Orion, the way he smiled at his new bride, clasping her hand tenderly in his own. He was delicate with her, careful with her veil and her dress, gazing at her with all the reverence of a handsome groom. Delphine matched his looks with innocent glances of her own. Her long lashes fluttered as she prayed, bashfully looking into Orion's eyes as she repeated her words, sinking into his touch as he lifted her veil, kissing her forehead, each cheek, and finally, her lips.

Arix couldn't tell if either or both of them were truly caught up in the moment or simply playing the part they had to play.

~

At the banquet, Arix stood beside the dais of the newlyweds, members of the Black Guard stationed at the entrances. Every guest's invitation was checked and double checked before they were allowed entry. Tables overflowed with food and wine, the painted ceiling above them draped with more of the transparent gazy material that had decorated the temple.

Course after course was brought out: geese stuffed with a cherry bread pudding, oysters and crab, swordfish drizzled in a heady beet lemon sauce with fresh basil and olive oil still sizzling in their platters. There were trays of olives and cheeses, roasted red peppers and asparagus laid over zucchini cakes. Rosemary and lemon cakes dipped in pistachio glaze were piled high at the center of each table, and the entire room smelled like absolute heaven.

Delphine's father made a toast to the couple—"Long may they both reign"—and then the party began. Arix didn't expect there to be any trouble at the party, and thankfully, there wasn't any. When the bride and groom had eaten their fill and been congratulated by nearly every guest in the room, someone called for dancing, and the expansive orchestra struck up a song.

It had been years since Arix had attended a wedding, but this one, even though it was for a king, was much like the other she had been to as a teenager. Then, she'd been working as a servant delivering trays of food to spy on the mistress of the house and had actually enjoyed the wedding, laughing at the traditions and the rules that had to be followed. Today was no different.

Normally, at the end of the night, a couple couldn't leave unless they snuck out and were not caught by the guests. Sometimes weddings lasted days because the couple simply couldn't sneak away. Even though Orion was the king, it seemed the rules still applied to him and his new bride. It wasn't until after midnight that the couple were finally successful in their escape.

Every time Delphine and Orion tried to sneak away, someone would catch them and pull them back to the party, guests laughing and cheering at the sheepish look their king gave them. Delphine, ever the bashful new wife, blushed right alongside him. After the fourth time of this, Arix was exhausted by the ruse. The next time they tried, she crushed a white mistletoe berry between her thumb and index finger and cloaked the couple, allowing them to finally slip away without notice. Others may have let this go on for days, but Arix had her own plan for the evening.

The moon was so full, it lit the streets as if it were the afternoon rather than the middle of the night. After making sure Orion and Delphine were well and truly away in their room, well guarded for the night, Arix slipped out of the estate, heading back to the temple at the fork of the River Helene.

Incense heavy with the smell of salt and citrus hung in the air as she made her way up the steps. She was still wearing her armor, and the few priestesses who were minding the temple at night didn't dare to stop her.

"The crypt?" Arix asked, her voice quiet. It seemed wrong to speak loudly in a temple.

The lower priestess dipped her chin, eyes to the floor as she motioned for Arix to follow. The pair descended past the main atrium, slipping down into the carved depths, the sconces becoming few and far between, and the shadows lengthened around them.

"Is there a particular family you seek?" The priestess's voice was light and airy, young.

Arix told her the last name.

For a moment, the girl's eyes flickered up, and Arix caught sight of the girl's face for the first time. She had to be around thirteen.

"I know the resting place you seek."

Arix didn't argue.

"Follow me."

They turned another corner, traveling down a long hallway before descending even further into the earth. Even though they were still surrounded by marble, Arix could feel the air changing as they moved further down. Were they under the river now?

Finally, they stopped, and Arix stared at the name etched into the stone.

"I shall leave you. Do you remember the way back?"

Arix nodded, unable to tear her gaze away from the name.

Without another word, the girl slipped away, feet as nimble as death. For long moments, Arix couldn't bring herself to move, to step any closer. She'd only come on a whim, and now that she was here, she wasn't certain she could go through with what she had planned.

It was one thing to decide something in your head, to decide on a course of action when you were alone at night, unable to sleep. It was another thing to actually be standing in a crypt deep under a sacred river and actually do it.

She took a step forward, fingers reaching to trace the name etched into the stone box. It was separate from the rest, most of the other family members entombed in boxes in the wall. The name was etched along the bottom, with the mother's and father's names below. Her fingernail caught on the letters as she ran her fingers through the grooves.

Celeste Ayala, daughter of Kilvea and Cheron Ayala.

"We all end up in the ground in the end," Arix muttered, the cool marble spanning under her fingers.

The silence of the crypt was her only response.

"You would do the same to me, you know. If our roles were reversed, and I was the one in the box? You'd have thought the exact same thing, made the exact same choices that brought me *here*." Arix punctuated the last word as she stabbed at the marble sarcophagus with her finger. Her mouth curved into a small smile. "If you could see me now, Celeste. You'd call me a coward if I *didn't* do it. Actually, you'd probably call me a lot worse."

Turning, she slid down until she sat on the cold floor, armor clattering a little as she rested her back against the box.

"Though I'm not sure what that makes me, that I've started thinking like you. I did look first, you know. I couldn't ask Lakai; he'd figure me out in a split second, know exactly why I was asking. But I had Nesrin find out. Nesrin's my secretary."

Arix chuckled lightly, realizing she was explaining herself to a dead girl. She tipped her chin up, following the curve of the ceiling above her, tracing the spaces between each carefully placed stone.

"There's so much more paperwork than I expected. And this trip is fun, this grand tour, but once we're home, it'll be back to more paperwork and missives and schedules. It's a lot of time spent at the castle. Which, of course, you'd approve of. Wouldn't want to get your pretty hands dirty. But I'm thinking of doing some good while we travel. Maybe connect with local places while we go.

"You know Ro Laris? Of course you do—you knew everyone at court. Well, he's one of my five Fingers now. He's the perfect person to help me figure out who's fucking whom and all that court gossip that I don't give a shit about. But I need someone like that for the rest of the realms. I've been thinking of getting rid of them all actually. My Fingers. They're pretty useless. What the hell do I need a headsman for, anyways? As if I couldn't just take care of people on my own…"

Arix sighed, scuffing her boot against a crack in the floor.

"I need people who *know* things. Who know more than how to dance and talk to dignitaries and say the right thing in front of what's-his-name. I need an ear to the ground. I need someone who knows the *people*. Then I could help. Better, you know? Of course you don't. You didn't think of anyone other than yourself."

Heaving herself up, Arix let out another low laugh. She circled the box slowly, running her finger along the edge as she went. There was a seam separating the box from its lid.

Instead of whispering the words out loud, Arix thought them, letting the cant slip through her mind, letting the magick happen without the physical components and the proper hand motions. She was the Black Hand, after all. That came with a few perks.

The sound of stone scraping against stone filled the space around her, grating, crushing, gravely rock sliding and pushing until the lid was askew.

She did it before she could think about it. She did it before she lost her nerve. Talking to Celeste had reminded her of something.

Celeste had been cold-blooded. She'd been selfish.

And Arix wasn't afraid to be the same. Not now.

But when she did finally look over the side of Celeste Ayala's final resting place, undisturbed on the night of a full moon in the middle of May, Arix's eyes grew wide. She'd expected to find the rotting corpse of the girl she'd killed in that glen three months ago. She'd seen plenty of the dead in her lifetime, but they'd all *looked* dead. Rotting flesh, eyes eaten from their sockets by birds, paper-thin lips, and hair falling out in clumps.

Celeste looked otherworldly. Other than being as pale as the marble box she lay in, she looked like herself.

Her golden hair was strewn around her like a halo, her face serene. The diamonds in her earrings and necklace shone, a golden and aquamarine dragonfly comb tucked into her hair. She was wearing a beautiful blue dress, hands folded neatly across her abdomen. She didn't look like she was sleeping, she was much too pale for that, but she looked…wrong.

Not how the dead should look.

Along the insides of the box were mementos, letters from her family, a journal, a jewelry box. Slowly Arix moved the lid further away, and firelight from the sconces spilled across more of Celeste's form. Arix's eye caught on the thing she'd come for, the reason she'd opened the tomb in the first place.

Gripped in Celeste's hands was her dagger. Her core.

Careful not to touch the body, Arix pulled out the dagger, pushing at the pommel between dead fingers until she could grab the hilt from beneath Celeste's grip and pull it the rest of the way free. The pommel was decorated with twisted gold and black metal, a crescent moon carved into where the handle met the blade. The blade itself was small, but with a wicked curve that hooked in a graceful arch.

Slowly, Arix turned the blade until she clutched the hilt in her grip with one hand and carefully removed the sheath with the other. The black metal of the blade caught the light, shifting in color like an oilslick.

She felt a thrum of power, a sigh. Electricity zinged down her arm—not painful, but not harmless either. It felt different from her necklace or Michael's ring. Her own core that hung around her neck felt like an extension of her, of her power. An external boost that thought like she thought, the curves of words and elements of magick forming cant lists in her mind's eye. Michael's ring had felt like a swirling wind of webs that connected everything together. The birds, the sky, herself, the ground she walked on. Michael's core showed her the harmony of magick, the flow of the world.

Celeste's core was the complete opposite.

As Arix gripped the dagger tightly in her hand, forcing her mind to connect with the core, she felt her train of thoughts shift instead to the unity of the world around her, but to also see the basic fundamentals of things. The roots and the history, the foundation, the raw power.

Michael's core was vast. Broad.

Celeste's was singular. Specific.

Paired together? Together, the cores could show her more facets of magick, more perspectives. Revena had always excelled in coalescent magick, combining cants together to create something that fit her needs. She'd had the kind of mind that could fit elements together, something Arix had never really been good at. But with cores like these, was that something she might be able to do better?

Arix glanced down at Celeste, so perfectly preserved in her little box. There was a faint line across the girl's throat, carefully stitched closed, where Arix had slashed it in the glen. She wondered vaguely if they'd used magick to keep her preserved like this. Gently, she pressed a finger along the line, feeling the small careful row of stitches. The skin was hard, with a strange texture.

Strange how the skin of her fingers looked almost as pale as Celeste. Odd.

Arix let out a slow sigh, pulling her hand from the box and carefully sliding the stone slab back over the top. As the shadow moved over Celeste's face, wreathing her in darkness once again, Arix felt a strange chill travel down her spine.

It was time to go.

The young priestess was waiting for her at the top of the stairs, and she peeked sideways at the dagger that was now tucked against the small of Arix's back. But she said nothing.

As the two neared the entryway to the temple, the girl faltered for a moment, catching Arix's attention.

"Arduinna."

Arix's heart skipped a beat. She stopped, surprised, turning to face the little priestess. "How did—"

"You go to the temple of the earth goddess next, do you not? Goddess Arduinna?"

Immediately, Arix's nerves settled a little, and she smiled. "Yes. We'll leave for Rohleach tomorrow."

"She will bless you."

Arix felt that strange chill slide down her spine again, all too aware that though the night should be warm, she only felt cold.

"What do you mean?"

"She yearns for your victory; the path that has been laid by Kaoss, she has blessed. You were blessed by Nereus, the sister, the savior." The girl's eyes were round, a strange sort of glint in them as she stared up at Arix. "The goddess of suffering knows you. She stands behind you, as does her mate, Osiris."

At the names of them together, Arix only felt more unsettled. These were the nicknames she and Orion had given each other, and it was strange sometimes to think that these were gods and goddesses who watched over the world.

"How do you know that?" Arix shifted to the side, realizing that the girl had gone still since she'd started talking. She hadn't even blinked once. "How do you know she'll bless me?"

Even as Arix moved, the girl's gaze stayed trained on a spot on the wall behind her. "They disagree. They argue over who to stand with: you or the messenger drenched in blood."

"Drenched in blood? What are you—"

The girl cut her off. "You are a servant of Kaoss. Nereus has blessed you, and so will Arduinna. But be watchful. The ethos is split, weighing itself in harmony or discord. They revel in it, the evercycle. The wheel. It turns for us all; even they must bend to its will. On which side of the scale do you stand, Bellarix Sable?"

The silence of the temple around them settled, and Arix felt the air warm again. The girl blinked, turned to Arix, and smiled.

"Have a good evening. Thank you for visiting the Helene River Temple."

And then, as though nothing strange had just occurred, the girl turned and walked away, leaving Arix standing on the steps, a strange copper tang in her mouth.

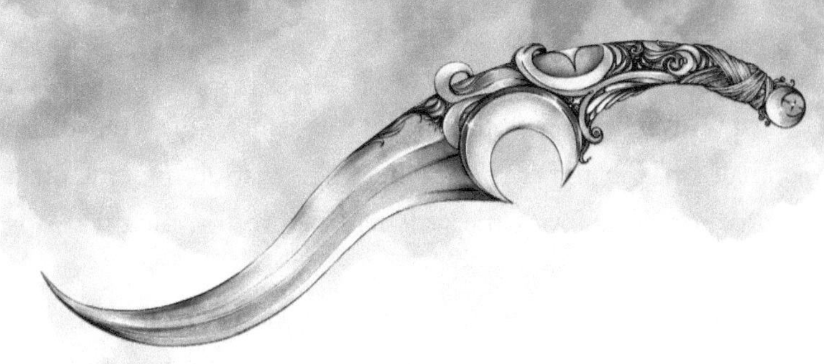

TWENTY

Arix knew she would not sleep tonight. She wandered the darkened streets of Coraven, walking along the river and thinking of what the little priestess had said. The disquiet in her stomach grew into a tangle, filling her with complete and utter grim expectancy. Even though she'd just taken some of the Well Water this morning, the insistent pain in her chest was back, worse maybe than before. But no matter how much it hurt, she couldn't bring herself to turn back to her bed. She wanted answers; she wanted truth.

She felt more unsettled than ever before. What was the truth? She didn't know.

She needed someone to explain the vision she had just witnessed. The girl knew things, knew that something was coming. Something Arix didn't know if she could handle.

She'd never been very religious. She'd never put much faith in the gods or the goddesses, especially not Kaoss' children. If anything, she had always thought fondly of the mother goddess who created the world for her children. She had always imagined a plump, tittering, and over affectionate goddess smiling sweetly as she watched her children play. If she were human, she'd be the kind of mother who baked tarts and pies, sang while she did the dishes, and scolded you with a small smile at the corner of her lips. Wistful, hopeful, quiet and comforting. Kaoss was the watcher, the creator, the great lady who watched from the perfect cosmos.

Kaoss stayed in the heavens. Patiently allowing her children, both gods and humans, to write their own history, live their own mistakes. Of all she knew about the goddess, 'invested' was not the word she would have ever used. Kaoss watched and waited. Nothing more.

And she stayed out of Arix's life.

To think that she had put some sort of seal on Arix's head, that there were games of approval and disapproval that the deities played, and she was a chess piece that they were supporting…

"Don't let it upset you."

Arix had stopped in the middle of one of the huge bridges that spanned across the river, staring down into the pitch waters swirling below.

"You need sleep. Perspective. Do not let the ravings of a little girl bring you turmoil."

Arix ignored the voice of the core around her neck and instead shifted her attention to the ring on her finger. Michael's core. She tuned out her own voice and listened to his instead.

"What do you think?" she muttered, staring down at the dull green gem.

It wasn't words that responded, not the way her own core spoke to her. But it was images, like watercolors of a painting, all shifting into each other and bleeding across a page. Abstract images and emotions were the resounding answer from the ring.

Images of the temple, of the girl. Feelings of apprehension, of careful, easy choices made with careful thought. Weighing of options; listening without bias of path. Images of Orion and Delphine's wedding. Feelings of pity, cautious comfort, *you're being strong, it's okay to be upset.* Images of Celeste's ghost-white face staring up at her from the marble box, feelings of warning. Warning of darkness inking in through cracks in her mind, taking hold of the goodness that lay there…

Arix cut off the images and the rush of emotions, squeezing her eyes closed until the darkness behind her lids was just that: darkness. No more swirling pictures.

Gingerly, she felt the knife at her back, Celeste's core. The tips of her fingers traced the carved out moon on the crossguard, feeling the cold, smooth curve of the metal against her warm palm. She opened herself to it, letting herself connect with the core, feeling it reach out to her in return, feeling along her spine and the edges of her mind. A gentle caress that ended in claws.

"YOU ARE NOT MY MISTRESS."

"No, I'm not."

"YOU TOOK ME FROM HER. YOU ARE THE THIEF. WE KNOW YOU."

Arix felt the talons of the core scratch gouges across the mental shield in her head. She wasn't foolish enough to just let the core have its way in her mind. She would shield, protect, and if she could connect with the core, then good. If not…

Arix glanced back down to the dark River Helene below. She would sooner chuck the dagger into the deepest part of the river before she let it control her.

"WE FEEL THE BLOOD UNDER YOUR FINGERNAILS, THE STONES BENEATH YOUR FEET YOU CRUSH EASILY. OUR MISTRESS WAS LIKE THIS. SHE TOO DID NOT CARE WHOM SHE CRUSHED. WE LIKE YOU AS WE LIKED HER. YOU ARE THE SAME."

White-hot anger flared in Arix. "I'm nothing like Celeste."

She expected the sarcasm and the laughter that her own core

might have responded with. The dagger only continued as though it hadn't heard Arix's outburst.

"WE HAVE HAD MASTERS AND MISTRESSES BE-FORE, SOME BLOODTHIRSTY AND SOME PATIENT. SOME HEROES AND SOME VILLAINS. YOU ARE NO DIFFER-ENT THAN THE REST THAT HAVE HELD US. WE DO NOT CARE FOR YOUR MOTIVES. YOU WILL EITHER FAIL, OR YOU WILL SUCCEED, BUT EITHER WAY, YOUR BONES WILL GRIND TO DUST JUST AS THE REST."

"You will serve me."

"YES. YES, WE WILL. AND YOU WILL SERVE US, AND TOGETHER WE CREATE OUR OWN UNIVERSE, LOOPING BACK UPON ITSELF IN DEED AND IN THOUGHT."

"I don't know what that means."

"NEITHER DID OUR LAST MISTRESS. BUT NOW SHE IS DEAD AND SHE UNDERSTANDS THAT EVEN AS POWERFUL AND AS BLOODTHIRSTY AS SHE WAS, HER DOOM MET HER ALL THE SAME. THE BLOOD THAT ONCE FLOWED IN HER VEINS NOW FLOWS FOR AN-OTHER PURPOSE."

"What did that girl mean, what she said in the temple? She said—"

"WE HEARD WHAT SHE SAID, STUPID INCANTOR." The dagger spat. *"WE MAY SERVE YOU BUT WE WILL NOT SERVE YOUR EVERY WHIM. REMEMBER THE WORDS ON YOUR OWN."*

Arix growled in frustration, hands gripping the hilt so hard that the intricately carved grooves of metal dug into her palm. "I do remember the words. *You* are here to help *me*. To serve *me*. So do it! What did she mean about the messenger drenched in blood?"

The dagger's voice reached a fever pitch in her mind, angry and red hot. *"ARE YOU A CHILD? THAT ALL MUST BE WET IN MILK FOR YOU TO CONSUME? USE YOUR TEETH! TEAR AND BITE AND PIECE TOGETHER THE TRUTH!"*

Arix mentally shoved back from the voice, pushing herself away and putting space between herself and the dagger. There was a cold settling through her, like frozen stones weighing down her limbs and pulling her until she sat on the real stone beneath her feet, one hand still gripping the bridge's handrail. She was tired in a way she hadn't been tired before, tired in a way that made her want to sink not just to the ground but to the bottom of the river, the calm and the cold pooling around her and making the surface disappear above her. She didn't want to be dead; she just wanted to be sure of something. Sure of the water, sure of the air seeping from her lungs.

Because right now she wasn't sure of anything.

~

The house was still raucous when she returned. Still partying, even though the stars had already disappeared and the first streaks of lavender-gray were seeping into the black of night. She stepped into the well-lit hallway leading to the honeymoon suite and nodded at the four guards she had posted by Orion and Delphine's door. They nodded back, confirmation that all was well. Abbas leaned against the wall at the mouth of the hallway and motioned for her to join him.

"Any trouble?" Arix asked, speaking in a low tone to keep her voice from carrying down the stone hallway.

"There was a guest who thought it funny to check in on his majesty."

"And?"

"He is sleeping off his bad choices in his room." Abbas didn't smile, but the corner of his mouth quirked up slightly at the corner. "Other than that, it's been quiet. Ulfur and the morning shift will be coming to relieve us soon."

"Good." Arix offered him a small smile. "Make sure you get some food before you head in, the feast is going to melt right into breakfast and there's more than enough."

Abbas nodded, and with a final salute, Arix slipped off to her room.

That ache in her chest was pressing, pushing at the back of her throat, and she felt like maybe she might be sick. Her rooms were quiet, pitch black, but Arix didn't bother to light a candle or pull up the magick orbs.

Sliding her hand across the softness of the bed, she went by sensation alone to guide her. Tracing the smooth lines of blankets up to the solid wood of the table that stood beside it; the cold metal of the latch as she pulled open the drawer.

Her fingers touched the one thing she'd left inside. The glass vial that Lakai had given her.

She felt for the stopper, pulled it, and drank down the rest of the Well Water. Thick and glossy, syrupy sweet and warm, it slid down to her stomach, instantly sending tingles up her spine. The ache and pressure behind her eyes disappeared almost instantly.

The feeling of loneliness, too, had faded. The lack of control she'd felt on the bridge was replaced by a calm assurance. This was a journey. The path that she was on now, whether of her own choosing, of the Gods', or just of simple fate, was her own now. Regardless of blessings or workings of the Carn, she had the power and the ability to do her job. To step back into routine and walk the line of nothing and something again.

Hadn't that been what her life up to now had existed of? Nothings and somethings all tangled into one? She was a lot of somethings now. And if she let all of it overwhelm her, she'd crumble under the weight of it.

With a sigh, Arix lay her head back against the pillow and stared at the ceiling. She didn't feel tired, not really. There was a sense that if she closed her eyes she might fall asleep, but she really didn't need sleep.

Now that the wedding was over, the journey upwards toward Rohleach would begin, and she would finally be back in the mountains. The last time she'd been in Tamhain's capital, she'd stolen Warden Aliska's prize horses from her. It had been early spring then; the snow had turned to slush, the roads a muddy muck. The mountains had been her salvation, slipping out of reach and disappearing into the Fyall range that ran along the north and east sides of their country.

As much as she enjoyed being near the salty sea air of the ocean, there was something different about being up in the mountains. The air had a bite, the tang of the pines crisp in the air. Soon, she would be able to look across the deep, dark lake and feel that snow-capped mountain air rush across her face. The grasses were thicker, the smell of hay sweet and earthy. But more would be waiting for her than just the wind and the mountains and the lake.

Arix thought back to what the young priestess had said to her in the temple.

"The goddess of suffering knows you."

The goddess of Earth was waiting.

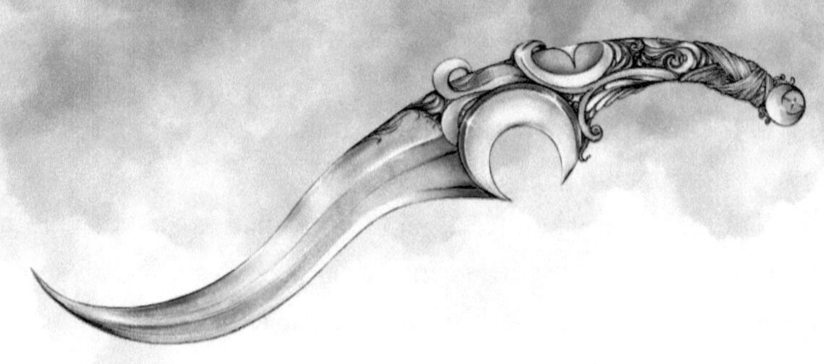

TWENTY-ONE

Entering Rohleach again felt grounding. Like the earth itself held you down and kept you firm. Osiris could feel it too, his steps surefooted and solid as he stamped his hooves. Even the cheering crowds had an air of stoicism to them. Deep timbered bellows and songs that had a deep steady rhythm to the cadence. In the distance, looming over them, the mountains were still capped with snow, even though the months had shifted into summer.

The air was warm with the smells of oil slicked leathers, fresh breads and roasting meats. Even with the season slipping into warmer months, there were fires that never stopped burning, and the smell of fresh burned pine, sweet sap, and dark smoky tobacco soaked into Arix's skin, rooting her to the saddle in a faint sense of home.

These people lived in long winters, cold and hard, nestled up against the Fyall mountains. It was how they liked it, separated from the rest of the country. The lake that Rohleach was built against was dark, a black mirror reflecting the city and the peaks and the cool gray sky above them.

Sieren and Coraven had bubbled with joy, bursting at the seams as they welcomed their new king. Streamers and ribbons and decorations of all sorts had been on display. Here, the banners were sturdy; woven so that they were stately and didn't titter and trail in the wind. The songs they sang had deep booming basses, a sturdiness to them that the songs sung in Nero did not have.

Zarak was known for its merchant traders, spices and textiles and stonework. Eldur was known for its artisans, painters and fabric weavers and vintners. Nero was known for their architecture and seafood. And Tamhain was known for its metalwork forges and mining.

Tamhain was also known for its songs.

Some of the best choirs in the country were made up of Tamhains, hitting low registers with ease, and writing epics of story and song that wove together better than any ever written down.

Arix felt the grin pull at her face. They were such perfect portrayals of the goddess of water and the goddess of earth. The north, sturdy and strong, grounded. The east, flowing and changing and full of movement. The two were so different. So different, yet the people that lived in them all desired the same thing: Peace and love, a fullness of life and a wide open world to grow safely in.

Arix's eyes fell to the two horses that rode in front of her. Delphine waved, her dainty wrist twisting as she watched the crowd with a delicate smile. Orion beamed beside her, offering his own waves and nods. Somehow, one nod could provide such assurance and promise.

It would all be well. Their king was here now.

They were so in their element, and Arix felt the warmth in her grow as she watched them. Was it too much to admit that she was proud of them? Proud of the king and his new queen?

And was she jealous? Not in the slightest.

For every eye that watched the king, their gaze easily swept past him and onto the figure in black that rode close behind. In the sunless day, Arix's armor seemed even more dark, sucking in the light.

Her white hair trailed free behind her, and she knew, seated up on Osiris' tall back, she looked fearsome.

She looked like death personified.

And that image thrilled her.

A drum was beating somewhere in the crowd, and to the beat, a song rose up amongst the cheers. Arix could just make it out if she focused her attention on the words. An old song, sung for heroes in battle, for champions.

> *The wind and rain and blood that falls,*
> *The hand of fate that watches all.*
> *Loss of life, loss of limb,*
> *Grappling death back from the brim.*

Deep in the crowd there was a deep baritone voice that seemed to be leading the song, and eventually Arix spotted him. He loomed over the people around him, bearded chin tucked into his chest as he thundered the words. Arix nodded to him, and he nodded in return.

Like two warriors acknowledging each other on the battlefield.

Arix's heart swelled. This was all she had wanted when she'd been a thief. She'd wanted the recognition, yes, but beneath it was something so much deeper. There was a bond here, a bond with the people that looked up at her. Looked up *to* her.

They saw her, *recognized* her as their protector. She was proud to be that for them. She was the protector of the crown, protector of the realm. She'd been blessed by Nereus and would be blessed again by Arduinna. She had the goddesses on her side, and she had Orion's back. What else did she need?

The other song that the crowd had been singing was slowly getting enveloped by the other until all she heard now was chanting of *"loss of life and loss of limb,"* and it took every ounce of her strength not to leap off her horse and kiss them all.

"Damn," Ulfur muttered at her side. "Who came up with such

abysmal words? The least they could do is sing som'thing *cheerful.*"

Arix chuckled under her breath, shooting him a sideways smile. She could tell he didn't mean it, and the crinkles around his eyes and the pink tips of his ears told her that he was feeling just as proud as she was. If anything, the complaint was just a way to dissuade his bashful pride.

And then everything exploded.

The force clocked her in the side, a bash that almost knocked her clean off her horse. Instinctively she let herself slide off the other side of Osiris, rolling across the stone street, keeping her focus on the king and queen in front of her. She'd kept a shield around them for the past day, and any attack on her meant that her assailant hoped to minimize her focus and drive her into dropping the shield.

"Black Guard!" Arix hollered as she rose to her feet. "With me!"

The crowds was scrambling, screaming. The songs and chants shifting to panic screams. Dragging wounded from the streets behind any cover they could find. Osiris snorted, his hooves stamping as he shied away from the blast, halfway ready to run in the chaos.

As her Guard were moving to obey, another force came flying from the right side of the street, slamming into the side of the shield barrier she'd placed around Orion and Delphine. It shimmered as the force hit it, vibrating so that the air waved and wobbled. With a snarl, Arix moved to stand at the head of the barrier, eyes trained on the crowd that was already dissipating on the right side of the street.

Nearly twenty figures stood, facing off against them. They wore hoods and capes, some keeping their faces down, shielded from view. Others stared across the space between them with confidence etched into their features.

They stood in a tight formation, and without even having to look for it, Arix knew they were shielded. From the front, maybe, but from beneath? The incantor had to be here. There was no way they could have found a way to bottle a shield that big.

Arix grinned.

As she thought it, forced it into being, it grew. A thorny mass of vines hurtled up from the ground, piercing through the bubble. It was so easy; she wondered for a moment if it was a trap. Only a fool shielded three sides of himself. *Her* defense shields were never this sloppy. A few of the Carn were able to sidestep, moving away from the threat of the thorns that entangled them, but many were easily wrapped. Arix waited for the retaliation, but it didn't come.

A skilled incantor would push back, make a counter-attack, something to disintegrate the thorns, ice maybe, or acid, or *anything.* Instead the Carn members in the bubble struggled.

Goosebumps crept up the back of Arix's neck. Something wasn't right.

A roar split the air and Arix spun, turning to the opposite side of thes street. Screams surrounded a man as his skin boiled and blistered, his form growing taller and his muscles bulging. The monster rose above the crowds, foam and spittle flying from his mouth. He ran at her Guard, picking one of her men up and kicking him down the road like a child might kick a small dog.

"No!" She scrambled past Osiris and shifted between the air, teleporting herself thirty feet forward until she stood behind the monster.

Celeste's dagger sliced at the tendons of his heel as she dodged, the monster's arm swinging back to stop her.

"FEED US!" The voice of the dagger screeched as the monster's blood ran in rivulets across the blade.

The monster was hot, his skin radiating heat, and she felt it wave over her as he spun, stomping to try and catch her beneath his feet. She dodged, but just barely, armor scraping and sparking against the stone.

A blast of fire rocked the earth.

Horrified, Arix glanced back to Orion and Delphine, still protected by the bubbled shield that surrounded them. Orion's face was set in a grim line, his eyes burning into her own. He held the reins of Delphine's horse as his new bride clutched at her saddle in terror.

Arix's gaze slid past them to her Guard. Even though the king was protected, her men were outside of the bubble. A moment of panic clawed at her throat at the flames that were still dissipating. Another band of Carn was grouped together, arms still upraised at the toss of their bottled magick.

The monster above her swung, and Arix used his momentum to slide past, twisting as she shifted her blade and cut again across his shins. He was tall, fast, and this time, she couldn't dodge as he backhanded her, the force sending her skidding across the street.

Her Black Guard was fine. She knew it in her gut that they were. After the initial Carn attack in Sieren, she'd incanted all of their armor to be able to take a hit, linking the spaces between the plates with magick. They could take arrows, hits with swords, fire attacks, weak acid, and even had protection from mind-controlling cants as long as they were wearing their helmets. She'd done all of this on the road, taking her time to improve on the magick as they traveled, reapplying the magick as they walked. They probably didn't even know she'd done it to their gear. She'd built it up over weeks of travel, and she knew it would hold.

But still…

Glancing toward their line, she looked for signs of damage, signs of death. A few had been knocked to the ground, but as their comrades helped them stand, Arix let out a relieved pant. They were all well.

The dagger in her hand shoved into her mind, and with the voice, she could hear whispers of her own core that was settled under her breastplate of armor, images from Michael's ring joining the voice.

"SEE THE WAY HIS EYES MOVE, BLACK HAND? SEE HOW HE OVERCOMPENSATES?"

She could see. The monster was charging, but as she shifted, dodged out of the way, slicing again as she moved past, his head jerked to try and follow her. While he might be a monster, he was still just a man underneath, relying on magick he wasn't used to, didn't know how to control.

Like trying to look through a spyglass to watch a dog that circled your feet.

Arix grinned. If he was having trouble seeing her, then she would make it even harder for him. Fog surged up from the ground around the monster and she twisted and ducked again, mixing into the magickal fog her favorite silencing incantation, making her practically invisible to the raging monster.

"DO YOU SEE, BLACK HAND? TOGETHER NO ENEMY CAN STAND AGAINST US!"

The monster was standing still, arms swinging with enough force to cleave a man's head from his shoulders, but Arix stayed low, waiting until he changed his tactics. It wasn't long before the monster bellowed in frustration, turning towards where she had last been.

Then she jumped. Used the magick to surge high above him, silent as a hawk, then to come crashing down, dragging the dagger down his spine, severing through bone and tendon and hulking flesh. When she landed she rolled, reaching a hand up and casting acid that surged into the open and gushing wound.

"FEEEEEEAAAAST!"

The monster howled, reaching around to claw at the gash in his back, the acid eating through the thick skin and into his heart.

Behind her, another explosion of fire hit her men, and Arix

turned, no longer watching the monster, even as he sank into the ground with a pitiful howl.

That little spike of fear that had surged through her heart earlier was replaced by fury, white-hot.

They wanted to play with fire? She would give them fire.

It was a good thing that the Carn had a bubble around them. A good thing they were locked away so protectively. It meant she didn't have to hear them scream.

The fire she lit scalded, and she watched their clothes melt into their skin as they writhed, trying to escape the enclosed inferno. Pitch-black smoke encased the bubble until it obscured her view. Then she turned, slowly, back to the first group on the right side of the road. The few faces she could see were twisted in shock, eyes glued to their companion's bubble on the other side of the road, to the melting monster that was dissolving away in a river of acid. Had they not expected her to retaliate? Had they not expected her to protect her own?

They had attacked her king. They had attacked her *men*.

She would watch them fucking burn.

They had thought the bubble would protect them, keep them safe from the big bad Black Hand. But they were wrong. Arix felt a smile twist at the corner of her lips, turning into a feral grin that split her face.

One by one, she had her vines crush the inhabitants. Crush them slowly and without mercy. Around her, she felt her Black Guard still, watching with gaping mouths, and she strode toward the bubble. Which of the Carn were fighting hardest; who were the others protecting? Surely, by now, an incantor would have dispelled the vines and removed the bubble, allowing those left to flee. But instead, the bubble remained up. The vines continued their work, and soon there were only three left.

Feeling the resistance of the bubbled shield, Arix pressed her hand against it, magickal current pulsating under her fingers. She could actually feel the vibrations of the inhabitant's screams thrum against the barrier, and glancing up, she could see who was still left alive. One woman and two men. They pulled against the vines, the woman desperately trying to saw the thorns from tangling around her thighs. Every tendril she cut, another rose up to wrap her further.

Then the bubble faded.

Arix stepped through, letting Michael's ring focus on keeping her own shields in place and striding closer to the three captives she held firmly in her vine's grasp. One of the men's left leg was bent at an odd angle, crushed in the vines. The other was wrapped up to his neck, flat on his back as he glared up at her from the ground. Only the girl was still standing, still frantically trying to cut away at the vines. As Arix neared, she swung her arm out, trying to catch Arix in the face with her blade.

"Well, that was stupid," Arix muttered, plucking the knife from the girl's grip.

"You killed them all!" the girl spat out, spearing Arix with a glare. "Fuck you, black-hearted bitch!"

"Oh, shut up."

She gave the man with vines wrapped around his neck a cursory kick and realized he was suffocating. She let the tendrils finish their job, focusing on the two that remained. A few members of her Black Guard stepped in, pulling the arms of the two Carn members back to restrain them and Arix let the tendrils of vines that held them creep back into the earth.

"Hold their hands up, keep them away from any pockets or bags. I want them stripped and their belongings kept from them until we know what weapons they might still be carrying. They need to be processed and held for questioning. I'll shield the cells they're put in.

I don't want a repeat of what happened last time." Arix pulled out a slice of purple glass the size of her palm and peered through.

Both of the captured Carn held no magick.

A quick scan through the crowd showed her that none of the other dead rebels or surrounding watchers held magick either. If the incantor had been here, she was gone now.

"Cowards." The muttered word came from Ulfur, standing beside her, mirroring her own thoughts.

"F'cking cowards." He repeated again.

"You've got this handled here? I've got to get the king and queen out of here."

Ulfur nodded, and Arix headed back to the center line. A group of her Black Guard still surrounded the shield she'd made around Orion and Delphine. The shield allowed her to step through, leaving no space for anything else besides her to enter.

Delphine's face was white as ash, her grip on her horse's reins tight. She was staring at the monster, dead in the street.

"Are we safe?" Orion's voice was clipped.

"Yes, I've got the shield up around you both. Nothing's going to hurt you. My men are taking care of this mess," Arix nodded to the monster, eyes roving the damage around them. One side of the road burned to char, and the other side strangled in vines. "There are two left alive, I'll question them later. In the meantime, let's get you both to Warden Aliska's home."

Orion offered her a nod before turning to his new wife. She clutched at his hand, her face upturned towards his with a grateful smile. Arix looked away.

The ride to the estate went without trouble, the rest of the court following behind them at a clipped pace. It wasn't until they were all within the safety of the walls that Arix felt she could breathe deeply again. She was livid. Furious that the Carn had attacked again. After the initial small attack in Sieren, the Carn had backed off, and there'd been no trace of them until now. And here it was again, the first day in a new city, with tripled numbers and a hulking monster to bolster them.

It was strangely predictable. It seemed like bad strategy, bad timing, and it made her nervous. There'd been only three of them in Nero, but they'd been fast. And this fight, though chaotic, only lasted a few minutes. The members of the Carn she'd just taken down had been untrained, nothing better than a ragtag team. Even with the monster, who had undoubtedly meant to cause more damage, had been sloppy. He hadn't known the reaches of his own power, his own limitations. Beating him had been almost simple.

They had been ragged. But a ragged team with magick, nonetheless. There had to have been an incantor that kept out of sight, offering them shielding and fire-power. But in the end, they hadn't done anything to save those who had just died. If it was Maeve, then this fight proved she lacked courage, lacked strategy. And from what little she knew about Maeve, it didn't match up.

Maeve, or maybe other incantors helping her, had kept the Carn hidden for *years*. Out of sight, always eluding the king's men. But now, here, they'd been caught so *easily*.

Something about this was wrong.

As they rushed the king and queen into the estate, Arix realized that Ro Laris was at her shoulder, following silently as she shifted to stand at the side of the courtyard.

"What have you heard?" Arix's voice was low as members of the court streamed into the walled courtyard. Warden Aliska had just arrived and was discussing matters with her counselors.

Ro's tone matched her own, his face drawn as his eyes continued to scan the gathered mass. "The Carn made a fatal error attacking again today. If anything, that little show has inspired more against them. There are some in the court that are grumbling. Lord Shaw had his carriage break a wheel when one of his horses bolted, so he's upset about that. I heard a few express their frustration at the lack of protection."

"Lack of protection?" Arix scoffed. "I turned a fucking monster into a puddle. I protected the king. That's my fucking job."

Ro's gaze snapped to her own. "Some are angry you didn't protect them as well."

"They weren't in any danger. The Carn attack was centered on the king and queen, not the rest of the court."

"Maybe, but some are still mad."

"Let them be mad. I don't work for them."

Most of the court members had arrived now, speaking together in groups and comparing stories on what had happened. Those who had been further back in the procession hadn't seen the attack first-hand and were getting varied stories and accounts relayed to them by others who had been further up the line.

"The people think you were brave. Did you hear the songs they were singing when you arrived?"

Arix couldn't keep a small smile from slipping across her face. "I did."

"Those songs will have ten new verses before the day is over, I guarantee it."

His shoulder pressed into hers, and she returned the pressure. It felt like a hug, even if only their shoulders were touching.

"You should head back to talk to Ulfur; I'll keep an eye on things here." Ro's grin was feral as he scanned the gathered crowd. "I'm sure there'll be plenty of chatter for my ears to pick up, and you know how I thrive on chatter."

"Do you have any people here?"

Ro quirked an eyebrow at her. "You mean, do I have any spies in

Rohleach? Of course I do."

"Find out how many were injured. I saw some of the damage, and I want to make sure we help. I'll provide healing if need be." Arix noted the room was quieting, waiting for instruction.

Lakai had just moved into the courtyard with Lord Bardon at his side, and Arix strode toward them, leaving Ro to slip back into the crowd to talk.

"Please continue to your quarters, and try to rest from all the excitement. Tonight's banquet has been postponed to tomorrow in light of today's"—Lord Bardon glanced Arix's way as she made her way through the crowd—"incident. Allow their majesties rest this evening, and the schedule will resume as planned tomorrow. Any questions may be directed to my steward."

As the crowd thinned, Arix moved in beside Lakai, her voice hushed.

"What is being done?"

"The king and queen will rest. But there will be an emergency council meeting in an hour. Warden Aliska has provided her council room for us."

Arix offered a nod, then turned back towards the gate. She needed to talk to her Guard, speak to their prisoners, maybe gain some information she could bring to the council meeting. None of her Black Guard had sustained serious injury, but they might need a little healing, which she was more than happy to provide. After all, there were perks to working for the Black Hand.

A hand on her arm stilled her from leaving, and Lakai guided her a step away from the dissipating group.

"You captured one of them?"

"Two. My Black Guard have them, and I'm about to head down to ward the cells so we don't have a repeat of what happened to the last Carn we captured."

Lakai nodded slowly, the blue of his eyes clouded. "Your men?"

"No fatal injuries. I'm headed that way now. I want to double-check them and offer any aid. The Carn rebels as well; I want to make sure they survive any questioning."

"What about you, Arix? That monster?"

"I'm fine." Arix shifted her shoulder, the one that had gotten clipped. "Nothing a little ice won't fix."

"If you need it, I can offer some healing."

Arix shook her head, waving him off. "No need. But I could use the company down at the cells."

"I'll come with you."

Together they rode towards the Warden's soldier's barracks, where they met Ulfur and Abbas. None of her men were seriously injured, except a young man who'd been knocked to the ground and had fractured his wrist while trying to catch himself. It was easy magick to heal, and by tomorrow the lad would be right as rain.

Just like they had done for the coronation, Lakai and Arix worked together to secure the jail cells, enforcing the doors, locks, and hallways.

Finally, Arix stood outside the woman's cell, watching and waiting. The girl had manacles on her wrists and her ankles, and the chain that secured her to the wall had been double-reinforced. Her clothing and belongings had been stripped, and she'd been given a coarse dress to keep her from getting too cold.

"What's your name?" Arix asked quietly. Her words echoed enough against the stone that she knew the girl could hear her just fine.

The girl just glared.

"This isn't the first time I've dealt with the Carn."

"Fuck off."

"I killed one of your men, you know."

"You killed a lot more than that."

Arix let a finger glide down one of the metal bars that separated her from the woman inside, her nail catching on the rough iron. "Not today. Last year. The first Carn I ever killed."

Eyes flashing, the girl gave Arix a challenging look, her lips pursing. "Good for you."

"I used my magick on him. Got him talking because he thought I was a friend. He gave me what I wanted so easily. You'll do the same."

Pressing out with her magick, she felt it slide around the woman, tendrils leeching into her mind. She was met with resistance, but it was weak, diluted. Arix only pressed harder.

"You will tell me your name."

All the tension that had held the girl's jaw in a murderous scowl loosened. "Alia."

"And your friend?"

"Kenji."

Arix let her fingers trail further down the line of metal along the door while she continued to focus the magick. There was a barrier there, set in place by someone else to keep deeper secrets safe.

"Who put that wall up in your mind, Alia?"

A flicker of deception. "No one."

Arix smirked. "I'll let that one go. It's not like I don't know your little incantor has been messing around in your minds. Brave of her. She could do irreparable damage like that."

Like a doctor might feel the joint around a dislocated shoulder, Arix probed through Alia's mind, feeling out the weakest points and softest spots where she could break through. It was simple work, with cracks in the foundation and bending joints. It wouldn't be hard work, but would take some time to break through without shattering the mind beneath.

Maeve might think she was protecting her people and keeping their secrets safe with a mind protection cant like this, but in all truth, it showed Arix the reality.

The girl was inexperienced.

A slow smile spread across Arix's face. It seemed the Carn's incantor was not as powerful as she pretended to be.

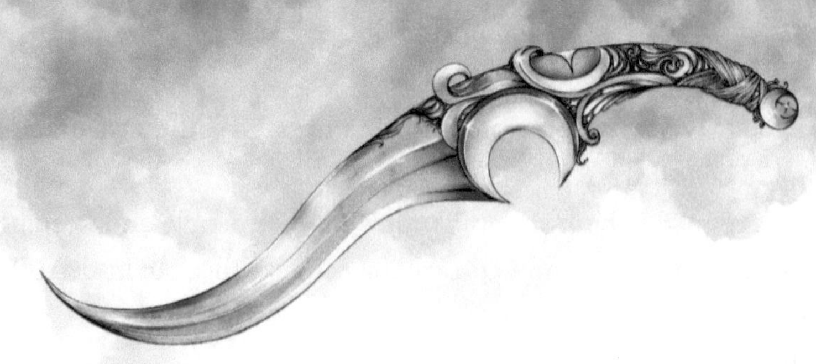

TWENTY-TWO

Arix stood outside Orion's door, her knuckles rapping lightly on the wood.

"Enter."

The hinges were silent as Arix slipped inside the king and queen's quarters. She just barely caught a glimpse of Delphine's dress skirt disappearing around a doorframe that led further into the king's rooms. Orion stood by the window, his back to her while he gazed out at the mountains that loomed over the Rohleach, all still capped in snow.

By the tension in the room, Arix had the distinct impression that she'd just interrupted something between the newlyweds.

"I can come back," Arix offered an apologetic smile as Orion turned to face her.

"No, no, it's fine. Delphine's tired from the trip and spooked from the attack. She just needs some time to rest." He stepped away from the window, his gaze trained on the now-closed door that Delphine had closed behind her. "It is…more trying than I expected."

Arix's eyebrows twitched upwards. "Trying?"

"To be a husband." Orion twisted back to look at her, and she could see the lines around his eyes deepening in frustration.

She let the silence linger between them, allowing him a chance to elaborate, to continue his train of thought, but he didn't. Instead, he ran a hand across his face, running his fingers through his hair before fixing his gaze back to hers.

An apologetic smile rose on his face, smoothing out the worry lines. "I'm sure you don't want to hear about my marital troubles. Should we go? You and I have a council meeting to attend to."

He led the way out of the rooms, but Arix kept close on his heels as they moved into the darker hallways of the inner castle. But after only a moment of walking, Orion's pace slowed until he stopped. Arix gave a glance at the guards following them, and they backed away until the corridor was empty.

"Orion?"

He said nothing, his back still to her. His shoulder rose and fell with each breath, but she gave him his space, letting him decide how and when to speak.

"Are you…" Orion's voice was low, the words quiet and the thought left unspoken.

"I'm fine. My men are unharmed."

"Good."

She wished he would turn around and look at her. When was the last time he had looked at her, really looked? He'd seen her riding in formation with her men, but when was the last time they'd spent time alone?

There were mornings she saw him while dew still lingered on the grass, the morning fog kissing moisture on her armor. He would glance around, looking for her, and maybe offer a small smile, but it was always so fleeting, so temporary. And she'd avoided him, avoided talking to him, avoided getting too close. There were other eyes here, watching her, watching Orion and Delphine. She told herself she was doing the right thing, but she missed him.

It was strange how things had shifted between them. It was all so odd to speak to someone every day, feel their presence and their gaze on you, feel their skin pressed against yours, and then in the very next moment feel it all disappear. She missed his touch, yes, but she missed the companionship they had shared. Orion had filled a hole in her heart when she'd lost Michael. And now it felt like she had lost him too.

She wanted to hold on to him. The fear of losing his companionship made her heart ache.

All Arix wanted was to be there for him, but was that her place? Stepping in between him and Delphine? It was a dangerous game to play, and she wasn't sure if playing the Mistress was something she ever wanted. But was she content to watch his life play out with Delphine? Without her?

"If you need to talk…" Her voice was quiet, the thick stone walls around them sealing in her intentions, her fears, and making her words bounce. "Know that I will listen."

When he didn't answer, she pressed a hand to his shoulder, feeling the corded muscle beneath. His fingers met her own as he clasped her hand to him, keeping it there. Then, slowly turning until he faced her, his grip on her hand moving across her fingers and up the back of her hand to grasp her wrist. He pulled her to him, gently guiding her into his arms, angling her chin up as his lips hovered over her own. It was so slow and deliberate, she knew he was asking, asking without words, to hold her, kiss her, press their bodies together. All to feel her again.

And she couldn't say no.

Achingly slow, he pushed until her back met the wall, one hand gripping her hip while the other pinned her wrist above them. His breath hovered at her jawline, skittering goosebumps down her spine as he moved his lips down, kissing the soft indent on her collarbone.

"Arix," he murmured, the warmth making her eyelids flutter. "I've missed you."

Heat raced across her cheeks as she felt just how much she'd missed this, missed him.

"I have to have you, Arix. I want the feel of you under my fingers, against my lips. You've been avoiding me. Don't avoid me anymore."

"I'm trying to give you space, the two of you." Arix could barely get the words out as his fingers flexed against her hip, sliding across her stomach. "People will talk."

"I am the king." He growled, nipping at the soft skin of her neck. "Let them talk. You are *mine*."

Shivers traveled across her scalp, pleasure mixing with guilt as she thought of Delphine all alone.

"You are my Black Hand, the most powerful woman in this country. You and I were made for each other, Arix. Made to rule this country, made to push the boundaries and make this nation the best in the world."

He crushed into her, and she could feel his arousal pressed between them. She groaned against the feeling, remembering so well how it felt to be buried into each other, wrapped in limbs and muscles aching from exertion.

"I don't know how much longer I can keep myself from you. Arix, I need you wrapped around me. Tonight."

Their lips crashed together, and Arix pressed into him, wanting his touch as much as he wanted hers. But she couldn't help the incessant thoughts that raced through her mind. Thoughts of Orion's beautiful wife, left alone in their honeymoon bed, wondering where her husband was tonight.

"Say you will, Arix."

"I don't—"

"I don't want anyone else. Only you."

Slowly, she pushed him back an inch, forcing their lips apart so she could think, breathe. Her body wanted her to say yes, was aching to feel their skin pressed together again. But her mind needed to think, to process, and being this close to him and feeling his breath on her skin was making it hard to think rationally.

"We shouldn't. You have a wife, a queen, and people will talk if we…" She left the end of her sentence unfinished. Orion had gone still at the mention of Delphine.

"Are you worried about them? Or about yourself?"

The bitter question speared through her, leaving her feeling hollow.

"Orion, you are the king. People will never speak out against you. But I'm still proving myself. Still proving to the people and the court that I belong here."

He released her wrist, stepping a few feet away from her, and instantly, she felt regret sweep through her at the loss of his touch. The lines of his jaw were hard, and he looked anywhere but at her.

"You know I had no choice in this, Arix. You know that I had to marry Delphine. And now, because I've done my duty and married a woman I don't even know, you're punishing me for it."

Arix blinked. "I'm not punishing you."

"You were the one who suggested it, Arix!" He let out a frustrated huff, motioning to her as he said it. "You told me to marry her, to form an alliance, to provide an heir. And I told you then and there that I wouldn't lose you to gain an alliance. I told you that very night that I wasn't going to lose you. We are too good together to let you slip between my grasp."

She could see the passion that had been there only a moment ago was disappearing. There was a kind of pain and desperation left behind, a man torn apart and shaking.

"What do you want me to do, Arix? Say that it was a mistake? I won't apologize for wanting you. I won't apologize for doing what I have to do as king. I will do my duty as king, and I will sire an heir who will take my place. But I refuse to beg your forgiveness for the choices I have to make. For the choices that *you* agreed with."

Everything in her was turning to dust. Crumbling and quaking and weighing so heavily in her chest that it felt like her ribs could not contain it all. She couldn't bring herself to disagree with him, to offer some kind of answer. She had known that things would change between them. Had known that Delphine would make loving him impossible. All those nights ago when they'd first talked about Orion taking a queen, she had known it, and she hadn't said anything. She'd let him believe that things would stay the same, that he could have Arix at his side and in his bed at the same time. That she could be two people.

But could she? Could she really let that be true?

"I need to think."

He scoffed. Turned away from her and paced a few steps before coming back to her. When he took her face in his hands, she let him, but the eyes she stared into were cold.

"You do that. You take your time, and you think, Arix, but remember this." His brows knit together, so much emotion mixed together with the words. "I *know* who I am, and I know who *you* are. You are my Black Hand. You are the missing puzzle piece in me, and I in you. And it kills me that you refuse to see that."

And then his touch was gone, his presence stepping away as he turned and continued down the hall towards the council room. Leaving her feeling emptier than before.

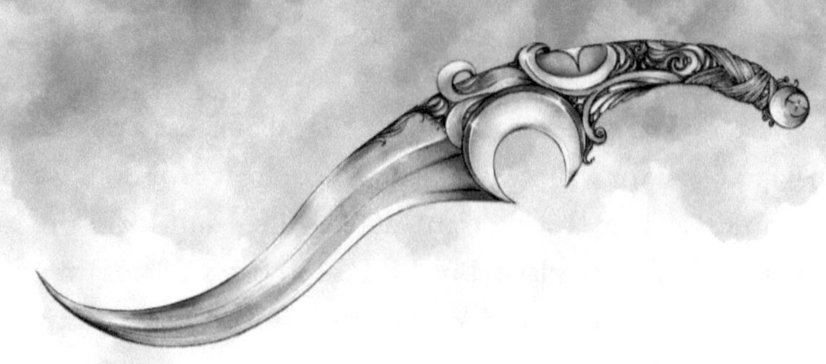

TWENTY-THREE

This was the first real council meeting Arix had been a part of. Her seat was beside Orion's, the loyal guard dog with sharp teeth sitting beside her master.

"Good evening, members of the council." Lord Bardon was standing at his seat, motioning to the king and to the others seated in Warden Aliska's hall.

The lofted ceilings towered above them, the long table and chairs placed near the back of the hall just down from the raised dais. Decorations for the banquet were draped across the windows, and the large candelabra of antlers suspended above them cast flickering light through the tower-tall thin windows that lined the outer edges of the wall.

"We'll skip the formalities this evening, as many of us are tired from the journey and still in shock after today's events." Lord Bardon glanced at the other members at the table, noting their nods of agreement before he sat, the meeting officially coming to order. "We need to discuss the Carn. After today's attack, it's clear that they've become emboldened. After the threat on Warden Los Ke's household at the beginning of the year and the interference with our competitors"—he glanced towards Arix with a nod—"it seems that they're not above using King Orion's tour as a way to make further statements."

Lord Bardon went on. "While the attack against Warden Ke's home was an undeniable act of unrest, their purpose, apart from killing the remaining competitors, is unknown. Even after interrogation, the information gathered was geared towards their inner workings rather than their immediate plans."

As he spoke, a dark pit was growing in Arix's stomach, the reminder of that mission still raw in her mind. They'd lost Idris that day, and if Arix hadn't remembered what Revena had taught her about the Lady Saguaro flower, she and the rest of the underground city of Pyesak would have been reduced to rubble. Her knowledge, in combination with Michael's magick, had been enough to defuse the bomb and save them all. What had come afterward was different.

She felt a chill run down her spine as she remembered the tang of blood in her mouth, the flecks across the back of her hands. The day she killed Micah. The day she lost Michael.

The pressure in her throat pushed against her tongue, and she fought against the churning in her stomach.

"The Carn has always been trouble for the crown, but their danger, even in recent years, has felt distant." Lord Bardon motioned with one hand to Reuben Corrigan, the warden of Eldur, and then to Aliska Sviengard, the warden of Tamhain. "In addition to outlying villages in Zarak, the Carn has attacked other secluded areas to the north and the south."

Warden Corrigan took this as a chance to speak up, stroking his dark blond beard that was just starting to tint grey wisps. "The largest of the Carn attacks were in Ewithwark, at our northern border, last year. We've sustained smaller attacks on our farming villages along the coastline, but losing Ewithwark has made it harder to move down from the mountain pass. Our trade routes out of Rökkur and into Nimbosia have been negatively affected by their hold of the city."

Arix remembered hearing about Ewithwark, a lake town that had been attacked and raided last year. It had happened right before she'd been captured by Lakai and brought to Castle Zma'ai.

Warden Aliska shifted in her chair, and those around the table turned their attention to her.

"We've had issues with border villages as well, and we've lost almost complete contact with towns in the Fyall Mountains. There are old routes, passages through the mountains that we believe the Carn are using to travel between Tamhain, Zarak, and Eldur unseen. My men have tried to map these mountain roads, but too much of the terrain has been changed."

As she spoke, Arix couldn't help but let her eyes shift to the huge figure that stood behind Aliska. Short blonde hair and eyes so blue they looked painted. She wore very little armor, just simple bracers of leather and interlaced with strands of metal. The design looked like swirls of waves or maybe clouds stitched together. In the midst of the design, pieces of glass glinted.

Arix narrowed her eyes while she watched the way the dim light from the windows caught the glass. Almost exactly the same as the magick glass Arix carried on her. Glass that showed the truth of a person and revealed whether there was magick flowing through their veins.

"I petitioned for more troops last year when we had a lead on them, but now it's too late." Warden Aliska continued, her gaze turning cold a moment as her eyes slid down the table to offer a pointed glare at Lord Bardon.

Lord Bardon moved on as if he hadn't heard her. "Warden Ke?

I understand your scouts have new information regarding the Carn's movements in the Sgudal Desert?"

Los Ke looked tired, his palms flat on the sturdy wood table in front of him. He seemed more weary than the last time Arix had seen him, deflated over the news that lay hastily scribbled on the letter in front of him. He nodded slowly before pulling the paper to him.

"Our nomadic tribes have done well thus far staying out of the Carn's grasp. But I've only just heard a few days ago that three of these tribes have not been seen or heard from in the past couple months. I worry they have been wiped out by the rebels for food, supplies, and horses."

"How many?" Lord Bardon asked.

"I couldn't say. The traveling nomads keep to themselves, but the numbers could number anywhere between five to ten thousand."

That was a sobering thought. The table hushed as the other members of the council paused to consider what it might mean if the Carn had their hands on ten thousand innocent people. With the stunt they had pulled at Pyesak, Arix didn't have a doubt in her mind that the rebels would kill anyone to get what they wanted.

"As much as I hate to say it," General Hawes spoke up after a moment of silence, "the maneuver that they pulled today might have actually been a good one."

As others made noises of protest, General Hawes raised his hands, the look on his face severe. "Hear me out. After this morning's display, we've seen a record-breaking number of volunteers for the military. Many are requesting to be transferred to the Black Guard."

Heads turned, and eyes met her own as members of the council looked directly at Arix. She felt her face warm with embarrassment, but pride filled her chest. Men and women wanted to join her Black

Guard. To fight with her. To fight *for* her.

"It is no surprise that my people rally behind the crown." Warden Aliska said, breaking through Arix's moment of pride. "But right now, we need more than just manpower."

"Agreed," said Warden Corrigan. "We need answers. The Carn have an incantor—this we know. But that *thing* today…" The others echoed his silence.

"How many of the Carn were taken prisoner?" Lord Bardon's question was directed at Arix, and she swallowed down the twinge of trepidation as others turned to look at her.

"We have two, a man and a woman." Arix kept her voice steady. "We haven't had the chance to question them yet."

"And you'll be doing the questioning?" General Hawes' eyes were cold as he stared Arix down.

"I will."

"Who's to say that you won't kill these like you killed the last one?"

The air stilled around them.

An icy grip clenched the base of her spine, locking it up as she stared at the man. "The fuck is that supposed to mean?"

"The last time you performed an *interrogation*, the man ended up dead, and we were down one captive. Your companions had a bit better sense."

Her chair scraped across the floor as Arix slowly stood, her blood thrumming under her skin. "My *companions* aren't here today. I am. The information I gathered that day was what I'd been tasked to find out. If Lord Bardon had had issues with my methods, he could have told me as much during the test."

Lord Bardon didn't answer, his posture casual as he leaned back in his chair and watched the display.

"If you'd like to be present during my interrogation of the two

Carn imprisoned today, you may make your request to the king." Arix remained standing, all too aware of the eyes around the table that shifted to her left where Orion still sat.

His fingers were steepled on the table in front of him, his shoulders drawn back. After a moment, he nodded to Arix, and she sat.

Anger shook through her spine, and it took effort not to let it show on her face. She had to remember that they hadn't seen her snap. They hadn't seen her beat Micah to a bloody pulp, hadn't seen how her fingers had flaked with his blood, sticking to her clothes and the latch and everything else. Did they know how she'd wailed after losing Michael only a few moments later? That day had been filled with loss and terror and self hatred. But it had been all her own. They didn't know about the torment they'd suffered that day.

Orion let out a frustrated sigh before directing his words at General Hawes. "The both of you will conduct interviews with the captives, but Arix will take the lead. After all, without her help, today's attack would have been a surprise that could have ended in the death of my *wife*."

The emphasis he put on the last word made more than one shift uncomfortably in their seat; the thought of their new queen or king being harmed was not a happy one.

"Yet..." Orion leaned forward in his chair, the muscles in his arms tensing as he spoke. "Even if we get answers about the attack from the prisoners, we're faced with the bigger question about the Carn: What do they really want? If we can find out, there may be a better way of resolving the conflict than how the rebel situation has been handled by the previous king."

High Priestess Esme Halotus' crystalline voice glided across the table as she spoke. "Indeed. We've entered a new age, with Your Majesty leading the charge. Perhaps this would be an excellent time to see if a treaty could be brokered with them."

Arix gripped the arms of her chair, her mouth falling open at what Esme was suggesting. She wasn't the only one who turned an accusing eye in the high priestess' direction.

"You suggest peace?" Lord Iman Holding demanded with surprise.

"I am suggesting that perhaps our king does not want to handle the rebels the same way as his father." Came her cool answer.

Lord Holding scoffed, looking to the others around the table. "You're suggesting that we forget the terror and harm that the Carn has done in Rökkur over the past decades. Even under King Taurus, their numbers grew, their methods secret and conniving. They have served their own purposes for too long. If you think that a treaty will solve our problems, then you are clearly disconnected from the reality of the situation."

Warden Corrigan backed him up. "Nero has not dealt with the same amount of discontent that the rest of us have experienced in our realms. Entire nomadic tribes are missing, with thousands dead over the years because of these attacks. Ewithwark is completely lost to us, and the mountain passes have been claimed and changed enough that our own people can't get through them anymore."

At the mention of the mountain passes, he motioned to Warden Aliska and the looming form that stood behind her.

Orion stood, and the others fell silent as he raised a hand to speak. "No one is suggesting that we haven't sustained incredible losses at the hands of the Carn. What I believe High Priestess Halotus is saying is that meeting the Carn with brute force, as my father attempted to do, hasn't worked."

He glanced around the table, making eye contact with every member of the council, lingering on each face as he spoke.

"My father's idea of control was one that held this country

in an iron fist. He saw the military as his weapon and the people as stepping stones in his tyranny. For how long did this council carry out his wishes even after he no longer clung to his sanity? Slipping further and further into nothingness? We all carried forth his wishes, even long after his role as the true king of Rökkur was removed."

"This is what he is good at," the voice over Arix's chest purred. *"Look at how they listen to him even when they do not agree."*

Arix could see it, the way that the members of the council quieted and listened.

"You have all trusted me to hold this seat of power, not only because of my royal family but also because you saw the need for a change. Our country and the realms have grown stagnant. Commerce is in decline, and with the mountains cut off to us, the Carn are controlling the routes with which we can trade with the rest of the world. If my father had had his way, the borders would have closed completely."

Orion's voice grew quiet as his chin lowered, and he stared down at the center of the table. "Sometimes I wonder if the Carn were just another way for my father to control the people of this country. If he does so still even from the grave."

The wardens around the table exchanged glances, and Arix wondered if they hadn't all been thinking the same thing. King Taurus had never been a truthful man, and from what she'd learned in her lessons with Desirae, he'd never really trusted his council about his dealings. How many of the people in this room had maintained their positions on the council out of sheer compliance with the old king's rule?

Even looking at them now, seeing the discomfort and frustration on their faces, she wondered if they knew more than she did. If the true actions of the Carn were steeped in more than just wanton destruction and demand for control. Did any of them know more about the Carn's true intentions than they let on? Again, her thoughts shifted to the magickal library back home. What answers did it hold, waiting for her return? Of the Carn, the Well Water, the Black Hands of the past? Surely if anyone held the answers, the library did.

"We will do what we can," Orion continued. "To learn the truths and the plans of the Carn. We will question them and work on a strategy. But in the end, there are too many empty pieces of this puzzle to know what their end game is. If it comes down to it, a treaty may be the best way to move forward to a peaceful solution. The fewer deaths of *our people*, the better."

Arix didn't miss the inflection he put on the words 'our people,' acknowledging to all those at the table that he was invested in each of their realms, in each of the five territories within his kingdom.

Even if the rest of the council didn't agree with him, he held them captive by his words. Arix herself felt more anger than most towards the Carn, but when Orion spoke, it was easy to picture the kind of world he described. Rökkur without the Carn? The trade routes opened back up again? It was an enticing idea.

And she might have been swayed by what he was saying. Might have been convinced that a peace treaty with the Carn was possible if she hadn't lived through seeing her village burn. If she hadn't watched her father die like a dog in the street. The Carn had taken too much for her to so easily be swayed by Orion's pretty words.

As the conversation shifted to other matters, Arix fumed.

She tried to focus as they discussed a few details of the banquet and the plans for visiting Tamhain's mountain temple to Arduinna, but her mind always shifted back to the thought of making peace with the Carn. Shaking hands with them, all in the name of reconciliation and newly forged alliances.

It made her sick.

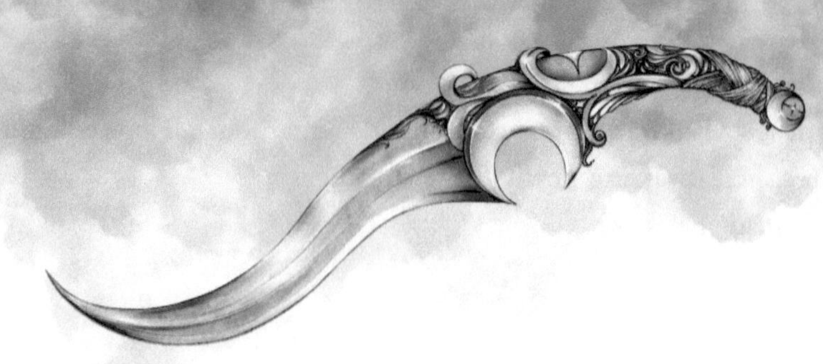

TWENTY-FOUR

She'd been nervous when they'd gone to the temple in Sieren, walking up all those white marble steps and having the memories of the paramour slide down her spine. Memories of death and destruction, bodies strewn about, the smell of sex and decay permeating the once holy space. She'd been afraid to go back, afraid of what kind of haunting memories might jump out at her, afraid that being back might raise all the thoughts of Michael back to the surface.

Being at the temple in Rohleach was worse.

Back in Sieren, she'd been surprised when she'd been blessed by Nereus. The water that had flowed up her body had been a strange and welcome phenomenon, leaving her breathless and full of wonder. Now that she knew she had received one blessing, she both craved and dreaded the next one, the war of the two emotions making Arix feel sick to her stomach.

What had the temple seer said in Coraven?

She yearns for your victory.

Arix had spent her entire life aware of the goddess, aware of the celebrations and rituals, the holidays and prayers. She'd gone to temples as a lost teenager, hoping to find some guidance in the holy words of the priests and priestesses. There were handfuls of gods, but they were petty deities, no more worshiped or prayed to than a quick muttering under one's breath for luck or to ward evil. It was the mother goddess and her children who were truly worshiped, who had temples and cathedrals built in their honor, men and women dedicating their lives to serve in reverence.

She had, much like many, only ever viewed them as myth and legend. Those who were there at the foundation of the cosmos but who watched the occupants below with barely anything more than vague amusement. Blessings were for kings.

Not for thieves.

"I'm not a thief," Arix mumbled under her breath, eyes training up the pathway she climbed, watching as it disappeared up between the rocks and zigzagged towards the open mouth of the rock wall above. "Not anymore."

Above them, Arduinna's Temple loomed, carved into the side of the mountain. With every step up the winding and treacherous pass, someone long ago had built shrines that told the goddess' story. Her creation of the world, her love with Death, the rape by her brother, how she had hidden herself away with a shame-ridden swollen belly and returned to the light after her child of monsters had been born.

When Orion had named her Arduinna all those months ago in the gardens, she'd been proud of the nickname, proud of the connotations it brought with it. Arduinna held the spirit of strength, of beauty, of form and ruin. If there was anything true about magick, it was that all magick centered around creation and destruction.

The temple itself was built into the rock as a homage to the months that Arduinna had spent deep underground, burying herself away from her brothers and sister, hiding herself and the betrayal away from all. As their group stepped into the mouth of the cave, weaving along the path between vine-entangled columns and moss-covered alcoves, Arix felt a chill down her spine.

She could feel the goddess here.

It was the feeling that someone watched you, standing just outside your periphery. But every time you turned to look, they were gone, leaving you wondering if your mind was playing a trick. The presence was a heavy weight on her shoulders, and by the way the rest began to hesitate, their steps slowing, Arix knew she wasn't the only one who could feel the change.

Pressing in on all sides, she might have thought the feeling was claustrophobia if it weren't for the fact that the cave was massive, and the cloudy gray sky was still easily visible if she turned to look.

No, the pressure wasn't physical. It was spiritual.

Strange to experience such a shift when, her whole life, she'd laughed at those who said they felt the goddess personally. Now she knew what they meant.

The further they stepped into the temple, the clearer it was that the earth had reclaimed the man-made carvings that decorated the interior. The columns that had been so exquisitely chiseled to depict Arduinna and the fates, with death watching from the edges, had long ago begun to erode. It had been decades since the temple had been hewn from the mountain, but since then, the goddess had taken back her temple, and the faithful who guarded it had let the moss and the vines and the flowers grow over the elaborate stone effigies, water dripping down from the rock above forming crystal pools and streams that ran along the stone path. Soon, they reached the small amphitheater, steps leading down to an oval stage-like center with roughly stacked stones that formed a table. Looming above them was a statue of Arduinna herself, carved into the rock, depicted with antlers and draped in garlands of flowers.

As Orion descended the steps toward Arduinna's high priestess, Arix moved to take a seat beside the other members of the court who had joined them to witness the blessing. There were more than a few glances angled her way, and the group that had joined them at the temple this time had grown since Sieren.

They were supposed to be watching Orion; instead, they watched her.

Arix hadn't wanted this, hadn't wanted to draw attention to herself during a moment that was supposed to be about their new king. But she couldn't help admitting that she liked the way the crowd shifted expectantly, peering and whispering as they watched her.

She'd spoken to Esme about the situation, knowing that there would be another blessing for her today, knowing that Arduinna would choose to bless both the king and his Black Hand. Should she hang back? Should she join Orion in the center of the room?

The high priestess had thought it would be better for her to wait in case there was no second blessing, and Arix kept her mouth closed about what the priestess seer had told her in the river temple in Coraven. She would default to what Esme thought was best when dealing with the goddess. There was always a chance that nothing would happen, and if she made a fool of herself pushing down to where Orion now knelt, she'd lose the respect that she was slowly gaining in her new position.

"King Orion Karcharias, step forward to receive the blessing of the Goddess of Earth." the high priestess said, her voice reverberating through the echochamber.

Orion was already standing in front of the stone table and knelt, his chin tipped up to accept the blessing.

"Mountains surging towards the sky, a portrait of majesty and strength. It is Earth that sustains us, Earth that births life. From the cradle of moss beneath sheltering trees to our graves beneath the soil, Earth nurtures and guides our very breath."

With each word of the prayer, Arix could feel the thrum of power reverberating across the walls and the ceiling above them, and the resonance of the priestess's voice had more resounding echoes with every word. The very walls were clinging to the words, holding them tighter and longer before releasing them to bounce back to the gathered listeners.

"Great Goddess Arduinna, favorite daughter of Kaoss, potter of land and mountains, mighty goddess of nature and nurture; we beseech you to fill our king with your fertile wisdom and nourishment of mind. Grant him the strength of mountains, the resilience of the mightiest oak, and the patience of a planted seed. Guide his steps towards the path of wisdom and understanding, that he may lead us under the hand of your blessing."

The priestess raised the carved wooden bowl in her hands, pouring the contents over Orion's head. Around her, members of the court craned forward, trying to catch a glimpse of what it was that cascaded over and around their king. It looked like tiny brown pebbles.

For a moment, there was dead silence as it seemed nothing would happen. Then, a small gasp came from the front row as they realized what the tiny pieces were. All around Orion, where the little seeds had fallen, grass began to grow up from the stone floor, and where they had caught on his clothes, flowers grew up from his sleeves and in his hair. A strange and beautiful sort of wreath tangled across his brow until he wore a crown of flowers and twisting branches.

Arix's own breath caught in her throat, the worry over her own blessing completely forgotten. As Orion stood and turned to face the rest of the room, his eyes slid to her, searching. He, too, was waiting to see if Arix would receive another blessing. Other eyes around the room shifted her way as well, and the scrutiny made Arix squirm.

It was a moment too long, everyone holding their breath. A strange moment of anticipation that bled into disappointment as nothing happened. No branches and flowers grew around her, no rocks trembled at her feet.

For a split second, a thought skittered across Arix's mind.

She could fake it.

She could use her magick, forcing flowers and vines to grow from beneath her boots, tangling up her calves and mirroring Orion's crown of branches across his brow. In this moment, who would know the difference? She would know; the goddess would know. But the rest of them? Arix couldn't help glancing back at a few of the onlookers, challenging them to continue staring, and she saw the look of curiosity, of disappointment. But there were a few whose smug glances and tittered whispers made her cheeks heat.

The goddess had not blessed her.

Not that she'd asked for any blessing in the first place. She'd never expected Nereus' blessing in Sieren, and the only reason she'd expected it here today was because of what the seer had told her would happen. Now that it hadn't, she felt cheated.

No one would know if she made flowers grow in her hair.

But she would know. And that was enough.

Glances slid away from her, focusing back on their king. The ceremony was over as quick as it had begun, and the gathered masses hadn't received what they'd been hoping for. Disappointment hung heavy in the air as the group filed out again.

As they descended from the temple, Orion walked ahead of her, talking lightly with Lakai, the flowers in his hair dancing in the mountain breeze. Arix offered Delphine an arm for the climb back down, and the new queen gave her a sympathetic look.

"Are you disappointed?" she whispered, her grip clutching Arix's left bracer.

The question caught Arix off guard, and the truth slipped between her lips before she could stop it. "More confused than anything."

Delphine made a small murmur of understanding.

"But I am a servant to the goddess," Arix quickly said. "It's not up to me whom she chooses to bless."

After a moment, Delphine squeezed her arm gently. "It doesn't make you less worthy, Arix."

And for that little bit of empathy, Arix was grateful.

As they made their way down the mountain, Arix couldn't help notice that Orion's shoulders were more relaxed, and he smiled as he chatted with those around him. He looked so at ease now, newly blessed with a flower crown to encircle his gold one. Had he been worried she would outshine his moment?

Come to think of it, had he felt that way in Sieren?

She'd seen the look on his face when the water had coursed over her, seen the look of hurt in his eyes. Had it been hurt? Had her blessing stung him?

If Arix was honest with herself, she realized she was disappointed, but that dismay she felt was fueled by something deeper. Resentment. She felt let down, and she hated that she'd put a small kernel of hope in the goddess Arduinna. After all, Arix felt connected to her. Connected in a way she didn't fully know how to explain. The seer had all but promised a blessing would happen. Now that it hadn't, it just made Arix feel like a fool.

~

There was nothing Arix wanted more than to drink and feast till she burst, and forget the strange itching feeling of shame and disappointment that crumbled like sand at the pit of her stomach. But her job was to remain vigil, keep an eye out for any more threats on the king's life. Lakai had mentioned how he didn't expect another attack soon, but Arix didn't want to take the chance.

So instead, she stood stoic with her Black Guard on the fringes of the banquet, held in Warden Aliska's main hall. In addition to their own large traveling party, Warden Aliska had invited many from Rohleach, and the long feasting tables were arranged in rows that ran across the stone floor. Benches packed elbow to elbow with guests who roared with laughter and merriment as they feasted.

Orion asked her to sit with him, to sit at his right hand side during the meal, but Arix excused herself. She couldn't bring herself to sit at the head table at the front of the room, on display for everyone to see. Even more eyes would be staring at her, more glances that asked the whispered question she'd already heard too many times today.

Why hadn't there been a second blessing?

It would have been better to shut them out, pretend that their words didn't bother her, but they did. Maybe even more so since the whispers came with accusing glances, as if maybe she'd done something to revoke the goddess' favor. But instead of avoiding the stares and closing her ears off to the gossip, she couldn't help but listen in. A quick cant, and she could enhance the voices around the room, amplifying their conversations about her.

It was almost macabre, the feeling of wanting to know what they said about her behind her back, slowly sliding deeper into herself and the dark pit in her mind that threatened to swallow her whole. She knew she should stop, knew that listening in would only make the dark feelings worse, but she couldn't seem to let it go.

"Arix, stop it. You're glaring." Ulfur muttered beside her.

She tried to soften her expression a little but couldn't. "Sorry."

"Don't apologize to me, lass. But you're just givin' the onlookers the fuel for their fire. They don't deserve any part of what you're thinkin', but it's written all over your face."

Instead of trying to steal her expression, Arix just turned away, moving to look out the window that stood behind them. You could see the lake from here, the edges of the water dark and dusky now that the sun had gone down. The full moon was hidden behind the dusty purple clouds that hung heavy. It was probably going to rain tonight.

"Is it wrong to be disappointed?"

"No." Came his simple reply.

Arix glanced over her shoulder, her gaze sliding over the sea of heads towards the front of the room where Orion sat with Delphine and the other council members. He was smiling and laughing with the rest, the branches and flowers still in his hair from this morning.

"He's happy."

Ulfur waited for her to continue, the pause in her thoughts lengthening the silence.

But she couldn't bring herself to vocalize the rest from her mind. The memory of how happy he'd looked when she hadn't received a blessing, when he'd been the only one to be honored by Arduinna. As king, it was his right to receive a blessing like this. It symbolized to all that the gods and goddesses approved of the new king, approved his reign.

"Has there ever been a king that didn't receive a blessing?" Arix blurted out.

Ulfur thought for a moment, shifting his weight back to lean against the stone wall behind them. "A couple, I'm sure. That'd be a question for someone other than m'self."

"Would Abbas know?"

"Probably. Tha' man knows damn near everything."

Arix glanced across the room to where Abbas was stationed closer to the head table, his hand resting casually at the sword that hung at his hip. He scanned the room slowly, keeping an eye on any potential dangers that might arise.

"How long have the two of you been friends? From child-hood, I gather?"

Ulfur chuckled, glancing towards Abbas as well. "The first day I met him was the day we were assigned to you."

"No way."

"It was a punishment, you know. Putting the two of us together to watch you. I mouthed off too much, and Abbas just has a way about him that puts other men on edge. They don't like that he keeps his thoughts to him'self. They thought he was a bit too big for his bri'ches; wanted to knock him down a peg."

"So they put the loudest man and the quietest man together to keep an eye on the little thief."

Ulfur beamed. "They did. An' fuck's sake am I glad they did." He jerked his chin towards Abbas. "He's the best of us, clever as a fox and no mistake. Pairing us up makes me look good by association."

Arix felt warmth bloom in her chest. "I'm glad they did, too. I'm lucky to have you both by my side."

"Til the end, Arix. Till the bitter, bloody end."

Her smile faded a bit at that, thoughts flickering to Michael and Revena. To the Carn attack. Would it come to that? Come to a bloody end? Was a war against the Carn on the horizon? They'd stayed in the shadows for years, but their grip was still a small one. If it ever did come down to brawn against brawn, the Carn would be completely obliterated, but so far, their tactics had been subtle and slow. They knew that an all-out attack against the king would see them all dead or worse.

Anger flared in her chest. Even if she had to burn their entire army alive, she'd do it. Anything to remove them from the game completely.

"You've got that look again," Ulfur said. "It's the look of someone who might burn the world down if a lad looked at ya funny."

"I just might," Arix replied before pushing herself away from the wall. "Gonna walk a lap. Let me know if there's trouble."

As she made her way around the periphery of the room, she checked in with a few of her Black Guard, swapping a few out for others so they could get some food themselves. Warden Aliska's men stood with her own, and she was glad to see a sort of camaraderie growing between them. As she moved around the edges of the room, Warden Aliska caught her eye, the tall blonde woman who stood behind her, guarding her back. Aliska tipped her glass to Arix very deliberately, and Arix nodded back. At last, she made her way to the front of the room and stood beside Abbas.

"We were talking about you, you know." She mumbled as she lightly brushed her shoulder against his.

A small resigned sigh was his only response.

"You looked so somber, I figured I'd come check on you."

His gravelly voice rumbled low beside her. "Would you rather me be kicking my heels in dance?"

Arix fought to hide the smile. "Maybe. I'm sure Warden Aliska would find it entertaining."

"I very much doubt that."

"What about other skills? Do you sing or play music?"

"Would that amuse you? If you require amusement, I'm sure the Warden has a fool that could do cartwheels down the isles."

"No, I only want cartwheels if it's you doing them." This time,

Arix couldn't hide her grin.

"Perhaps a distraction is what you need. I have heard the whispers."

It was a gut punch for Abbas to bring it up. But he'd lowered his voice as he'd said it, the meaning clear behind the words. He was worried about her.

Her smile turned warm. "I've heard them, too. I'm alright, really. Once I get some food in me, I'll be better."

"You should eat. The rest of us have the perimeter under control for now."

Arix gave him another glance, and this time, he dipped his chin to look down at her. While there wasn't a change across his features, she could sense his gaze soften on her. Without warning, her throat squeezed as she realized just how much Ulfur and Abbas cared for her. Ulfur's comment about staying by her side till the bloody end had been true. The kind of loyalty these men had for her, that all her Black Guard had for her, made her heart crack.

She didn't need approval from any goddess. She just needed their trust.

That alone was all the inspiration she needed.

Abbas' gaze flickered for a moment, glancing up at her hair as lines of confusion crinkled on his brow.

"What?"

Even as she asked the question, there were gasps splitting the room, and more than one of the gathered crowd was pointing at her.

Then she felt it.

The undeniable rush of adrenaline, sparks flying in her belly and goosebumps raking down the back of her knees. Her fingers rose to her brow, feeling what she already knew would be there. Flowers were sprouting and tangling in the braid she wore, and tangling up from the crown of her head were branches. She could barely feel their weight, but the thick branches were sturdy under her fingers as she felt them curve up and away from her head.

"What do they look like?" she asked Abbas in a hushed whisper, the voice craggy and cracked with emotion.

"Antlers. Like the horns of a great stag rising from your head." Awe filled his voice as he said it, and the room had gone silent.

She hadn't been chosen this morning in the temple of Arduinna, but here it was, the overwhelming presence of the goddess laying like a shawl over her shoulders, comforting and true. Arduinna was the goddess of nurture, of growth, and it had never really clicked in her until right now. Kaoss might be called the mother goddess, but Arduinna was the true welcoming embrace of a mother. An embrace that Arix had not felt for a long time. She felt so safe, so wanted, so loved. The kind of unconditional love that all parents held for their children.

The tears that slid down her face felt like they were branding her, carving marks into her very soul.

The goddess had blessed her after all. Without temples and priestesses, without the pomp and ceremony of it all, the goddess had blessed her anyway, right here in the middle of Warden Aliska's banquet hall.

Arix didn't know what to say, what to do. All those eyes were staring at her, whispers growing anew, and she had no clue how to respond to it. Luckily, it was Esme who came to her rescue.

"Another blessing from the heavens!" Her clear voice rang out strong, and people turned to look at her as she rose from her seat at the table and came to stand at Arix's side. "What a glorious day that our Goddess Arduinna has chosen to appoint her favor on our king and his Black Hand. Blessed be!"

The crowd chorused the response, and Esme led Arix to her seat to the right of Orion, pulling out her chair for her and encouraging her to take her proper place.

"Smile, Arix. And for goddess sake, relax your shoulders. Drink some wine, catch your breath. And when you're done, stand and make a toast to King Orion." Esme whispered in her ear as she appeared to lean down and give a light kiss to Arix's still tear-stained cheeks.

Arix did as the High Priestess told her, taking a sip of her drink and pushing her face to form a smile. It felt wrong to be in front of so many. The feeling that filled her up was something she wanted to hide away for herself, to treasure in the solace of her privacy away from the prying eyes. It was too intimate a moment to share with all of these people.

After a moment, once Esme had retaken her seat and a few seconds had passed, Arix stood, raising her glass high. The room stilled, their own glasses raising to meet her own.

She pushed down the discomfort, pushing her voice to boom across the already silent room. "I raise a toast to our ruler, King Orion, blessed by the goddess Nereus and the goddess Arduinna. Long may he reign!"

As she said it, she looked to her left at Orion, but what she saw turned the rosy feelings in her heart to ice.

He was furious.

His smile did not reach his eyes, and his grip on the goblet he held was knuckle white. To anyone watching from the feasting tables around the room, it might look like he watched her with contented joy, but Arix knew better. Beneath the smiles and the nod of approval at her little speech was the white-hot anger of a man who felt as if he'd been upstaged. Embarrassed and humiliated in front of his court and his subjects.

Arix felt fire flare in her. And she smiled back at him.

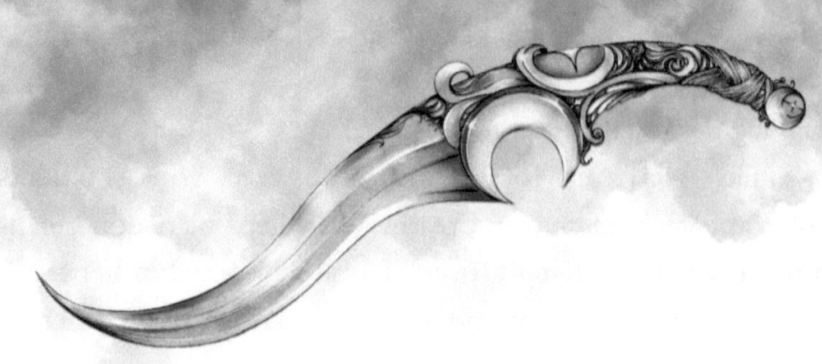

TWENTY-FIVE

When Arix awoke the next morning, the antlers were gone, the flowers that had woven into her braid nothing more than dried petals on her pillow. She stared at the ceiling of her room, aware that she should get up, begin her day, and interview the Carn rebels who sat in Warden Aliska's holding cells. She had a long list of items to deal with today, including another meeting with the council later this afternoon and an inspection with her Black Guard. Then there was the trip to plan, as it seemed Orion was more than happy to move on from Tamhain, ready to journey on to Zephyrus' temple in Zarak.

She wanted to talk to Ro, learn what he'd heard after last night, anxious to know if anyone else had picked up on the anger that had seethed at her from Orion's pores last night. He'd avoided looking at her for the rest of the evening, and Arix had chosen to do the same. Asking him how he felt or checking in on his emotional state was something she decidedly wasn't going to stoop to. If he had an issue with how Arduinna had chosen to bless her, he could take it up with the goddess herself. Arix wouldn't feel bad for how it had happened.

After all, she hadn't asked for this.

Orion had planned this trip to solidify his claim as king, and while historically, the king usually stayed in the capital and requested the priestesses come to him, he had chosen the spectacle of a three-month trip around the country. He'd go to each temple with the sole purpose of receiving his blessing. Arix had only ever gone as his Black Hand.

He didn't have a damn reason to be angry at her.

With a sigh, she pulled herself out of bed and stepped into the adjoining sitting room. Nesrin was up, standing near the door as she and Ulfur talked in low tones. As she entered the room, the two turned to glance her way. She couldn't help but notice Ulfur's eyes slide up her face to the empty space above her head where the antlers had been last night.

"Morning, you two." Arix took a seat on one of the couches strewn with a soft caribou pelt and poured herself a cup of tea from the service on the table.

"Yer horns are gone." Ulfur nodded his head in her direction before coming to stand beside the table.

"Good thing, too. They were a bitch to sleep on."

Neither Nesrin nor Ulfur laughed at the joke, and Arix felt the smile slip from her lips.

"What happened?"

Ulfur's mouth was set in a grim line. "They're gone, Arix."

Slowly, Arix set down her cup and leaned back carefully in her chair. "Alia and Kenji?"

Ulfur nodded.

For a moment the three were silent, Arix simply staring at the little bowl of sugar and carafe of milk for the tea. Nesrin shifted uncomfortably from one foot to the other, then moved to finally sit beside Ulfur on the opposite couch.

"Was it the same as last time?"

Once again, Ulfur nodded.

"Our men?"

"Ten dead, about eight others knocked clean out, not counting the Warden's people. They've got some kind of magick put on 'em."

"When?"

"Came here as soon as I found out."

Arix stood, grabbing her bag as she headed for the door. She needed to see this for herself.

~

The air reeked of magick.

Even if she hadn't been trained to recognize it when it appeared, she probably would have noticed its presence. It was like a metallic tang in the air, like an oil slick that touched everything in the vicinity.

The walls, the cells, her men, all of them stank of heavy cantwork; it almost made her sick to her stomach. This had been no ordinary magick. This had taken time and effort, and whoever had cast it didn't care that Arix knew they'd used magick.

Maeve.

It had to be.

Arix stood in the doorway of Kenji's cell, staring at the shackles that *she* had incanted, hanging limply from the stone wall. The Carn's incantor had simply waltzed in and undone the chains, and just like that, Arix had lost her prisoners. *Again.*

With a roar, she kicked the door, the heavy metal groaning as it slammed into the stone wall. She turned and hit the stone wall where the chains taunted her with a blast of acid, melting the metal and the stone together as they sludged down into a sticky mess that pooled in the corner.

"Fuck!"

The Carn's incantor had been right here, under her nose, stealing her prisoners and killing her men. And she'd been sleeping in a warm bed, dreaming of stags without their antlers.

Arix stormed back out of the room, heading back up the stairs from the depths of the keep until she was back outside again. Fury so white hot that it felt cold devoured her insides, tearing her apart. She'd lost ten good men and women, and the warden had lost more. She'd sworn to protect them, to find answers, to win, yet here she was again feeling even further from the answers than she'd been before.

But it was more than just the loss of men, the loss of her captives. She'd underestimated Maeve *again*.

The mind cants on Alia and Kenji had been shoddy work, and Arix had looked forward to ripping them apart. She'd assumed—incorrectly—that the sign of poor cantwork was the sign of a bad incantor. But a bad incantor couldn't have done *this*.

Lord Bardon, Lakai, Warden Aliska, and Aliska's looming guard were waiting for her when she stepped into the office, Ulfur and Abbas right on her heels.

Aliska's expression was pure venom.

"Thirteen of my men are dead, Bellarix Sable," she spat out. "And both of our prisoners are gone. What the hell happened here?"

"The whole place stinks of magick." Arix threw herself into a chair, slouching as she rubbed her temples. "Their incantor was here, Maeve. It's the only way they could have pulled this off."

"Our wards?" Lakai asked.

"Dispelled. They came in through the north gate, cast some sort of sleep cant on most of the guards, and killed the rest. The trap we laid was walked clean through, like they knew it was there."

Arix paused. She repeated the words again, but this time slower.

"...They knew where our traps were."

The room stilled.

Slowly she rose, eyes wide and accusing, the breath growing louder as the idea sunk in.

"This fucking bitch knew where our traps were. She knew every enchanted lock, every precaution we set into place."

"How could the Carn have known that?" Lord Bardon asked.

"Ask him." Arix sneered as she stared at Lakai.

"Me?" The old man was indignant, angry at the accusation. "You have a lot of nerve accusing me, Arix."

"Who else did you tell about what we put in place?"

"No one!"

"Who else knew about what we did?"

The room was silent as the seven glanced around. After a moment Abbas broke the silence.

"To my knowledge, Arix and Lakai set the traps and knew of the details of each cant. But anyone in the keep who was here when you put your magick into place would know which parts you incanted. The list of possibilities is long, Lady Black Hand."

Arix let out a long sigh, scrubbing her hand across her face as she sat back down. There were too many eyes on her; even if she did suspect Lakai, it was better if the others didn't know it.

"I apologize, Lakai. I don't know what's gotten into me."

"DON'T APOLOGIZE. YOUR SUSPICIONS ARE GROUNDED." The dagger at her back growled.

In response, she felt Michael's ring swell with worried caution, careful discretion to keep her suspicions towards Lakai hidden.

Even though he said nothing in return, the tension in the room dissipated a little.

"The question now is what to do." Lord Bardon offered, taking a seat across from Arix. "We've lost what little leverage we had. What is the plan now?"

Warden Aliska sat behind the desk, her fingers steepling under her chin. "King Orion wishes to leave for Zarak. The new queen is already restless to be settled back in Mergur. It seems the length of the trip has been trimmed down a bit."

Arix snorted, feeling the unapproving glare of her old teacher. "So we leave for Zarak and prepare for another attack? If anything, the Carn has proven consistent. They attacked that first day in Sieren and again on our first day here. If they hold to pattern, they'll attack Orion again when we arrive in Ramal, only with more men and more monsters. And in Eldur, it will be more of the same."

No one had anything to say to that. She knew she was right. Regardless of whether the Carn had a larger plan, they'd consistently attacked on the first day of Orion's appearance in each realm's main city, and it was foolish to think it wouldn't happen again.

"Maybe we should cut the trip short. Orion should travel back to Mergur—"

Lord Bardon cut her off, his voice hard. "The king will not run like a coward back to his castle before the tour is complete. There are still two more temples to visit before he can return to the capital. He is insistent upon completing the tour."

"Truly, it's not Ramal we should worry about," Warden Aliska cut in. "But the journey between Ramal and Vingard. Portions of the route cut into unreliable territory. The roads aren't exactly unsafe, but if the Carn plans to pull a full-scale attack, it'll be there."

"We have the Black Guard as well as the soldiers we brought from the capital. Just because the rebels have pulled off a rescue mission doesn't mean they're capable of an all-out assault against the king." Lord Bardon nodded to Arix. "They've proven that already."

"Actually…"

They all turned to look as Arix leaned her elbows against her knees and stared up at them through a grimace.

"I don't think they've had Maeve with them at all during the last two attacks." Arix glanced up at Lakai, whose mouth was set in a disapproving line. Fuck him. Keeping something like this from the rest of them was a bad idea. If they were going to come up with a plan to protect Orion, they'd need to have all the facts.

She reached into the small satchel tied at her hip and carefully placed the small red vial on the desk in front of Warden Aliska. The warden leaned forward to look at the bottle but didn't touch it.

"What is this?"

"What the Carn didn't get a chance to use in Sieren. I pulled it off of one of them, studied it, and basically,"—Arix glanced around at the others as they stared down at the stoppered glass vial—"it's bottled magick."

No one said a word, the small bit of cantwork emanating the tiniest of red glows.

"As far as I can tell, this one produces fire. And there are others."

One after the other, Arix placed the other bottles on the surface of the desk beside the first, each of the colors emanating the smallest glow of the liquid through the glass.

As she set each bottle down, she listed what they did. "Healing, speed, poison, and fire."

Lakai let out a sigh before stepping closer to the table and motioning to the potions. "It seems that the Carn does not need to have their incantor present to use such magick. They've found a way to bottle it and utilize the magick on its own, separate from the source."

Warden Aliska leaned in to look more closely at the bottles. "Is this how that man turned into a monster? Some kind of bottled magick?"

Arix nodded. "Probably."

"Can we replicate this?" Warden Aliska asked.

Lakai glanced at Arix, who shook her head.

After a moment, everyone sunk into their chairs. The small glowing vials changed the way their enemy was fighting them, putting magick into the hands of anyone. Anyone who held a grudge, anyone who wanted to take the rebels' cause into their own hands, and all they needed to do was break or drink from a bottle.

Finally the warden spoke again. "They used shields, too, didn't they?"

"They did. Not very good ones, but yes. Also most likely from a bottle."

Aliska moved her thumbs up to her temples and rubbed in slow circles. "Arix, be honest: do you think Maeve is more capable than you?"

For a moment, indignation flared in Arix's throat, but she pushed it down. It wasn't a question meant to offend. What she was asking was fair. If pitted against one another, would her own power match Maeve's? Or would it fall short against the Carn's incantor's capabilities?

"I don't know." Even as the emotion flared in her, Arix shoved it away, determined to answer honestly despite the image she'd been trying to build for herself. "I haven't had to use my magick at full strength yet. Ever since I became the Black Hand, the magick I've done has been minimal, simple stuff. The protection magick on my Black Guard, the shields I keep on Orion, the security and perimeter traps I set around the estates he stays in, it's all fairly simple. Even the attacks, all those cants were simple ones against an enemy that didn't have any *good* defense."

As she said it, a chill ran down Arix's spine. If Maeve had moved through her and Lakai's defenses so easily to free her own men, how easily could she have slipped past Arix's own traps and safeguards to kill Orion?

Either she'd tried and failed, or she hadn't tried at all. Was Orion really safe in Arix's hands?

It seemed the others were thinking the same thing, exchanging glances with one another. Immediately, the anger was back, pulsing through her as she shame burned her throat white hot.

"I can protect the king," Arix ground out, hackles rising at the implication that she couldn't do her job.

Aliska shot her a look. "No one doubts your loyalty, Arix. but we need to be realistic about what their incantor is capable of. She's shown today to be skilled. But we need to know how her skill will compare to yours in an all-out match. And we need to know if she has eyes within the king's confidants. After what happened today, it would be foolhardy to underestimate her or the Carn. We must be careful. Very careful."

Arix let out her breath slowly, trying to reign in the frustration that boiled at the base of her spine. The ache in her chest was quickly returning and setting her nerves on end. She was wasting her time here, talking with them. There were too many variables they wouldn't be able to account for. And the question of her own capabilities only reminded her of her own limitations. What was she truly capable of? She still didn't know.

Arix stood abruptly, heading for the door before she paused, turning back to the others. "Whatever you decide, I will do my duty. I will protect the king."

Slamming the door, she turned on her heel and left the warden's barracks. She was done reacting to these rebels. It was time to go on the attack.

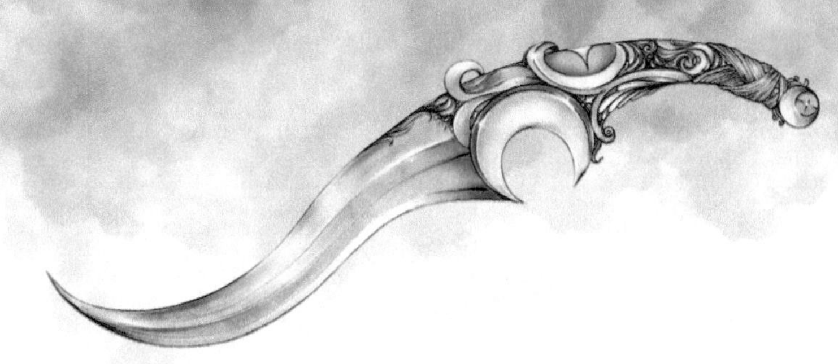

TWENTY-SIX

Before the week was over, their traveling party had moved on again, leaving Rohleach behind and heading south into Zarak. The mountains on their left remained constant, the peaks rising distant in the waves of heat that turned the horizon wavy. Summer had settled in around them with finality, and as they moved further into the desert, the midday heat bore down on them without mercy. The nights were a completely different story. Colder than the nights in Tamhain, the desert dipped down into freezing levels that made Arix's teeth chatter at night.

Arix was able to assist their travel with her magick; she kept up a breeze that cooled them throughout the hottest parts of the day and fires that blazed extra warm through the night. The road had been easier to traverse from Nero into Tamhain, with packed dirt roads so solid and flat they felt like stone. The roads in Zarak were rockier, twisting between mountains and sloped hills as their caravan moved slowly toward their destination.

While plenty of their party grumbled, Arix loved the change in terrain. She disliked the flatness of Northern Nero and Eastern Tamhain and preferred the mountains and scraggly bushes of vegetation that dotted the rocks. And while she may have disliked the pounding heat of day, the cold night sky was brilliantly aflame with summer constellations. Ever since she'd been a child, she'd always been fascinated by Zarak's animal life. Giant lizards stayed far from their traveling party during the day, but at night, the sandmice snuck close to catch a glimpse of the newcomers, their black eyes shining in the firelight.

There were cants to talk to animals, to coax them close enough to trap or eat, but Arix left them alone. She didn't need to convince them she was safe and let their instincts guide their behavior instead.

The stars felt more real here in Zarak, brilliant pinpricks of light woven into a river of starlight that swung from one tip of the horizon across the sky to the other. Even when they'd traveled through Tamhain, the stars had been different, the sky a silken blue. In the desert, it was the color of black oil, spilling over them like a tipped lamp dotted with glittering jewels.

Orion no longer tried to seek her out on their travels, and Arix was surprised to find herself content with this distance that had grown between them. She missed him, yes, but she realized that while it had been good to slide into Orion's bed in those first weeks upon becoming the Black Hand, she'd craved the companionship most of all. And, to be honest with herself, she'd found that companionship again but with Ro and Nesrin, and even with her Black Guard. There were days when she caught Orion watching her, but she stayed to her own bonfire. Time would tell what they would become.

Throughout the journey, Arix noticed that Warden Aliska's looming guard spent more and more time away from her mistress, choosing to bed down with the Black Guard instead of staying near Tamhain's dignitary's tents. She was quiet, often listening to others talk and remaining quiet herself.

When she reached out into this mystery woman's mind, she

found only a flat stormy sea.

Very few were guarded against mind-delving cants, and those who were usually set up mental walls to protect themselves. This woman was different.

Strangely, it didn't raise Arix's hackles. She could sense a strange aura around the woman. Not quite something she would see on Lakai or another incantor, but there was *something,* even if she didn't know what.

One night, after a particularly hot day on the road, Arix found the woman sitting next to her as she joined her Guard for dinner around the fire.

"Lady Black Hand. I would speak with you if you are amenable." The woman's voice was deep, each word even and planned as though she'd rehearsed them again and again in her mind.

"Please do." Arix leaned back against Osiris' saddle, which was propped into the ground as a backrest. "I've been meaning to talk to you as well."

"I have sought my mistress's permission to join your Black Guard, and with your approval, I would join you in your duty to our king."

Arix let the words sit as she slowly stirred the bowl of stew in her hands, tucking her fingers against the metal bowl's lip. "Is that so?"

"It is."

The woman sat perfectly still as she stared at Arix, her own bowl sitting on the ground at her side, untouched.

"I don't even know your name."

"Kloevendirr, Lady Black Hand. Semmer Kloevendirr."

"Well, Semmer, why do you want to join the Black Guard?"

Semmer's spine straightened, prepared to give another rehearsed answer. "I am a skilled fighter. I seek to serve. I have spent over a decade under the service of Warden—"

Arix set her bowl down, leveling a hard look at the woman in front of her. "Semmer. If you are so skilled, why is Warden Aliska willing to give you up?"

"She has released me from my bond to her."

"Your bond?"

"Yes."

Arix waited for Semmer to elaborate, but she didn't. "This would be the time to explain, Kloevendirr."

"I…" For a moment, Semmer faltered, her eyes dipping to the sand before snapping back up to look at Arix. "That is something I keep between myself and the Warden."

Letting out a slightly exasperated sigh, Arix shifted, angling her body away from the rest of those around them. "Why do you want to join the Black Guard?"

Again, the look of a confident practiced answer as Semmer opened her mouth. Arix raised a hand, stopping her before she could begin.

"I want the real reason. You could join the Warden's military ranks or even the King's Guard. But you want to join the Black Guard. And more than that, Warden Aliska has given her *permission* for you to join me. Why?"

Semmer did her best to hide her nervous swallow. "I have certain…talents that I believe can assist you with the fight against the Carn."

Arix kept her gaze level. "What talents?"

She felt out with her magick, peering at Semmer Kloevendirr with a deeper insight. Again, she found the stormy sea, the sense of vast waves of mental barriers that separated them.

"You are trying to read me," Semmer murmured, leaning in, her eyes wide. "Right now. And I felt you try before, too."

"And?"

"And what do you sense in me?" Semmer pushed, almost excited at the idea that Arix was trying to read into her mind.

"Nothing," Arix admitted, picking up her waterskin, uncapping and recapping the seal. "I've never met anyone who warded themselves like that."

For a moment, the two women stared at one another, each trying to discern something of the other. Finally, Semmer yielded.

"I…am willing to lower my shields. If you will allow me to join you."

A small smile threatened to spread across Arix's lips, but she held it back. "I set the terms of my men and whether they join the Black Guard or not, not you."

Semmer nodded. "Of course."

"And instead of lowering your guards, I want you to tell me what you are."

The woman across from her stilled, Semmer's eyes flashing against the firelight. Her words were even as she asked, "What do you mean?"

"You know what I mean." Arix held her gaze.

There was something different about Semmer, something magickal that wasn't magick. Something else that Arix was unfamiliar with. The cores around her neck, on her finger, and at her back held their own kind of magick, and this woman was no different. She was tapped into it somehow. Tapped into the grains of the universe, tapped into the energy that flowed and spread and morphed around them.

"You are not an incantor," Arix said.

Semmer was still. "No."

"But you are *something*," Arix pressed.

After a moment, the woman dipped her chin in assent.

"Tell me," Arix breathed, finding herself leaning in and closing the distance between them.

"I do not… I cannot mold magick the way you can." She shifted, eyes glancing around to make sure no one was listening before looking back to Arix. "At least, not here."

It took all of Arix's energy not to demand for Semmer to continue. But she waited, letting the woman work out her words.

"I am what my people call a Stormsinger."

Arix racked her brain for the memory of the title but couldn't remember ever hearing the name.

"I come from a very small island on the other side of the world. It was washed away a long time ago, but I made my way to Rökkur as a child. To Warden Aliska's service. She discovered what I could do, so she kept me close. Had me trained. I have protected her ever since."

"A Stormsinger," Arix repeated the name.

"Yes."

"What makes your magick different from mine?"

"Your magick is delivered from the Goddess Kaoss. It flows in your blood, combines the elements that make up the world. Water, earth, air, fire, and spirit. My magick is not based in these elements; it is connected to the aether."

Semmer watched Arix for some recognition, but when Arix only knit her eyebrows together in response, the Stormsinger inched closer, trying to explain further.

"We draw our energy not from the air or the sky but from the storm. The divine energy that surrounds us, encases our world and keeps the stars at bay. We tap into the storm's energy, the force of the rain, the constant of the wind, the weight of thunder, the speed of lightning."

Arix found she had been leaning further in until the two women were huddled close, the Stormsinger's secrets quietly filling her with a sense of wonder.

"Your magick," Arix said, keeping her voice low. "You said you can't do it here? In Rökkur?"

Semmer shook her head. "I do not know if it's the polarization of the planet or the difference in hemispheres, but my singing is weak here. My heartbeat cannot find the rhythm of the storms. All I receive are inclinations, feelings of the storms as they form and shift. It is useful for predicting the weather and perhaps shifting a storm that is in progress, but little more than that."

A grin spread across Arix's face as she moved to cup her palms between them. If she had done this for anyone else, she could have merely simulated a storm with an illusion cant. But Arix had a feeling that if she tapped into an actual storm, she'd learn a lot more about the Stormsinger's abilities.

As the miniature galeforce started between her fingers, Semmer's eyes widened, and she stooped down to better see the storm.

"I can feel it!"

Arix waited, watching as Semmer adjusted her posture, then slowly began drumming a fist against her chest. With the beat, she added a guttural song, throaty and deep to match the pace of each pound. Arix watched as the storm she had formed in her hand began to take on a new shape, the curling wind that crushed against her fingers changed direction, tiny pinpricks of rain forming against her palms.

As the cool air ran across the soft skin at her wrists, goosebumps raced up Arix's arm.

She watched the Stormsinger focusing on the miniature storm, her steady singing and drum beat setting a pace that the tempest listened to. And with it, Arix could feel her own blood rushing in rhythm to the song.

Then it was over.

As quickly as it had started, Semmer stopped drumming, and Arix let the storm die in her hands. Once again, they were back around the fire, surrounded by the casual conversation and general camaraderie of a regular evening. Semmer glanced up, a look of surprise on her face.

Arix immediately understood the feeling.

For a moment, she and the Stormsinger had stepped into a world all their own, the magick shared between them sparking something beautiful. Whether it was the cantwork, the song, or the beat that Arix still felt drumming through her veins in a slow fade, it had made them forget that they were surrounded by people. The little storm had made them feel in a world all their own.

"Join me," Arix said, eyes trained on Semmer's.

The woman smiled. "It would be my honor to join the Black Guard—"

"No." Arix shook her head, leaning in closer until her forehead almost rested against the Stormsinger's. "Join my inner circle. Join my Fingers."

Semmer blinked.

"I want you close, Semmer Kloevendirr. I want you close for whatever might come next. If Aliska will release you to me, if you'll sign my contract, if you will join us, then I want you."

Semmer blinked again, and Arix was surprised to realize the woman was blinking away tears.

"It would be my greatest honor."

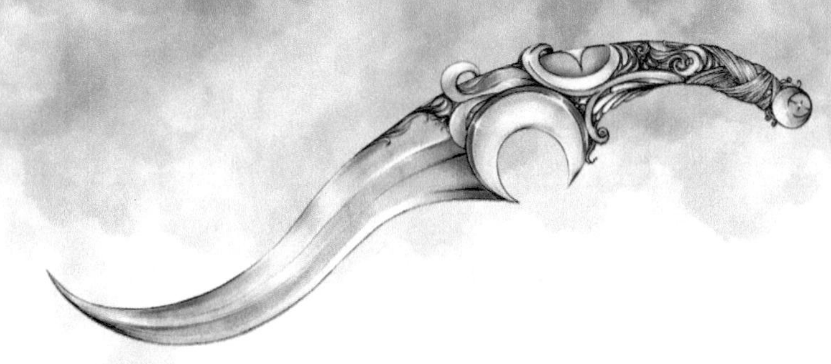

TWENTY-SEVEN

Arix was almost disappointed when they neared Ramal, the last red of sunset disappearing as they neared the city. The shield cants were doubled this time, and the protective coating she'd canted onto her men's armor had been triple-checked in case the Carn decided to attack again. Not only were her protective cants in place, but Arix had prepped a few others as well. She wasn't going to let them get the drop on her again. This time, she'd capture more of them, have more of a bargaining chip. She'd be ready and she'd hit them back just as hard.

Entering in the dusky space between day and night might have been an issue if they'd been stepping into any other city, but Ramal thrived in the nighttime, and the city spilled light from it like its own golden sun. At every corner, streetlamps shone brightly, painted glass reflecting colored light across the street like scattered jewels. The streets were tighter than in Rohleach, so the party had to weave and turn as they made their way to the center. The whole city smelled of pepper and ground coriander and licorice. And much like Sieren and Rohleach before it, the city cheered as Orion and Delphine rode past.

They'd changed their clothes before entering the city, matching the flowing shawls and heavy veils that were popular in Zarak. Orion was dressed in gold again; the curtain of fabric draped around his neck was stitched with gold, and he smiled and waved as the crowd cheered for him. He was their sun king, and he had dressed the part.

Delphine complimented him in a rich red-orange detailed sari that was the color of saffron, her hair braided around her head in a crown. They paired so well like this, smiling and waving, leaning into each other to whisper and laugh at little jokes. It was all for show, though.

"They play their parts so very well. They deserve each other," the voice from her pendant noted.

Arix stayed only a step behind them, riding in her black armor, the darkest night only a step behind the sun king and his sunset bride. She'd seen the way they'd begun to talk to each other, or perhaps, how they didn't talk to each other. Delphine didn't like the travel, was afraid of the rebels, and wanted to cut the trip short. Arix actually agreed with her, but after voicing her concerns in Rohleach to Warden Aliska and Lord Bardon, she remained quiet on the subject. She was here to guard. She was here to protect.

And the more they traveled, the more she saw how weary Orion became as well. He always had a crease between his brow, thinking or talking in hushed tones. After the rebels had attacked them in Rohleach and killed their men, they'd set off for Ramal almost immediately, giving Arix and Orion no chance to talk again.

The anger she'd felt the night she'd been blessed had faded in the bright light of day, realizing that the rift that had come between herself and Orion had started long before the goddess had given her antlers. It was more complicated than that, more intricate. Since his marriage to Delphine, a lot had changed between them.

And Arix couldn't decide if it was a good thing or not. This was all still so new, still so fresh, both her position as Black Hand, as well as Orion's new role as king. In the early days, they'd had chances to slip away, to walk the gardens at night, to talk in the library. But on the road, the eyes that watched them had tripled, and the intimacy of even a few words felt strained.

There was one thing that Arix was sure of, as her eyes trained across the faces of the gathered people, cheering and singing, she was tense. The muscles in her neck, her insides drawn taut like a bowstring; she was restless. Lakai had encouraged her to drink more of the Well Water to help balance out her nerves, and though she took it, she hated her reliance upon it. She didn't like the idea of being so dependent on bottled liquid she knew next to nothing about.

It might be easy to say that it was the stress that had her wound so tight, but she knew that the anxieties of their travels and the looming threat of the Carn were only part of her frustrations. She missed Orion. Or maybe she missed the companionship they'd shared, the raw and jagged space in her heart that he had stepped into so easily after Michael had died.

Maybe she just missed having someone in her bed. Just like her senses had sharpened, so had her appetites, both for food and for life.

She could taste every ingredient in the food she ate, could taste the individual minerals that made up her water, knew what wood barrels had been used for aging her wine. She could sense the differences, taste the detail. She slept deeper, burned angrier, and yearned for the hot touch of another person between her sheets.

She had plenty to choose from—Ro and Nesrin had both apparently fielded offers from more than one of their traveling party. Ro had even invited her to a few of his own private events, but Arix had so far refused. It felt strange to slip into someone else's bed when she and Orion had left so much unsaid since the last time they'd really had a chance to talk. But what could she say? She didn't want to encourage any kind of ill will between herself and Delphine. She didn't want to be the reason that Delphine and Orion fought.

Though, as Arix watched them, they both played parts so brilliantly well, smiling and waving when just a few miles outside the city they had been icy cold towards each other, that perhaps Delphine would welcome any distractions Orion might chase. It was hard to know. The girl was unreadable. As of yet, Arix hadn't tried to probe further, giving the queen the privacy of her own thoughts.

As they turned another corner and the road straightened out, Arix startled at the walls that marked Warden Los Ke's estate. There'd been no Carn attack this time. Her gaze moved across the faces of the crowd, looking for any signal of discontent or gathered suspicious figures. There were none. Either they were biding their time, or there would be no attack today.

Her spine stayed rigid, overly aware of the faces that moved around them until the entire traveling party was safe behind the estate's wall. The lack of attack made her tense, putting her nerves on edge in a way they hadn't been since the competition.

"No attack?" Ulfur muttered beside her as they stood near their horses in the courtyard of the Warden's home.

The rest of the members had mostly slipped away to their rooms to bathe the sand from their skin and turn in for the night, but Arix's blood still rushed in her ears, adrenaline from the potential attack thrumming through her.

"Appears not," she replied. "But I wouldn't count on it being a quiet night. I know the Guard wants rest tonight, but have them patrol in shifts. I'm not convinced the Carn haven't got something planned."

Ulfur nodded before moving off, and Arix let out a sigh. She should sleep. Or patrol with her men. The lack of a fight had left her nervous, and her senses felt aggravated. Every movement caught her eye, and she felt like a hound on a hunt, looking everywhere for a bushy-tailed fox.

When she'd been in Ramal before, after she and Michael had saved Pyesak from explosion, they'd stayed with Warden Los Ke's family here for a few days before returning to the capital. She hadn't had a chance to see the sights then, and she was itching to now.

"You just want to explore." Her core grumbled contentedly against her sternum.

"No," Arix muttered back. "I want to *investigate*. There's a difference. If the Carn are planning something in town, maybe a little skulking around will reveal it."

In truth, she was curious about more than just the city itself. She had a faint recollection from her childhood, when she'd been to the underground night markets long ago, but the memory swirled with color and lights and no discerning detail. In Nero and Tamhain she'd spent next to no time in the cities. She wanted to feel the thrum of people around her, listening in on their conversations and enjoying the simple pleasures of a market.

Her armor remained behind, and she pulled a hood over her white hair in the hopes that it might disguise her from recognition. A little extra magick and she would slip through the crowds unnoticed.

The first thing to hit her was the smell.

Spiced hot drinks on every corner, carts selling paper cones of clove and cinnamon candied walnuts, stands with skewers of meat dripping with fat and paprika, stalls that held baskets of spices that mixed in the air and danced like the stars in the sky. Lamps that lit the street were all different, hand-carved, with the blown glass colored with whorls of patterns and pictures. Metal-plated signs and banners that hung above shops and tiny metal price plates besides their wares, all reflected the light from the lamps; crystals that decorated shop walls and pop-up tent stalls sent rainbows of spiraling lights across the city.

Arix was sure that if she stood at one end of the market and shone a light straight through the twisting streets of stalls, it would bounce and reflect and come clean out the other side.

She ordered a spiced mead, dark and red, and drank it down with a wooden bowl of saffron orange rice mixed with dried berries and cuts of the softest lamb she'd ever tasted, the flavors singing across her lips. She strolled between stalls that sold hammered metal plates and bowls and the tiniest handle-less teacups, then waited in line to peruse the glass-blower shop as he demonstrated his technique.

Yet even among all the colors and lights and flavors, Arix kept an ear open, listening to snippets of conversation as she passed.

"I wonder if the queen's sari was made by Ori Gan Mendi's shop near the square. I'd recognize that detailed stitching any-where."

"Serves them right, attacking the king like that. Burn 'em like they burned us, I say."

"I haven't heard from my sister in over two months. She was part of the clan that's disappeared in the desert."

"I heard the Black Hand fought three hulking bears in Tamhain when they arrived. She cut them down without a word spoken."

"There's trouble coming, I tell you. With new kings always comes trouble."

"Hush now, hush! They say she can hear like an owl trailing a mouse in the darkest woods."

"I thought she'd be taller."

"Da says he saw her once. Back when she was just normal like the rest of us. Saw her in a tavern near the west road all bundled up and eating like she hadn't seen a meal in weeks. Her hair was red back then, but Da swears it was her."

"I don't like it. King Taurus dying the way he did, and now this marriage alliance with Sieren. The three of them waltzing into the city, all smiles and song like they haven't a care in the world. There's something going on, I tell you. Something dark is coming."

"Great horns, he said! Like an elk!"

Each time Arix caught a conversation, she hovered, waiting to see where the stories would lead. The ones about her were always exaggerated, and while most of the talk was bubbly and joyful, some were worried, upset, and angry over Orion's arrival and what it meant for their country. She'd hoped to get more information on the Carn, but they were rarely mentioned, and when they were, it was done in hushed whispers like you might tell a ghost story.

After two hours, Arix headed back to the Warden's estate. She'd seen only a small part of the city, but the adrenaline that had raged through her at the start of the night had faded with good food and drink and left exhaustion in its wake. She remembered the underground baths she had visited the last time she'd been in Ramal, and suddenly, her skin itched to sink into the steaming pools.

The hallway that led down underneath the house cooled with every step, and she took the rock stairs slowly in the dim lamplight. She'd expected maybe a few others soaking themselves before bed, but her bare feet were the only sounds as she padded down the stone tunnel and turned into the first room. Stripping down, Arix left her things folded on the wooden bench before moving through the adjoining doorway into the next room. A trough of running water dissected the room, with small cups sitting beside it. The water she poured over herself sloughed across her feet, rolling down the slight slope in the floor and disappearing through a slit underneath the stone trough. After she'd worked most of the dust and sweat from her skin and wrung out her hair, she moved into the next room, steam clouding around the four pools set in tiers into the floor.

Arix groaned as she let herself sink down to the underwater bench in the pool, relaxing her head back against the rim as the hot water curled around her. She was alone, the only sound the echo of lapping water as it bounced off the stone walls. Small lamps had been placed around the room, and the light flickered across the surface of the water, casting wavy shadows that rippled on the ceiling above her.

She'd been here, what? Only six months ago? It felt like it had been years.

Somewhere, incense was burning, and the smoke wove in with the steam of the baths, filling the air with a spicy aroma of sandalwood and amber. The heady scent, in combination with the hot water, pushed away the adrenaline, leaving behind only exhaustion. She'd been prepared for a fight when they'd entered Ramal, and now she found herself slipping out of consciousness against the warm water.

It wasn't until the water rippled, and the echoing sound of another body slipping into the pool, that she cracked an eye open, realizing she had indeed fallen asleep. Esme's dark form slipped into the water across from her, her arms outstretched against the sides of the pool as she lounged in the water, her legs shifting in slow lazy kicks.

Even with the steam from the room and the heat of the water, Arix felt goosebumps shoot down her arms and across the tops of her thighs. Esme watched her, heat searing into the look as her gaze trailed down Arix's neck and collarbones and down her shoulder.

For long moments, the two stared at each other, the tension and heat rising around them. Arix wondered if she should say something, cut through the silence and relieve some of the tension between herself and the High Priestess. But she couldn't think of anything to say.

Perhaps she didn't want to say anything to dim the spark between them, heightening with every passing second.

"She is inviting you in. You should accept."

And so Arix did.

She slowly stood, raising the upper part of her body out of the water and relishing the feeling of each droplet of water as it trickled down her and across her skin. Her body responded to the movement, nipples pebbling in the steaming air as she slowly walked across the pool toward Esme. She was giving the other woman a chance to move away, a chance to say no or put space between them, anything that would have given Arix a sign that she wasn't interested.

Esme just held her gaze, her eyes sparkling gold in the low light, tipping her chin up to hold Arix's stare as she moved closer. Slowly Arix, straddled the other woman, settling down in her lap as she looped her arms around Esme's neck, their breasts pressing together in the steaming water.

Their lips hovered over each other without touching, the tickling of Esme's breath dancing across Arix's. Their lips parted delicately and then came together in a gentle sighing kiss as Esme wrapped her arms around Arix, her pointed nails gently dragging down her spine. Heat pulsed between them as Arix tangled her own fingers in Esme's hair, guiding her head back to rest against the edge of the stone pool. She moved down from Esme's lips, whispering delicate kisses along her jaw, nipping at the priestess' earlobe as she traveled down her neck, gently sucking and biting at the soft flesh. Esme let out a low moan, her grip becoming tighter as she pulled Arix's hips down further into her lap.

Arix kept her kisses feather light as she teased her way across Esme's collarbone, tasting the lightly salty sweat of her skin mixing with the heady, incensed air. All the tension she had felt the last couple of weeks was amping up into a fever pitch as she ground further into the woman beneath her. One hand left the back of Esme's head and moved to trail fingers down Esme's chest. She let out another moan and arced into touch, nails biting into the skin at Arix's hip.

Arix teased a few moments more, relishing the way that Esme squirmed beneath her touch, all too aware of the heat that screamed through her. Esme's own mouth moved, unable to sit still, latching to Arix's throat and dancing trembling, desperate kisses across the skin. Her fingers moved across Arix's hip and slipped between them, sliding and dancing and building up a fire that roared through them. A low growl rumbled from Arix's chest, biting down on Esme's shoulder as the two collided against each other.

All the stress and anxiety were melting away, replaced with a persistent new tension that rose with every sweep of Esme's deft fingertips. Even the subtle hint of her nails scraping across Arix's skin made her shiver, the pressure building in her stomach as they pressed into each other. Desperation was winning out over Arix's intention of slow, patient teasing, and she found Esme's entrance with her own fingers, thrusting into the other woman with building force until they were both panting against each other.

Their mouths clashed together, nipping and biting until their lips were swollen, and soon Esme was stiffening in Arix's arms, her echoing cry hitting the stone walls and resonating back to them. The sound alone might have made Arix finish on her own, but Esme's fingers didn't stop working, and Arix quickly followed her ecstasy with a hard bite and a growl into the woman's shoulder.

The two lay collapsed against each other in the swirling water, hands stilling and shifting as Esme moved her fingers to Arix's exposed back, scratching and rubbing in long strokes down her spine. The skin contact felt so good, and for a moment, Arix thought she might fall back asleep again while being held like this. It was strange how through it all, neither had spoken a word, only groans of pleasure filling the air between them as they chased each other's pleasure.

When Esme rose to leave, she took Arix's hand in her own and led her back to her own rooms. And for the first time in weeks, Arix didn't sleep alone.

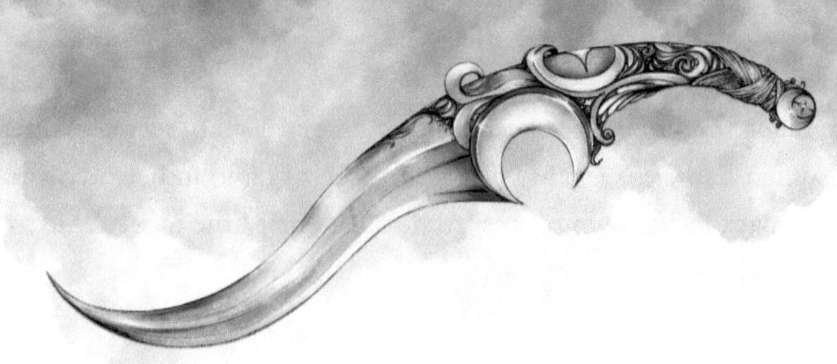

TWENTY-EIGHT

When Arix awoke, Esme was curled up beside her, fingers tracing gentle circles across her ribs. Neither said a word, the new light of day filtering through the intricate glass panels of the window. Patterns and swirls were etched into the frosted glass, making it impossible to see out but allowing the beautiful morning gold glow to spill across the bed.

She'd slept well with Esme curled up at her side, but now that she was awake and the haze of last night was slipping away, Arix felt a twinge of guilt slide down her spine. The tension between herself and Orion was reaching a point that she could not turn back from, and she needed to mend the space between them before it grew too vast. Even if they weren't lovers, they were friends, weren't they?

If nothing else, she was his Black Hand. And that was a strange bound loyalty she wouldn't betray.

But even as she thought it, her glance drifted back to Esme's hand on her chest, fingers tracing the black lines that spread from her heart. The veins had grown, clustered now as a black ink blot that speared up from her sternum and traced across her breasts and up her collarbone. It was getting harder to hide the lines with her clothing, though the armor still covered most of it.

The headaches were coming back as well, and more than once, she had succumbed to taking Lakai's potion on the road to Ramal. As much as she hated the idea of drinking something she knew nothing about, she hadn't had the time to research it more in Tamhain, and an open road beside a campfire didn't seem like the right place either. Her thoughts shifted to the library back home—not the first time she'd done so on the road. There had to be research, information that past Black Hands had gathered. Now that they were settled in Ramal, perhaps now would be a good time to discover just what the little vials contained.

"You have such a serious face right now, lover." Esme's voice was gravely with sleep, and she shifted in Arix's arms to look up at her. "What worries you?"

For a moment, Arix considered telling her. About the headaches and the dizziness and the vials of Well Water that Lakai had given her. But Esme's specialty was spiritual rather than magickal, and sharing something like that didn't sit right. She'd known Esme for a short time, and one night in the woman's bed didn't make them confidants.

"Are you worried about the blessing?" Esme offered, guessing at Arix's silence.

"A little," Arix said, finding the truth in the words.

"You've been blessed by both Nereus and Arduinna. That is a tremendous gift. To expect the same from Zephyrus may be too bold."

"What, you don't think he likes me?" Arix grinned, sliding down the pillows and turning to her side so she could see Esme's face better. "What did I ever do to him?"

Arix had meant it as a joke, but a small line creased between Esme's eyebrows, and she took a moment before she responded.

"Zephyrus is different from the rest. He is unpredictable. Spiteful at times. He may refuse a blessing to you simply to spite his sisters."

If Esme had said this months ago, back before the first blessing, Arix might have scoffed. Might have laughed at the sincerity with which Esme said the words, like the god was real and had emotions that impacted his decisions. But after receiving the blessing from Nereus in Sieren and Arduinna in Rohleach, she was more willing to believe that the gods and goddesses kept a closer eye on humanity than she'd previously thought.

"A seer told me it would happen. In Coraven, I talked to a seer who said Arduinna's blessing would happen." As Arix spoke, Esme's eyes widened slightly. "I didn't really believe her, and then at the temple in the cave, when Orion was blessed and I wasn't, I thought that was the end of it. I never asked for this. I don't really know what the blessings mean."

Esme sat up, drawing the cool orange-toned sheets around herself as if suddenly cold in the morning's warmth. Her brow furrowed as she stared at Arix, her finger rubbing absently against the edge of the fabric.

"What else did the seer say?"

"I don't really remember. She talked about Arduinna standing behind me, and Osiris. She said something about how the 'goddess of suffering knows me.' She said not all of Kaoss' children agree. I sort of guessed that meant that I might not receive blessings from all of them."

Esme was nodding, her gaze trained hard on Arix's face. "What else, Arix? What else did she say?"

"Something about being drenched in blood. That they had to choose between me and the messenger drenched in blood."

Esme's face paled.

"Did she say anything else? The seer?"

Even with the golden morning warmth seeping into the room, Arix felt cold. Esme was serious, worried. Maybe she should have told the priestess sooner about all of this.

"She said other things, but I don't remember. It was weird. It happened over a month ago when we were in Coraven for the wedding."

"Which temple?"

"The one at the split of the river, the Helene River."

"Which seer was it? Lulienne?"

Arix pulled herself up in a sitting position to match Esme's posture. "I don't know. She didn't say her name. She didn't look like a seer—she was young. We were talking, and all of a sudden, her voice changed, and her eyes glazed over. I don't know, Esme, I'd never seen anything like that before."

The high priestess stood, sliding out of bed and striding across the room to dress.

"Esme. what's going on?"

"I need to go."

"Go where?" Arix sat in the center of the bed, sheets draped across her lap as she watched Esme pull on clothing and drape a veil around her head. "What's going on?"

Esme finally stopped, glancing towards the bed from the far side of the room. She looked worried and for a moment, maybe scared. Then, suddenly, the lines smoothed out across her brow, and she offered Arix a practiced smile. The smile of a woman who knew how to manipulate people, knew how to display the right kind of charm that made hearts melt and made you want to trust her.

"Don't worry, lover." She swept across the room, the thin fabric of her dress billowing behind her as she gracefully sat at the end of the bed and reached a delicate hand towards Arix. "I need to commune with the gods. You've been blessed, and you've heard directly from the most high. I'm going to the temple to pray, to worship. Take your time here, eat breakfast, and I will see you later."

When Arix finally took her hand, Esme placed a kiss to the palm, letting her fingers trail gently across Arix's wrist with the seductive kind of touch that said their night could pick up where it left off later.

Arix knew it was bullshit.

She was spooked by something, and she was running away to confirm whatever theory she might have had about the seer's words.

But Arix was as adept as Esme when it came to masks. When it came to hiding yourself in plain sight.

With a sweet smile, Arix rose up on her knees and leaned forward to capture the High priestess' chin and kiss her. "Of course. Go, I'll see you later."

But when Esme was gone, Arix grabbed her things and left. She didn't want to sit and have breakfast when she needed answers. Orion's blessing was happening this evening, and she needed a plan before then.

~

Arix was running out of time.

There was a private library connected to the temple, but Arix didn't go with the possibility of running into Esme. Instead, she double checked her wards and cants, and she patrolled with her men. She'd hoped the tasks would help her brain focus or maybe let her forget about her conversation this morning with the high priestess. But instead, she only grew agitated and snapped at more than one of her Black Guard. It was only after Ulfur snapped back and told her to leave them in peace that she went back to her room and paced instead.

She poured through Revena's journal and then again through her own notes before slumping to the floor with frustration

"Calm down," the voice of her core over her heart sounded annoyed. *"You'll make yourself sick."*

"I'm trying to remember exactly what the seer said."

Arix pulled off the necklace and laid it on the bed, placing the ring and the dagger beside them. Michael's ring was offering her waves of peaceful serenity to calm her down, but it wasn't really working. Arix turned her focus to the dagger instead, the core that saw the miniscule details.

"THINK, INCANTOR. WHAT DID THE GIRL SAY?" The dagger's voice was also twinged with annoyance.

"She said a lot of things."

"THINK."

The words from a few weeks ago swirled in her mind. "She said that Arduinna would bless me. That she backed me the way Nereus had backed me. They were splitting up, the gods and goddesses; they were split between me and…"

"AND?"

"And the messenger drenched in blood."

"AND?"

"And she asked if I stood in harmony or discord. Like there were sides, and I needed to choose."

"YES, YES, YOU SAID THIS ALL ALREADY TO THE PRIESTESS. GO BACK."

"Back?" Arix pressed the fabric of the bedspread between her fingers, rubbing it back and forth like it somehow might have the answer she was looking for. "She said the goddess of suffering knew me—"

"NO! YOU HAVE MISSED IT. MISSED THE DETAIL, MISSED THE SLIP. THE PRIESTESS TOLD YOU WHAT SHE WAS TOLD TO TELL. BUT SHE SHARED TOO MUCH. LET TRUTH SLIP INTO THE RIDDLE. TOLD YOU A DETAIL THAT YOU HAVE ALREADY FORGOTTEN."

Arix racked her brain, thinking back to what the girl had said, desperate to remember. "I don't… I don't know what detail you're talking about."

"THINK, BELLARIX SABLE, THINK UPON THE THING YOU HAVE FORGOTTEN. WHEN YOU REMEMBER IT, YOU WILL KNOW."

Arix felt the core's consciousness slip back, further away from her. And like a dream you try to chase, the harder you run, the further it pulls itself from you. Why couldn't cores be a little more *helpful?*

Now, the sun was setting, and the trek to the temple was about to start, but she was nowhere closer to an answer than she'd hoped. So she did what any good leader might do.

Delegate.

"…specifically the term 'messenger drenched in blood' and any information about the blessings. I want to know what they're for. Not just the kings—I want to know what the original purpose was. Who was the first king to be blessed, things like that."

Ro lounged on the couch in front of her, nodding as Nesrin helped fit Arix into her armor. When Arix had asked for his help, he'd volunteered without question.

"After the blessing, there'll be another feast, so you should be free to do whatever snooping you want."

One of the straps on her side jingled as Nesrin fought with the buckle, then stepped aside as Ro stood and moved to help secure the clasp.

"Don't worry about a thing, Arix. I'll get you the answers you need." He stepped back to admire his work, but the gaze turned soft as his eyes connected with Arix's. "Are you going to be ok?"

"I'll be fine."

"Arix."

She moved away from the two, securing the sword at her back and the pouch at her side. With a light touch, she checked that Celeste's dagger was still at the small of her back. "Really, I'll be ok. It's not like I haven't done this already twice before."

Ro and Nesrin exchanged a small glance.

"Of course," Nesrin started slowly, amping up to what she really wanted to say. "But you also mentioned that there might not be a blessing this time. A lot of eyes will be on you. Can you handle that? They'll be whispering, trying to find an excuse. They'll assume you've lost favor."

Arix clasped a hand on each of her friend's shoulders and grinned. "Fuck them. It'll be fine."

The corridor outside was lined with her Black Guard, and they followed silently as she headed down the hallway towards the door. Having Ulfur and Abbas at her back was comforting. Especially now.

The procession towards the temple was more subdued, the sky above the lit streets a pitch black contrast against all the glowing orange lights. Arix kept her eyes peeled, watching the crowd that lined the streets. When no attack from the Carn had marked their entrance into Ramal, Arix had been unnerved. Her anxiety had only grown as she waited on pins and needles for what felt like an inevitable attack.

Watching the faces along the road, Arix felt like she was doing them a disservice, eyes seeking out trouble amongst a throng of people who danced and sang for their new king. Parents with young children on their shoulders, keeping them up late to see the procession, young maidens throwing flowers at the sun king as he passed, all of them joyous and celebratory. And yet she saw past it, glanced over it all with a roving eye looking for trouble, for anger, anything that might give a sign to another attack.

But there was none.

It was the billowing fabric that caught Arix's eye, and she looked up, realizing they had arrived at the temple. The temple to Zephyrus was open to the air, with only columns to hold up the roof rather than walls. Between the columns, swathes of sheer fabric were the only walls separating the outside from the in, and every time a gust of wind blew from out of the desert, the curtains would shift and billow. A constant reminder to the god of air for which the temple was built.

The atmosphere was tangy with citrus and spicy with the incense that burned from metal lanterns. They stepped beneath the parted curtain, and Arix felt something shift inside of her, goosebumps traveling down her spine.

Even though the air had been warm only a moment ago on the street, it had grown colder the moment she'd stepped into the temple, the hair on the back of her neck rising. Incense that had only a moment ago smelled bright and fragrant turned sour and sickly rotten.

"You are not wanted here." The voice of her pendant was firm, insistent.

"WE MUST LEAVE." The dagger tucked into the sheath at the small of her back rarely spoke, but its voice was also adamant, with a twinge of something else hoving underneath. Fear?

Even her finger, where Michael's ring fit her snuggly, was ice cold, as if it too wanted her to go, to turn around and run.

But she wouldn't.

Arix grit her teeth against the churning in her stomach, moving further in and stepping to her place at the side of the room.

Watching as Orion moved towards the priest at the altar, she tried focusing on him rather than the faces of the court that glanced at her as well.

No one else seemed to see a problem, seemed to notice the change in the atmosphere, all simply vying for the best place to stand to watch the blessing proceed.

The priest in simple white robes stepped up, clearing his throat before speaking. It came out loud and authoritative, the sound jarring as it bounced against the stone pillars.

"King Orion Karcharias, step forward to receive the blessings of the God of Air."

As Orion moved to kneel, the robes he wore billowed, and whispers began to titter around Arix. It seemed the blessing was starting even before the prayer had officially begun.

The priest had to raise his voice to be heard as the wind around Orion picked up even more, whipping his hair back away from his face.

"Breath inward, breath outward, a rhythm of life unseen. It is Air that is the invisible current, the very essence of life itself. It is Air that whispers through leaves and howls in the storm, bending us to its will."

People were ducking back now, pushing backward from the wind that howled around Orion. Though he faced the priest and no one could see his face, from her vantage point, Arix saw the corner of his mouth twist up into a smile.

"Great God Zephyrus, cursed son of Kaoss, boundless unseen weaver of the wind, we beseech that your secrets of life be whispered into our King's ear…"

The wind had shifted directions now and was lifting, Orion's form sweeping upwards to hover a few feet off the stone floor. His arms were swept wide, and his head tilted back to embrace the currants that surrounded him.

Arix's stomach twisted even harder as she felt the backlash of that wind pushing her like it was trying to force her to her knees. Gritting her teeth, she pushed back, focused on staying upright beneath the gust.

"Grant him wisdom's clear breeze, fill his heart with purpose, strong as ancient trees that sway beneath the galeforce wind. Let clarity guide him, like the air currents guide winged birds above, navigating the perils of the skies and seeing all that may come."

As the last words of the prayer died out, the wind began to die down until only the light breeze from before remained. Orion touched back down to the marble floor and turned, smiling, to the rest of the gathered mass.

And something about the look in his eyes made Arix's heart flip. Made her stomach plummet and carved out a dark, hollow feeling inside of her.

He was enjoying this.

Not the way he had at the first blessing. Not with humility and the grace of a new king. The smile he shot her was haughty, arrogant, a look that said he deserved this. That this blessing was owed to him.

Arix felt the chill again, ignoring the stares from the rest of the crowd as they parted for him to exit the temple, watching and waiting to see if something similar would happen to her.

She knew it wouldn't.

Orion had been changing ever since the tour had begun. Ever since he had become king. The space between them had only yawned wider in the past months, and the more time that passed, the further she drew away from him.

But the question that haunted her, that stole the air from her lungs and made her feet feel as heavy as lead, was this:

Had he grown into this? Had the power of the crown started to change him? Or had he concealed his true nature from her all along?

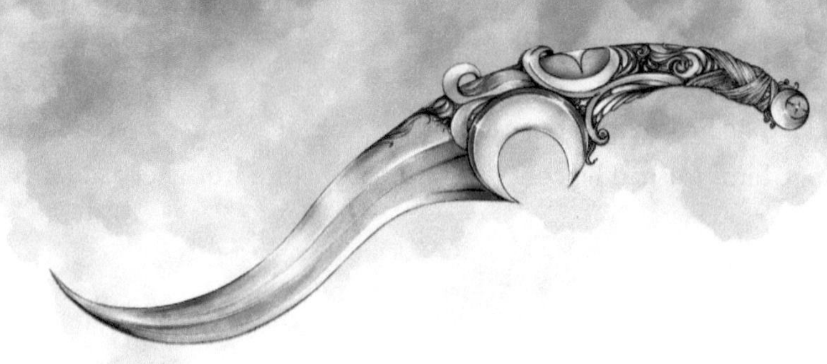

TWENTY-NINE

The people of Ramal lit a bonfire so high and so hot that once it was ablaze, no one stepped within twenty paces of it. Tables overflowed with fruits, and spices filled the air. Eight oryx antelope roasted on a spit over a trench of coals set back from the main fire. As the turners rotated the carcasses to keep them from burning, the skin crisped, popping and sizzling as fat dripped and filled the air with the aromatic scent of mustard seed and coriander. People danced, holding hands and following each other as the leader led them 'round the fire again and again, chanting the steps to those who were unfamiliar with the dances.

Arix stayed back from the fire, from the food, her eye trained on Orion as he stood beside Delphine, one arm around her waist, talking with Warden Los Ke. He was smiling, jovial and laughing at some joke the Warden had made, squeezing his queen into his side as she blushed and looked away.

But the role suited him. He preened in the light of the crown, basked in the sovereign glow of his title as the Golden King. When he waved at the smiling crowds, they shouted their favor. Their love for him was clear. But was he deserving?

"There is a way to know for sure." The voice was a rumble in her mind. She felt like one set of eyes among four that watched the king as he moved and laughed as if he'd been preparing for this his whole life.

Maybe he had.

There was magick she could use. Cants that would reveal his true nature, showing the worst of himself to her, and she would finally know if the apprehension that was growing inside her was justified or just her imagination. It wasn't complicated magick.

But she couldn't bring herself to do it.

Couldn't bring herself to use any magick on Orion other than the shielding cants that were in place to protect him. It would have been *too* easy. After all they had been through, both before his rise to the throne as well as after it, if she had to use magick to see the real him, then she was a fool. A patsy who had been tricked and manipulated from the beginning. And even the thought of that as a possibility pushed bile up her throat.

It was a game she refused to play with herself.

At least for now.

Maybe it wasn't Orion who had changed. Maybe she was the one who had changed towards him.

"Enjoying the show?" Ro's voice was light and merry, with only a slight slur to his words as he tipped his drink up for another swallow.

Wordlessly, Arix took his cup and finished off the contents: a sweet honey wine with hints of clover.

Ro winced. "That bad?"

"You heard?"

"About the blessing? Of course. And you"—he snapped to a nearby servant who quickly filled the cup back up to the brim—"are sulking because you received nothing."

Arix snapped her head to glare at him. "I'm not sulking."

"You are." Ro took the now full cup back from her and took a long sip. "But I don't fault you."

"Tell me a secret," Arix said, hoping the subject change away from herself might be encouraging enough for Ro to drop it.

It was.

His grin was face splitting as he leaned in close and subtly pointed to their right, where a few tables of local high-value vendors were selling some of their wares. "I heard that Lord Vermoin had his entire enterprise bought out from under him by his head saleswoman. Apparently, she settled him into enough debt that he had to sell his trade at a loss, and she bought it right out from under him. She's moving the entire operation to Mergur."

Arix watched the woman draped in lilac purple cloth that looked almost silver in the firelight sip her drink as she spoke with a few of the court ladies, gesturing to the spectacularly woven fabric on display.

"What's her name?"

"Lydia Skonos."

"And other than her shrewd business skills, what makes her special?"

There was a twinkle in Ro's eye as he turned his gaze away from the vendor tables and back to Arix. "She knows everyone."

"You know everyone."

"I know almost everyone." Ro waved away the compliment with a wagging hand. "*She* knows *everyone*. Has a mind for names and faces. Lord Bardon's secretary offered her a seat in his private cabinet, but she refused."

Arix's eyebrows rose. "Interesting."

"She asked to speak with you when you have a chance. I think she could be an asset. I like her."

"You like everyone."

"No, I *smile* at everyone. I like very few people; there's a difference."

"You like me." Arix let the small smile slip as she glanced over at him.

Whether it was the wine or the friendship, Ro's eyes danced in the firelight. "I do."

Someone nearby laughed loudly, and Arix glanced around, eyes skittering over the crowd as she lowered her voice. "What else did you learn today?"

Ro passed her the glass again, and she took another sip. "I found something, but it's going to take a lot more digging before it starts making sense. Nothing about a 'messenger drenched in blood' but there is a bit about the blessings. Apparently, it originated not with a king—but with the first Black Hand."

"Luthren Chestail."

"That's right. He was a priest of Kaoss and discovered something, some relic or holy ground that tapped into magick in a way that other incantors couldn't. He used it and became the first and most powerful incantor in the world. King Venen, the ruler at the time, knighted Luthren to help fight his war, and together they won. The blessings came afterwards, once the war was won and King Venen was crowned the high ruling king of modern-day Rökkur."

"I remember reading something about him," Arix squinted into the fire, trying to remember the little she'd read last year in her lessons with Desirea. "A little about his life, his husband, and some other tidbits."

Orion was moving, leaving Delphine behind to talk with the Warden's wife as he moved around to the other side of the fire. Arix motioned for Ro to walk with her as she shifted positions to keep Orion in her sights.

"I couldn't find much more about the blessings," Ro went on, keeping a steady pace beside her as she inched around the outer edge of the crowd. "But it seems they're pretty heavily tied to the king and his or her Black Hand. The roles go hand in hand, pardon the pun."

Arix sighed, completely ignoring the joke. "Unfortunately, none of this is new. I'll have more answers when we get back to Castle Zma'ai. The library will have the information I'm looking for. In the meantime, I just need to wait it out."

Ro linked arms with her, pulling the cup back out of her hands and taking another swig. His smile lit up his face, and the gold hoops in his ears glinted in the firelight as he looked at her. "Cheer up, Arix. The night is still young, and there's plenty of good food to drink. Beautiful women to dance with to get your mind off your troubles."

Arix raised an eyebrow at him, squinting as she had to pull her head back away from his sloppy embrace, her smile only partially hidden. "My troubles?"

"Just because you didn't get another blessing doesn't mean you aren't special." He said it as though he was talking to a child, comforting someone who hadn't gotten the starring role in a school play. "I'll still love you if you're only blessed by two of the gods."

Arix couldn't help the laugh that bubbled up as she swiped back the cup. "Go away; dance with the pretty girls and boys and fill your belly with apples and antelope. I have a job to do."

She waved him away and was happy to watch him scamper off and join a small circle of partiers. He deserved the revelry for all his investigating, even if it was all information she already knew.

Warm arms slid around her torso, and Esme's sultry voice echoed in the hollow of her ear as she whispered, "Dance with me, lover."

It was slow, simply swaying back and forth to the music that rang out around the fire, but Arix gave in to it, allowing Esme to guide her. She kept her eyes trained on Orion but leaned her head back to rest it against Esme's shoulder as they rocked together.

"Have you eaten?"

"I'm alright."

"I came back to my room later, and you were gone, Arix. I had hoped you would wait for me." Esme's words were as smooth as the silk kaftan she wore, though considerably cheaper.

Suddenly, the comfort Arix had felt only a moment before faded and was replaced with a hard hollow stone in her throat. She pulled away gently, turning to face Esme, squeezing the woman's hand before extracting herself from her grasp.

"I had work to do today. And I'm working now."

The look in Esme's eyes shifted, knowing full well that she was being rejected. "Of course. Come see me again, please, Arix. While I turn most away from my door, it is always open to you."

Arix nodded with a small smile. She didn't doubt the words, but she knew the game Esme played. Perhaps it was a game she needed to learn better herself. But right now, becoming Esme's regular lover was not part of her intentions.

When Esme walked away and Arix turned back to the fire, she found Orion's eyes locked to her own, a smoldering fire in his gaze. Jealousy mixed with desire. It flared something equally hot within her, and Arix suddenly found her throat dry, overly aware of the parts of her skin exposed to the warm desert air.

She still wanted him. Maybe not the way she had before, not with the emotional attachment, but she still wanted his hot breath pressed against her skin.

"PATHETIC." This time, the voice came from the dagger at her back. *"FUCK HIM OR DON'T. JUST DECIDE."*

Arix chose the latter.

A few ladies were moving away from the vendor tables as Arix approached, and they eyed her as they left, whispering to themselves as they moved away.

"Arix Sable, the Black Hand to King Orion Karcharias. It is my greatest pleasure that you would speak with me. Thank you." Lydia smiled from behind the sheer purple veil that covered the lower half of her face, and Arix realized the woman had scars that ran up her throat and across the left half of her lower jaw. "Have you been told who I am?"

"I have," Arix answered, eyes sweeping across the table that stood between them. "Ro Laris was impressed with your history."

Lydia inclined her head to the compliment before motioning that Arix step around behind the table and join her away from the crowd of revelers. She still had a line of sight to Orion, so Arix joined the woman and sat on a chair that Lydia gestured to.

"Can I offer you something to drink? I don't drink alcohol myself and prefer tea to keep a clear head. I have chilled jasmine if you'd like."

"That sounds excellent."

Lydia removed the lid from a stone jar beside her, then fished through the water to pull out another smaller stoppered jar. She refilled her own cup, then poured a new one for Arix before replacing the smaller jar within the larger.

"Chilled water," Lydia commented when she saw Arix watching. "To keep the tea cold within."

"It's smart. But I can do you one better." Arix twisted her finger, using one of Revena's modified cants that kept items cold, focusing the magick on the outer jar. "Now your jar will stay cold, no matter what you put into it."

Lydia glanced down at the jar, pressing two fingers to the side of the clay to feel it. She glanced up again with surprise. "It's cold."

"It is. And it will stay cold. Not forever, the magick will wear off in a week or so, but it's my gift to thank you for the tea."

The woman cocked her head slightly, eyeing Arix with an appraising look. "You are not what I remember."

Something jolted inside her. "We have met before?"

Lydia nodded.

"It has been years now—I am positive you do not remember. But you lived for a time in Zarak with a nomadic family. I knew you then, though your hair was red, and you were not an incantor in those days." She offered Arix an evaluating look. "In some ways, you are the same. In others, you are not."

Uneasiness mixed in her belly as Arix took a tentative sip to calm her nerves. She'd always expected to run into people she knew from the old days, people she had stolen from, people she had helped. But so far, she'd been spared the awkwardness of a run-in. At least until now.

"Ro mentioned you wanted to speak with me."

"Yes." Lydia's manner shifted and became all business as she straightened. "I wish to join your council."

Arix blinked. "My council?"

"Your Fingers. You have five, do you not? Ro Laris, Nesrin Yara, the Stormsinger. These are all members of your council, your inner circle. I wish to join them."

"That's a bold request."

"It is."

"And why do I need you as one of my Fingers, Lydia Skonos? What do you bring to the table that Ro and Semmer do not already offer me?"

"I know things. I remember faces and names excessively well, and I have a talent for seeing through disguises."

"I can see through disguises with my magick. I don't need you for that."

"I have connections," Lydia went on, leaning forward in her seat a bit as she spoke, her voice rising slightly. "Intel that Ro Laris does not always have access to."

Arix said nothing, allowing her silence to encourage Lydia to continue.

"For example, I know that you seek some information regarding the blessings."

That got Arix's attention. "Ro needs to learn a bit of self control."

The lightweight fabric of her veil shifted as Lydia shook her head. "It is not Ro who told me. I have little snakes that speak to me. Little snakes that listen and pass on messages to me. They hear all manner of things, and I make it my business to collect what they hear and make sense of it. When one of my little snakes hisses in my ear that Ro Laris is reading up on the first Black Hand, that High Priestess Esme Halotus spends all day locked in Zephyrus' temple fasting and praying for revelations, I hold this information tightly. I wait. I use it to the best of my advantage."

"And you offer this to me," Arix said.

Lydia nodded. "I do."

"All of my Fingers are oathed to me."

"I know."

Arix huffed, leaning forward to match the woman's posture. "Why? Why become a Finger to the Black Hand? Your business is thriving, your name is already well known. The information you have is already highly sought after. Ro tells me you refused Lord Bardon."

Lydia nodded again, a sly smile spreading across her face. "That man is a different kind of snake."

"And what makes you think that I am not?"

For a moment, the two women were quiet, the sound of music

and crackling fire echoing around them as their little conversation remained apart. Lydia considered the question seriously, eyes locked on Arix's own until Arix felt the urge to look away under the scrutiny.

When Lydia finally spoke, she did so slowly, her eyes glowing warm in the orange blaze of the fire. "I know what you've done."

Arix fought the urge to swallow down her panic, to break eye contact, but she held her ground, staring straight back.

"I know what you devoted your life to doing. And I know how you are going to try and spend your life as the Black Hand, continuing to fight for the small little people in it. Ro collects and holds secrets. I collect and hold names and faces. You collect and hold hope in your hands. The dreams and hopes of people who are afraid of the exploitation and the system that treats them with disrespect. They do not care how you right the scale as long as it is righted."

"So, you know about my past. So, what? A lot of people know who I used to be. That doesn't mean I'm the same person now."

"You ask how I know you are not a snake in the weeds, waiting and watching for the right time to bite. I tell you this, Arix Sable, you are more like a wolf pretending to be a dog."

"You're very open for a woman who has built her career through skill and patience."

Lydia's grin was feral behind her veil. "I have learned the art of timing. There is a time for it all. A time for silence and patience, a time for bold words and unflinching action. Is it true you bit out a chunk of her arm?"

All of the blood drained from Arix's face, and she felt the tips of her fingers grow numb. "Who told you that?"

"It doesn't matter who told me." Lydia shifted in her seat, reaching into the double jar to pour them each more tea. Arix had barely touched hers. "What matters is if it's true or if it's just a good bit of gossip some servant girl made up."

Arix chose not to answer.

"The reason I ask is this: When you were in those woods, your death inches away, were you finally behaving like your true self? Were you tapping into a raw and brutal part of your nature that you didn't know you had? Or were you lifting back the curtain to reveal the beast you already knew was waiting?"

"I did what I needed to do to survive."

"But are you proud of it?"

"I—"

"Because if you aren't, then your reign will be short and pointless. You will remain the king's attack dog, trotted out like a stud horse to prance and show off, all to the glory of the great Sun King." There was an edge to the woman's voice, brutal and honest, in a way that reminded her much of the voice of the pendant that now hung silent around Arix' throat. "But if you are…"

Lydia leaned forward, her chin tipping low to stare Arix down.

"If you truly are proud of the things you did that day, you will be a Black Hand whose name will live on through the ages."

It was strange, how Lydia Skonos' words were matching thoughts of her own. What was her purpose, really? Right now, she was a glorified bodyguard. She did as she was told, following Orion and the rest of the court as they traipsed around the country seeking the god's blessings, but her heart wasn't in it. When had she felt most alive?

Fighting the Carn?

Her blood flowed hot, even at the thought of the adrenaline that had pumped through her veins that day in Rohleach's streets. She'd felt useful, like a warrior. And the people had seen it and shouted her name and written songs about her heroism. But it had been more than the praise that had set her heart racing. It was the knowledge that she wasn't just a small corner of the grand tapestry of the world;

she played a role in the center.

Maybe she'd always wanted to be at the world's center. At *history's* center.

And maybe, just maybe, standing in Orion's shadow wasn't good enough.

Arix leaned back in her chair, sipping her tea as a slow smile spread across her face.

"Let's draw up the contract. Welcome to the Black Hand's Fingers."

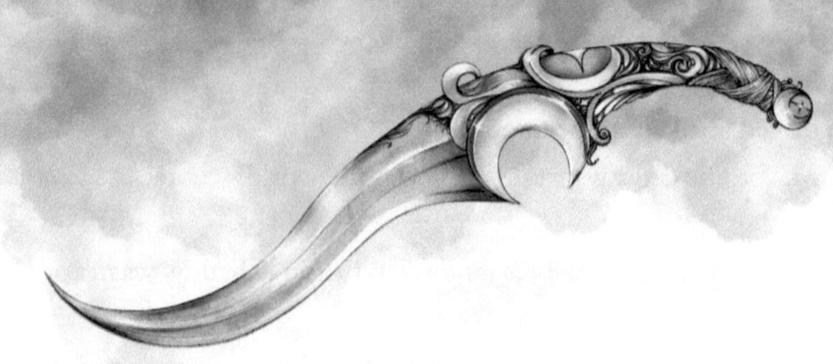

THIRTY

The fire was dying, the blaze worn down to a heap of charred logs as Arix kept a ten-step pace behind Orion and Delphine as they returned to Warden Los Ke's estate. Delphine's voice was pitched up an octave, and she leaned heavily on Orion's arm as she teetered. Arix had offered to retrieve a horse or a carriage for them, but Orion had insisted they walk instead.

It was practically dawn, the inky black of night giving way to the dusty lavender of early morning, and there was something about the orange glow of the lanterns that seemed different at this early hour than they did in the early evening. The walk back wasn't long, so Arix gave them some privacy, keeping back but close enough to offer assistance if it was needed. Delphine let out a snort and a tittering of laughter, and Orion mumbled soft words to her in response.

To her surprise, Arix found herself annoyed at that. At his patronizing tone, shushing her with a soft reprimand, like a parent might to a child that's become a nuisance.

"Do you want me to carry her?" She moved up a few paces, nodding to Delphine as the queen slumped slightly, her knees buckling a little as the three of them paused on a side street.

"I've got her."

Orion wrapped an arm around Delphine's shoulders, his other arm swooping beneath her knees as he pulled her up off the ground and into his arms. She mumbled something incoherent before pressing her face against the embroidery of his jacket and promptly falling asleep.

Instead of stepping back, Arix kept her pace with Orion, quickly casting a cant to make the sleeping woman less heavy.

"Thank you."

Arix only nodded in response.

"I was watching you tonight," Orion spoke, his voice quiet so as to not wake Delphine. "You and Ro scheming away on the opposite end of the fire."

There was something in his tone… It was too casual, too nonchalant for there to be anything more than a hidden meaning beneath the surface of his words.

"I asked him to do some research for me."

"About the first king?"

Arix bit her tongue to keep from asking him how he'd known that. More than ever, she was glad that Lydia Skonos had been added to her inner circle. Orion had his own informants, and she needed to stay one step ahead of them.

"Just curious about the traditions."

Orion scoffed, shaking his head in frustration. "You're keeping things from me, Arix. From *me*. It's one thing not to share my bed out of respect for Delphine; it's another to snub me altogether."

"Snub you?" This time, her reply snapped out before she could stop herself. "I have done nothing but support you, Orion. When you wanted a queen, when you refused to end the tour early, I supported your decisions. How have I snubbed you?"

"Don't think I didn't notice the way Esme was wrapped all up in your arms tonight. People were staring, Arix. Don't you realize the effect your actions have? How they reflect poorly on me? If you want to fuck the high priestess, that's fine, but keep it in the privacy of the baths and not in front of the entire court."

For a moment, Arix had no response, her mouth hanging open as she stared at him. He had never spoken this way to her, never used this kind of cruel language. It was brusque and out of character.

"To be honest, I'm surprised at you." Orion went on, his voice taking on almost a pitying tone. "I'd have thought you would choose better bed-mates than a temple prostitute and the most infamous man whore in our little traveling party. You could do so much better, Arix. I only wish you had more self-respect."

His words stopped Arix in her tracks, and Orion walked a few more paces before turning back to look at her.

"Coming?"

He said it so casually that she could only stare after him, any response gone from her mind. They walked the rest of the way in silence, and even when they arrived at Orion's door and Arix held it open for him to enter with Delphine, he said nothing more. It wasn't until she was in her own bed, staring at the shadows on the ceiling brightening with every passing minute as the sun rose over the desert, that Arix found the words.

But she had no one to say them to now, and a biting retort, no matter how witty, didn't have quite the same meaning when whispered angrily in an empty room.

~

It would have been right to tell someone where she was going, either Lord Bardon, Lakai, or Orion, but she'd decided against it.

Nesrin and Ulfur and Abbas knew where she'd gone, and she'd told them she'd return to Zarak's capital in two days, plenty of time before Orion's caravan departed again and headed south to Eldur.

Most people were still sleeping off the previous evening's party, and the streets were empty as she fled on Osiris out of the city limits and headed further east into the desert. She hadn't meant to take this trip, not at first. But after talking with Orion, Arix knew she needed to get away, even if it was only for a few days. She needed distance to think, to decide what to do and say.

As Osiris' hooves pounded against the sandy roads, leaving a trail of dust running like a river behind them, Arix cut thought from her mind and let the hot sun bake into her back. She rode low, hunched down in the saddle, and gave Osiris his head, feeling his stride lengthen as the giant horse took her lead and ran wild. Every step resonated against the sand and stone, the power of his stride amplifying their ride. The sand muffled his hoofbeats, so instead of sounding like a horse running along the road, it sounded more like the deep rush of water echoing against the canyons that surrounded them.

Arix watched the red rocks loom in the distance, marking the way that Lydia had told her.

After Lydia Skonos had signed the contract, binding herself and her loyalty to Arix, she'd offered some advice. Advice that Arix hadn't at first intended to take.

But here she was, regardless. Sprinting through the desert with only a single rock formation guiding her path. It would be a long way to travel, but when she arrived at her destination, she wanted to be able to stay. To rest. To feel and connect and breathe.

She'd slept only a little during the day, choosing to leave after the worst of the noon sun had passed, and it was near dark when the first sighting of what she'd come to find dotted the horizon.

The village was modest, small. Built against one of the smaller canyon walls, red rock carved away into a tiny cluster of homes. Pens of wild dogs and desert horses with their stockier legs and shorter necks were off to the side, happy to rest as the sun dipped behind Arix's back.

A woman stood outside, hand shading her eyes as she watched Arix dismount and approach.

"I'm looking for the Kali family."

The woman's voice was velvety and sure. "You've found them, stranger. How may we help you?"

Arix searched the woman's face, looking for some recognition, some kind of sign of familiarity, but she found none.

"My name is Arix Sable."

The woman's eyes grew round, and she clutched the fence post beside her. "You're here."

"I wanted to pay my respects."

"Of course, of course." The woman rushed forward, and as she neared, Arix realized she was pregnant. "I'm Malina. Please feel free to leave your horse here; there's water. I'll take you to my mother."

Osiris was more than happy to chomp away at the dried grass bundle Malina hung for him against the fence post as Arix followed the girl inside the large house at the center of the village. She stooped a little to enter the door frame and paused as her fingers caught on the rough edge of the stone.

Markings, carefully carved vines and runes, had been painstakingly engraved into the rock around the edge of the doorframe. Arix pushed her fingers against one of the leaves, feeling the smooth wear of other hands having touched this very spot, evening out the rough edges with use.

Pain choked in Arix's throat. She'd promised herself she wouldn't let emotion cloud her, not here. Not when she had things to say.

Malina led her further into the house, past a large dining room that was already set with dishes of bread and dark meat. Two children around the age of ten were setting out plates, and another emerged from an adjacent room with a bowl of syruped dates. The boy stopped when he saw Arix, frozen in place until Malina gently pushed him to the side so that she could pass him into the kitchen.

Arix followed, ducking again as she stepped through the doorway. Two women and a man were in the kitchen, one slicing a thick loaf of bread while the other two leaned over a pot, tasting from a spoon. All three glanced up as they entered, eyes skimming past Malina to stare at Arix. Questions pooled in their gazes, and Arix felt the back of her tongue grow as dry as the sand dunes outside.

She'd had things to say, had a speech prepared and words that might help them know her for who she was. Malina faltered as well, gesturing for Arix to introduce herself. But before she could, the woman cutting the bread let out a small gasp, the words falling out of her mouth in a whisper.

"You're Arix, aren't you?"

With her name finally spoken, it broke the tension, the momentary pause of uncertainty replaced with surprise.

Arix cleared her throat, finally finding her voice underneath the lump lodged in her stomach. "I came…" This wasn't going how she'd planned at all. She took a moment, then started again.

"I'm so sorry."

Tears welled in the first woman's eyes, and she put down her knife to round the edge of her worktable to approach Arix. She put her arms around her and pulled her into a desperate embrace.

That was all it took, the tears trickling down Arix's cheeks, wishing she could pull together her composure, wishing she could say something, anything, that might express all the emotions that welled up inside of her.

But instead, she just cried. Sagged against Revena's mother as she held her tight, resting her forehead on the motherly shoulder as the tears turned into body-wracking sobs.

She'd cried for days after Revena's death, avoided food and sleep, and turned inward, heartbroken and feeling so alone. The way that her friend had died left no body to mourn over, no corpse to wrap up and send home to be buried. Revena had pushed Arix to safety, sacrificing herself in a terrible death, and now, as Arix sobbed, she realized how much she wished she had a grave to visit, a resting place she might stand next to. To beg forgiveness. To beg for absolution.

Coming here—to meet Revena's family, to apologize and explain—was the only way she could think of to close the final chapter, to move on, to seek the kind of peace that Revena would have wanted for her. She'd expected a certain level of welcome, but Arix had thought it would be out of politeness, a desire to curry favor with the Black Hand. She'd thought that they would see her as the girl who lived so their daughter could die. She'd even known there was a possibility that Revena's family wouldn't see her at all. That they would kick her from their home, and she would return to Ramal emptier than when she'd left.

But this?

She had not expected this. This embrace emptied out all the tears she had left, all of the heavy burden of loss. This embrace gave her closure.

And when the tears were over, and Revena's mother released her from her embrace, Arix joined them all for dinner, sopping the thick bread into the stew, licking sticky date syrup from her fingers, watching as the Kali family interacted with each other around the table.

They laughed together, parents smiling fondly as the younger children told stories of their day, everyone so easily avoiding asking questions that Arix wasn't ready to answer yet. They treated her like one of their own, like a neighbor simply visiting for the evening, and not the reason that there was a missing place at the table that had once belonged to Revena.

After dinner, Arix checked on Osiris, settling him in for the night before returning to the house. Malina was overseeing the five other children as they worked to clean the kitchen, washing dishes and putting away uneaten food. Revena's mothers, Liala and Genni, and her father, Oli, moved into the sitting room, pulling Arix in after them to sip a heady tea before bed. They pulled her down to the low, comfortable couch and tucked her in with a blanket as they talked and laughed softly.

Much like dinner, they didn't press her with questions but left gaps in their conversation to give her a chance to speak up if she wanted to. It was so welcoming, so open and unhurried. Genni, who had hugged her in the kitchen, stayed close to Arix's side, offering her occasional smiles and encouraging glances.

It was nice to simply sit and listen as they talked about their day, about the plan for their annual migration during the final month of summer. They laughed softly, inside jokes and sweet glances intermingled with their words. She felt safe here, maybe for the first time in a long time. No wonder Revena had been so wonderful if these were the people who had raised her into who she'd become.

The minutes slipped into each other, and before Arix knew it, she'd fallen asleep to the lulling sound of their quiet companionship.

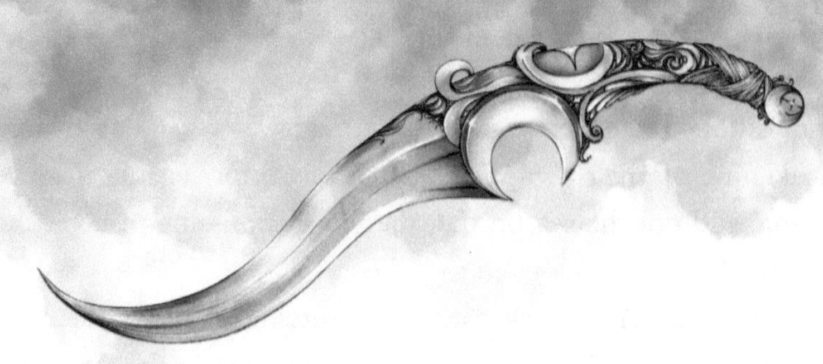

THIRTY-ONE

It was the door that woke Arix in the morning, the soft squeak of the hinge and quiet, hushed voices as someone slipped outside. It was barely past dawn, the darkness of the house still slowly awakening to the brilliant orange light of dawn. Arix pulled her boots back on, hurrying to fold the blanket on the back of the settee and help with the morning chores. It was the least she could do after they'd fed her and given her a place to stay last night.

But when she followed the hushed voices and stepped through the squeaky hinged door, she found a small courtyard off the side of the house. Genni sat in a chair, her legs folded up underneath her with a steaming mug in her hands. Her face was upturned to the orange red sky, and she held out a hand with a smile for Arix to take a seat on the adjacent chair.

"Beautiful, isn't it?" Genni motioned to the blooming sky, tipping her cup to her lips as she gently sipped the dark contents. "I like to take a moment in the mornings like this and watch the day spring to life."

They sat in silence for a moment, and Arix watched the cloudless sky swirl with color as light brightened the world around them.

"You know," Genni's voice was soft as she contemplated the color shift. "Revena used to sit out here with me in the mornings. My sweet little morning dove."

Tears burned the corner of Arix's eyes at the emotions in the nickname. She remembered the last moments she and Michael and Revena had had together, coming up with silly nicknames in the barn last winter.

"She saved me." Arix felt the words rush out before she could stop them. "She's dead because of me."

Genni stilled, watching Arix with a careful look.

"I don't know what they told you."

Genni took a moment before responding, shifting the mug in her grip. "They didn't tell us anything. Only that she was gone."

The lump that had been in her throat yesterday returned, but this time without the tears. This would be the hardest part.

"It was during a test." Arix started, trying to keep her tone level. She watched Genni, but the woman kept her gaze down, staring into the dark liquid of her cup. "We were sent to retrieve a box deep under the castle. When we got down there, a dragon was waiting."

At the mentioned monster, Genni's gaze snapped up, locked on Arix. Confusion, dread. She already knew what Arix was going to say. The legends, no matter how old, were stories that everyone knew well.

"We ran, and we were so close. But in the end, we weren't fast enough. She pushed me out of the way. She…"

Arix couldn't say it. She couldn't say that Revena burned. But the memory was hot in her mind… The smell of seared flesh, of burning hair, the bite of the metal box wrenching out of her hand, her senses tingling as the memory brought it all up to the surface.

"She saved me. There wasn't anything I could do. I tried to go back for her—you have to believe me, I tried. They wouldn't let me retrieve her. They said…"

Once again she couldn't get out the words.

But Genni knew. She stood, her back to Arix, and stepped further into the courtyard to stand beside a small fountain.

"It's because of her that I'm here today. She had notes, journals, pages and pages of her research on magick. After she…was gone, I stole them, copied them, kept that as a part of her that I could hold on to. Her research helped me win. She's the reason why I'm still here today."

"No, Arix." Genni turned, a small smile on her lips as tears tracked down her cheeks. "As much as you might believe it, Revena is not the reason why you're here. If you had been any less worthy, you wouldn't have made it to the end. You wouldn't be here now as the Black Hand. I have to believe that the goddess planned this all. I have to believe that there is meaning behind her death, or I will go mad with guessing."

Arix stood, joining Genni by the pool's edge. "I wouldn't be here without her."

"I believe you were always meant to be the Black Hand, Arix."

"It should have been her."

"But it *wasn't*." Revena's mother reached out and pulled Arix's hands within her own. "It wasn't. And you cannot live your life thinking that you were only a cheap replacement for what my daughter could have been. If you live like that, thinking that you are second best, your life will crumble around you.

"If you trust anything I say, Arix, trust this: You are the Black Hand for a reason. Kaoss placed you in this position for a reason. There is a divine plan. You must trust it."

She believed it, Arix realized. Genni believed every word she said, her entire being trusting that all the pain and suffering, even the loss of her daughter, was part of the goddess's intention for the future. For Arix's future.

"My daughter was a great incantor. She was brilliant." A bright smile came over Genni's face as she thought of Revena. "It was like she knew how to perform cants in her heart long before she read the instructions in a book. From when she was little, I knew she was different.

She was always walking around the house, muttering words, trying out how they sounded in her mouth, trying to coax the magick together."

Genni's gaze shifted to the pond, and Arix followed the line of sight to stare down at the water. Lily pads dotted the surface, two lazy koi fish swimming beneath the stems. Down at the bottom of the pond, a glint of something caught her eye.

Was that…?

Arix knelt down beside the pool, dipping her fingers into the cool water, pressing past the lily pads until her fingers closed around the shiny circle at the bottom. Beads of water dripped off the smooth surface, running down her arms and wetting her rolled-up sleeves.

Even though she knew the magick, knew what it was, it still hit her square in the chest, a hollow ache at the reflection that looked back at her. It was inside the house, propped up on a shelf, overlooking the family room. On the left side of the mirror window, she could see the corner of the wooden box that the other half of the mirror window had sat in.

"That was her first cant that worked. She used it with her sister to spy on us, to pass notes, to tell secrets." Genni's voice was soft. "When she left for Mergur, she took one of the mirrors with her and left the other in the pond so she could watch the fish."

The knuckles on Arix's hand whitened as her grip turned hard on the smooth surface. She had a sudden urge to smash the mirror, smash the last bit of magick that remained of Revena. Instead, she carefully put the mirror back in the water, placing it gently against the bottom of the pond again.

Genni's hand squeezed Arix's shoulder as the two women paused to watch the fish, watch the glint of light off the little circle of mirror.

"Why did you tell her to keep her feelings for me a secret?" Arix mumbled, unable to tear her eyes away from the shimmering surface.

"To protect her."

"If I'd known—"

"If you'd known, it wouldn't have changed anything." Genni cut her off, pulling Arix's shoulder until she was forced back up on her feet. There was pain written in the lines of her face, a desperation that caused the chocolate of her eyes to turn even a darker brown. "My daughter would still have died, Arix. Even if you did love her the way she'd loved you, it wouldn't have made any difference to the results we now stand with today. My daughter is dead. And you are the Black Hand."

Arix couldn't bear to look at her. To see the pain there. But Revena's mother tipped her face, forcing her gaze up.

"I am trusting Kaoss that it was not for nothing."

Genni pulled Arix into a hug, and once again, she felt the overwhelming feeling of comfort, of relief. Is this what it felt like? To be held, safe and sound, in a mother's arms?

"I miss her." Arix found herself muttering into Genni's shoulder. So softly that she hoped the other woman hadn't heard her.

And whether she had or not, Genni said nothing. Just held her tightly.

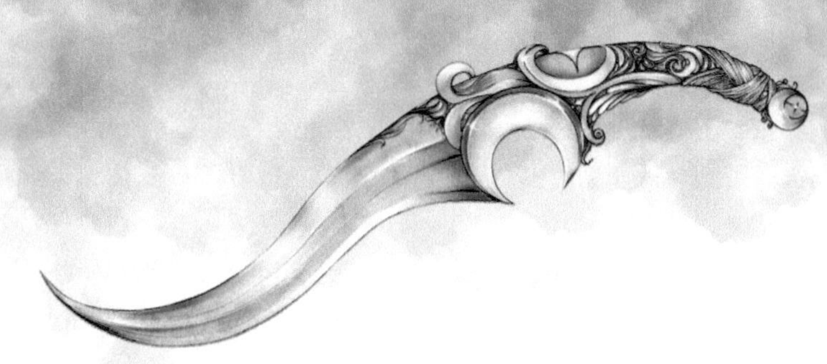

THIRTY-TWO

Orion didn't say a word about her disappearance, nor did any-one else, though after she'd returned, Lakai gave her dirty looks. He refused to talk to her, instead trying to punish her absence with his silence. It was all the better; Arix didn't want to talk to him either.

The party was back on the road quickly, staying even a shorter time in Ramal than they had in Rohleach. It wasn't a surprise, really. They were nearing the end of their tour, and Delphine was sick of the travel, ready to settle into her new home at Castle Zma'ai. Most of the rest of their traveling party felt the same, especially now that summer was setting his hot feet upon the realms and Vulcan's sun was scorching their backs. Eldur would be cooler than the dry desert of Zarak, and by the time they arrived back in the capital, the swel-tering heat would be giving way to autumn.

On the road, Arix was pleased to find that her own little travel-ing party made the road less boring than their trips in Nero. Lydia Skonos often rode beside her, with either Ulfur or Abbas on her oth-er side, and if Ro was feeling adventurous, he'd leave his carriage and join them as well. Semmer usually stayed a pace behind, silent but listening intently. The conversation between them all came so easily, and sometimes Arix would simply sit back in her saddle and grin as the merry little band talked over each other and laughed at the stories and jokes they told.

It was *fun*, Arix realized, to have friends again. Allies that wouldn't disappear through tests and trials. And it was even easier to forget that they all had signed contracts in blood, binding themselves to her service.

"But if you want th' absolute best basted eel," Ulfur continued, reigns gripped in one hand as he gestured wildly with the other, "then ya need to visit Gareth's ale house down in Bordin. Serves it with the most amazing seaweed salad. It's all crunchy an' soft an' slimy but in th' best way."

Lydia was nodding her head. "I do love a good seaweed salad. But I don't partake in fish, myself."

"Eels aren't fish!" Ulfur countered, looking offended. "They're like a type o' snake."

Nesrin leaned forward in her saddle so that she could look over the top of Osiris' hulking neck at Ulfur, her brow furrowed. "No, they aren't."

"Well, I don't eat snakes either," Lydia sniffed.

"I had to eat snakes a few times when I lived on the road." Arix offered with a shrug, "The big ones taste like fish."

Ulfur was grinning at her, nodding along enthusiastically while Lydia's nose wrinkled a little underneath her veil.

"But you really should cook them with a good spicy seasoning. Without that, they're pretty bland."

This launched Ulfur into a long tirade about spices, which turned very quickly into a back-and-forth between him and Lydia regarding tradesmen in Mergur and who had the freshest supply.

Arix was more than content to sit back and enjoy listening to them bicker.

She'd relieved Harksten Gregory, her Master of Coin, of his post and officially replaced him with Lydia. Now, the only two that remained of the Fingers Lakai had assigned her were the Lady Doral Kel, whom she hadn't seen once on their journey (and wasn't entirely sure whether the woman was even still alive or if she'd perished somewhere along the road,) and Tamsin Olsfair, her Master of Woe, who seemed quite content to be demoted to simply her Black Guard.

Arix found she actually liked Tamsin quite a bit, but it seemed he preferred to settle into the comfortability of the Guard than reside in the limelight her Fingers basked in. She didn't mind letting him melt into the background, and he obeyed her orders with a simple nod and a quiet diligence in his work that she appreciated. She'd replace his post with someone else eventually. And of course, she'd replace Lady Doral Kel, too, whenever the old woman showed her face again.

The road south smoothed out the further they stepped away from Zarak and into Eldur, the landscape transitioning from the red rock canyons and dunes of sand into lusher tree clusters and fields of green grass that butted up against the mountains.

This was Arix's home realm. This was where she'd grown up. The green rolling hills jutting up to the towering mountains of the Southern Fyall range. The further south they went, the closer they would get to the sea, where cliff faces plunged down from the rolling hills, dropping away into the churning gray-blue tides below. It was all so familiar, drenched in the nostalgia of her youth, yet completely at odds with the memories that surrounded her. Arix had left Eldur when she was young, and while the mountains remained a looming monstrosity at the edge of her vision, she had thought them even bigger as a child.

The mountains had guarded them for ages, marking the lines between Zarak and Eldur, marking the lines between the borders of

Rökkur and the rest of the world. They were protectors, guardians. Yet, Arix had traveled them herself when on the run a few years ago. She'd learned that there was an art to traversing them, an art to the paths you picked. One wrong step and you would be plunged down the side of the mountain.

"And if you put nutmeg in it, it's even better," Nesrin said with a sigh. "That's the first thing I'll drink when we get back home. I'm sick of travel food. Maybe when we—"

With a slick, sickening thud, Nesrin toppled off the back of her horse, her body landing in a sudden heap on the road.

Arix couldn't get her shield up fast enough. Around her and back down the line, riders were falling from their horses, drivers falling from their perch above carriages. Ulfur and Abbas were turning, each peering at the terrain for a sign of the coming onslaught. Lydia slipped from her horse, using its giant body as a shield as she bent above Nesrin.

Osiris was moving before Arix could tell him to, turning around and bolting back down the line towards Orion's cabin. The driver was still alive, hunching in his seat as he gripped the reins. He saw Arix coming and nodded as she motioned him to stay where he was. Their caravan was still too far away from anyplace safe, so there was nowhere that they could run to. They'd have to stand their ground and fight back.

The shield around Orion's carriage was still intact and holding well as she approached, situating herself on the East side of the road and putting herself between the carriage and any line of attack.

"Get down, stay hidden!" Arix shouted, eyes darting up the line frantically evaluating who was still standing. Her Black Guard seemed fine; their armor had taken care of any beatings. But there were others, bodies littering the ground where they'd been taken out by something else.

Mentally, Arix cursed herself for not checking on Nesrin. For not giving the girl some sort of protection. She'd blindly assumed that Nesrin would be fine if she stayed beside Arix, that somehow she would have been protected.

Heat coursed through Arix's body, searing down her legs as she squeezed them into Osiris' side. He pranced in response, his back legs dancing in place as they held their ground.

"Magla," Arix muttered, hand shooting out beside her, fingers outstretched.

All around her, down the line of their party, fog surged up from the ground. Arix pushed at the magick, forcing it further and further until the cant could cover no more ground. The fogbank wouldn't help to stop the attacks, but they would make it harder for individuals to be seen, obscuring them from being picked off one by one.

The only problem with the fog was that it was hard to see through herself, and she needed to be able to spot where the attacks were coming from. She couldn't hold too many cants at the same time, and the magick it took to extend the fog sapped more from her than she liked.

Arix glanced down at Michael's ring on her finger. She felt out with her magick, locking onto it and pulling the power she needed from it to keep the fog in place. The fog held.

It was hard to tell exactly, but the attacks slowed and then stopped altogether. The fog had been a good idea after all. At least to keep her people protected. But without the attacks, Arix couldn't tell from which direction they were coming from.

Long-range attacks could have been coming from the ridgeline above them, but there were clusters of trees that dotted the hillside now that they'd moved into the woodier climate of Eldur. Their road sloped between steep hills, the forest running along their left side, angling up into the mountains. Arix huffed with frustration as she forced Osiris back into the cloud, obscuring herself from view. The line of fog only covered them as a wall, but past it, the air was clearer, and Arix found Ulfur and Abbas organizing the Black Guard into lines.

"Nesrin?" Arix asked, eyeing Ulfur's brandished sword and the grim line of his mouth.

"Some sort of black acid hit in the chest near her shoulder. Lydia says it's seeping into her lungs."

"Fuck."

Lakai moved into the grouping, standing beside her. "I've extended the fogbank down the line—should offer a bit more protection. We need eyes on them, Arix."

"I know, I know. Bird's eye view, maybe?" Arix watched him, brain filtering through the cants that could help them. Before Lakai could respond, she was already shaking her head, shifting course in a different direction. "It'll take too long for you to cast. Fuck that. No, wait, let me think."

"I can find them, Arix." Lakai's voice was calm, irritatingly so, reminding her that he had actual battle experience, and she was still so new at this. She was good in a pinch, good fighting one-on-one like she had with Celeste. But this was different. She had to split her attention between defensive positionings to keep Orion and the rest of them safe and offensive attacks against what could only be the Carn.

"Do it."

Lakai slipped away again, hurrying down the line, no doubt back to his horse for supplies.

"Lakai!" Arix called after him.

He snapped his head back to look at her, the wisps of his beard trailing after the quick motion of his head.

"Here!" Arix whipped the satchel that hung from Osiris' saddle through the air at him, which he caught with ease. After a quick glance to be sure the pouch contained everything he needed, he set to work right there in the grass.

If she could let him focus on finding their opponents, she could focus on prepping her men for a fight.

"Abbas, take a few men and find out how many we lost; get as many behind the wagons and carriages as we can. There'll be no outrunning this. Ulfur, hold the line, prep the Guard for another attack. I won't hold this fog forever, and we'll make our stand here."

The men moved to obey without a word, and Arix shifted back to Osiris' side to grab a few things from the saddlebags. She found Lydia holding the reins, the edges of her veil soaked in blood.

"How bad is Nesrin?"

"Bad, Arix."

"Show me."

She was wasting precious time, she knew, but she'd vowed to keep Nesrin safe. To keep all of her Fingers safe, and she wasn't about to let a single one of them die.

Semmer had dragged Nesrin out of the line of fire and held her in her arms, careful to keep from touching the black ichor that was eating into the girl's chest.

Arix knelt, feeling with her magick, pulling on the healing power of Michael's ring for guidance. She wiped the rest of the acid off with her metal bracer, knowing that it was canted against acid. Beneath the acid, the flesh was angry and red, bits of bone and white sizzling fat being eaten away at the residual corrosive material. Some of the acid bit into her fingers as she pressed her into the wound and healed from the inside out. Air hissed between her teeth as she bit back a curse, focusing on the cantwork and letting the pain hurry her in her work. The pain in her fingers grew as she dug out the acid black glop, using two cants in unison to heal Nesrin and prevent damage to herself in the process.

It was taking time, precious time, to knit the flesh back together, to clean the acid away, but Arix did it anyway, healing until the worst of the damage was fixed. She wiped her bloody hands on the grass before standing.

"It's all surface wounds now. Bind her up and get to safety," Arix muttered. "Ro's carriage is shielded; hide in there with him."

Lydia nodded as she handed over Osiris' reins.

"I wish I could help you, Arix. But unfortunately, this fight is not something my skills can assist with."

Arix didn't respond, and Lydia was already turning away and disappearing in the direction of Ro Laris' carriage while Semmer carried Nesrin. Out of the corner of her eye, she could see the pool of blood and black ichor on the ground, and it took more strength than Arix cared to admit to keep from staring. For some reason, Lace came to her mind. Both girls had been too young, knocked from their horses in mid-sentence. She wouldn't let Nesrin share in Lace's fate.

That thought burned in her with a white-hot fury, and suddenly, Arix's skin felt too tight, her hair pulling at her scalp. Her skin crawled as frustration tore at her. Hiding behind wagons and counting their dead wouldn't help end this fight. She was angry, angry enough to do something stupid. She found Lakai still knelt in the grass, the edges of the fog clinging to his sleeves.

"Well?" Arix asked, squatting down beside him.

"Just a moment more."

"We don't have a moment. I don't want to waste my time having to renew the fog."

Even as she said it, Arix could feel the pull of the magick, the strain to hold the cant over so much space and for longer than it had intended to be held. Her shield cants were fine for now, but if her resources dwindled, she'd choose the shields over the fog.

Lakai didn't spare a moment for a response; he was snapping tiny bones in half, grinding the shard edges with soot and eggshells.

Arix knew the cant; she knew all the cants. He was taking too long.

With a huff, she stood, pacing at the edge of the carts, glance switching from Lakai's hunched form to the rush of men and women hunkering down for safety. Abbas was heading her way, and Arix rushed to meet his long stride.

"How many?"

"Twenty-eight dead."

"Black Guard assembled?"

Abbas nodded. "Together with the king's guard and the other private bodyguards that came with us."

Arix saw his gaze flicker past her shoulder to see Lakai on the ground with her pouch of ingredients.

"Don't worry about him—he's trying to get us eyes on the enemy."

Abbas' voice was low as his gaze flicked back to hers. "I could go. Scout them out for you."

"No."

As badly as she wanted to send him, she knew there was too high of a risk that the Carn would spot him and cut him down long before he was able to get close enough. She'd almost lost one friend today; she didn't want to lose another.

"No," she repeated with a sigh. "I need you here. If anyone's going, it'll be me."

Abbas' eyebrows shot up slightly. "Is that wise, Arix?"

"Maybe not." Arix gave him her best devil-may-care grin.

"But I'm sneakier than you."

He didn't respond, but there was a line of worry that creased along the bridge of his nose.

"I have to do something, Abbas."

His nod was slow. "Let me help you, Arix. You do not have to do this alone."

Behind him, Ulfur was talking to a few of the other commanders, his expression stern as he gave them their orders. Arix watched for a moment, realizing that the decision needed to be made now. Abbas could travel as quietly as anyone, and maybe together, they could actually do something.

"Come with me."

She pushed past him until she stood beside Ulfur. He nodded to her, stepping away from the others so the three of them could talk.

"News?" He asked.

Arix grinned at him. "I've got an idea, and it's a really stupid one."

Ulfur's mouth twisted up into a matching smile. "I love stupid ideas."

~

Arix stayed low as she ran, keeping herself hidden behind the trees and shrubs as best she could. Abbas was on her heels, staying as quiet as she was as they moved together through the underbrush. As they sprinted between the trees, momentarily visible between the foliage, Arix prayed to Kaoss that if Maeve was here, she wasn't looking in this direction. In the end, no matter how many rebels were hiding in the woods, she really only had to worry about Maeve.

They found the first grouping hidden behind a band of rocks, eight men with potion bottles laid out between them, sticky with black ichor. Each of the men held slingshots, and they watched the fog-covered traveling party, waiting for an opportunity to lob another bottled curse in the direction of the road.

"USE ME. USE ME!" The dagger at the small of her back sang, and she could practically taste its hunger, its craving.

Arix slowly pulled the core from its sheath, relying on her invisibility as she moved from her hiding place. The men were spaced apart, and she approached one from the back of the group. Her hand hovered at his shoulder, ready to grab him as her other arm circled around his kneeling form and prepared to slice. He didn't even blink in response. He couldn't see her. As the blade sank through his skin, she felt the relief of the blade, the instant gratification, the swell of satisfaction, and the thrum of magick through her veins as blood slicked down her arm. He slumped, gurgling slightly as Arix clutched him, her magick shifting to the dying body as he, too, vanished from sight.

Abbas was right behind her, following her lead, even faster with his own dagger than she was. They didn't waste a single moment, slitting the rest of their throats before the little band of Carn even knew what had happened. Not twenty yards away was another small collection of rebels, and they were dispatched just as quickly.

The anxiety that Arix had felt only moments before on the road was quickly being replaced with a kind of adrenaline-fueled glee every time she felt warm blood coat the fingers that grasped her blade. She was so tired of having people taken from her, it felt good to be the one doing the taking. To be the one deciding fates.

She didn't kill all of them, just most. The ones she left alive were held down by vines that sprouted from the earth, tangling over mouths and around throats to keep her captives quiet. She and Abbas moved through the woods until they reached the center.

A flicker of movement at the corner of her eye caused Arix to look up, spotting the hawk that circled in the trees above them, gliding between the branches as it eyed the figure below. By the way the bird watched her, tracking her invisible steps as she slipped between the trees, she knew it was Lakai and that he could see her as plain as if she hadn't been canted at all. She grinned, feral, holding the hawk's gaze as she tore through another throat with the dagger. The hawk stilled, watching as she and Abbas took down another dozen Carn rebels.

The bird made no movement to stop them, to signal or get her attention, but watched and waited until every last member was dead or restrained.

Satisfaction burned in Arix's chest.

While Lakai had snapped his bones, she had snuck out here and taken care of the problem. Let him watch her succeed. Without a thought, the magick of the invisibility cant faded, and Arix and Abbas shifted back into the visible plane, glancing around them.

Arix grinned. "That went significantly better than I thought it would."

Abbas' face was stoic as he stared down at the bodies around their feet, but Arix saw a flicker of satisfaction in the small smile he gave her. "That was…interesting."

"How did you like being invisible?"

The small smile at the corner of Abbas' mouth turned into an uncharacteristically feral grin that cracked his face nearly in half, something Arix had never seen him do before.

"I liked it," he said plainly, though the smile said a different story.

All the tension and frustration that had been pent up in her, all of the pain and anger, ebbed away, and Arix laughed loudly, the joyous sound echoing in the trees as the hawk took flight and floated far above them.

~

All in all, Arix and Abbas had killed exactly twenty-eight Carn members hidden in the trees. Whether the number was purposeful or not, Arix thought it was only a small price for the twenty-eight of their own they had lost. Thirteen had been taken prisoner and were currently under heavy watch at the back of their traveling party. The supplies that these rebels had stashed in the woods, as well as horses and a cart, were taken into possession of the king and added to their party.

When they finally reached Vingard, news of the attack had already spread ahead of them, and the streets were beyond packed with people. The noise was so loud, Arix could hardly hear herself think. But even as she rode, trying to keep from wincing at the volume, she beamed, waving at the people who cheered her on. The songs they had sung about her in the north had apparently traveled south but with a few changes.

She noted, with no small amount of satisfaction, that the eyes of those gathered shifted past their new king and queen, gazes trained on Arix, who rode behind them. Even Delphine, whose hair was braided up into a crown on her head with seashells woven into them, turned in her saddle to look at Arix, a strange look on her face.

A sick little pebble of satisfaction gathered in Arix's throat, the pride of the victory melting together with the swell of the roaring crowd. It had been so *easy*, so simple, to use her magick and sneak behind the Carn, the precise slice of each cut of her blade like running your fingers through tall grass. If it weren't for that pebble of satisfaction, Arix might even think she felt guilty that it had been so easy. That in no time at all, she'd dispatched their enemy and ridden into Vingard as a victor.

She caught the edge of the verse as the crowd sang around her, the words barely audible mixed together with so many voices.

And vict'ry snatched with tooth and claw,
She steals their fate from 'neath god's maw.
Queen of black, queen of night,
Queen vict'ry, her enemies take flight.

At the last line, Arix could feel the pull of the crowd, the energy crackling all around them. Orion might have been at the head of their procession, but all eyes were on her. Beside her, Ulfur beamed, and Abbas remained as stoic as ever, but she could see the pride shining in his eyes.

With a quick draw, Arix pulled her sword from its sheath and held the blade aloft, and with a roar, hundreds of hands followed her motion. Fists pumped the air as she thrust her sword high, and the cheering of the crowd turned to a deafening roar. The song was completely gone now, replaced by the shouts and hoorahs, and all eyes were trained on her.

She knew it was her place to sit back, to ride demurely behind Orion, to let him take the center of the crowd's cheers. But she was tired of sitting back. Tired of doing what she was told. Tired of obeying men who were weaker than her.

And clearly, the masses agreed.

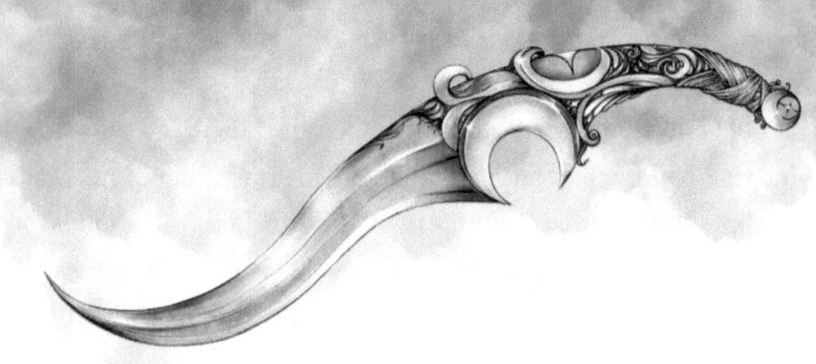

THIRTY-THREE

Warden Reuben Corrigan's estate sat atop one of the sloping hills of Vingard, its gates protecting a huge plot of land that stretched acres into one of the most beautiful gardens of Eldur. His lands contained vineyards and rolling meadows where horses ran freely. It was a beautiful home, and each room seemed more elegant than the last, with marble sweeping staircases and high ceilings that loomed above them, paintings that traveled up the walls and swept across the ceiling above their heads.

Arix had lived the beginning of her life in Eldur, second wealthiest realm of Rökkur, and yet she'd never been in estates like this, never. As she stood on the balcony attached to her room and watched the distant rolling hills dotted with wild horses, she wondered if this was the life Michael had led. There had been such a gap in the way they'd grown up, and yet they'd become the best of friends. He'd lived in Vingard his whole life, had probably been to this estate plenty of times, had maybe even stood where she stood now.

The pang she felt now, missing him, was less than before, and the thought filled her with a strange uneasiness. Was she forgetting him? Forgetting the loss of him? Forgetting their friendship and the hole that had been left behind in her heart when he'd died?

Her visit to Revena's family had changed something in her. Had patched up some of that emptiness. As she turned, the sounds of voices inside her apartments bringing her back to the doorway to stare inward rather than outward, Arix smiled.

Ro Laris was reclined back with his head very nearly resting on Nesrin's now-healed shoulder as the two chatted with Lydia, who sat on the floor. Between them, Ro poured a heavy cup of fig wine, setting the bottle down beside a spread of cheeses and fruit. Abbas, Ulfur, and Semmer stood near the door, wrapped up in their own conversation; the two tallest listening intently as Ulfur talked, animatedly moving his arms with every word.

She may have lost Revena and Michael, but this new family had filled in that emptiness. It had filled in some of the darkness that Arix knew was growing inside of her. These men and women she trusted with her life. Not just because they'd signed a contract agreeing to it but because they'd proven their loyalty and bravery with their actions.

Her gaze was pulled away from the group as a figure entered the room. Ulfur stopped mid-sentence, glancing to Arix for approval, but she waved him back to his conversation and beckoned that the old woman join her on the terrace.

Lady Doral Kel eased herself down into one of the balcony chairs while Arix settled herself back against the railing.

"Lady Kel. A surprise and a pleasure to see you. Are you settled into your rooms?"

Her Mistress of Quill, whom she hadn't really seen since their journey had begun, gave her a sidelong glance that made Arix want to both run and laugh at the same time.

"No need for the sass, young lady. I have my own servants enough for that, checking if I have enough pillows or enough wine in my cup. I don't need you meddling over me, too."

"Would you like a glass of wine, Lady Kel?"

"Well, since you've offered, I won't say no. But don't think that I'm the kind of old woman who spends all her time drinking"—she paused long enough to take the cup from Arix's hands— "and doesn't pay a lick of attention to anything going on around her. I've had my eyes wide open, you know, and I've been watching *you*."

As she said the final word, she thrust a knobbled aged index finger at Arix, who had returned to her position by the railing.

"Me?"

"Yes, you."

Arix tried her best to keep the smile from her face. "And what have you seen, Doral Kel?"

The old woman took a long sip of her drink before responding. "Don't think I missed that little stunt you pulled today."

Arix's smile quickly faded, and annoyance curdled in the back of her throat.

"No, no, no, don't look at me like that, young lady." Lady Kel peered a keen eye across the space between them, eyeing up the sudden rigidity of Arix's posture. "You wouldn't be anywhere near the position you're in today if you didn't have a shrewd mind in that pretty head of yours, and I know what you did today was tactical. Waving your sword around to encourage all that cheering."

Lady Kel leaned back, and in a moment that completely surprised Arix, she smiled a perfectly blinding white smile. "It was a good move."

Arix blinked, taking a moment to regain her composure. "You… It was? Lady Kel, I half expected you to scold me over it."

The woman's smile shifted into a smirk as she brushed at a bit of lint on her sleeve. "I still might, you know. But I'm not senile enough not to realize that your actions were tactical to the core. When a crowd behaves like it did today, it would be foolish not to respond.

If you'd pretended it wasn't happening, like you did in Rohleach, I'd have a mind to bop you over the head."

Lady Kel placed her wine glass down, resting her forearms on her knees as she leaned forward in her chair. She eyed Arix with a cool gaze that was clear as crystal. "You don't really know what to do with all that power you carry, do you?"

Arix glanced towards the terrace door, listening for a moment as the voices inside rose and fell in rhythm. After a moment, she pushed off from the railing and gently closed the door, the voices fading as the latch clicked into place.

"No, I…don't think I do."

"You thought you would."

"Yes." Arix moved to sit in one of the other chairs on the patio, settling herself in and tucking her feet up under her. "I thought that I'd know what to do. Know how to make the changes I wanted. But—"

Lady Kel cut in. "But you've spent the last three months traipsing around behind our new sun king, wondering when the real work will start?"

Arix nodded.

"You are his lap dog, after all." Lady Kel shrugged. "Your job is to obey, not to think."

For a moment, Arix thought of denying it, of challenging her role as the Black Hand. But she herself had described the role that way to others. She was the attack dog, the guard dog, the show dog to Orion. Without the power she carried, would he have ever offered her a second glance?

"But today," Lady Kel said slowly, drawing out the words so that Arix would hear every single one. "Today, you thought. You played to the crowd; you validated their praise of you. You could have, *should have*, stayed humble and quiet. A good dog on your leash. But you didn't. Instead of a dog, you were a warrior."

"They cheered me because of my magick, not because I'm a warrior." Arix countered, shaking her head.

"Bullshit."

"It's not bullshit." Arix felt a smile pull at her lips as she argued. "I'm not a warrior. I fought dirty—I used magick, snuck up on my enemies with a trick to win."

"You think the Carn didn't fight dirty? Didn't use bottled magick to kill our men today?" Doral Kel leaned forward in her chair, her face a breath away from Arix's as she grinned. "Besides, if I recall, you won your title by playing dirty, too."

Arix could feel the blood drain from her face as she stared at the old woman. "Does everyone know about that?"

"The rumors have made their way around enough now that some version of your victory, whether true or imbued with additional details, is well enough known."

Slumping back into her chair, Arix stared at the tips of her boots, wondering what kind of rumors might have flown about her fight with Celeste. It was a wonder she hadn't received a harsher welcome in Coraven for the wedding.

"You know," Lady Kel continued, sipping from her glass. "I knew Celeste Ayala. I knew her father, did business with her grandmother on more than one occasion. She was horrid as a girl, a perfect little liar. She was a crafty one, smart; she learned how to use magick very early, had some of the best tutors to prepare her for the inevitable. But that girl had been trained to fight others like her. Highborn twats who had noble magick in their noble veins. She was trained to cast the same way she was trained to fence. Even in magick, I'm sure there are rules of engagement."

Arix glanced up, watching Lady Kel's face as the woman reminisced. She stared over the balcony's railing, crystal eyes following the slopes of the hills that stretched beyond the estate house.

"You fought her dirty. You took her life, and you won."

"Yes."

"And if I'm not mistaken, you took something else of hers as well." Doral Kel gave Arix a pointed glance, indicating to the small of her back where Celeste's dagger was strapped to her.

Arix's eyes widened.

Lady Kel nodded thoughtfully at Arix's reaction. "Good. That girl deserved it."

In a gesture that felt almost motherly, Lady Kel patted Arix's knee before she slowly stood, groaning a little, and her limbs clicked into place.

"I know I'm just an old lady to you, Bellarix Sable, but I've seen a lot of people come and go through the palace. I've seen great families fall great distances, and I've watched the world change as I've grown older."

Arix stood as well, placing her hand into Doral Kel's outstretched knobby one. The lines on the old woman's hands wrinkled like fabric, and Arix could feel how thin her skin was, stretched taut over the gnarled bones beneath.

"I'm glad to have a seat in your inner circle, even if for only a short while." Lady Kel patted the back of Arix's hand and squeezed as she spoke. "Even if you do plan to replace me with someone younger."

"I don't know about that..." Arix started, but the old woman waved her off.

"I saw how you replaced that snotty little Colin Calel with Ro Laris." She glanced behind her at the closed glass doors that led back into Arix's rooms. "What a tart that man is! But he's got the keenest eye and the largest ear, and he'll be a boon to your inner circle. The rest of them, too—they're all good in their own ways, and they'll help you figure out what you want to do. They'll help you carve out the kind of world you want to rule in."

"They've all signed contracts, you know." Arix offered with a grin. "You could sign one, make you an official member of my five Fingers."

Lady Kel wrinkled her nose. "I had hoped you might change the name. Not sure I like being called an appendage."

Arix shrugged. "The Five Fingers of the Black Hand? Sounded poetic to me."

"Maybe so, maybe so. I imagine signing a contract would bind whatever years I have left to your service?"

"I wouldn't say service."

"Well, whatever it'd be, it would guarantee loyalty, would it not?"

Arix's smile softened. "Yes. It keeps them all from playing two sides. Trust may be something that has to be earned, but I just don't have time for that."

Silence lengthened between them as a breath of wind gently blew through the patio, pushing a strand of hair into Arix's face. The leaves of the trees around them rustled in the warm summer air, branches knocking together in the wind.

"I suppose you don't." Doral Kel said softly, patting Arix's hand. "I suppose none of us do anymore."

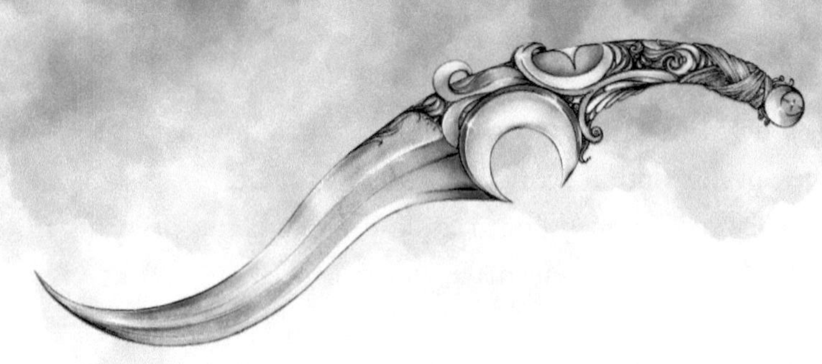

THIRTY-FOUR

It was right after dinner when the note came, calling Arix to a council meeting. Ulfur and Abbas came as well, posting themselves outside the door to Warden Corrigan's meeting room to wait, even though Arix had told them their presence was unnecessary.

Orion was already seated at the head of the table, his stance casual as he leaned back in the tall wooden chair. As the others took their seats, Arix took her place standing at his side, just to the right of his chair, between him and Lord Bardon.

"They loved you, today."

Arix didn't realize who it was that had spoken until she glanced down and realized it was Orion. There was something about the way he said it, something too calm in his voice that pricked a point of unease in the pit of her stomach.

"I am the hand of the king," she said simply. It was one thing to acknowledge what had happened today with Doral Kel, but it was another to say it to Orion. He'd been so different the past couple weeks. So different from the man she'd come to know last year.

Orion's voice was thoughtful as he watched the rest of the council members file in and find their places at the table. "Perhaps. Perhaps they see you for who you really are."

Arix didn't know what to say, so she stayed quiet.

It was impossible to interpret the mood he was in, to interpret what he was thinking. She'd maybe expected a bit more resentment or condescension, but he seemed content. Resolved, almost, not to fight her or push her.

It made her nervous.

"WHAT'S HE DOING?" the raspy voice spoke, and she felt the dagger warm at the small of her back as the words flooded her mind. *"WHAT NEW GAME DOES HE PLAY?"*

Arix felt, rather than heard, her necklace hum in agreement.

But there was nothing she could do but wait. Wait and see what Orion was planning. He'd called this meeting for a reason, and now that they were all here, she was about to find out why.

The voices in the room faded into silence as Orion slowly stood from his chair and spoke. "Thank you all for coming. I know you're tired from the journey and the excitement, so I appreciate your willingness to meet so late. After what occurred on the road into Vingard, I've thought about ways to deal with the Carn. Ways to deal with the violence and the bloodshed. My father chose to deal with the rebels as if they were a plague. Stomping them out where he could, and this council helped him do it."

Orion motioned to Warden Aliska and Warden Los Ke as he continued. "Your military force has helped to drive the Carn into hiding but has forced them to resort to sneak attacks and an unnecessary loss of life. I, for one, am tired of the bloodshed."

He paused, and for a moment, an eerie chill passed down Arix's spine. Something was wrong. Something—

The doors at the far end of the room swung open, and Arix saw that Ulfur and Abbas were restrained in the hallway, on their knees with swords to their throats, held at bay by a group of nearly twenty. Through the doors strode a tall man, his cloak streaming behind him as he confidently stepped inside the room.

"It is time for some semblance of peace," the man said, moving towards one of the empty seats at the far end of the table.

Arix didn't let him reach the chair.

With a growl, Arix thrust her hands forward, moving to point a finger at the man.

"**S T O P.**" The word she ground out was deep, thrumming with magick, reverberating with a tone more similar to a gong than the human voice.

The intruder stopped in his tracks, obeying the command, his hand still outstretched to pull the chair out for himself. Behind him, his men in the hall tensed, pulling Ulfur and Abbas tight against the blades held at their necks. The council members were silent, Warden Uellen Vod and General Hawes standing, glancing at Orion to see what he would do.

"That's enough, Miss Sable," Orion said, his voice strangely calm. "Allow our guest to sit, if you please."

Arix tore her gaze away from the intruder to stare at Orion. The look in his eyes was cold, calculating. Anger tore through her, the urge to ignore his order thick on her tongue. He had his own agenda, his own aspirations to greatness, and she had gotten in his way today. This was his retaliation.

Slowly, she dropped the magick, disgust and frustration burning in her eyes, and the man at the end of the table moved to pull out a chair for himself. He grinned at her as he did so, the contempt clear on his face. In the hall, his men relaxed a bit, and two more joined their leader, standing on either side of his chair. Behind them, the door closed, and Arix felt a ripple of fear twist in her gut.

Kaoss, she thought, *keep Ulfur and Abbas from harm.*

"I've asked Lazh Mendir to join us today," Orion continued once the man was settled, "to broker a sort of temporary peace."

Arix's head snapped up at the name, remembering what Micah had told her during the test. He was Maeve's uncle, one of the leaders of the Carn. It was he who decided where they went, where they hid, where their band moved and attacked.

Lazh leaned forward, placing his elbows on the table as he grinned at them. "It is an honor to be invited here, King Orion. It's our hope to be able to come to some sort of…understanding here today."

Every muscle in Arix tensed, ready to silence him again if she needed to. If Lazh was here, was Maeve? Would she finally get a chance to meet the Carn's incantor face to face?

Orion took his seat again before addressing the rest of the council, motioning that they all follow his example. "There has been enough bloodshed even in the past week. On this tour, there have been attacks from both sides. What I said in Rohleach still stands. You've trusted me to this seat, trusted the vision I have for a better and brighter future for Rökkur. We cannot continue to live divided in this way. Each day, our enemies see us growing and fighting and wait for us to kill ourselves so they can pick our bones clean. After some thought and prayer, I reached out to Lazh to better understand what it is the Carn want. I believe my father used the people's fear to control them. I am king now—not to demand loyalty, but to ask for your trust. Trust that we might come to a better solution than the insurrection we've teetered on for the past twenty years."

Around the table, Arix could see the others on the council listening with guarded expressions. No one cheered him or nodded their assent. They watched and waited. They were hesitant, wary of what Orion was doing. Too many of them hated the Carn, she knew. But were any of them willing to put their hatred aside long enough to trust Orion?

Hatred ran deep, and no amount of trust could truly cut it all out.

Orion had brought Lazh here, into Warden Corrigan's home, without discussing it with the rest of them, without seeking their counsel. Only Lord Bardon, Lord Heseth, and Lakai remained unsurprised, probably the only ones at the table who had known what Orion was planning. Lord Bardon, she could understand; he'd helped Orion rise to become king. Even Lord Heseth made sense; his insight into military strategy made him an obvious choice when considering the potential for war or peace within Rökkur. And Lakai? Arix avoided looking at her former mentor. Somewhere along the journey, Orion had turned to him instead of her.

"In the pursuit of peace, Lazh is here to broker a temporary treaty," Orion continued before shifting his attention to the intruding general and gesturing toward the man. "I understand you've brought some terms to discuss with us today, General Mendir. Our ears are open to what you have to say."

"Thank you, Your Majesty," Lazh said with such an unhurried tone, such an air of confidence, as though he held all the cards in this exchange. "And I speak on behalf of not only myself and the twenty-five thousand men and women that stand with us but also for our true leader, Maeve Mendir."

The others in the room knew the incantor's name. But only a few of them knew that it was Maeve that had been bottling her magick to attack them in the streets of Rohleach and on the road to Vingard.

Lazh leaned forward, placing a piece of paper on the table, and pushed it towards the center. No one reached for it.

"King Taurus had a name for us," Lazh went on. "He called us rebels; he called us outcasts. And for a long time, that was what we were. A fringe sect on the edge of society, doing our best to protect, to restore, to—"

"Shut your mouth."

All eyes shifted to Arix as she ground out the words, her teeth bared together as she glared across the table. She gripped the hilt of her sword so hard her knuckles buckled white, anger rolling down her spine in waves.

Lazh's eyebrows shot up, but not with surprise. She could see the amusement written all over his face, the game he was playing so obvious that it made Arix feel sick.

"You aren't protectors." Arix spat out the words, feeling sick to her stomach as images of the devastation she'd seen at the hands of the Carn ripple through her mind. "You destroy, you burn, you steal. King Taurus was right to hunt you all down, to kill you all, to wipe you from the face of the—"

Arix had begun to stride forward, to end it here and now, to shut Lazh's mouth of lies forever, but her feet had stopped in their tracks. She glanced down, then slowly let her eyes flick up to the only other person in the room who could be holding her in place. Lakai gripped the edge of the table as he focused on her, cants muttered under his breath to restrain her.

The edges of her vision darkened, and Arix could feel the swell of magick coming before she could stop it. Her attention was shifted now, all that anger now directed at her old teacher, who kept her stilled when she wanted to strike. She could feel the voices of the pendant, Michael's ring, and Celeste's dagger, all muddled in her mind as they traced the outline edges of the magick that held her. Feeling the cracks and crevices of his cant.

It was shoddy work, she realized. Haphazard and thrown together. There were weak spots in the boundaries where the cant held her legs, her feet, bracing her arms in their positions. And she could feel her own magick responding, so simple and easy to feel the weakest points and snap them.

Arix cocked her head at Lakai, letting a smile spread across her face. "No one can hold me, old man. Especially not you."

And she simply *pushed* through his barrier.

She saw Lakai's eyes widen, and she heard the gasp in the room as she stepped out of the cant that was supposed to hold her and drew her sword. Lazh stood from his chair, and the men at his side stepped backward, eyes growing round as she advanced towards them.

"You promised us!" Lazh shouted as she rounded the table, glaring at Orion as he and his men drew their own swords. "You promised us safety, Orion!"

"Arix!"

She stopped.

It took every ounce of willpower to do it, every fiber in her being screaming and clawing to ignore his command, to ignore his voice, to ignore what he was asking of her. Her cores, too, screamed in her mind, the dagger spewing threats and vile accusations, her pendant going hoarse with rage, and waves of hurt and disappointment from her ring. It took all her energy, her will even, to obey him, to lower her sword and go still only inches away from Lazh and his men.

But she did it. She took a shaking breath, felt the anger pooling white hot in her throat, and fought the emotion that screamed and thrashed in her chest.

"I promised them safety," Orion boomed, his voice loud enough to rattle Arix's bones. "And safety they will have. Come, Arix. You will not fight them today."

There was such authority and satisfaction in his voice. He knew he had control over her, knew she would listen to him. He knew that here and now, when he whistled, she would come like a good little guard dog.

And she did.

It broke something in her to do it, broke that part of her that had held on to her hatred and anger. Broke the part of her that trusted him, that maybe trusted anyone.

Arix turned, deliberate steps the only thing keeping her upright, as she returned to her place at Orion's side, standing guard beside his chair. Her sword slid back into its sheath, her hands shaking with the effort.

Orion reclined back in his chair at the head of the table, satisfaction written on his face. "My apologies for the outburst. You have to understand, after over twenty years of devastation and death, it is not easy for anyone here to trust you, Lazh. But let us leave the past in the past."

Lazh was still standing, his men with their swords drawn, and Arix noted that the General clutched a bottle in his hand. Ready to throw it, ready to react with the bottled magick if he needed to. If he tried, she wouldn't give him a chance.

Orion motioned for General Lazh to retake his seat. "Please, sit. We aren't here to forgive and to forget the past. Clearly"—he glanced over his shoulder at Arix with a smirk—"the anger towards the Carn runs too deep for that. Instead, let us look at the present with a mind towards the future. Your attacks will stop. You will cease your operations until the tour is complete. Let the people celebrate and revel in peace. Let them receive their new king and enjoy the rest of the summer season without fear for their lives."

Lazh still had not sat back down, but the men behind him had relaxed a little now that Orion was proposing a peaceful, if temporary, solution.

"When I am back home, in Mergur, we will revisit a more lasting treaty. Your demands will be discussed, and perhaps then we can come to a more realistic outcome."

"And what will the Carn receive for our restraint?"

"The men we took captive outside of Vingard… I'm prepared to give them back to you."

More than one of the council members shot a confused glance at Orion, frustration writhing around the table. But not a single one spoke up. Not a single one disagreed or fought or coughed or said a *damn fucking thing*.

Arix seethed. Her jaw popped with the pressure as she ground her teeth together, fighting the urge to say something, *anything*.

She should have killed every last Carn she'd found. Should have taken no prisoners, should have slaughtered every last one of them. If she'd known that Orion would be handing them back like this, she should have done so much worse.

Lazh considered Orion's offer, eyes flickering back to look at the men who stood beside him. One of them leaned down to whisper in his ear, stretching the silence in the room.

But there was something else, something deeper than the uncomfortability, the sense of betrayal. Orion was too smug, too relaxed. There was something else she was missing, a piece of the puzzle that might put this into perspective, a sliver of truth in the woven tapestry of mistrust that surrounded this meeting.

Casually, Arix ran her finger down the chain of her necklace, feeling the stone warm between the pad of her thumb and forefinger. The magick responded, flowing from the tapped power of her core pendant. Tendrils flowed from her mind, stretching across the room, ignoring the other thoughts and feelings of the council members who sat at the table but reached for Lazh's mind. He was the enemy, after all, no matter what false peace might be brokered here today, and she would give him no privacy of his own thoughts.

It was a strange thing, peeking into someone's head.

It took concentration and a fair bit of magick. She had to be careful, prod slowly forward, and slip as easily into her opponent's mind as she would slip into a still pond. The more she thrashed, the more ripples spilled outward, disturbing the surface.

Her reach was cut short, hitting the hard impenetrable wall that surrounded Lazh. Arix's brow quirked. He was warded.

As if he knew what she was doing, his gaze flicked away from Orion to settle on her, and a small smile played across his lips.

She turned her reach to his companions, but once again, hit a wall. All of them were warded; all of them were kept safe from someone stealing into their heads. It was difficult magick. Magick that took time and energy and immense amounts of *power*. Arix herself wore three cores to help her channel her own magick, and even with them, she knew her own limits. Knew the limits of how far her cantwork could reach.

This was damn near impossible.

"Your incantor," Lazh spoke, keeping his gaze pierced at Arix even though he spoke to Orion, "meddles where she shouldn't. It is impolite, I think, to read the thoughts of those around you."

More than one head turned at that, and Arix clenched her jaw in response.

Orion said nothing, but he only seemed to relax more into his chair at Lazh Mendir's accusation.

"General Mendir," Orion said, tone casual, "I assure you that it was not meant with malice. My Black Hand only seeks to protect me."

Lazh snorted.

"Do you agree to our terms?" Orion asked.

The Carn general slowly stood, his hands braced on the surface of the table as his chair scraped back across the carpeted floor. He smiled.

"We do."

And then he turned, and they walked out of the room, his

men opening and shutting the doors to leave the council in silence. Arix could hear the retreat of their feet, fading away. Out
of reach, out of her grasp. They had come and gone in less than
ten minutes, and in that span of time, everything had changed.

Fury raged in her. It filled her up like hot bubbling molasses,
spilling down the sides and leaving her shaking with the savagery
of it.

"Would you die for me, Arix?"

Orion's voice was quiet as he asked.

Something about the way he said it was wrong. She'd expected
anger, fury to match her own, but he seemed so calm. Arix could
feel the eyes of the council burning into them, feel their stares
boring deep through her sternum and into her very heart.

"It is my duty to protect you, Your Majesty," she ground out.
"As Black Hand, I would gladly lay down my life for—"

"Of course you would." He cut her off, standing abruptly and
causing the chair he'd sat in to fall backwards, crashing to the floor
as he spun to face her. "You're sworn to serve. Me. My rule. Not
your rule."

Arix crushed her jaw closed at the accusation.

"I am king here. In this realm and all the others. I am the leader
of this nation, the Sun King who will pull Rökkur out from darkness and into a new age. I wear this crown, and it is I who must
make hard decisions for the good of the survival of my reign and
this country. Do you understand what that means, Arix?"

She couldn't look away from him, couldn't let the white-hot
emptiness around the edge of her vision show on her face. Embarrassment and fury burned the tips of her ears red as he shamed
her in front of the entire council.

"I do, King Orion."

The words she bit out felt as black as pitch dripping from her mouth.

"And do you understand your role here in this court? As my Black Hand? That you are here to serve, protect. You listen to *me*, obey *me*. If I tell you to stand still, you will do so. If I tell you to throw yourself from the highest cliff, you will do so. You will be my shield, my sword, my wrath, my dog. Your magick may give you a seat at this table, but do not ever forget that you still answer to *me*."

She said nothing, biting the inside of her cheek to keep from lashing out, to keep from hitting him square in the jaw. He deserved it, and she might have, if they'd been alone. But here? Would she gain or lose the respect of the council?

He stepped closer until they were chest to chest, the black of her armor brushing against the rich gold thread of his vest.

Orion's voice was low, quiet and even. He was speaking so only she could hear as he lifted her chin to meet his gaze. "You will never undermine me like that again. Do you understand?"

There were tears biting at the outer corners of her eyes, but she forced them away. Slowly, Arix dipped her chin in a small nod.

"Say it."

She moved to pull away from his grasp so she could speak, but he kept a firm grip on her jaw.

"I understand, King Orion." The words held venom.

It would take nothing, barely a thought, to pull from his grip. To use her magick to force his hand, to give her strength, to shrink him to the size of nothing and stomp him out if she wanted. But she understood better now than she ever had before that this was all about power and perceived threats. This was not about her. It was about him.

He didn't like being undermined. She was his guard dog, teeth sharp as knives, but a guard dog that wasn't obedient to its master was put down. And Arix knew that if she posed a threat to him, if he saw her as a potential problem instead of an ally, he would remove her from the equation. She might have been the most powerful in the room, but it didn't mean anything as long as she served him.

Cold, icy fingers of realization encircled her throat, grasping it so tight that she thought she might choke on the air in her lungs. How had she never realized what she was to him? Who she was? All the words he'd said to her, all their late-night conversations whispered in the dark… Goddess, she'd been such a fool.

"Good." Orion finally let go of her chin, stepping back. "You're dismissed."

Arix didn't hesitate this time. She turned on her heel and strode out of the room. Around her, she could feel the eyes of the council looking away, avoiding seeing her disgrace. None had spoken up for her. Why would they?

As she pressed her hand to the wooden door to open it, she glanced back, catching the gaze of only one who stared back at her. They held each other's gaze before Arix forced herself to look away, shame catching her squarely in the throat.

But even long after the door had closed behind her and she had walked the full length of the corridor, her steps echoing into silence, Lakai stared after her, pity filling his old eyes.

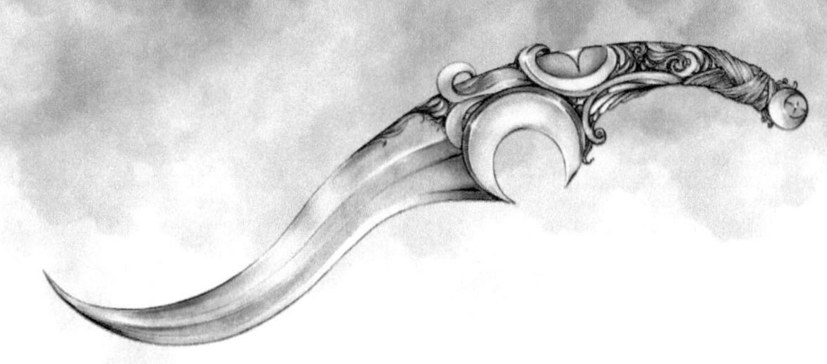

THIRTY-FIVE

Arix did not sleep that night. Instead, she returned to her rooms, locking the doors behind her. She banished Nesrin with a glare that could have frozen an ocean and ordered bottles upon bottles of honey brandy. She drank each glass slowly, steadily, slumped in a chair on her balcony, letting the thick syrup of the alcohol coat her throat until her vision swam and her stomach churned. And then she vomited it all back up over the railing, lying her head on the cool tile of her veranda floor and staring at the shining stars that waved pinpricks in her vision.

Even then, exhausted and wrung out, alone and woozy, she did not sleep.

The shame in her heart would not let her. The humiliation ate at her mind and would not offer the mercy of rest, instead playing back every memory, every moment, every glance and kiss she'd shared with Orion over the past year.

She picked apart their talks, their interactions, cracking open the shell and dissecting every word. There had to have been a sign, glaring, blatant proof of what Orion had been all along. But lying in the dark, humid night, she cursed herself for not seeing his actions for the facade they were.

That was perhaps the worst of it. If she'd thought back, realized the moments of his lies with clarity, she could have forgiven herself, forgiven him even. But she hadn't seen it. There had been too much going on, too many pieces in play, and he had seemed so sincere in all of their talks.

Had he lied to her? Or had she only lied to herself?

When the sun finally rose, it rose dead, a gray husk that dragged itself over the mountains and spilled into a gray-shrouded sky. It felt fitting. Like, for once, the weather matched the darkness in her heart. Why shouldn't the sun mourn with her? Why shouldn't the sky cry, raindrops slowly pricking the leaves of the trees in a steady and sure rhythm to dull the ache in her head.

It was the knowledge that Nesrin would come knocking on her door any moment that urged Arix to finally rise off the cool tile floor and run a comb through her hair. A simple braid down her back was good enough for what needed to be done today. The blessing wasn't until tomorrow at dawn, in the temple of Vulcan, but the feast would come tonight, and they would eat and drink through the darkest hours to celebrate Vulcan's wife, Nyx, with the full moon.

She didn't need to take part in any of the preparation for the banquet, but Arix had her own duties to attend to, her own role she still needed to play.

After she'd left the council room last night, she'd refused to answer Ulfur and Abbas' questions, and she felt their anger at her back as she'd stormed away to her rooms. She owed them an explanation, an apology, for how she'd behaved. By now, they all probably knew, but she was their commander. And they were her friends.

She found Abbas first, talking quietly with two of her Black

Guard outside Vingard's outpost. As she approached, her Black Guard saw her first, their shifting glances giving her away and then scurrying away before she could get close.

"Good morning, Arix." Abbas' voice was solemn. "We must speak."

"I know."

"Ulfur is upset."

"Yeah, we all are."

Without another word, he turned towards the larger of the garrison buildings, and Arix stayed silent until they were both in the general's office, the door closed behind them. She slumped in the chair behind the desk, resting her head on the cool wooden surface as Abbas settled across from her.

"Ulfur will be here soon."

Arix could only manage a mumble in return. Her head was splitting, and her mouth was dry. She hadn't eaten, and her empty stomach clawed at the underside of her ribs in agony. It was only when the door squeaked on its hinges that Arix picked up her head, bloodshot eyes connecting with Ulfur's from across the small space. He was angry, his jaw clenched as he took a seat.

"They're gone. All the prisoners. The Carn just came in with King Orion's men an' took 'em. A few of our men fought it—we didn't know wha' to do, Arix. You weren't *here*." He intoned the last word, frustration and anger piled together.

Arix sighed slowly, letting the air hiss out between her teeth in one long slow stream. "I know. You're right. I should have been here."

"Why?" Abbas asked, his low timbre rumbling the question that all three thought.

"Lazh was here."

"Aye, we saw that." Ulfur spat.

Arix's gaze shot up to glare at him. "He surprised all of us. No one knew what he was doing there, and when I tried to stop him, Orion intervened." Even as she said the words, the anger seeped out of her, worn out through sheer exhaustion.

"He betrayed me." The words came out so soft, embarrassing words that Arix wished she could shove back in her mouth.

She stared hard at the surface of the desk, her hands laying flat and open on the wood. What else could she say other than that? What else could she tell them? That she'd been a fool?

That he'd shamed her in front of everyone? That she was afraid that Orion had come to despise her?

"He betrayed more than you last night, Arix." Abbas' voice was firm and even, but even that couldn't make Arix raise her head to look at him.

"I'm sure people are talking," Arix said with a mirthless chuckle. "I'm sure everyone knows by now."

"Do not worry about them."

"I do worry." Arix finally raised her head to look at Abbas. "I do worry about what you think of me, what the rest of the Guard think of me. He said terrible things in front of the council; he put me in my place. And he did it because he knows I'm becoming dangerous."

Ulfur and Abbas traded a knowing glance.

"What?"

Abbas spoke slowly. "There is talk that the blessing will be a public event."

Arix felt the blood run cold in her veins. "What?"

"People are talking about having the blessing ceremony for King Orion in the amphitheater rather than in the temple. It will be full seating—many will come to watch him."

"And me."

Abbas nodded.

"They'll be disappointed."

"Why?" Ulfur asked. "You donna think you'll receive another blessing?"

"I know I won't," Arix responded simply. "A seer told me when we were in Coraven that I'd receive blessings from the first two but not the others. If Orion is planning a whole spectacle, then somehow, he knows. Somehow, he knows that I won't get a blessing. It's another way to control public opinion of me."

"I donna understand why he's doin' this to ya, Arix. Why has his opinion changed so much for ya?"

"I…" Arix faltered in her response. Did she know? When had it happened? "I don't know. Maybe I fooled myself into believing things about us, about him. But something changed, and the air between us is stagnant now."

"Whatever King Orion has planned, it is good that you know now. You have time to plan." Abbas offered.

Arix scrubbed her hands over her face, trying to wipe away the exhaustion.

"Did ya sleep, lass?" Ulfur asked, his voice gentle. "You donna look like ya caught a wink o' it."

Pushing herself up from the desk took more effort than Arix had expected, and as she stood, Ulfur and Abbas stood with her. "I need to move. I need to drink some water, eat something, and *move*. Is there training today?"

"A few of the younger ones are training in the courtyard." Abbas offered.

Ulfur grinned. "I'll get ya some food for your belly; you go down and suit up. Swing a sword 'round and show th' little ones who's boss."

They made their way back out of the office and headed toward the courtyard, where Arix watched a few of her men training while she stuffed down the bread and cheese Ulfur had brought. After giving her stomach a chance to settle, she joined in, letting the pull of her muscles take over her mind. The turn of the blade, the shield cants to block… It slowly replaced the dark thoughts that loomed, and after an hour, she had almost forgotten.

It felt good to train again, to clash swords with her guard, to spend time with them. She could tell by the way they looked at her, talked to her, that they respected her. A few joked, pointing out where she was rusty, but it was always with the utmost regard, never speaking too comfortably. They still saw her as their commander, and the knowledge of that gave Arix a little bit of hope. Even when she was humiliated, there were men and women at her back who followed and looked up to her.

Maybe things would be different when they returned to Mergur. The fuss of Orion's tour would be over, they would all be home again, and she would be able to slip back into the routines of daily life. She'd stand watch over Orion and Delphine like a good guard dog, but she'd have her Black Guard and her five Fingers, and she'd be able to do research into her magick. A safe sort of comfortability that she could lean into. Orion's scrutiny would turn to running his kingdom, and she would simply fade into the background.

Maybe that was best.

"Maybe you are a coward." Her pendant whispered.

Arix pretended not to hear.

~

By the time she'd finished her training and returned to her room, she felt a little better. Food and a hot bath only added to her mood, and somewhere between the soaking hot water and a buttered biscuit,

Arix felt almost back to normal. She changed into simple high-waisted, wide-leg black trousers and a billowing black shirt with long cuffs before heading down to the main hall of the Warden's estate.

Servants spilled through the doors leading into the main ballroom, carrying decorations or stacks of dinnerware. The banquet was only a few hours away, the ceremony planned for dawn. She simply had to make it until then, make it past the stares and the whispers and then she could focus on the return trip to Mergur. Once the blessing was over, she could return to her incantor tower in Castle Zma'ai and fade back into the backdrop again. She might find peace in it, and maybe, finally, the burning in her chest would stop.

Arix fingered the small vial of Well Water in her pocket, trying to decide whether or not to drink it. It still felt so wrong, and even if she couldn't place a finger on *why*, the feeling ate at her. She'd been taking the Well Water that Lakai had given her, taken it when her headaches pushed her to the brink, taken it when hollowed-out pain inside her raged so violently she thought she might pass out again. And she wanted to take it now, the churning in her head and her chest almost too much to bear.

She let the vial stay in her pocket.

As she stood in the doorway to the ballroom, she felt a presence join her, Lady Doral Kel's recognizable stooped form hovering at her elbow.

"Lady Kel." Arix offered a smile. "How are you this afternoon?"

"Well enough to know you have no reason for smiles, Lady Black Hand," Doral Kel countered. "And I've heard the blessing will be public, too?"

Some of the energy Arix had regained after food and a bath fizzled away a bit at the reminder.

"Does it matter if the king's blessing is public or not? It'll be the final blessing before returning to Mergur."

Lady Kel let out something between a scoff and a curse. "It matters, Arix. You know why he does it."

It wasn't a question. The two women knew there was more to this choice of venue than just Orion's desire to connect with his subjects.

Arix wanted to say something, a retort, a response that would satisfy both herself and the old lady, but she couldn't find the words. The exhaustion was still eating away at the edges of her being, and she was too tired to find the fight in herself.

Doral Kel seemed to notice this, and instead of pressing, she wrapped her bony fingers around Arix's upper arm and leaned into her, her entire posture and tone shifting. "Won't you walk with me, Lady Black Hand? Through the gardens for a moment. It's a beautiful day, and these old bones need to stretch a bit if I'm expected to stay up all night and into the dawn of morning."

Arix eyed her with a suspicious glance. "It looks like it's about to rain."

"Pish posh, don't you think these bones are old enough to know that it won't rain just yet. My elbows speak to my knees, and they confer with my hips that the rain will hold off for at least another hour."

That pulled a laugh from Arix as she turned and escorted the old woman out the back door and into the hilled gardens behind the estate. Dark earth packed the path beneath them as together they slipped between the trees and hedges, picking nectarines and pears off the trees as they strolled. Doral Kel kept the conversation civil and tame for the majority of the walk, but the further they stepped from the estate, the more Arix wondered if there wasn't an ulterior motive to their little stroll.

"Lady Kel." Arix finally said, "Shall we maybe take a moment and rest here?"

The gazebo was hidden away between more of the fruit trees the two had been wandering between, and they sat under the sloped rooftop as the first drops of rain splattered against the dirt pathways.

"You cannot let him win."

Doral Kel's voice was almost impossible to hear over the sound of the slow patter of raindrops on the wooden roof above them, and Arix had to lean in close to the old woman to hear what she said as she went on.

"You must stop him." Doral Kel's storm-gray eyes watched the leaves of the trees around them shift underneath the weight of each drop. "He's gone too far with this trick, Arix. Peace with the Carn will ruin Rökkur. All of the power is poisoning him and dragging the council along with it."

Arix said nothing, watching instead the lines furrow into Doral Kel's forehead as she spoke softly.

"You must fake it."

"Fake what?"

"The blessing." Lady Kel twisted, those gray eyes now boring into Arix. "He's chosen the amphitheater for a reason. Orion wants the spectacle; he wants the witnesses. To prove that you aren't as special as he is."

"I don't think it's about how special he is," Arix cut in, feeling that defensive cut of emotion rising up her sternum. "It's about his power. About proving I fall under him, not above him. That's why he traded the rebels for a temporary peace. It was to prove that even as powerful as I am, I obey him."

"Any man who has to tell you he's in charge, isn't. And any man who utters the words, 'I'm not afraid of you,' is secretly quaking in terror." Doral ground out. "You have to prove to him, and more importantly, to yourself, that you won't be cowed."

Arix only stared out at the rain.

"He treated you like a dog." Disgust was etched into each syllable as Doral Kel spat out the words.

"Like a dog," Arix echoed.

Her conversation with Lydia Skonos rippled through her mind, and for a moment, she let that thought rest. She was a wolf, underneath it all, chained to Orion and trained to come at his whistle. She would heel when he told her to and bare her teeth when he commanded.

"I don't understand why you aren't angrier."

Arix sighed. "I'm too tired, Doral. I'm too tired to fight him, not after last night. And after…"

She trailed off, the words unspoken as the rain came down harder around them.

"You don't know what I did, Lady Kel. You don't know how I helped him become king."

Arix felt the old woman's fingers slip between her own as they lay clasped in between them on the worn bench.

"It's alright. I know. I think most of us know, if not suspect. The timing was too perfect for it to be anything else."

For a moment, she thought she might cry. But the tears didn't come. Instead, she felt hollowed out, empty of the emotion that should have been raging in her. Arix wasn't sad about losing Orion's companionship or angry at his turning on her last night. She didn't feel alone or disappointed or heartsick.

She felt nothing.

"I killed Taurus for him."

"You did it because you thought it was a mercy."

"I did it because I was selfish." Arix retorted, pulling her hand from Doral's grasp and standing by the opening to the gazebo. "I killed an old, helpless man because I wanted to be the Black Hand. Because I saw a future for myself standing at Orion's side. I still do. I still see the good I could do as Black Hand if we worked together. But last night proves that we can't. The future I saw, he never did. Maybe I was always a pawn to him. A chess piece to move around the board at will."

"If you are a chess piece, Arix, you are the queen. You move how you will, and the only restrictions you have are the ones you hold on yourself." Doral Kel practically had to shout, the rain was coming down so ferociously now.

Arix didn't want to hear. She stepped out into the deluge, water instantly soaking through her clothing, pressing her hair against her skull. Who was she if she was not Orion's incantor? If she was not his attack dog?

The person she had been before was gone. There was no going back to hiding away on rooftops. And the person she had become, the competitor, was gone too. In the past few months, she'd stepped fully into her role as Black Hand. She felt it more in her bones than she'd ever felt anything before. But in her mind, she'd always been the Black Hand that stood beside Orion.

Arix angled her chin up, letting the water run down her face in streams, squeezing her eyes tight against the water drops. Slowly, carefully, she erased Orion from the picture in her mind, letting the lines of his jaw and the flow of his shirt sleeves, the wave of his hair, and the blue of his eyes fade into nothing. She was left with only one figure.

Herself.

Moving from the side into the center, taking the centerpoint in the frame. And stepping in from the darkness behind her, her five Fingers. Nesrin, Ro Laris, Semmer Kloevendirr, Lydia Skonos, and Doral Kel.

It was a new idea, something she'd never thought of. But seeing it now in her mind's eye, it was a beautiful thing. A smile slowly spread until she was laughing, the rain practically choking her before she spun back around to face Lady Kel.

"I have an idea."

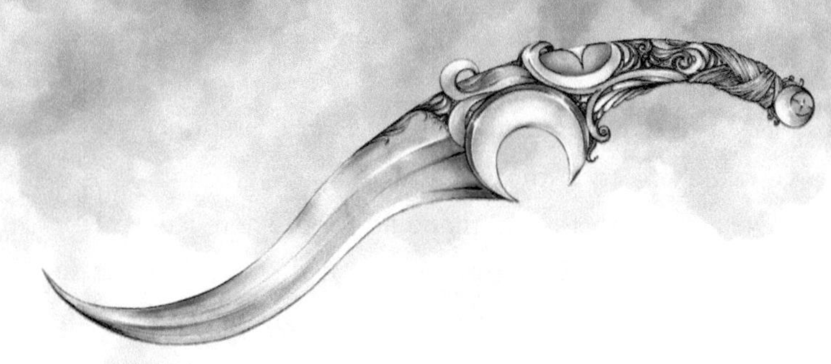

THIRTY-SIX

The banquet raged around Arix, a storm of laughter and gaiety swirling around her quiet stance behind Orion's chair. It didn't touch her, the sounds and merriment fading to a whisper in the space around her. She tuned them all out, eyes watching but mind somewhere else. Mentally, she flipped through cants, piecing together what she would need.

Her stomach was curled into knots, and Arix took moments to sip from the vial of Well Water until the knots faded to a dull ache. She would be focused, and she would be perfect, and she would fool them all.

The air was charged, different from all the other times before; laughter was extra boisterous, and the alcohol flowed so freely that Arix wondered if anyone would be able to stand once morning came. It felt like everyone in the room was trying a little too hard, and the tension that built slowly, minute by minute, drink by raucous drink, amped up into a soundless whine that made Orion's temperament drop.

He could tell, like she could, that the revelers around them, the court and the Warden's dignitaries, invited guests, all pushed themselves past the underlying truth of what Orion had done.

He'd made a treaty with the Carn.

That was not something Arix could forgive and, it seemed, that was not something some of the others could either. No one spoke out, not publicly, but it was easy to tell just by watching from the center of the head table; uneasiness ate away at the ambiance of the room like a cancer.

Arix could not help the small smile that quirked at the corner of her mouth.

By the time the night had played its course and Lord Bardon announced that it was time to head to the amphitheater for Vulcan's blessing, the crowd was beyond tense. Heads shifted to watch her, and the whispers that trailed behind them on their way grew louder with every step.

The amphitheater was packed with people, those too late to enter parting to allow their king and his court to enter. The lilac-gray tinge of the sky was so still that the shuffling of their feet sounded louder, and their whispers echoed through the stone passageways and expanded through the carved arches. People clasped fists over their hearts as Orion passed, and he nodded to them with all the humility and serenity that a good king should.

Arix refused to lower her head.

For as many onlookers gazed up at Orion with adoration, just as many looked to her, fire blazing behind their eyes. So many of them were angry, looking to her for a trace of indignation, for a sign that she felt the same resentment that they held in their hearts.

As they passed through the final archway, Arix felt a crumple of paper press into her palm, and she glanced down at the tiny hand that held hers. A little girl stared up at her, eyes wide as she gripped Arix's hand. The girl's mother was there only a moment later to pull her away, but Arix held the little girl's gaze until they had passed too far into the amphitheater, and the girl was lost.

Uncrumpling the paper, Arix read the words scrawled in a messy hand in the cool light of morning:

Good luck.

Arix smiled softly, folding the paper back up and sticking it in between the panels of her armor, settling the note into a spot against her collarbone.

The hard sand of the theater gave way under her feet, and Arix stepped forward out of the tunnels and into the swelling center, watching the light that spilled over the tops of the stone wall slowly start to tinge orange as the sun moved ever upward. At the center of the arena, the priestess had placed Vulcan's altar beside a roaring braiser that crackled with fresh wood, ready for Orion to approach and the prayer to commence. Hidden by the tall circular walls that surrounded them, the center was still shrouded in morning darkness.

The near silence of the colosseum faded into nothing as the priestess raised her inked hands.

"King Orion Karcharias, step forward to receive the blessings of the God of Fire."

Orion moved forward, stepping towards the priestess, his face lit up by the orange glow of the flames.

"Burning flame, flickering bright. It is Fire that warms our hearths, Fire that sustains the forge, Fire that burns and purifies. From the loneliest, darkest winters to the brightest sunshine of a summer's day, it is Fire that endures, a constant fiery sun in our skies."

At the words, the fire swelled, flickering higher as Vulcan responded to the words. The clouds above them tinged pink, the sky ablaze with colors as the sun continued to rise, still yet to crest the outer walls of the arena.

"Great God Vulcan, honorable son of Kaoss, burning light of flame; we beseech you to forge within him a bold heart, kindled with purpose and confidence in all he does. Scorch all doubt from him, all manner of weakness, and sear ambition to his soul. Let fire burn away all who oppose him, trampled like embers beneath his feet. Let the blaze of victory follow behind him, lighting the darkest night."

The priestess stepped aside, motioning for Orion to step forward toward the fire. He did, moving a hand outstretched towards the blaze. The crowd gasped as he stepped close, moving until his whole arm had been swallowed up by the fire, licking around the sleeves of his golden embroidered jacket. The fabric sizzled on contact with the fire, burning away as pieces of charred fabric were carried away by the breeze. But the soft of his flesh beneath did not burn, and the fire merely kissed past it. The small crease between Orion's brow faded, and a smile spread across his face as he removed the arm and held it aloft.

All around them, the crowd surged, cheering and shouting praise to Vulcan.

Arix took a deep breath. It was time.

Behind Orion, the logs that formed the fire shifted, a piece of flaming wood crumbling and cracking under the burning weight. The crack was deafening as the wood splintered, spilling out of the metal confines and crashing into the sand. Orion jerked his head to look, fear spreading across his face as he stumbled back from the burning wood.

Without warning, the *sand* caught fire.

The priestess screamed, turning to flee. Orion scrambled backward to avoid the flame, sand skidding under his feet as he moved out of the path, the voices of the stands around them calling out in warning.

But Arix stayed where she was. She took one cautious step forward as if she was being drawn towards the fire rather than away from it. More calls for alarm filtered down from the stands.

There was a pressure at her back, like someone pushing against her, against the flame. But she held it at bay. Lakai would not stop her, not now.

She took another step. Another. Until she was surrounded by the flames. They burned hot, her hair singing around her face, the smoke smudging her skin black. She raised her arms as the fire licked around her legs, up her torso, obscuring her vision of those around her.

But Arix didn't need to be able to see the crowd. She could *hear* them. And she could hear the dagger at her back, laughing.

The leather tie that held her hair up burned away, her long white hair falling in waves down her back but not burning up as it flowed around her in the waves of heat that emanated from the flames.

Then, as quickly as it had started, the fire was gone.

Arix looked up slowly, squinting as she watched the sun finally crest over the walls of the colosseum and bathe her in perfect golden morning light. She turned slowly as if she was in a daze, letting everyone in the stands see that she was unharmed.

And the crowd went wild.

It took every ounce of strength not to smile, not to revel in their response and bask in the success of it. Her gaze shifted, falling to look at those standing behind her.

Lakia was furious. He knew it had all been magick, all been a trick, and he seethed with the indignity of her lie. But he made no move to out her, no attempt to claim what had just happened was falsity.

Beside him, Orion simply stared. Not in shock or horror or

anger. He simply watched her as she stepped back into her place at his side, ever the good dog who obeys her true master.

And then he smiled.

A shiver ran down Arix's spine at that smile. Orion knew. And he would not soon forget how she had undermined him today.

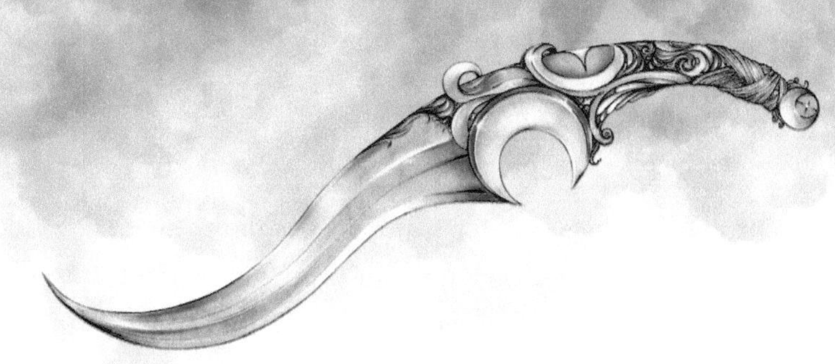

THIRTY-SEVEN

For the second day in a row, Arix did not sleep. She was exhausted, her body bruised from the use of the magick, but the adrenaline that coursed through her blood wouldn't let her rest. Even after the colosseum had emptied and she had returned back to the Warden's estate with the rest of the court, she found herself back in the gardens wandering between the morning lit hedges, letting the memory of the cheers screaming her name echo in her mind.

Nesrin had offered to stay with her, even mid-yawn, but Arix had pushed the girl to her room and told her to go to bed. Ulfur and Abbas hadn't taken no for an answer but respected the fact that she might need time to process, trailing behind her in the garden a good twenty paces away. Their quiet support and presence were so comforting, so sure, it settled a peace into Arix's chest that she felt maybe hadn't been there in a long time.

After the display in the arena, she'd downed the entire bottle of Well Water from her pocket, and the clawing in her chest had immediately subsided. It soothed a dark part of her that burned, and her reliance on it made her uneasy. It was better not to think about it and focus on what the contents could do to help her.

"It waits for you in the darkness." The voice around her neck said softly. *"You avoid the truth because you are afraid of it."*

Arix pressed the heel of her hand against the pendant around her neck, a useless way to silence the thing. It might be right. But she did not want to think about it today.

"Good morning, Lady Black Hand."

Arix glanced up, startling at the man who stood in front of her. He looked oddly familiar.

"Morning, sir…?" Arix searched for the title.

"Lord Woodhale."

The air stilled. Even the birds stopped singing, the garden around them—which that had been abuzz with life only a moment ago—deathly silent.

"Lord Woodhale," Arix repeated.

She could see it, the resemblance. The wavy brown hair, though he had his combed back, receding around the temples, and he grew a goatee that covered his chin. But she could see Lord Woodhale's resemblance to his son. It was their eyes. Exactly the same eyes as Michael.

"My apologies for not introducing myself sooner," Michael's father continued. "I had intended on making the introductions as soon as you entered the city, but with the chaos of the blessing and the feast, didn't quite find the chance."

He paused, allowing space for Arix to say something, but she only stared. The light smile that had been on his face only moments before faded as he squirmed under her gaze.

"Ah. I wanted to speak with you since…since you knew my son. I hear you were good friends with him."

"And where did you hear that?" Arix asked. She could feel Ulfur and Abbas approach, standing behind her. "I don't believe Michael ever sent you letters."

The man blanched at that, taken aback by the force in her voice. The lines between his brows crinkled together, anger taking over the features.

"I loved my son."

"Did you?" Arix pressed forward until she was nose-to-nose with him. "Michael was a good man. A great man. He wanted peac; he wanted love. And you…"

She couldn't even say it. Emotion was welling behind her eyes, sticky with rage.

She could see Michael's face in her mind, lit up by the moon on the ship as they'd returned home from laughing about their lives. His expression, even almost a year later, was as clear as crystal. The twist of his brows, the sorrow in his eyes, the shame as he talked about his father, about his duty, his obligations. The soft and sad yearning of a son who wanted his father to love him for who he was.

Arix swallowed, her voice evening out. "He was the best man I've ever known. He knew who he was, unapologetically. He died doing what he thought was right. He died his own way, on his own terms. His last actions were his own, not someone else's. I respected and loved him. And I miss him."

Lord Woodhale's eyes pinched, and Arix wished she would have seen the worry in them. Wished she had seen compassion, regret, sadness. But instead, she saw only the pitiful, confused gaze of a man who could never have truly known his son. Lord Woodhale never knew the Michael that she had known. Had never seen his son the way she had seen him; dirt under his fingernails from the tomato plants, head thrown back laughing as they jumped again and again from the roof. Michael's father had missed more than the joy; he had missed the vulnerability, the heartache, the loss that Michael had known.

She wanted to hit him, to knock him to the ground and slam her fist over and over into his face, to break his jaw. She wanted to press her fingers into the soft skin over his sternum, to dig inside his ribs and look for any semblance of a heart. To seek out the last remnants of love that he might have for his dead son.

But instead, she walked away.

She left behind Michael's father, speechless in the garden, wishing that he might wonder. Because maybe, if he wondered what he had missed, what he had overlooked in Michael, he could have a fraction of the guilt that she felt. He might feel a sliver of the sadness she felt. He might know the smallest portion of what it meant to lose someone who saw as much, shared as much, and felt as much as Michael had.

~

When they left, the king's party departing from Vingard on the final trek home, Arix could not bring herself to wave on the roads to the screaming crowds. She could not bring herself to sway with the songs they sang about her. She could not stop the feeling that she was finally, truly, leaving behind the last pieces of Michael.

All of those pieces had been left in the gardens with Lord Woodhale, just like she had left the last of her grief with Revena's family in the deserts of Zarak. Maybe it was better that way. Maybe it was all part of the new person she was becoming. Maybe leaving the grief behind was a way for her to leave her old self behind as well. Leave it burned up in the arena.

Because the moment she pretended that blessing, the moment she lied in front of hundreds of people, the last bit of the old Arix died too.

And she couldn't decide if it was good or bad. If it was part of some great plan, like Genni had said it was.

Her companions knew to leave her to her thoughts, and Nesrin rode silently beside her as they left the last outlying streets of Vingard behind and rode home.

~

"My bed," Nesrin said with a vehemence Arix hadn't often seen from the girl. "That's what I've missed most. My room is across from Arix's, and I swear that bed has to be stuffed with feathers because you can sink in and die of happiness."

Lydia chuckled, ripping her loaf of bread in half and handing it down the line. Semmer took it with a nod and a smile, tearing off her own piece.

Ro passed the bread without taking any, then fell back onto the blanket he'd placed on the ground. "I've been meaning to ask, do we get emblems or pins or something? To differentiate us?"

"You don't like the notoriety alone?" Lydia laughed. "You need a pin to show the world you're special."

Ro matched her grin. "Yes."

Arix didn't speak up, but she'd already been thinking about it anyway. Having a brooch or emblem wasn't a bad idea. But would having something so easily recognizable put her Fingers at risk? So far, they'd been on the road back to Mergur for two weeks, and there had been no reports of a single Carn attack or sighting. But the peace wouldn't last for long. The treaty would be in effect only as long as Orion hadn't returned to the capital.

They were close, maybe only five days away from returning home. Then the treaty would be absolved, and an attack could come at any time.

It was strange, after having been on the road for so long, to now be so close to home. Her room, the library, all her research, a normalcy she hadn't felt for a long time… It was less than a week from Arix's grasp.

And what would she do when she was back? She had ideas for the city itself and, after a few conversations with Lydia, knew where she wanted to start. The merchant's guild needed to be reformed, as most of it was run by propped-up nobles who used the guild as a byway to push their own ventures and snuff out smaller local sellers and farmers who came from small towns. Lydia Skonos had a few ideas already and had broken some of them down for Arix.

Her motivation for rebuilding the merchant guild was tied into another of Arix's plans. What she'd recently learned from Semmer proved that there was so much about her magick she still didn't know. Arix wanted to keep learning, keep researching, and source ingredients from all over the world. She wanted to learn how other countries and cultures approached magick. It would take time, and exploration expeditions, and men and women that were trustworthy, rather than beholden to some nobleman's beck and call.

With a new system in place, she could sponsor those types of journeys, expand her knowledge. She could maybe take the study of magick further than ever before. Magick was dying, but she could build it back up. Maybe. It would just take the right kind of research. Once she was home, she could spend her time researching in the library, finding out more about the previous Black Hands.

But all that was all big picture plans, long term-strategies that would take years or decades to implement. Her immediate worry was the Carn.

Orion had to have a strategy for when they returned to Mergur. He wouldn't have made the treaty or agreed to Lazh Mendir's concessions without having something else in mind. He simply hadn't told her what they were.

Arix didn't doubt that Orion had something planned. Some trick up his sleeve that might save them the loss of more lives, but she knew without a doubt that the Carn would never agree to a permanent peace. They'd burned towns and murdered thousands over the years. They'd grown in number, grown in power, and now they had an incantor.

There was a good chance that whatever Orion had planned, Arix wouldn't like it. So that meant having her own plan, her own contingencies to put up against Orion's.

The question was, would Orion listen to her? Maybe not. But she had to try. And maybe she could use a bit of magickal persuasion to do it.

"It's been a little over a year and a half since I was in Mergur," Lydia said, sipping her cup of chilled tea. "But there is a lovely stall near the square that sells the highest quality herbs and spices. The owner is an old friend, and he creates all kinds of lovely blends and sells them in sachets. You could put them in your bath or in your tea, stews and poultices. I think the first thing I will do is oblige him with a visit."

"Does that mean you could technically drink your bath water?" Ro asked, wrinkling his nose. "That sounds…unappetizing."

"And you, Semmer?" Nesrin asked. "What are you looking forward to in the capital?"

Semmer glanced around the group, surprised at being asked to participate. "I have not been to Mergur before. But I am excited at the opportunity to see the training grounds built in the wall that surrounds Castle Zma'ai. I've heard they're expansive."

"Aye. Arix did a bit o' her own training there when she was a competitor. Commander Zaran does a good job with his men," Ulfur said.

"I look forward to seeing it." Semmer offered a rare smile before her eyes slid over to Arix. "What about you, Lady Black Hand? Is there anything in particular you are looking forward to when we arrive in Mergur?"

Arix's thoughts instantly slid to the library. Her first priority upon her return would be to research the Well Water. To find the histories of the Black Hands of the past and understand what the blessings meant. If she could understand her own history, she might better piece together her present.

"I miss my bed, too," she said finally, throwing a glance at Nesrin. "And my offices. Just the way the stone feels underneath your boots. Castle Zma'ai became a home to me while I was a competitor. And I think she still holds a great amount of secrets yet to be uncovered. I'm looking forward to uncovering them all."

"Surely not all the secrets," Lydia smiled behind her veil. "For some things do not give up all their secrets simply because another wills them to."

Ro raised his glass. "Quite philosophical. A toast to beautiful things and their secrets."

The rest of them laughed as he downed his drink, and Arix laughed along with them, knowing Lydia was right. The castle would not quickly offer up what had been hidden for so long.

And Arix was more than happy to spend the rest of her time in Castle Zma'ai figuring them out.

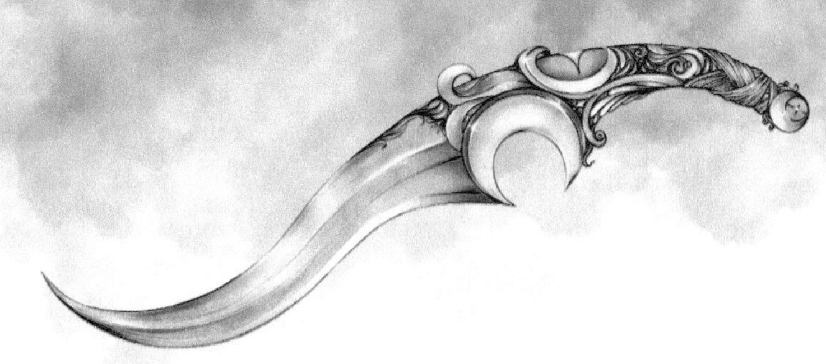

THIRTY-EIGHT

It felt so good to be home. Mergur's streets, lined with screaming crowds and waving banners, brought out a deep breath from Arix, the weight of the journey and the blessings finally lifting a little and letting her lungs fill with air again. The sounds and scents of returning to a place that she had thought of as home for some time now brought with it pangs of memory and nostalgic expectations for the future.

Castle Zma'ai loomed high above the city, its black towers piercing the perfect blue sky.

Arix loved the sight of it. Home was only a few streets away, and then, she told herself, she would finally breathe normally again.

Osiris stomped his hooves, picking up his feet and performing for the crowd, feeding off of Arix's excitement and his recognition of home. Being back in Mergur meant warm, familiar stables, apples and carrots and his favorite mash. But it also meant only taking occasional leisure rides rather than spending day after day on the road. The further they moved through the city, the more his pace quickened, and Arix had to fight him every step of the way to keep him from racing ahead of the group.

Delphine rode beside Orion just ahead of Arix in the most beautiful flowing cream and gold dress. It looked similar to the dress she'd worn on her wedding day, and it was like she was being presented to the city as a fresh bride for all to see.

As they neared the central square, Orion raised his hand for their procession to stop and raised his hands for silence. He glanced back at Arix and tapped his lips. Arix urged Osiris forward a bit and cast a simple cant so that his words would carry above the crowd.

"My people!" Orion's voice carried louder than any normal voice could have, and the gathered multitude hushed to hear him. "It is so good to be home again, back in our loving Mergur. I bring with me three things, gifts that I bestow now to all of you upon my return."

Arix kept her eyes on the crowd, watching to make sure there wouldn't be any unwelcome surprises during the unexpected speech.

"The first is news that I have received the blessings and favors of all four of Kaoss' children!"

The crowd broke into raucous cheers, and Orion beamed and let them scream and sing for a few moments before he raised his arms again for silence.

"The second… I bring with me your new queen, Delphine Vod, daughter of Nero!"

Again, he paused for the shouts and cheers of joy. People threw flowers towards Delphine, and she blushed prettily under the attention. Yet even through the chaos around her, she only stared at Orion lovingly, the perfect picture of a doting wife and humble queen.

This time, Orion did not wait for them to quiet down again before he motioned to Delphine and shouted, his voice carrying louder than the throng:

"And third, that Delphine is with child! Rökkur will soon have a prince!"

Arix felt the blood drain from her face, and prickled skin race up her arms as her gaze switched from the crowd to stare stunned at Orion and Delphine. Delphine flushed, her cheeks tinging pink as she gently folded her fingers over her flat belly and the crowd exploded with joy. Orion's guards as well as Arix's Black Guard had to step in, keeping the throng away from rushing the smiling couple.

It took nearly ten minutes to clear the road enough that the group could continue moving again, and Arix followed behind Orion and Delphine, completely dumbfounded. She shouldn't have been surprised. The two had been married since early summer, and having a child meant Orion could solidify his line's claim to the throne. He'd married Delphine to form alliances. And nothing cemented alliances faster than a royal baby.

Arix could only feel numb. The ties that had connected her and Orion had broken long ago, and she had felt her own feelings die throughout this journey. More than just his marriage, more than this child now between them.

Maybe it was a good thing. This final tie snapping between them, however expected, was still jarring. They had been friends once, before they had been lovers. She knew better than anyone that life changed circumstances. That life got in the way of the best laid plans. This was simply the final cut to break her ties with him.

As they climbed the hill and passed through the final gates into the castle grounds, Arix felt the numbness give way to the familiar scents and sounds of the grounds. The men and women who guarded the walls, the gathered court members who had stayed behind. She caught sight of Bishop Forir among them, a huge grin on his face, waving like a madman, even though with every gesture, he looked like he might tip over from the effort of the motion.

There was an air of finality, of exhaustion, of relief, to be back somewhere familiar, back in a place that many of them considered home. All around her the men and women that had traveled with her all summer dismounted from their horses or stepped down from the carriages, stretching the aches and pains out of their bones.

After Orion and Delphine were passed over to the king's guard, Arix dismounted herself, feeling the familiar crush of white gravel under her boots. She excused her five Fingers, telling them all to rest and eat, and for Semmer and Lydia to settle into their new rooms. Then she took her time brushing down Osiris and sat in the grass of the pasture with him as he rolled in the open field.

"Rest now, Arix," the voice around her neck said. *"Rest while you can."*

The words had a sense of warning behind them, and Arix's mind instantly flickered to the unstable treaty that Orion had agreed to with General Lazh Mendir. What would happen now that the king was safely back at the castle with his pregnant bride?

~

When Arix awoke, it was still dark, and she took a moment to reorient herself to the space of her room, running her fingers across the cool sheets, pressing her head back against the feather pillow. By the look of the inky sky out the window, she still had a few hours before the sun came up, but she was wide awake. After months of sleeping on the ground, it seemed her body still needed to get used to the softness of her mattress.

She pulled her feet slowly out of bed, scrunching her toes against the carpeted floor, feeling the weave of the design as she contemplated what to do.

Grabbing a blanket off the end of her bed, Arix stepped lightly towards the door, lifting the latch to leave her rooms. The sound of her bare feet padding against the stone was the only sound as she made her way through Castle Zma'ai, shifting invisible as she passed the posted guards and following the old familiar path until she reached the oak doors.

There was a fire in the fireplace, crackling gently as she entered, the flicker of the orange light dancing across the spines of books standing patiently in the rows and rows of the library. Her old familiar chair was right where she'd left it near the window, a book on the sill, waiting for her to return.

"Hello, again," Arix breathed with a smile.

There was no response, but Arix felt as if the books were listening all the same. Or maybe not the *books* but the *library*.

Stepping towards the window, she picked up the book on the sill, flipping through the pages until she found her bookmark, then settled into the overstuffed chair to read by the fire. For a moment, she was transported, slipping away to another world and leaving her body behind. That was how all books were, portals to other worlds where the reader could be anyone and anywhere they desired.

The sky outside was barely starting to tinge lilac when the door to the library opened, and Arix twisted in her chair to meet Orion's gaze.

"Hello," she said.

"Hello."

"I couldn't sleep."

Orion approached and leaned over the back of her chair, peering down at the book in her hands. It felt so familiar, like old versions of themselves, back when they were connected by more than physical bonds.

"What are you reading?"

"A fairy story." Arix showed him the cover. "I must have left it out before we left for the tour. It was waiting for me."

Orion smiled. "The library does like to do that. Leave the right book out at just the right time."

Arix nodded.

A moment passed without either of them saying a word, letting the silence do all the speaking for them.

But even the silence was too intimate now, too close, and Arix could feel it pressing against her throat. She stood from her chair, moving to place her book back on the windowsill, and leaned against it, putting space between herself and Orion.

"Congratulations," she offered with a small smile. "On your news. I'm sure Delphine is overjoyed."

Orion watched her from his position behind her chair as the sky slowly lightened in the window behind her. "She is. She'll have someone to love now."

"She loves you."

"She doesn't." Orion hung his head slightly, a resigned smile on his face. "Not really. She loves the attention, and she loves the notoriety her new title brings. But she'll love this child because it's part of *her*, not because it's part of *me*."

Arix tugged the blanket around her closer. "It'll be part of you both."

"Yes. And when I die, he'll be king."

"The Karkarias rule is secure." The voice against her sternum was snide, mocking.

"Or she," Arix offered, ignoring the voice. "You could have a daughter."

Orion laughed, then joined her at the window, his smile genuine. "Goddess help us all if I have a daughter. She'll have all of us eating out of the palm of her hand."

They laughed together, and Arix felt a pang of what they'd once shared, before things had gotten so complicated.

"What happened to us, Arix?" Orion asked, turning to her, voicing the thoughts in her own mind. "When did you stray so far from me?"

She flinched, feeling the barb in the words, as if it were she who was to blame for all of it.

"You know what happened."

"You told me to marry her, Arix. *You* told me to do it."

She could hear the subtle tone of anger underneath the words, his frustration leaching through.

"I did."

Orion stared long and hard, waiting for her to continue. But she couldn't. She didn't have the words for him that he wanted to hear. She didn't have the solutions; she didn't have an answer other than she knew her duty and he knew his. She and Orion had been doomed to fail since the beginning, their roles doomed to be one of shadows and secrets. And Arix didn't want that anymore.

"I love you, Arix."

Arix winced at the words. Even now, it sounded like Orion barely believed it, barely hung onto the idea behind the words, hoping that saying them out loud would bring her back to him.

"Don't say it," Arix said in a half whisper. "Please. I don't want…"

Orion pulled her into a kiss, his hand slipping into her hair to cup the back of her head. There was anger in the kiss, frustration, and sadness so cold that Arix thought their skin might freeze together.

She pushed back, a steady and sure motion until he released her.

"You are hers, Orion," Arix muttered softly. "You are hers. And you must know that things changed between us a long time ago. I will serve you as Black Hand. As an incantor. But that is all."

His fingers dropped from her arms.

"Why can't you understand?"

Arix took another step back from him. "I understand that we all have roles to play. But you need to understand that I have my pride. I am not a toy. And neither is Delphine."

When he didn't respond, Arix turned toward the door, giving him a final glance as she hovered in the doorway. She'd hoped to find understanding in his gaze, sadness, or even acceptance. Instead, it was a look similar to the one she'd seen in Zarak when he'd carried Delphine home from the bonfire and again in the amphitheater in Eldur.

A kind of determined arrogance, a justified pride.

And it sent a shiver of warning down her spine.

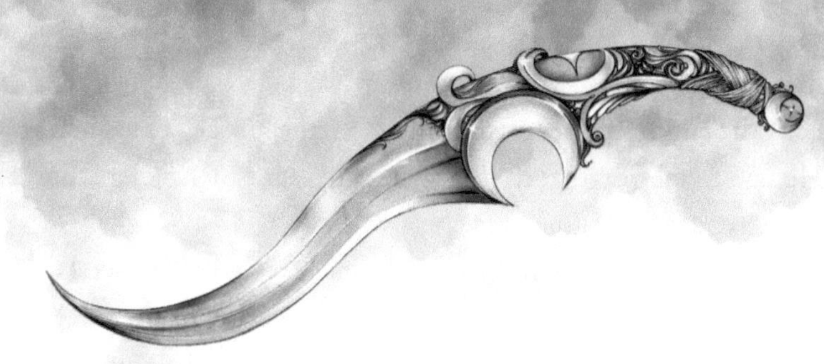

THIRTY-NINE

Arix felt the air shift.

She could smell it, smell that something was wrong on the air that blew through her window as the sun streaked orange across the sky. She could hear the clatter outside in the hallway, the boots rushing, the frenzy and the adrenaline pumping through her veins long before Abbas threw open her door.

She didn't need to look at his face; she was already pulling on her armor, lacing up her boots.

"The Carn have attacked Mergur." Abbas gripped his barbed spear in a white-knuckled grip. "They have brought their incantor."

Arix settled Celeste's dagger at the small of her back, and she sidestepped Abbas and ran down the hall. The Carn had kept their promise and had even given them a day to rest. And now they were here.

"Where?"

"Southeast road into the city; the lower third is already on fire. The king's men will remain here, and General Hawes has already dispatched his troops into the city. They're cutting off escape routes and routing citizens to safety and putting out fires. They're going to gridlock the city, keep the Carn from advancing any closer to the castle. He said to tell you that if you come across any of his men, they'll obey your orders as if they were his own."

Arix was halfway down the main stairs now and could see Lakai in the entryway, speaking with Lord Bardon. When he spotted Arix, he stepped into her path, already knowing what she planned to do.

Lakai's voice was firm. "You cannot go, Arix."

"I need more Well Water."

He grit his teeth. "You have a vial already."

"I need more, Lakai. Do not deny me this. Not when I'm trying to protect people."

Her old teacher said nothing, the lines of his mouth settling into resolute determination.

"Then I'll do it without your help."

She pushed past him with a scoff. His grip on her arm was strong enough to stop her, swinging her back from the open door to the castle.

"Your place is here with the king," he growled as she yanked her arm away from his grip.

But Arix was already moving past him, boots crunching on the gravel.

"The king is safe behind the wall," Arix called back. "My people are dying out there."

Her Black Guard was already waiting for her in the courtyard, suited in their armor and ready to follow her orders. Arix didn't stop, checking the tack on her horse and mounting up as she shouted orders.

"Split into two groups. Group one will join General Hawes' men in closing off the grid of the city and cutting down the rebels. Your armor will protect you from most of the flames, but don't be stupid. No one else is going to die today because of these fires. Group two will come with me. We'll put an end to the fires, then rejoin you. Go!"

As she moved to go, she felt a press against her leg and looked down. Lakai was staring up at her, his outstretched hand holding two more vials. The two said nothing as Arix pocketed the Well Water and turned.

Osiris tore out of the courtyard, gravel flying behind him as Arix rode low on his back through the gates. Behind her, her Black Guard thundered to follow. From the hill, she could already see a third of the city engulfed in angry orange flames, licking at rooftops and spreading down to the harbor.

Their biggest threat would be the fire that raged over the city. It was huge and couldn't have been started by accident. The chaos that would ensue would provide the rebels with cover to move further into the city, and the troops would have to divide their forces between fighting and dousing the flames.

Arix made a beeline for the harbor, noting that Ulfur stayed with the first group, saluting to her as they turned off towards the center of the city. Ahead, a group had already started a line of men passing buckets from the harbor into the city, putting out buildings on the edge of the blaze to keep the fire from spreading. Instead of joining, she moved down the line, her men following behind her as she rode further into the burning portion of the city. The horses, including Osiris, balked against the wall of fire, and Arix swore under her breath.

"Dismount!" she called, leaping to the ground as she moved further into the burning section. The smoke that curled around them was already dense, and Arix's eyes watered against the sting.

She swore as she moved, realizing that while her men's armor might protect them from the heat of the flame, it wouldn't protect them from the smoke that would rip apart their lungs.

"Stay close behind me! As I clear the flame, check for survivors and pull anyone you find to safety. Ugushi!" Arix shouted, arms outstretched to a portion of a house as she cast a fire mastery cant. Instantly, the flame flickered out of existence, black smoke billowing in its place.

Mentally, she switched to a new incantation, pushing her palms apart to part the black smoke enough for her men to advance.

"Rasprshi."

Semmer stepped up at her side, drumming against her chest with her fist and singing low under her breath as she focused on bolstering Arix's cants with a breeze to gently push the smoke away from them.

Again and again, Arix switched between the cants, extinguishing the fire and then clearing the smoke. Over and over, she and her men pulled people from their homes, merchants from their shops, some coughing and scrambling for safety, some burned beyond recognition. The smell of it, the burning wood and the burning flesh, seared into Arix's mind, and waves of nausea rolled over her as memories hammered her.

After only a few streets it was clear: the bodies her men were retrieving were past the point of saving. The best they could do now was to put out the rest of the fire.

"Half of you!" Arix called, motioning to the line of soot covered men and women that still worked to put out the fire with buckets, "stay here and help. The rest come with me, and we'll rejoin the others. Let's go!"

As she mounted Osiris again, she saw the toll their efforts had already started to take. Her men moved slower, their armor smudged with black smoke residue. Lines of black marked their foreheads and the creases around their mouths where the soot and ash had pressed into their pores. The skin in and around her nails was black from it too, but Arix didn't care. The horses beneath them were skittish from all the smoke and fire, and it took a moment for the rest of them to follow her as she moved further through the city. General Hawes had already marked roads, barred with troops and wooden barriers moving slowly through the city in a grid to corner the rebel units.

As they wove between the barricades, Arix could feel her anxiety rising, the use of the magick taking a toll, and the knowledge that Maeve was here crushed together and filled her mouth with ash. Luckily, she had three vials of Well Water in her pocket. She downed one after the other, feeling the surge, her heart speeding up at the boost of adrenaline.

She needed a leg up; she needed to be able to *see*.

Abbas nearly ran into her as she came to a sudden stop, swinging down from Osiris' back and tucking her fingers tightly into his bridle. The cant she was about to perform wasn't an easy one, and she'd need to be grounded to another living thing.

"Don't let anyone near me," she said to Abbas, squeezing her eyes shut and focusing hard.

Seeing through an animal's eyes was one thing; she'd done it while training with Osiris and had watched through the eyes of hawks and deer. But what she was going to try was different.

She felt her eyes roll back, slumped slightly against her horse's bridle, and let her mind slip. It squirmed through the consciousnesses of the men and women around her, sliding past them like hot oil, seeking and slithering until she felt her mind brush the mind of someone else. Soldiers, fighting and burning, their emotions curled around her mind, and she felt them fight against the hold that tried to grasp them. But she was stronger than they were, her mind sharp as a blade, slicing through them like it was nothing. It was so ridiculously *easy*.

She found a mind wrought with fear and targeted it. The fear left gaps, gaps for her to fill until she could feel him inching away from her, releasing control to her completely.

Arix blinked.

She was standing somewhere else, a glass bottle of yellow liquid in her hand, a sword in the other. Around her, rebels fought against troops in Orion's colors, the yellow liquid from the vials pooling and sucking and killing anyone who touched it. Arix reeled her arm back and threw the vial in her hand, feeling the mind of the young man whose body she'd taken fight her for control. His grip tightened at the last moment, and instead of throwing the bottle, it slipped and fell straight down, crashing to the ground beneath the young man. Arix felt the pain, the agony, felt the boy's scream crawl up her throat as he howled against the acid magick that ate at his legs.

Arix pulled back, stabilizing herself back into her own body, eyes blinking open as she slumped into Abbas' arms at the disorientation. Her fingers were still tucked into Osiris' bridle, tangled so tightly that the leather cut bloody marks into her palms.

"—rix! Are you well?" Abbas was pulling her up to a standing position, tugging her hands free from the leather bridle.

"Five streets up," Arix choked out, fighting through the nausea. "Two over. There's a group of rebels. We have to go."

She could feel Abbas hesitate, but she pushed past him, pulling herself back up into the saddle. Blood slicked the reins, but she muttered a quick healing cant before sprinting off again, turning through the streets of Mergur to find the rebels.

They were easy to find—Arix just followed the screaming.

The boy was dead by the time they arrived in the small square, the sickly mucus-colored pool of yellow acid spread out across the cobblestones. More of General Hawes' men had arrived, but so had more of the Carn. A trench of the acid separated the square, and seeing the bodies that already littered the ground spurned more fury in Arix's heart.

"You like acid so much?" Arix was shouting, riding Osiris straight for the acid line, pushing him to jump the substance to land on the other side. He balked at the last moment, and Arix nearly hurtled out of the saddle.

A scream tore at her throat as she thrust her palms out, sending streams of acid towards the rebels. The effect was instantaneous.

The air around them turned acrid as the corrosive liquid took hold, eating away at clothing and limbs. But even if the magick acted quickly, the acid did not. Arix watched, sat atop Osiris, as the rebels burned, their flesh and bones eaten away over the next few minutes. Eventually, the screams faded, and an eerie silence stretched across the square.

She could feel the eyes of the soldiers around her, boring into her back, as she watched the Carn melt away. She felt the rage building, thick with ash under her fingernails, snaking up the back of her legs, gripping her spine and a steel vise.

For a moment, all was quiet.

Even the crackle of distant fires faded to a hollow whoosh in her ears. The nervous shifting of boots against the cobblestones, even Abbas standing beside her… It all faded into nothing. There was something else that took all her focus. At the edge of her reach, at the periphery of her magick, she felt it.

Maeve was here.

Arix turned slowly, eyes rising upward to stare at the towers of Castle Zma'ai that pierced the air above Mergur. That was where the incantor was. She could sense the girl's magick like she could smell a storm.

Boiling rage grasped her so tightly, Arix gasped, huffing air into her lungs to offset the emotion that coursed through her. Abbas was pulling at her arms, yelling at her, but she could not hear him. She swung herself into the saddle, the magick laced in her words as she leaned low over the great black horse's neck and whispered, "Run."

And he did.

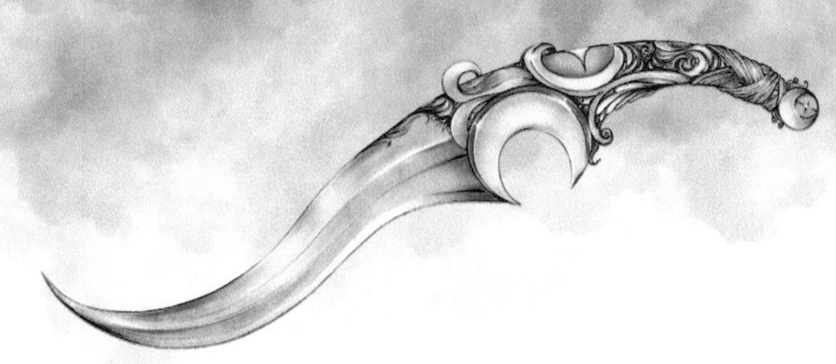

FORTY

Osiris, frenzied by the magick, tore through the streets, leaving Abbas and her Black Guard behind. Everything inside her was screaming with every step closer to Maeve. They were drawn together like a magnet, pulled together by the magick that coursed in their veins. Magick that brought them together and wrenched them apart.

As they neared the gates, Arix reached out a fist and they were pummeled. The guards that stood waiting for the Carn were sent flying, and Arix careened past them into the courtyard, white gravel flying out behind her. Osiris was frothing, great foaming gobs dropping from his mouth as his eyes rolled, pulling to get away from her. Before her feet had hit the ground, he was off, tearing around the side of the castle, galloping straight through the hedges to get as far from Arix as he could.

She stood in the courtyard, the gravel torn up around her, waiting in the silence that echoed past her pulsing heart, even the blood whooshing in her ears going silent.

The girl was coming to her, had been calling to her with her magick, and now they were so close that Arix could taste the Maeve's scent on her tongue. Taste the confidence, taste the trickery.

A grin spread across Arix's face. "You cannot hide from me, little girl."

A motion to her left.

Arix swung low, easily ducking the blast of energy that surged over her head. Behind her, a corner of the hedge burst in an explosion of leaves and snap of a hundred broken branches.

Another—a surge of magick, again from her left, but closer now, aimed at the ground so she couldn't duck away. It was rudimentary, something Arix would have done when she was new to magick.

This time, she didn't dodge it. The blast hit her shield with a sizzle of sparks and a force that shook the ground, vibrating against the metal of her boots.

"You're going to have to try harder than that," Arix called, eyes trained on the spot the cant had come from. The motion had disappeared, and the courtyard of the castle had gone quiet again.

Instead of listening for a sound or looking for a ripple in the air, Arix closed her eyes. She pushed against the magick, searching it out with her mind letting instinct take over as she felt it again at the edge of the courtyard.

It was moving, crouched low but moving in a definitive circle. She waited, feeling it slide, the magick growing stronger with every step. When Arix realized what the girl was doing, her eyes flew open, staring straight at the spot she knew Maeve was, invisible, tracing a circle into the stones around them.

"You think drawing that circle will help you?"

She felt the girl falter, the magick pausing for a moment as Maeve balked. It was all the hesitation Arix needed.

Her own bolt of energy surged out, and the girl couldn't hold all three of her cants without being blown away. Her invisibility cant dropped as a rampart cant took its place, and Arix's magick bounced off the shield, sputtering and sparking. But even with a powerful shield, the magick thrust her backwards, the heels of her silver armored boots digging grooves into the ground as she was pushed back a foot.

"To fight you," Maeve called out, "I will take all the help I can get. Especially the assistance of a casting circle."

The girl looked even younger than Arix had expected. She'd known Maeve was still only a teenager, but she'd expected at least a semblance of maturity to her features. Maeve was small, shorter than Arix by a few inches, her spotless golden armor glinting in the morning sun. Her mouth was set in a grim line, determination and confidence encased in the lines around her eyes as she glared at Arix.

Her hair was white, cropped short around her face with bangs that curled slightly on her forehead.

That white hair, waving gently in the wind was like a punch to Arix's gut, a force that could have knocked the wind out of her. How had she gotten it? Who had given it to her?

With a wave of her hand, Arix disrupted the stones the girl had moved, erasing what little of the circle Maeve had drawn in the stones.

"You shouldn't need it. You're the Carn's incantor. And by the looks of things, you've had your own taste of Well Water." Arix pushed her own white hair over her shoulder, narrowing her eyes. "Your power should be just as strong as mine."

Maeve was studying her, and Arix could feel the girl's magick trace down her legs, across her chest, feeling for weaknesses, feeling for another attack. Just like she and Celeste had evaluated each other in the glen, Maeve was doing the same to her now.

"I am not like you. I am not a Black Hand," Maeve spat.

It was strange. All the anger Arix felt was still there, surging in her veins, but mixed with it was curiosity at the girl's power. It caused

Arix to pause, to wait. She was stronger than Maeve. She could feel it, feel the disparity between them.

Maeve had more magick in her veins, had more natural ability. A quick evaluation cant had told her that right away. But the girl was… new. She hadn't been taught the same way Arix had, hadn't learned the same incantations. She was determined, that much was clear. But there was something missing, and Arix couldn't quite tell what it was.

There was a commotion to her left, and Arix glanced to look. Two people, a man and a woman were stalking into the courtyard, empty bottles dropping to the ground at their feet even while their skin bubbled and expanded. They grew, taller than the monster she'd fought in Rohleach, muscles rippling and splitting their forms. She could see from here that whatever bottled magick they were using had been improved upon. Their skin was thicker, and bumps grew along their hairline until the skin split, and rows of pointed horns emerged from their scalps.

Arix backed up, stepped into the garden, pushing between the hedgerows and guiding Maeve further in. There would be more material she could use as a shield, and the pathways of white gravel that crisscrossed between the foliage and trees reminded her of her fight in the glen with Celeste. Another thing she could use as an advantage against Maeve and these new monsters.

The hulking once-humans were catching up now, stomping alongside their mistress as she stepped between the hip-tall, manicured bushes. They had grown so big that they simply stepped over the hedges into the garden.

"Didn't think you could fight me on your own, little girl?" Arix called out.

Maeve didn't respond, but her hands moved, fingers twitching, and Arix felt the heat of the firebolt before she saw it tear up from the ground around her. Even as she dove backwards, scrambling through a hedge, she felt the skin of her face blistering red against the heat.

The green leaves were burning up between them, and Arix could see Maeve approaching through the gaps in the branches. It was time to change tactics.

The monsters advanced, but they weren't moving towards her; they were hulking towards an illusion. A false copy Arix had created in her place while her now invisible form slipped away. To them, it looked like she was hurt, scrambling to get away from them as she huddled on the ground, injured and scared. The real Arix was moving, silently cutting down the path and circling around behind Maeve, invisible to all.

Maeve paced forward, through the hole in the hedge she'd created with her fire, stalking towards the illusion. Her monsters came from the side, reaching the illusion a few steps before the Carn's incantor. Arix didn't wait for them to realize it was a fake.

The ground near her illusion flash-froze, the air popping from the change of temperature. The monsters howled in pain, and Maeve's shield was too slow to save her from the frostbite that pricked her skin. Arix almost laughed at the chaos, the whirling of Maeve's blue cape as she spun in place, trying to find the real incantor.

The girl's domed shield was up again, but Arix could see the cracks in the girl's lips, the red flush of her cheeks. She'd embarrassed her.

Arix dropped the invisibility cant, and Maeve finally focused her eyes on her target.

"I didn't know we could bring friends," Arix called, nodding to the hulking monsters who were still scrambling their way out of the radius of cold. "Why didn't you say so?"

She'd never done this next cant before. Never needed to. But now seemed like as good a time as any to try.

She remembered the words, the motions, and Michael's ring showed her the images of her textbook, the dagger at her back surging with power and confidence.

"Do it," urged the necklace against her heart.

The ground began to quake, the white pebbles of the path shaking as a large figure rose between Maeve and her monsters. It was nearly as tall as the monsters themselves, glowing in white light, a sword and shield in its grasp. Above its head, great antlers rose up, enough to make any beast or man topple from the weight.

Maeve spun towards Arix, anger glinting in her eyes. "What have you done?"

Arix couldn't keep the feral grin from splitting her face. "Spectral Goddess. Did you not learn that one, Maeve? Pity."

With a roar, Maeve rushed at Arix, the monsters and spectral Goddess caught in their own fight and leaving the two incantors on their own.

The first of Maeve's firebolts was wide, followed by another that was even sloppier. She was using the same kinds of spells over and over, and Arix couldn't help but wonder why.

"What do you feel, Maeve?" Arix asked, lacing magick into her words.

The girl's expression remained unchanged, her pace consistent as she continued her sloppy attacks.

Arix grinned. She cranked the dial of her power, amping up the cant as she spoke again. "What do you sense from me? What will I cast next?"

The furrow in Maeve's brows tightened, and she blinked rapidly, her mind reeling to determine reality from the visions Arix was giving her. Funny how she was using the same cants here that she had used against Celeste.

The dagger at her back growled, and Arix grinned at the sound.

In that moment, Maeve moved, her feet planting in the ground as she brought up a hand, and Arix felt the oil slick of a curse slide over her. The magick was good…

…almost.

The curse slowed her movement, impeded her mind, forcing her to add more effort behind her magick, and it might have worked against another incantor. But Arix could feel the surge of power from Michael's ring, reacting against the cant and adding to her disruption of it. Against anyone else, the cant might have been strong. It might have broken her. But Arix had more than just the power of three cores on her side. She had the three vials of Well Water screaming through her veins, and that made all the difference.

Slowly, she reached out a finger, sliding it along the purple, oil-slick sheen of magick that covered the black glint of her armor. She held Maeve's gaze and raised the finger to her mouth, drawing it across her tongue in a long slow lick.

The necklace around her neck purred.

She could taste the bitter tang of the magick, feel it tied to Maeve, feel the intentions that were woven into the cant. Arix pressed against it, drawing on the power from Michael's ring to heal and Celeste's dagger to burn away whatever final remnants of Maeve's curse remained. And within a moment, she felt the curse leach off her and melt into nothing.

Maeve's eyes widened, her shoulders sagging a little at how quickly Arix had disrupted her curse.

"Disappointed?" Arix drawled, pushing past the shiver that ran down her spine. "Expected to beat me easily?"

Maeve's spine straightened, jaw tightening as she ground her teeth together. "I knew this would be a test for me. I knew fighting you would be more than just a battle of magick and wits."

"Wits?" Arix's laugh bubbled through her lips. But the grin and the shine in her eyes were anything but humorous. "You didn't burn down my city with your wits, little girl."

"No. I did that with fire."

A low rumble spread across Arix's chest, a growl of irritation as her smile dropped. "And how does burning a city fit into your plan to beat me? Innocent lives taken in order to…what? Make me mad?"

"Sometimes, it's necessary to burn the whole house to cleanse it of the plague."

"We're incantors!" Arix shouted, feeling the spit that flew from her lips as anger surged through her. Images of the bodies seared in her mind. "We can cure the fucking plague!"

"ENOUGH OF THIS CLAMBERING FOR A FOOT-HOLD," the dagger screamed. *"STOMP HER OUT!"*

A bellowing call filled the gardens around them, and both Maeve and Arix turned to look as the Spectral Goddess stood over one dead monster and plunged her sword into the other. Arix could feel the drain of magick the spectral was pulling on, feel the damage her glittering guardian had taken. With a sigh of relief, Arix banished the specter, and the garden grew quiet once again.

"Finally," Arix breathed.

As Maeve turned back to face her, Arix saw the disappointment on the other incantor's face. The defeat.

It filled Arix with glee.

"And now…" Arix felt a smile split her face as rage roiled in her chest. "It's my turn."

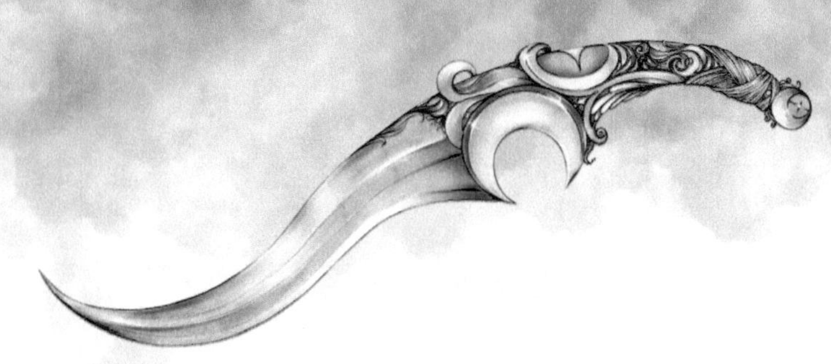

FORTY-ONE

It was so easy that it almost wasn't fair.

Arix advanced without mercy, without hesitation. Maeve was disheartened, her monsters having been wiped out with one powerful spell. She didn't have the mental fortitude to fight, and Arix could tell that the girl was losing heart.

It was easier to break someone who already wondered if they'd lost.

There were mind cants that Arix had learned, that she had used, to dig into someone's thoughts. To tear down the barriers that they'd built to protect themselves. This was something darker, harsher, like a surgeon using a cleaver rather than a scalpel.

Arix had spent her whole life without magick, had learned to use her sword and her words and her confidence. But now, she leaned into her magick, into the damage that it caused: ruthless and unforgiving.

Maeve fought her every second, fought the cant that wormed into her mind, reading the emotions that leached off of her. She shook her head, drawing up shields around herself. But every wall she raised, Arix pummeled through, finding the cracks, and ripped them apart to slide further in, barbs holding fast.

"Get out of my head!" the girl screeched, and Arix almost felt sorry for her.

"You came here to prove something," Arix said, her tone flat, even as the rage seized at her lungs. "That the Carn is stronger? That we will bow to you? That Orion will bow to you?"

Maeve cast out a fire bolt, but it swung wide, missing Arix entirely. More useless fire. The second bolt was on target, and Arix had to raise her own shield to avoid being hit. It set her back a little, but her mind worm remained, and she fed off the girl's fear, the emotions.

"Did you come to kill Orion?"

Another mental wall surged up, cutting off access to the deeper thoughts behind the feelings. This time, it took more effort to break through the wall.

Fragments and flashes of thought flickered through Arix's mind as Maeve fought her. They were jumbled, and she couldn't make sense of the little that she could see. That was fine. Arix could be patient. She could keep digging.

"You didn't come to kill him?"

The words continued, conflicting against each other as Maeve fought to keep her thoughts simple, not to reveal any more.

"Did you come to kill his child?" Arix prodded.

Maeve's brow furrowed as she concentrated on pushing Arix out. But with every action, every defense, it gave Arix a glimpse at what was behind the wall, behind the barriers Maeve was setting up for herself.

"Not his child. Interesting." Arix moved a step closer and Maeve cast another bolt to keep her from getting too close. It too sparked off her shield.

"This is exhausting," Arix said with a sigh. "You could just tell me. Then I wouldn't have to go *digging*."

On the last word, Arix whipped a hand up, and the ground around Maeve's feet churned as vines grew up around her ankles, tangling the incantor's feet and dragging her to her knees. But this was something Arix had used before, and Maeve was prepared. The dispelling cant was already withering away the vines before Arix could drag another crop of thorns from the ground.

Arix saw the shift in Maeve's mind as the girl moved to a different incantation, something more powerful, trying to oppose Arix's mind worm with one of her own. Even before the girl could perform the kinetic movements, think the words of the cant, Arix was forcing up more defenses, and she easily sidestepped the ice shards that speared from the ground around her.

One of the ice pieces shattered against the edge of Arix's right bracer, clipping her arm and shoving her slightly off balance. Gritting her teeth, Arix only shoved harder into the girl's mind, the two half-frozen as they fought against the mental barriers the other tried to traverse.

"You won't win this," Maeve ground out as she stared Arix down.

Arix only grunted, shoving her hands up to shift the shield as more ice speared up from the gravel.

"And do you know why?" Maeve continued, shifting to her feet and slowly drawing out her sword. "Because there is good in the world, and there is evil. And good always wins against evil."

Arix almost dropped her concentration, laughter bubbling up from her throat. "You're fucking kidding, right?"

Maeve's hand glided down the blade of her sword, a golden glimmer covering the metal. Then she swung, and Arix felt the force of it put a crack in her shield.

"I am the Red Hand!" Maeve declared, slashing again. "The hand of Time holds me, guides me. We will find the Conclave, and we will protect what little there is left. I will fight your evil with the power that Aion has bestowed on me!"

This time, her slashing blade cut clean through the shield and the force knocked Arix back, gravel tripping up her steps as she threw herself out of the way, tumbling to safety.

"What the hell are you talking about?" Arix called, not sure whether to laugh or rage. "I'm not the evil one here. You and the Carn are the ones burning a city to the ground!"

Arix still had enough of a hold in Maeve's mind that she felt the surge of emotion that washed through the other incantor's thoughts.

A sense of rationalization. A sense of self-assurance.

All humor disappeared from Arix's face. "You think you're justified, Maeve? In burning a whole city to the ground?"

She closed the distance between them in a heartbeat, knocking the girl flat on her back, pinning her throat against the gravel. The blade in Maeve's hands was momentarily caught between them, and Arix felt the searing hot pain as the blade slid between a panel of her armor and scored the flesh of her side.

"I am the messenger drenched in blood," Maeve choked out, fighting for breath.

"You will tell me," Arix breathed into Maeve's face, magick heavy in every word. "Tell me what the fuck is going on here."

Maeve choked, fighting against the lack of oxygen, the air being squeezed from her lungs, and instantly parts of her mental wall crumbled.

An image crackled through their mental link: *Arix burning in the center of the amphitheater. The great lie she told that day, the thousands of faces that watched her, believed her, trusted her. The image shifted to Orion, to his face as he watched her burn. The look that she had missed, his eyes turned to slits and his mouth set to a determined line.*

Maeve's chest heaved, fighting to regain air, the corner of her lips tinged purple.

Realization washed over Arix as she stared into Maeve's choking face. She barely felt the scratches that raked her arm as the girl clawed for release.

More images flashed, visions from gods and words spoken in the dark. With each new image, Arix felt her heart plummet. She didn't want to believe what she was seeing. Didn't want to acknowledge it, even as she watched the memories flicker through Maeve's mind. All of it was the truth.

"When did he make the deal?" Arix choked out, letting off the pressure at Maeve's throat. The girl gasped on air, and Arix shook her, slamming her back down against the stones. "Was it back in Eldur? Last night?"

Maeve didn't respond, but Arix didn't need to read her thoughts to know the truth. She'd seen it plain and simple in Maeve's mind. The secret that Orion had been keeping from her this whole time. The reason Maeve felt justified in burning Mergur.

"I did what I had to," Arix spat. "The people needed to believe, to trust that I'm as powerful a force as Orion is. That he might be their king, but I am their protector!"

"You're not their protector," Maeve wheezed, blood staining her teeth. "I am."

"And he thought you could beat me? ME?" Arix let go and reeled her arm back, slamming a fist into Maeve's jaw.

Maeve rolled, and Arix stood, striding across the rocks to keep up with her, flexing her fist as the pain washed up her knuckles. But the pain was good—it gave her clarity.

Her mind cant was slipping, fading as her anger raged, but Maeve still struggled to breathe as she tried to drag herself away.

The bloodied and enraged incantor on the ground was reaching, fiddling with the straps of a pouch hidden behind her cloak. But Arix was faster. Before Maeve could get a grip on the bottled cant, Arix was already kicking it out of her hand, watching as it sailed down the path, breaking into a surge of fire that lit their features in hot orange light. Maeve was reaching for more, but Arix wrenched the entire satchel from the girl's waist and flung the entire bag as far as she could into the depths of the garden.

The explosion of color and magick shook the ground as the bottles in the bag shattered. Fire and acid and a bubble of a shield combined in a destructive mass. Maeve wailed, the loss of her bottled cants as great a blow as if Arix had plunged a blade into her.

"What kind of incantor do you think you are?" Arix spat, glaring down at Maeve. "You have access to it *all*, and you resort to simple magick in a bottle?"

The girl had almost crawled to a split in the hedge and was trying to pull herself out of Arix's line of sight.

"Oh, no you don't," Arix muttered. Only a few strides closed the distance between them and she yanked Maeve off the ground by the collar of her breastplate, dragging her kicking through the hedgerows, back out of the charred gardens and into the center of the gravel courtyard. With every step she felt the scrape of the stones across Maeve's decorative gold armor, and her hatred grew.

This time, when she dove into the Red Hand's mind, she didn't go slowly, didn't take her time to slip between the stones of Maeve's mental wall. This time, she crashed through them with enough force that she knew she would be leaving scars.

The girl's mouth fell slack, her eyes so wide that Arix could see the red veins in the whites of her eyes. She was crossing a line, she knew. And she didn't care.

Images flared, hazy red, as Arix shuffled through them until she found what she wanted.

Lazh talking with a figure, scowl turned down as they spoke. But this image was older, maybe by a few years and the other man was cloaked in shadow…

"Explain," Arix choked on the words. "Explain this. Who is he?"

Answers flooded Maeve's mind, giving clarity, giving insight, but Arix refused to believe them. Refused to believe what she was seeing even though the truth was right there in front of her. The man in Maeve's memory stepped from the darkness and familiar lines of his face made Arix's heart sink in her chest. Orion and Lazh, standing beside each other, shaking hands, laughing. Familiarity and ease in their manners and conversation. These men knew each other; they were friends.

"Explain this!" she roared.

Maeve stuttered, fought for words as the raw instincts of her mind kicked in to keep her alive. "They're cousins. Orion's mother was Carn. He is one of us."

Heat and anger and bitter disappointment filled Arix's mouth, rising like bile, too many thoughts that jumbled together to form a complete picture. The truth of it was there, as clear in Maeve's mind as if she'd seen it herself. And yet, she could not wrap her mind around it.

"All this time…the bright future Orion wanted to build," Arix slowly said, heart heavier with each word. "The peaceful Rökkur he wanted to create… It was with you. The blessings, the attacks, the men and women that died… All of it was to build on what the Carn started. And I helped him do it."

She'd been used. From the start, Orion had manipulated her. Like a puppet, he had pulled her strings; like a toy, he had played with her, and she had done everything he'd asked. She'd never once questioned that he might be working with someone else.

Arix let go, Maeve's body dropping to the ground, too worn to hold herself up. Arix pulled herself to her full height, eyes trained upwards, watching the sky. She shifted her gaze as she followed the line of Castle Zma'ai's dark spires.

A new clarity washed over her. A simple and calm truth that filled her up to bursting.

The answer was simple. The doubt that had washed over her a moment ago gave way to perfectly plain resolve.

"S T A Y," Arix said to the girl that lay unmoving on the ground. "Stay until I come back for you."

The gravel that crunched under her feet rang out like cracking bones, the smell of smoke in the distance as raw and burning as if she stood in the center of a fire. And far, far above, the caw of a raven as it circled the sky, like the scream of something dying.

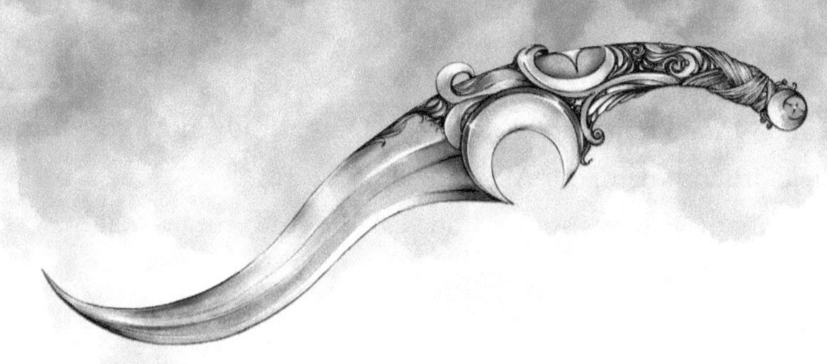

FORTY-TWO

She found him sitting on his throne, elbows resting on his knees as he watched her enter. All around him, his guards held their weapons pointed at her. But she could see it in their eyes; they didn't want to fight. They knew they would not win.

Beside Orion, Lakai stood in *her* place next to the throne. His hands stayed in front of him, ready to rebuff the magick she might use. Even from here, she could see the old man's hands shaking. Arix smiled.

"They won't protect you, Orion. Not from me."

Orion didn't respond.

Arix could read his posture—the way his knuckles whitened against the pressure of his steepled fingers, the way his brow furrowed, unmoving. She could read him now better than she'd ever been able to read him before.

Each step echoed in the hall as she strode forward, raising her palms together as she walked. With a flick, she parted her hands, flinging them wide, and with the motion, Orion's guards were flung sideways, clearing a path as she neared the dais. The crash of their body-clad armor colliding with the walls was instantaneous, thunderous, and Orion jumped to his feet. Lakai was already moving to form a shield around them, but Arix pressed forward.

Lakai's magick was strong, and years of study meant that he was almost matched to her.

Almost.

But Arix had things that Lakai never had. She had three cores. She had the Well Water. She was the Black Hand. And she had a new determination that settled the fears, settled the insecurities, settled all thoughts of doubt.

Arix pressed back with her own magick, feeling for a crack in the shield, for a weak joint in the protection cant that Lakai tried so hard to maintain. Silently, the two incantors fought, their magick straining against the other: the man who had taught her everything, the woman who had surpassed him. And slowly, Arix felt his magick give way to her own.

It yielded, inch by merciless inch, and with every decrease, she took another step forward until she simply *pushed through* the shield.

Lakai was panting, sweat dripping down into his beard as his chest heaved. Blue eyes, so steadfast, stared back at her.

"Lakai," she said simply, watching his gray-blue eyes shift back and forth between her own. "For the sake of the magick you taught me, for the sake of the trust we once shared, I will only say this once: go."

She thought he might stay. She hoped, maybe, that he might fight her so she could feel the satisfaction of his admission. Admission that he too had lied. That he'd given Maeve the Well Water. That maybe by fighting him, she could fight for the answers that the trapped incantor in the courtyard had given her so easily.

But he didn't.

Without a word, Lakai vanished, blinking out of existence.

Arix could feel his magick disappear from this place, wholly and completely, leaving her alone with Orion.

"You fought her? Maeve?" Orion asked.

She could hear his blood surging through his veins even while he tried to remain calm. Even while he soothed his breathing and relaxed his brows, she could *feel* the way his heart raced in his chest.

"I did."

Orion nodded slowly, a smile playing at the corner of his mouth. "I had hoped you would."

Her head tilted slowly to the side as she watched him. "You had hoped one of us would die."

"Of course." Orion said it like she was stupid. He said it like a man who was trying in vain to convince himself that he hadn't stepped directly into the path of a poisonous snake.

Arix took a step forward, her voice quiet as she spoke, pressing a palm to his chest. "You, Orion Karkarias, betrayed me. Today, yesterday, the night I killed your father. The night I killed Celeste, the day we met in the garden. All those days and all the days in between."

His skin paled, and the terror that bloomed on his face gave her a rush of euphoria.

She leaned up on her tiptoes, guiding his chin down so that their lips brushed gently.

"You lied to me," she whispered against those lips.

"I never lied to you, Arix," he breathed back, throat catching on the deception even as he spoke them into her mouth. "I just couldn't tell you."

His arms wrapped around her, embracing the viper who was poised to bite him. The embrace was so familiar, so recognizably Orion's. She knew that even with her senses gone, she would always recognize his hold on her.

"Whatever she told you, it isn't true."

A smile curled at the corners of Arix' mouth.

"And what, do you think, she told me?" Arix asked carefully.

"The Carn lie. They always have. Whatever it must have been, it wasn't true."

He lied so smoothly, so evenly, that Arix wondered if he hadn't been lying his whole life. Stacking them up one on top of the other until he lived his entire existence propped up on them.

"Tell me," Arix said slowly, holding his gaze as she wound her arms around his neck to pull him closer. "When King Taurus fucked your whore mother, did he know he was fucking a Carn rebel? Did he know he was going to sire a son who would destroy everything he'd built?"

Orion stiffened in her arms, trying to extricate himself from her hold, but she only gripped him tighter.

"And when you grew old enough, was it your bitch mother that told you to vie for the throne? To usurp your father and use me to do it?"

He was gripping her waist, trying to push her off him, but she held tight, forcing his chin down to look at her.

"This is why I didn't tell you." His tone was firm, the tone of a scolding parent. "I knew you wouldn't be able to see past your hatred. You wouldn't be able to see the future I know we could achieve together. Together, Arix. *With you*, not against you."

Arix scoffed, slowly shaking her head as she stared at him.

"It truly amazes me," she whispered, "how many lies you've wrapped yourself up in. Can you even tell them from the truth anymore?"

"Not lies, Arix," Orion said softly, leaning his forehead against her own. "Just secrets. To tell you when you were ready."

Arix closed her eyes against the touch, leaning into the embrace. "So did you pick me because I was the only one stupid enough to believe you? Stupid enough to be charmed by you; stupid enough to—"

"A smart man never bets on only one horse," he interrupted.

Arix stilled. She spoke slowly, carefully, keeping her tone even and cool as her hands traced the collar of his jacket.

"And I was just one horse? Who was your backup plan?"

Orion laughed softly, stroking a finger down her cheek. "You *were* the backup plan. You surprised me, Arix. You proved yourself the strongest against Celeste. Not even I had planned for that."

When she said nothing, he went on, pulling far enough out of the embrace so he could look her dead in the eye.

"You should have seen their faces that day. We watched you through Lakai's orb, battling Celeste in that glade. Every single one of those council members were on the edge of their seats. They didn't consider you even part of the equation. But you proved yourself. You proved me right."

When she didn't respond, he continued with a small frown. "I had hoped you would be able to move past this. That *we* could move past this."

"And you sent her to kill me."

"Only to prove that you were stronger! That you could beat her!"

"You backed Celeste to become Black Hand."

"Only at first, Arix—"

"And you settled on me when you realized I had a chance of winning instead."

"Arix, stop this. It was strategic—for the good of the crown!"

"You manipulated my emotions, knew I was drowning after losing Michael and Revena, and you used my desperation against me."

Arix spoke every word with precision, every bit of the pain of losing them brought back with a vengeance. But this time it only fueled her fury.

"You used my need for companionship, for physical intimacy, to control me."

"You really think that?" Orion was incredulous, false pity and hurt spread out across his face. "I didn't kill them, Arix. I didn't bring about their deaths. You can't blame me for that."

"And what about the blessings?"

Arix saw the shift in his eyes. It was so subtle, so small, but she could see the change from manipulation into frustration.

"You shouldn't have done what you did in Eldur. Your strength was beautiful once." Orion stared past her as though looking back to the day they had first met in the garden under the moon.

"And now?" Arix reached out a hand, gripping his chin as she forced his gaze to hers. She smirked. "Are you intimidated by it? By the way it has grown? Or maybe you've realized that I have outgrown you."

Anger flashed in his eyes, and he stepped back from her. She let him go, slowly letting her arms fall to her sides as she watched him. All their time together, all of the manipulation, and it was finally now, here on the dais, that Orion seemed to understand. To come to the truth of it all.

"You've become dangerous, Arix."

"Finally," the pendant over her heart breathed. *"The truth."*

"No, Orion."

His brow quirked. "No?"

"No." She smiled, reaching a hand forward, towards him. "I have always been dangerous. You have just underestimated me."

And then she *reached,* though the fabric of his jacket, through the skin of his chest, past the splintering of his sternum, and clutched his heart.

A spray of blood flecked across her face, and for a moment, his heart continued pumping in her palm, hot blood sluicing from the torn veins and spilling across her fingers. She yanked and the organ came free, bones cracking out of the way as Orion's body crumpled back to sprawl on the golden throne.

"Always dangerous," Arix said again, watching as the heart stopped beating, watching as rivers of blood ran down her arm and soaked her sleeve. Slowly, she let the heart slip from her fingers, landing in a wet splat on the marble floor. "Always underestimated."

A gasp pulled Arix around to see Delphine standing at the bottom of the steps. Her eyes were hollow orbs as she stared up at Orion's body, slumped on the massive throne. Arix moved quickly, closing the distance between them, but Delphine made no move to run as the Black Hand who had murdered her husband came to stand in front of her.

"Is he dead?" Delphine asked, the hollows of her cheeks and the pallor of her skin more visible in the dimly lit throne room.

"He is dead."

Arix waited for tears, for indignation. For howling anguish or even for the queen to faint in her arms. Instead Delphine's shoulders eased, and a huge sigh of relief washed over them both.

"There is no future left for his line. For you. For your child."

The queen shuddered in revulsion. "I do not want his throne, Arix. I do not want it for myself or for my child. If I am to be free of him, then I want to be free of *all* of it."

"Then go, Delphine. I will not hunt you."

Delphine finally looked away from Orion, the long curl of her lashes kissing her cheek as she watched Arix carefully. Her words came out shuddered, barely a whisper. "You know…what he was like?"

Arix chose not to answer the question. Chose not to tell Delphine that she hadn't seen Orion for who he truly was until today.

"He drugged me. The night of the bonfire. At least, I think…" Delphine's eyes glinted, jaw set in a grim line. "And then I was pregnant."

When Arix reached forward to offer a comforting hand, Delphine pulled away.

"What now?"

"I want you to go. Find solace with your family, raise your child in safety, and tell your father that I do this in exchange for Nero's fealty." Arix's breath rattled in her chest, adrenaline slicking through her veins. "Nero will stand with me. Stand by me. Orion was a liar and a manipulator. He brought about his own death by siding with the Carn, and he was going to use you and I to build the empire he wanted. And it is you and I who will not allow that future to come to pass."

Delphine was staring past her, at the puddle of blood slowly dripping down the stairs. It was spreading closer, the tip of her slippered shoe dangerously close to soaking in the crimson blood like a sponge. She made no move to step away from it.

"Do we have an understanding?" Arix asked, her voice low.

Slowly, Delphine turned, calm resolve in her eyes. "Yes."

"Then go."

Delphine wrapped her arms around herself, holding the unborn in her belly in an embrace as she turned to leave. After a few steps, she turned back, spearing Arix with a stare that tore through her very soul.

"You have saved us both."

Arix waited until the padding of her shoes disappeared down the hallway, taking a moment to stand in the stillness of her actions. She breathed in the tang of Orion's blood, felt the cold of the stone beneath her feet, stared at the slumped soldiers who lay scattered along the walls. The sunlight that flowed golden through the high windows of the throne room remained unchanged in the face of the new order. In the face of the actions she had just taken.

Arix let the stillness envelope her.

If she moved even an inch, it might all disappear, fading away into a dream filled with never-ending loops of lies and deceit she would never be free from. She felt the waves of relief at the realization that this was real.

But the silence didn't last long.

There was a groan from one of the men, the clattering of armor as they moved to rise. Arix remained where she stood, simply watching as the lone guard blinked, glancing around him, glancing up at the throne. She saw his eyes widened, watched him sit up, straightening for a better look; then watched his gaze slide along the trail of blood to rest on her. Shock registered across his features, then slow realization as his eyes grew wider, and he stiffened under her gaze.

"The old king is dead," Arix said, her voice echoing against the marble pillars. "Long live the queen."

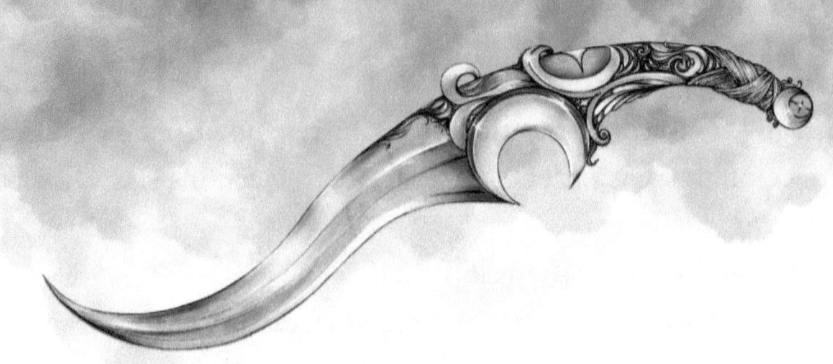

FORTY-THREE

The stone around her grew cold as Arix descended. Each step brought a new wave of calm, an assurance. If this was real, all of it, then what she was about to do would either solidify her actions or wipe them away to dust.

All the shades of gray had disappeared for her. All the in-between, the doubt, the insecurities, had faded the moment she had killed Orion. All that remained in its place was the assurance that what would be, would be. Her only choice was to walk the path. And it would either lead her to victory or to defeat.

Stale air, compounded by the pressure of going so deep, encased her, and some weak part of her mind begged her to turn around, begged her to rethink what she was about to do. There were other ways, other routes she could take. This path wasn't necessary for victory.

"But it is," Arix said aloud, and that tiny fearful voice in her mind stilled.

The doors reached high above her in the darkness, but Arix pushed them open, letting her magick be the strength as she opened one door and then the other. There would be no escape this time, no rushed retreat. She would walk face first into the den of death and face whatever consequences arose.

Her throat clogged at the smell. It had been months, but charred hair and flesh still lingered in the stale air. The floor was clean, any remnants swept away, bones crunched or swallowed whole or maybe burned into ash and adrift in the air.

Instead of taking the stairs down, Arix moved toward the balcony that overlooked the giant room. She lit the channel of oil with her magick and watched as the orange glow of the fire traveled down the stairs, around the outer edge of the massive space, flickering quietly.

"I know you hear me," Arix called, letting the cant change the manner of her voice, expanding the sound so that it boomed. To her, it still sounded like her own voice in her own language, but she knew that the cant had changed the shape of her mouth, the shape of her tongue so that the one she spoke to could understand her. "I come with a gift. A proposal. A request."

For a moment, her voice was only met with silence and the faint flicker of the flames. And then the tinkling of gold coins, sliding and spilling across the floor. Behind the piles of treasure, of paintings and cloth, and behind piles of jewels and gold, the dragon rose. Her eyes trained on Arix as she slowly moved from her nest, each step shaking the stones and causing more of the melodic tinkling of coins and gems to roll across the worn stone floor.

Arix waited until the dragon neared, until she could feel the heat radiating from her, feel the waves scorching hair, until the heat was almost too much to bear. But Arix did nothing to stop the pain, cast no cant to lessen the temperature of the dragon's body.

"Please speak freely. I will be able to understand you," Arix said slowly. "To whom do I have the honor of addressing?"

The dragon was close enough now that her head loomed mere feet from the balcony's edge, her third eye blinking slightly out of sync with the other two.

"There is not a word for my name in you language."

The voice was so deep that Arix strained to make out the words, graveled and rich.

"I remember you, human. You have returned to me, returned to the place of your death."

"I am Arix Sable, Black Hand and"—Arix stumbled over the word—"queen."

The three eyes blinked, lighting fast as the dragon simply stared.

"You killed my friend."

The dragon chuckled, and Arix remembered the sound. She'd heard it last time she was here, when their ice cants had not worked, when Helios had been caught in the flame, his skin blistering and bubbling like candy.

"And I will kill many more. I will kill you, if I like." The dragon snapped her jaws, and Arix glimpsed the rows of sharpened brown teeth, layered like a shark.

"I came to offer you a deal."

"I have no interest in your *deals*," the dragon growled. "It was a *deal* that trapped me here, trickery of the mind and trickery of the words of men. And now I am forced to eat the children I bear who will never live, cut off from my kind, rotting with the only comfort I know."

Her tail flicked, the barb at the end spearing through one of the paintings, splitting the canvas and shattering the gilded frame.

"Stupid humans. You think that dragons are drawn by wealth, by treasure? You thought that this would satisfy me?"

Arix was forced to take a step back as the dragon huffed molten air, her nostrils flaring as her anger rose.

"It is the passage of time that matters to us. The change of history, of dynasties breaking and building, of changing culture and the evolution of economies." With every word, the dragon swung her tail, scattering the piles of wealth, bolts of fabric catching on fire, coins melting against the heat. "It is the metamorphosis of culture we crave. Not the things themselves."

"But they didn't understand," Arix said quietly, watching the treasure below melt and burn.

"No." The dragon snorted, her tail finally slowing like a cat. "The incantor who trapped me here did not understand. And I was too young to grasp the fallacy of his words. He sealed me with his magickal doors and left me here to waste away."

Arix had questions, wanted to ask which incantor had done it, but she felt like if she stopped the dragon now, if she interrupted, the mystery would be broken.

"Ask your question, incantor."

"How many years?"

For a moment, she just blinked, and Arix watched the small scales around her eyes click lightly as the muscles beneath shifted with every closure of the three eyes.

"What do they call this place? This great fortress they have built above me?"

"Castle Zma'ai."

Even as the words came out, translated into Draconic, Arix suddenly understood their meaning, understood the trick hidden in the very name of the castle she'd come to call home.

The corner of the dragon's mouth curled, and a stream of smoke drifted between her teeth. "You understand?"

"Yes."

"The name meant nothing to you, would mean nothing to those

who did not know the language of the dragons. To them, it would be pretty words. But to me... I have been trapped here since the forming of the stones, the building of the spires high above me. In the Castle of the Dragon."

"Do you want to be free of it?" Arix asked, the words coming out like a plea.

The red dragon went totally still. Even her tail ceased thrashing, her eyes stopped blinking, and Arix felt her looking deeper than the surface.

"You say that what dragons really want, what they really desire, is to see kingdoms rise and fall. To see time take its toll the world. I offer you this.

"Upstairs, the king is dead," Arix said simply. "I ripped out his heart."

The dragon snorted, leaning her head over the railing and forcing Arix to either give way or burn. Arix stood her ground, feeling her skin quake against the heat, blistering red under the proximity.

"Why, little incantor? Why did you rip out the king's heart?"

"He wanted to control me."

"No." The word came out with a growl, the teeth snapping dangerously close. "No, there is another reason, Black Hand. Why did you rip out the king's heart?"

"Because..." Arix paused.

There were so many reasons. His betrayal, his lies. He'd used her as a pawn, had sought to control her. He'd wanted her dead, and she had emerged victorious. But was any of that the real reason she had ended his life? She could have controlled his mind, turned the puppet master into a puppet himself. She could have ruled through him, but she'd chosen the hard path instead.

"Because he could not see me. The real me. Not just the incantor with all my magick. He couldn't see the truth of me."

Arix thought of Michael and Revena. Revena who had died right here, protecting Arix from the flames that burned her alive.

"I think only a few might ever see me for who I am. And Michael and Revena were the closest to it. But they're gone. And I remain."

"And you have come here to speak to me."

"Yes."

"To offer me a new deal."

"Yes."

The dragon moved, slowly raising a leg and hauling her body up onto the balcony. It was too hot, too deadly to remain where she stood, and Arix was forced to move backwards as the towering creature climbed up to loom above her. The dragon's talons dug into the stones, gouging marks to hold herself steady. Arix had to look straight up as the dragon bent her head down, the two practically nose-to-nose.

"What do you propose, little incantor?"

"Freedom. For one year, I ask that you help me hold the throne I took. When the year is up, your fealty to me is over, and you can go. Seek out your own kind, find your freedom in the mountains or over the sea. But in that one year, help me. Because I can't do it alone."

For a moment, the dragon said nothing, and Arix let the waves of heat wash roll over her. Strangely, with every breath, the heat lessened until it felt no more stifling than a summer's breeze.

"A bond like that," the dragon said finally, her nose pressing slowly into Arix's chest, "should be sealed with a name."

"I am Bellarix Sable. Queen of Rökkur."

"My name, you would not understand. But it translates to a fate I believe has come to pass for all of my species. I am Maer Dáinn, Mother of the Eternal Dead."

"Maer Dáinn," Arix repeated carefully. "Do you agree to form this bond with me? To fight at my side for your freedom?"

Maer Dáinn's gaze flickered to the doors behind them, at the magick seal she could see embedded deep in the door's surface. Without turning to face it, Arix reached out a hand, pushing out with her own magick and dissolving the cant that locked the dragon deep within the bowels of the castle that loomed above.

A rumble shook the stones, and Maer Dáinn took a hesitant step forward, her belly sliding low to the ground as she took a tentative stride through the doorway and into the great underground hall of Castle Zma'ai beyond.

Only after she was all the way through did she turn around to face Arix.

"I will forge this bond with you, Bellarix Sable, Black Hand and Queen of Rökkur."

Arix felt a surge in her chest, her magick responding to the invisible bond that now linked them.

Maer Dáinn grinned, her teeth snapping in the air. "May your rule be carved into the chronicles of history."

Arix let her own smile spread before joining the great red dragon on the other side, leading the way back to the surface and to her new kingdom of chaos that awaited her.

ACKNOWLEDGMENTS

The absolute biggest thank you to everyone who helped The Black Crown come into being, and those who have championed this series from the beginning. Your continued support keeps me writing, keeps me focused, and keeps me looking towards the future. I can't wait to close out the series with you in the next and final book, The Black Kingdom. I truly hope to wreck you all emotionally, in the best ways possible.

To Allan, my husband and partner, thank you for letting me talk through my plot holes and problems, walking round and round our block to let me rant, reminding me of the bigger picture, and talking me down when I'm overthinking things.

To Lisa, my writing partner and bestie, I wouldn't have been able to write this book in a year without you. Writing together every Wednesday night, keeping each other accountable, it was the only way I ever had a chance of putting this story to paper. I've loved writing with you and look forward to all the other books we'll write together over Discord. I'm immensely grateful for you and your friendship. I hope our Marco Polo rants go on forever.

To my cover designer, Nevena Jevtic, thank you so much for

creating the most glorious cover art and seeing the vision even before I did. To my chapter header artist, Jo Ramos, your talent deserves so much more notice, and I'm honored to have worked with you on the chapter header art and coloring page of Arix and Ro. To Choco, thank you so much for the stunning artwork of Arix on the bookmarks and banners on my website and social media. Thank you so much for bringing my world and characters to life through your beautiful artwork and talent. You have my gratitude.

To my editor, Charlie Knight, who did the absolute BEST job at turning my scrappy manuscript full of misspelled words and grammatical catastrophes into a coherent and beautiful book. I wish we'd met a lot sooner, it would have saved me a lot of grief with The Black Hand. I look forward to working with you again on The Black Kingdom.

To my beta readers, who read an early draft of this book and gave me the notes, gasps, and emojis to craft an even better version. I hope you love the changes I've made, inspired by many of your comments and questions. You were on the front line, reading before my editor had fixed the million mistakes, and I'm so thankful you could still see the gem of this book underneath the mess.

To Maz, for your amazing support and help with the pronunciation guide. You've been such an irreplaceable cheerleader through all the TikTok writing, through both of my books, and your friendship and support have meant the world to me. I hope I can give you the same kind of support when you're ready to unveil your own story with the world.

To the gang, Kayla, Michael, Jacob, Christa, and Nik, you guys are the best. Thank you so much for supporting me and letting me rant and rave about the perils of being an author. Thank you for being the kind of friends who encourage creativity and growth.

You all have been the best kind of friends; the best kind of companions in life.

To Lindsey, probably my longest-running writing fan, thank you so much for your support. Hearing you rant and rave about these characters slays me in the absolute best way. Thank you for loving me and loving these books.

To mom and dad, who don't read fantasy, but have always supported their dramatic daughter. I'm so glad that even though you buy my books, you don't read them; I'd hate to scandalize you, and I'd really rather you continue thinking of me as writing happy stories about dragons and adventures rather than the death and gore in these pages. Thanks for loving me, even when I write "bloody stories with depressing endings." Love you both to pieces.

To my dear friend Camille, who regularly reminds me that I write for myself, first and foremost. I write for my younger self, who felt so very lost in the world and found her greatest comfort in fantasy worlds and made-up stories. Thank you for encouraging me and challenging me to continue piecing together all the things that have made me who I am today, and for pushing me to continually seek growth.

And last, but never least, to the amazing book and writing communities on TikTok and Instagram, thank you so much for your support and views. It's been a process, and you've shown up and showed out to support this series as it grows. I see your likes, comments, views, and shares, and they mean so much to me. Your support is for more than just this series, but for me as an author as well. Thank you.

H. M. REINHARD

Hannah is a storyteller, first and foremost. In addition
to being a writer and avid reader, Hannah co-hosts a book
club podcast, sews costumes and ren faire clothing, loves
cooking, and enjoys playing Dungeons and Dragons whenever
possible. Hannah lives in South Carolina with her husband and
their three cats, Bunty, Beckford, and Birdy.

Find H. M. Reinhard on Instagram and TikTok
@h.m.reinhard_author
www.hmreinhard.wixsite.com/books

www.ingramcontent.com/pod-product-compliance
Lightning Source LLC
Chambersburg PA
CBHW020325010826
48973CB00005B/1123